THE JUDGEMENT
OF
OLERON

by

DONALD MOORE

London

HODDER & STOUGHTON

Copyright © 1960 by Donald Moore

MADE AND PRINTED IN GREAT BRITAIN FOR
HODDER AND STOUGHTON LIMITED, LONDON
BY C. TINLING AND CO. LIMITED, LIVERPOOL,
LONDON AND PRESCOT

"A ship is lyeing in a haven and tareyth for the freyghte and tyme to departe, the mayster ought take councell with his felowes and saye, Mates how lyke ye this wether? Some wyll saye, it is not good, lete it over passe. Other wyll saye, the wether is good and fayre. The mayster ought agre to the most, or els if the shyp perysh he is bound to restore the value as it is praysed, yf he have wherwith. This is the judgement."

The Judgementes of the See.

PART ONE

PART ONE

ONE

I

THE four of them sat in the jukebox uproar, waiting. They did not know why they waited, nor did they wonder. It was necessary only that four Canadian Ryes should be brought to them each twenty minutes and that they should be able to watch the swirling skirts of the girls in the smoke-laden air; drinking, occasionally speaking (speech not amounting to conversation, for it was pointless to converse in the belting rhythm), just sitting and drinking and staring, the four of them: Goldstein the Jew, Schirmer the Swede, da Falla the Eurasian, and Lord Birkenhead, an indestructible negro colossus possessed of all the majesty of his race, debased only by the company he had been obliged to keep since he had slid into the cotton field from his mother's womb.

They watched the girl in the cosmetic mask whose expression was unalterably incredulous because she had changed the natural shape of her lips and the configuration of her eyebrows. She was small and pinched, dressed in a short pleated skirt and a striped woollen sweater which did as much as could ever be done for her ill-fed frame. Her hair was ringleted, lacquered and dyed, tortured with irons, caught in steel grips. When she turned her skirt flew up in the half-light and they could see her tight black knickers.

Perhaps Goldstein was upset by this brief attire. Or perhaps it was simply the whisky. But whatever the stimulus he snatched at her as she passed and pulled her on to his knees, sharp buttocks against soft male thighs, and pressed his wet lips against her make-up and patted her and felt her and said in his hoarse ghetto-cockney, "Hello, dearie, how about you an' me goin' outside for a bit, eh?"

She pushed her fist between his thighs and looked at him with her astonished doll face. "How much you got?"

"How much you want?"

9

"Five bucks, an' you pay me right here."

" 'Ow abaht four-fifty?"

"Take it or leave it, sailor. I got work to do."

Goldstein must have been drunker than he looked or he would never have done it, never have inflamed or defied or even merely annoyed Svenson, the big Swede who had been dancing with her, who was very nearly as tall and broad as Lord Birkenhead, who just stood looking down at Goldstein's big-hipped body as if he were waiting for a dog to finish scratching itself.

The jukebox stopped when Goldstein stood up and faced Svenson in the silence. Svenson said softly, "Get out, Jew boy!"

Goldstein licked his lips and moved one hand behind his bottom to see if the girl was still there and felt the nap of her sweater and wanted to turn and push his head into the softness of her tiny breasts and hide himself there.

"Dirty Jew bastard!" Svenson said.

Goldstein was unable to see Svenson clearly for his vision was beginning to swim, but the whisky answered, "Flip off! Can't you see I'm busy? It's a free country, ain't it?"

The bottle shattered into the silence on the edge of the table and Svenson was holding the neck and pushing the jagged edge into Goldstein's face. Goldstein stared at it. "Steady on, mate, steady on. 'Ave an 'eart." His companions closed up behind him but Svenson just went on devising variations on 'Dirty Jew bastard', until his voice became a shout and the brown beer-flecked glass lunged towards them.

Lord Birkenhead hit Svenson in the stomach with a fist that moved like a flying lump of granite. Svenson's body sailed across the room and came to rest below the winking lights of the jukebox, jolting it into life. "Mr. what d'you call 'em, what you doing tonight? Hope you're in the mood 'cos I'm feeling just right."

The dancing started again and Goldstein took the girl outside into the street and had her in a doorway for five dollars, quickly, for it was cold for a man with his trousers down.

II

Erik Jacobson, Captain of the seven thousand ton Swedish merchantman, *Oleron*, climbed the companionway to his bridge towards the end of the forenoon watch and took up his customary position near to the port wing. The fog was clearing before a freshening breeze and already he could see the Commodore's ship at the head of the centre column. A slack swell swept down lazily from the north-east, nudging the sixty-three ordered vessels, but not deflecting them from their dogged course.

It was the winter after Dunkirk.

Jacobson gazed morosely at the oily seas heaving below his bridge. His distrust of the future was profound. He was inescapably enmeshed in an alien machine that had taken his crippled ship into Liverpool, repaired her, stored her, fuelled her and despatched her in convoy from Liverpool to Halifax and back again. It was the fate of all Swedish ships caught defenceless without the Skagerrak barrier; damaged neutrals were the fair game of hard-pressed belligerents and *Oleron*, Jacobson's *Oleron*, was no exception.

Once *Oleron*'s new purpose had become generally known to her crew, trouble had swiftly ensued. A proportion of the crew had deserted, some in Liverpool, others in Halifax. Men had been unaccountably taken with obscure diseases and detained in hospital. The First Mate had gone off his head—finally and unquestionably—and killed the cook with his own blood-stained chopper, and the Second Engineer, who had sailed with Jacobson and *Oleron* since she had been launched at Swan Hunter's on Tyneside before the war, had developed DT's for the last time and vanished over the side one rude Atlantic night.

Now Jacobson found himself burdened with a scratch crew dredged and driven from gutters and gaols of the Canadian sub-continent; that such a miscellany of gruesome ne'er-do-wells should be ensconced in *Oleron* was an intolerable affront to her name and the susceptibilities of her Master. His chagrin was intense.

Even his officers were unknown, and, it seemed, unlikeable quantities. Theodore Busk, the First Mate, who was standing the forenoon watch, was a tall ramrod of a man from the south of England, an angular, bony figure with a sallow hatchet face divided by the whitest set of dentures Jacobson had ever seen.

His thinning brown hair was parted carefully in the precise middle of his head and swept back in a V to terminate in a rich curtain above his scrawny neck. His eyes were too small and his nose too thin and his mouth too big for Jacobson ever to have taken to him easily; yet Jacobson was a man prepared to go to extreme lengths to like a man, particularly an officer in his ship. It was clear to him that Busk treated him with a kind of offhand indifference, almost insolence, as if he, Busk, were in command and Jacobson a mere neutral supernumerary. He invariably addressed Jacobson as 'sir' but accented the word, giving it a half-derisive twang. But he appeared to know his job; for this, at least, Jacobson was thankful.

"It seems to be clearing," Jacobson said in his slow correct English.

Busk did not look at him but continued to stare straight ahead. "Yes, sir."

"I think soon the Commodore will increase speed. Keep a good look-out."

"Aye, aye, sir."

Jacobson leaned against the bridge rail below the glass screens and watched the dissipating fog-clouds sweep over the cork-screwing bow. Then he went into the charthouse, looked at the barometer, read the latest signals and consulted the chart. Everything was in order. The ship rumbled and throbbed methodically under his feet. Perhaps he had simply been tired; he had been on his feet all night and to be tired was not unnatural. He passed a hand over his smooth brow and returned quietly to his corner of the bridge.

Something nudged his right arm and he turned and saw Busk looking down at him, grinning with artificial teeth and plastic gums. "Cigarette?" Jacobson glanced at the proffered packet of Players. "I smoke a pipe, Mr. Busk." When the packet did not move he added, "I do not wish that my officers smoke on duty. I first give permission—by smoking myself."

Busk answered, not at all abashed, still holding out the open packet, "That's not the way in British ships."

Jacobson's blue eyes blinked. "But this is not a British ship."

"It's a British convoy."

Jacobson's voice remained mild and gently reproving. "That may be. But this, Mr. Busk, is a Swedish ship."

Busk did not retreat, did not take the grin off his face, but just stood holding out his cigarettes, waiting for Jacobson to give way. His experience of this dapper little man was dangerously limited. "I ask you to obey my orders, Mr. Busk. Please, to your duties!"

Busk put the cigarettes in his pocket and sauntered amidships to his station. Jacobson returned to his contemplation of the weather. Soon he brought out his pipe and filled it with Balkan Sobranie Mixture and made much of lighting it and when it was burning furiously he left the bridge with short, crisp steps. "Smoke if you wish, Mr. Busk. Call me when convoy speed increased or zigzag resumed."

He returned to his cabin on the upper bridge deck to plod once more through the convoy communications orders, to make quite certain that he understood them in all their unfamiliar complexity. He was relieved that the first trial of strength had occurred.

But this Busk, he was a queer fellow.

III

The messenger knocked on the door of the Second Mate's cabin on the starboard side of the boat deck.

"Yes?" Dawson called.

The messenger pushed open the door and inserted his untidy head into the cabin, leaning on the frame with his shoulder as the ship rolled. Dawson, who had the afternoon watch, and had already eaten dinner, was putting on his coat. "Captain wants to see you in his cabin."

"Now?"

"Yes. Now."

"O.K. Coming."

The messenger left the cabin door open and swayed aft. Dawson turned forrard and made his way up the ladder to the upper bridge deck where he knocked on Jacobson's door and waited in the draughty passage, listening to the rising sough of the wind in the towering derricks.

He was a powerful man with tremendous shoulders. He stood six feet four in his socks. He might, at one time, have been a boxer or a wrestler, but if so his face revealed none of the ravages of the profession. He was even handsome in a Hollywood, nondescript kind of way: his features were so regular, so perfectly formed, that they ceased in Jacobson's view to project the character or even the personality of an individual, and became, instead, the mask of a type—specious, perhaps; or empty; it was impossible to tell. His hair was dark and abundant, immaculately but naturally waved. He was no more than thirty-one or two.

"Come in."

Dawson smoothed his hair and entered the cabin. Jacobson was standing by the scuttle, screwing down the brass retainers more tightly, and Dawson could see over his shoulder and through the salt-wet glass to the see-sawing convoy beyond. The fog was almost gone. Jacobson turned and regarded his Second Mate who stood almost a foot taller than he did, smiled genially, and sat down at his desk. He did not believe that he liked the look of Dawson any more than he liked the look of Busk. He did not approve of the almost swashbuckling air, nineteen-forty style, that Dawson affected. Yet, it was highly necessary that he should be able to rely on one of them and it seemed unlikely that he could rely on Busk. "Please sit down, Mr. Dawson."

The Second Mate lowered his immense frame into the rexine-covered chair and waited for Jacobson to state his business.

"You are Canadian?"

"That's right, sir. Born right there in Halifax."

"And your last ship?"

"Er . . . the *Golden Eagle*."

"Where is the *Golden Eagle* now?"

"That I don't know, sir. She sailed when I was asleep—as I told you. When I woke up she was gone. But I was told . . . there'd be no questions asked."

"There will be no more on this voyage, Dawson. But what happens in the few days ahead of us could, perhaps, influence your future. You understand? I wish to remind you. That is all. We have not enough crew and there are too few officers. But *Oleron* will continue as if she sailed with her full complement. I make myself clear?"

"Of course. Yes, sir."

Jacobson wondered how heavily he drank; in his experience it was extraordinary how much some mariners could drink and yet retain their physique, if not their wits. He watched him carefully, but Dawson's eyes did not falter. "I am not satisfied with the tarpaulin over the forrard well-deck cargo hatch, Dawson. The Bos'n, he must change it during the afternoon. Please see to it, will you?"

"Aye aye, sir."

"That is all. You have nothing to fear in this ship. But you must obey my orders, yes?"

The Second Mate picked up his cap and departed, leaving Jacobson to sit and stare at the photograph of a pleasant-faced plump little woman which hung on the bulkhead in front of him. He held his rounded chin in one hand and thought fleetingly of his wife in Stockholm, his children, even his dog and the kennel he had made for it when last he was at home; and he speculated on the character of his Second Mate. What had passed through Dawson's head as he had sat before him? Anything? Or nothing? What exactly had gone wrong in his previous ship? He wondered whether Dawson had anything in common with Busk—who had undoubtedly reflected on the tenuous nature of a captain's authority in a ship full of strangers, most of whom were not even his own countrymen, most of whom were involved in a war in which Jacobson could have no part.

The voice-pipe whistled. He leaned over and answered it. It was a constant effort to remember to speak in English.

"Convoy speed increased to eight knots, sir. Zigzag to be resumed at twelve-thirty There's no need to come up, sir. We can handle it."

"Thank you, Mr. Busk. I come at once."

He stood up, pulled his reefer jacket straight over his corpulence, straightened his tie, placed his cap with its gleaming gold company badge quite straight on his head, and made his way up to his bridge.

IV

The engine revolutions increased as he reached the top of the ladder. The fog had almost entirely dispersed and Dawson had relieved Busk.

He made his way out on to the port wing and watched *Oleron*'s high bow slicing and knifing through the tumbling green-grey hills of water, conscious of the swelling drive of the engines beneath his feet. It was exactly twelve-thirty when the executive signal hurried down the halyards of the Commodore's ship; at the same moment he heard Dawson's laconic order to turn and felt the tilt of the deck as the ship's head swept across the murky horizon. *Oleron* turned with the convoy on to the new course.

Jacobson was happy; that is to say, he knew a supreme contentment or if not a mere contentment then a kind of joy; he could never be otherwise, whatever the provocation, in the company of his excellent vessel. He was a man who loved. He knew a fierce pride in all ships, but in none more than *Oleron*: his, his dwelling-place, his world, his beginning and doubtless his end. As he stood by the bridge screens watching the hungry, mile-eating, spray-crowned bow biting into the sea, his pudgy hands grasped the varnished teak rail until the bones showed white through the pinkness, and his rotund body, so precisely attired, straightened and became rigidly erect. He loved; of this there was no doubt.

Yet he also hated the sea. When he had first become a seaman he had sailed in a four-masted Swedish barque carrying grain to Europe from South America. He had been young then, little more than a boy, an apprentice with much to learn. During his second voyage his ship encountered a hurricane, an explosion of Atlantic insanity, and *Oleron*, as that ship also was named, sprang a leak in her mighty timbers beyond the capacity of all the pumps in the world to master. Every boat in the ship was destroyed and in the storm's aftermath the crew manned the futile pumps and pumped until backs cracked and palms frayed red on the handles. Yet, however hard they pumped, *Oleron* settled ever more deeply into the bottomless water—an inch and then two inches and finally three and four inches an hour, day and night, until the slack seas washed insolently over her decks and the bare feet of men at the pumps. Towards the end the crew just collapsed into the sloshing water, too exhausted even to take to the raft they had improvised on deck. They were saved by a providential freighter as *Oleron* sank beneath their scrabbling feet. It had been Jacobson, the boy, the apprentice with much to learn, who alone had urged the men back to the pumps and kept *Oleron* afloat until the boat was alongside. Since that day, that hour, that minute when he had watched the great ship sucked into her grave, it had been his unaccommodating purpose, a part of his love and a part of his hate, to defy and defeat the sea without which he could not live. Now, for the first time in his life, he began to wonder whether he could continue to win.

His blue, mild eyes watched the bow and he felt for his pipe in his jacket pocket. Then he seemed to change his mind. He turned to Dawson. "I shall go below for lunch. I am in the saloon if I am required."

As he walked off the bridge he heard screaming abaft the funnel. He paused, and looked at Dawson who also had heard it. "And ask Mr. Busk to report to me on this . . . disturbance."

V

There were three tables in the small, neatly panelled saloon, the first and largest presided over by the Captain, the second by the First Mate, and the third by the Chief Engineer. The smaller tables were empty but the five passengers waited motionlessly at the Captain's table like figures in a museum. In the enclosed space of the saloon, where the scuttles were screwed down hard, they had not, apparently, heard the scream. There was no sound by the ceaseless hum of the ship and the creaking of her bones as she moved to the motion of the sea. So much the better if they had not heard, Jacobson thought. Busk would now be investigating the incident or whatever it was; meanwhile, he decided, the Captain would be better employed supervising the comfort of his passengers.

He bobbed his head in a perfunctory bow. He had never entirely been able to accommodate himself to the idea of passengers in his ship; their very designation offended his sense of the fitness of things. "Good afternoon to you. I apologise for keeping you waiting but just now the convoy increases speed."

He began, methodically, to untwist the intricate flower that Chan Sam, the saloon steward, had constructed with his napkin. The passengers acknowledged his greeting and waited.

They were a curious collection, none of them having anything in common with the others except the shared imminent danger: Stockmann, the thick-set, over-dressed Swedish industrialist;

Harris, Second Engineer of the British tanker *Bristol*, now resting on her savaged side on the bottom of the Atlantic, and which, in the agony of her going, had released a scalding jet of steam into the Second's left eye and blown it right out of its socket; Gerda Olstein, a physically magnificent but curiously down-at-heel Swedish stewardess who had been mislaid by her ship in mysterious circumstances in Buenos Aires; and Mr. and Mrs. Albert Reed, he a woollen manufacturer from Yorkshire and she his devoted wife of thirty years, neither of whom felt it right, even at their age, for their country to engage in a war without their being there to see it won.

"How goes the war, Captain?" Stockmann asked in his rasping mock-jocular voice when the tinned tomato soup was served. Jacobson examined the fleshy, horn-rimmed face and the magnified eyes and saw how the beard would grow if allowed to develop—in twin tufts on the chin, like the beard of an overfed goat. There was something cold about the eyes. "Well, I believe."

"You are enigmatic, Captain. For whom does the war go well?"

"For us, shall we say?"

"We can, but does it?"

Jacobson did not reply. He conceived it to be a part of a captain's duty to take command of the conversation at his table; he had no wish to involve himself in argument with Stockmann.

He addressed himself to Harris, unreasonably aware of the black patch over the hollow socket in the hollow face, as if the patch and not the good eye were watching him. Everything about Harris suggested hollowness, his body a mere empty receptacle of pain. He played with the soup as if it nauseated him.

"You look forward to returning to England, Mr. Harris?"

"I suppose so."

The voice was weak, entrenched in a nameless Midlands accent, faintly truculent. He asked quickly, almost slyly, "Has the escort joined up yet?"

"No. Not yet. It is expected this afternoon."

"Well, I wish it'd get a move on. Bloody Navy!"

Alice Reed's warm north-country voice was indignant (the Reeds were practical, uncomplicated people who believed, as an article of British faith, that the Navy could do but little wrong).

"I don't think you can blame the Navy, Mr. Harris. They have a lot to do." She sought corroboration from Albert, her husband. "No, I don't think you can blame the Navy," he said.

"Perhaps the British are short of ships," Jacobson suggested mildly.

Harris snapped. "At this rate they won't have any ships to be short of."

"I think you are right," Stockmann said.

Harris turned a blazing eye on him. "What's that to you?" His voice was irate, offended.

Stockmann shrugged and Harris turned in his seat and called to Chan Sam. "Steward! Take this away and bring me a brandy-soda."

Jacobson was filled with distaste. He turned to the girl who sat with her head down, never looking at the others. She was perhaps thirty; well-built and strong, with a mass of lank, streaky-blonde hair. She wore a tweed skirt and roll-neck sweater and her breasts under the taut wool were heavy and pronounced but not unshapely. There was more than a hint of prettiness in her face—except that there was too much of it to be altogether pretty; even of comeliness—except that it was, perhaps, too angular to be comely; and about her expression seemed to hover the barely perceptible shadow of bovinity, or if not bovinity then a disinclination to concern herself with what went on about her or even with what happened to her. Jacobson wondered about the grief in her eyes—most assuredly, he decided, it was grief. He spoke to her in English. "You return to Sweden, yes?"

She answered slowly, "I am sorry. I do not speak English well. But yes. I return to Sweden to my people."

When she spoke her vacant face became instantly alive. Her voice was quiet and well-modulated and Jacobson, heartened by her smile, warmed towards her. Then he became aware of Busk casting a shadow over the table, and when he turned in his chair Busk was saying: "Can you come at once, sir? There's been something of an accident"—saying this and yet not looking at Jacobson, allowing Jacobson to receive an impression of his First Officer's disembodied mouth opening and shutting itself in space while his cheeky, confidential eyes devoured the girl at Jacobson's side.

Jacobson put down his napkin and rose from his chair. "Please, you must excuse me," and then, "Will you lead the way, Mr. Busk?"

VI

Jacobson strode into the crew's quarters aft and halted inside the doorway. Busk had acquainted him with the essential details, en route from the saloon.

He said in his most executive but still moderate voice, "Well? What is it?"

Busk, behind him, began to speak, but Goldstein stepped forward from the ring of sullen, shaken men and said, "It's like this. We was . . ."

Jacobson looked at him, not speaking, just staring him out of countenance.

"Sir," Goldstein said.

Jacobson inclined his square head the merest fraction, "Proceed."

Busk again interrupted but Jacobson gestured for silence. "Let this seaman speak, Mr. Busk, if he has anything to say."

"Well, it were like this. Sir . . ."

The men watched Goldstein and as his story progressed they moved nearer so that towards the end they were gathered in a half-circle about him, facing Jacobson, Busk, and behind them the squat efficient bos'n, Frieslund.

"It were the last night in 'alifax an' we was in Barney's Bar and there was a fight, see, over a girl, an' Birkenhead 'it Svenson —not that 'e didn't 'ave it comin' to 'im. Maybe it were my fault fer larkin' abaht wiv the skirt but Birk don't know 'is own strenf an' either the 'it or the fall must've affected Svenson's 'ead 'cos 'e goes proper queer ar'er it, an' that's a fac'. We was all a bit pissed, Cap'n."

"Pissed?"

"That's right, Cap'n. Pissed."

"He means drunk," Busk said.

"I see. Go on." Jacobson was understanding very little of the staccato Cockney rattle, but even so was understanding enough.

"Anyhow, this Svenson says 'e'll get Birkenhead if it's the las' thing 'e ever does. Sir. But 'e waits 'til we leave port, see, and this forenoon starts knockin' back the old 'ooch."

"Ooch?"

"Drink, sir," Busk said dubiously.

"Drink, Mr. Busk? And from where did he get it? It is against my orders."

"I know, sir, but he obviously had it hidden away."

"Obviously, Mr. Busk. Proceed . . . what is your name?"

"Goldstein. Sir."

"Proceed, Goldstein."

Jacobson was suddenly weary and passed a hand over his forehead and pressed his palm against the unlined skin. He had no stomach for the low life of his crew. They offended him.

"Well, when Birk comes below for 'is dinner Svenson's orready 'alf seas over an' 'e says to Birk 'e says, 'We don't want dirty niggers 'ere,' but Birk don't take no notice but goes an' sits dahn an' gits on wiv 'is grub like I said. But this Svenson won't let 'im alone an' goes on sayin' that Birk's—an' Birk's me oppo —a lousy flippin' black . . ."

"In English, Goldstein, please," Jacobson said in his sternest voice.

"Eh?"

"English, I said."

"But this *is* English, like me muvver taught me."

Jacobson's voice came as near to a roar as it could ever come, "Proceed, Goldstein!"

"Yes, sir. Sorry. Sir."

Jacobson put his hands in his jacket pockets but with his thumbs hooked over the edges, and spread his short legs farther apart.

"Well, like I was sayin', Svenson kep' sayin' that Birk was a dirty murderin' swine, which ain't true—is it, mateys?—'cos Birk's—although 'e's so big an' strong—strong? yer don't know what strong is 'til yer've seen Birk in action, strong as an ox, strong as the mainmast—kinda gentle, gentle as a little kitten. Well, Svenson gets Birk a bit narked and Birk jus' pushes 'im away an' before yer can say Tottenham Court Road out comes the knife, clickity-click, just like that, faster 'n light as yer might say, click! 'E bends dahn low an' watches Birk gettin' to 'is feet, ever so slow like, while 'e crouches an' 'olds the knife flat on 'is fingers stretched art in front of 'im. Nobody can go near 'cos as I said 'e'd gone crackers, this Svenson—nobody 'cep' Birk who says in 'is deep voice, 'Drop it, Svenson,' an' walks slow towards 'im but Svenson don't take no notice 'cep' 'e backs away some. 'Drop it,' says Birk, still gentle—I'm tellin' you, sir, still gentle and persuadin'. 'Drop it,' 'e says again but all Svenson does is call 'im a lousy nigger an' goes on callin' 'im that an' circlin' low down as if 'e was goin' to wrestle wiv 'im 'cep' 'e's got a knife in 'is 'and.

"Then Birk stands still an' lifts 'imself up to 'is full 'eight, like a bloody tower, and 'olds out 'is great 'ands as if 'e was appealin' to Svenson an' then—Jesus, honest to God nobody saw it—the knife was stickin' an' quiverin' in Birk's neck, right up to the 'ilt, an' the blood spurtin' an' runnin' dahn 'is chest an' 'im starin' like 'is eyes 'ud pop art of 'is 'ead and Svenson still watchin' 'im an' waitin' for Birk to fall dahn.

"But 'e don't fall dahn—ha!—'e don't fall dahn at all—an' yer shoulda seen Svenson's face when 'e don't fall dahn. Terrible, it was.

"An' then, with the knife stickin' in 'is neck, Birk moves towards Svenson, not walkin' so much as staggerin', but all the time movin' towards Svenson who's still crouchin' an' when 'e sees Birk comin' when 'e shoulda bin dead, when 'e sees 'is 'orrible face, 'e gets yeller like anybody would if they'd seen Birk's face comin' at 'em. Then Birk's right up to 'im with the muscles swellin' in 'is body an' the veins standin' art fit to bust an' 'is 'ands goin' up in the air. An' when Svenson sees 'e's 'ad it, 'e don't bolt but kneels like 'e was paralysed an' screams an' puts 'is 'ands together like 'e was prayin' to a black god wiv a knife in its throat, sayin', 'Don't 'it me, Birk, for the lova Christ don't 'it me.'

"The edge of Birk's 'and comes dahn an' 'its 'im in the back of the neck like a sixteen-inch brick, an' it's curtains for Svenson right enough. An' when 'e'd done this thing Birk lets out a terrible great sigh and falls on top of 'im."

Jacobson spoke into the silence. "I see. Thank you, Goldstein. Why do you tell me this?"

" 'Cos Birk's me frien', sir, an' I'm tellin' yer what really 'appened. Birk's a good man, tho' there's some of 'em 'ere what don't think so."

He looked round truculently and Frieslund the bos'n stepped forward. "Birkenhead is still alive, sir. They pulled the knife from his throat and wrapped a towel round his neck. The windpipe does not seem to have been hurt, nor the veins nor the backbone. He may live. He's in the sick bay and we've bandaged him up."

"Thank you, Bos'n." Jacobson turned back to the men and held out one hand. "The knife, please."

Goldstein said, "Who 'as the knife?"

Not a man stirred. Only the ship moved and rolled about their perpendicular figures. They looked at their feet or the deck or the back of the head of the man in front of them, but not at Jacobson.

"The knife," Jacobson repeated.

Again the shifty embarrassed refusal.

"I warn you," Jacobson said. "The knife."

It clattered into the silence at his feet and the bos'n stepped forward and retrieved it and wrapped it in his handkerchief to keep the blood off his hands. The crew had demonstrated their respect for their erect, pink-faced Captain with his cap dead-straight on his head.

Jacobson said, "Very well. We shall see about this," and turned to go, but a sepulchral voice spoke up from the rear of the men and Jacobson waited. "Let 'im die, Cap'n. 'E's a Jonah. A Black Jonah. You know what a Jonah is, Cap'n? 'E's a bad omen. You 'ave to get rid of 'im. You want to know something? Birkenhead's been sunk three times and every time 'e comes back. Every ship 'e's sailed in 'as bought it. You wouldn't like that to 'appen to us, sir, would you? You with your smart ship. That's why Svenson wanted 'im dead. Let 'im die if you ask me. Let 'im die."

The men kicked their feet against the deck and mumbled. Jacobson stalked angrily away, slamming the door behind him, and returned to the wholesomeness of his shining bridge.

VII

Jacobson remained on the bridge for the afternoon watch. At 14.30 the armed merchant cruiser *Conway* hove in sight and by 15.00 had taken up her station in the van of the convoy.

Although he wanted no part of what he took to be other men's wars, Jacobson experienced an immense relief when he saw her. Yet she was a symbol of war and he deplored her necessity and looked forward to the day, not necessarily when the war would be over, but when he himself could be rid of her and all ships like her. He turned his back on *Conway* and stumped into the charthouse and checked the dead reckoning and went on into the wireless office where he drank a cup of tea with the Radio Officer. Only after thirty minutes was he able to bring himself to return to the bridge and face the inescapable presence of *Conway*'s churning black stern.

But in the ships of the convoy, men by the hundred came up into the biting wind on deck and looked with professional, appraising eyes at the brave, long-fo'c'sled ex-liner tearing through the water at eighteen knots, boldly zigzagging ahead of the convoy, her white ensign taut in the wind.

They drifted below again in ones and twos, back into the warmth of their ships, and although some accepted the situation without question, others asked themselves or their shipmates what one ship, however diligent, could do to help so many in an emergency, and if any of them received an answer to their enquiry, it could not have provided them with very much comfort.

At 15.30 a morose Jacobson sent for Goldstein, and when that slack-bodied voluptuary was standing before him, as near to attention as he could manage without actually hurting himself, Jacobson said, "You believe in Jonahs, Goldstein?"

"Me, sir? Blimey, no."

"I do not, either. I have considered to signal for a doctor but I think you can be of greater use. I relieve you of all duties except that of attending to Birkenhead. You must nurse him so that he will live."

Goldstein showed all his broken teeth in a smile that spread in a huge crescent below his gargantuan nose.

"Aye aye, sir," he answered and actually doubled off the bridge.

Jacobson returned to his brooding contemplation of *Conway*'s stern. Night was not far away.

TWO

I

CAPTAIN RICHARD AINSLEE, RN, in command of HMS *Conway*, spoke to his Chief Engineer on the bridge telephone. "Chief, we may need all the revolutions you can give us . . . Yes . . . No, just a precaution. All right?"

He replaced the receiver in its cradle on the bulkhead and found his Officer of the Watch, Lieutenant Mallet-Jones, RNVR, staring at him in disbelief. Ainslee coughed, and frowned at the worsening sea. "Now that we're with the convoy we'll go to action stations at dawn and dusk. Usual thing. Sound off action stations"—he pulled back his woollen glove and glanced at his wrist watch—"in ten minutes' time. At 16.00, that is. Before the hands go to tea."

"Aye, aye, sir."

"It will, I fancy, be a sensible precaution."

"Er—yes, sir."

Conway, still far more of a liner than a warship, was a comfortable billet from which to wage a war; the crew's quarters were spacious to a degree and the accommodation for officers luxurious. The bridge was wholly enclosed and not at all the windswept, often seaswept platform of a naval vessel. Yet no one on board still laughed at jokes about luxury cruises. *Conway* was almost never in harbour, almost always at sea, slogging through the steep Atlantic seas with convoy after convoy, running a shuttle service between Halifax and Liverpool and back again, and turning round in these ports in as much time as was necessary to take on stores, fuel and ammunition. The faces of the crew had become drawn, not merely from weariness or the constant possibility of disaster but because *Conway*, for all her proud bearing, was a dangerous, semi-impotent ship from which to fight a battle.

But now there was something more than the familiar obduracy in Ainslee's face, something new, half exhilaration, half apprehension. He swept the horizon ceaselessly with his binoculars and called several times to the look-outs for redoubled vigilance. He could no longer stand still and moved restlessly from one side of the bridge to the other, as if seeking a better vantage point for each successive examination of the horizon. Mallet-Jones watched him and discovered that apprehension was contagious.

The Petty Officer signalman said to the signalman of the watch, "What's up with the skipper? Look at him! Like a cat on hot bricks." The signalman answered that he was flipped if he knew what was up with the skipper but that beyond all doubt something was up.

The first look-out said to the second look-out on the starboard wing of the bridge, "Why don't the skipper stand still? 'E's makin' me dizzy. What the 'ell's eatin' 'im?" The second look-out answered that he was flipped if he knew what was eating the skipper but that beyond all doubt something was.

Ainslee drank the tea his steward brought him but even as he picked up the cup and tilted it at his mouth and grimaced as the hot liquid tumbled down his throat, he watched the horizon.

He was an exceptionally handsome man with a tall athletic figure. Although his mouth was thin, sometimes almost cruel, his eyes were kind, unmistakably those of a man of the sea. He was a disciplinarian, his ship preceding all other loyalties; he governed *Conway* and all who sailed in her ruthlessly, but always with a scrupulous regard for what he believed, passionately, to be justice. He was something of a fop and, although he wore his cap a little farther back on his head than was customary among senior officers, his sole sartorial concession to the rigours of the Atlantic winter was a submariner's white jersey beneath his jacket and a spotless duffel coat which actually fitted him. He was nearly fifty and looked a young forty.

Ainslee had retired from the Navy in the early 'thirties, a Commander and a disillusioned man. Towards the end there had been little love lost between the service and this driving, clear-thinking man who apparently dedicated himself to the discomfiture of more senior, less brilliant officers. When he had taken himself off to Warwickshire and married a beautiful girl some fifteen years his junior and established himself as a market gardener, their Lordships had been wonderfully relieved to see him go. Let him, they said, expend his undoubted talents on the problems of raising vegetables. Things would run more smoothly, less acrimoniously without him; there would be fewer irreverent minutes, no more prodding and shoving upwards from below instead of from the top downwards. But they were thankful enough to see him back when war was declared. Within a year he had been made Captain and given command of *Conway*.

He had never been happier. His letters to Jean, his wife, still living at 'Manningtrees' and running the market garden with the help of his mother (who, when she was not gardening, was knitting him better and thicker seaboot stockings) were full of the excellence of the *Conway*. Jean accepted the divided love and comprehended the attraction of the great ship.

Ainslee often thought about the decision he had made when he had left the Navy; it had never ceased to disturb him. Before the war, immersed in the continual problem of making ends meet, he had been able to forget for long periods of time; but the doubt had always returned: persistent and nostalgic. He had tended to avoid places which could remind him of his former association; his uniforms had been packed away in moth-balled boxes, out of sight but never wholly out of mind. Secretly, he had wanted war.

The scar of amputation had never entirely healed and since he had taken command of *Conway*, the ship which had brought him such intense satisfaction, he had occasionally wondered whether he was not afflicted with some weakness of character, some defect of staying power.

He raised the binoculars to his eyes again and swept them through one-hundred-and-eighty degrees across the racing waves and the sea-sprayed six-inch guns on the fo'c'sle. The wind moaned and howled about him. Otherwise nothing, nothing but the sea and the grey sky, the silent ships and his own intuitive conviction of imminent peril.

II

Lieutenant Peter Mallet-Jones's greatest fear was that he had left Third Officer Gwendoline Baker in Liverpool with child. Not that he did not intend to marry her; he was anxious only that he should be able to marry her before her condition became generally apparent, if, indeed, she was pregnant at all. He wished desperately that he could know.

Wherever he looked, at the sea rushing under *Conway*'s bow, at the compass, at Ainslee still pacing across his bridge waiting for action stations to sound, he tended to see her: in the operations room, dwarfed by the immense representation of the Atlantic, so infinitely desirable in her uniform; and as he had seen her on their last night together before he had sailed, without her uniform or any of her clothes, lying with him in the hotel bed they had decided not to lie in until they were married.

Afterwards she had cried, crying and then not crying, but smiling with wet eyes as he held her in his arms and kissed her face and her fair hair and her throat until, it seemed he was ready to start all over again, no longer caring or even thinking, but possessed only by his love and his longing. Then she had eluded his arms and darted into the bathroom, and when she had emerged she had dressed and applied her make-up again in that strong-willed inflexible way that women have, while he had lain on his back on the bed and watched her.

"It was wonderful," he said, "bloody wonderful."

"Yes."

"I suppose we shouldn't."

"No."

"But you're not sorry, are you, darling?"

"No, of course I'm not sorry."

"Come over here."

"No. Get dressed."

"Just for a minute."

"Get dressed."

"Do you still love me?"

She had laughed, her fair hair falling in waves over her cheek, and had come towards him. "I still love you, darling. But now it would be better if you would get dressed. The food will be off."

They had gone down to dinner, the ostensible Mr. and Mrs. Mallet-Jones in whom no one believed, very young and very gay, and had drunk too much, telling themselves that they regretted nothing, but regretting it all the same; but happy, glad beyond all expectation.

Then he had returned to the darkened *Conway* and sailed the next morning with joy and a certain amount of anguish in his heart.

He watched Ainslee tramping from one side of the bridge to the other and noted again the expectant, preoccupied face. "Should I warn the ship's company that it will go to action stations in five minutes' time, sir?"

Ainslee halted and squinted at Mallet-Jones's youthful face, as if he had heard but not understood. "Hm?"

"Should I warn the ship's company—?"

"Yes, better do that."

Ainslee resumed his tramping and Mallet-Jones, becoming alarmed by his Captain's demeanour, asked of the retreating back, "Is there anything wrong, sir?"

Ainslee smiled at Mallet-Jones's concern. "Wrong? Yes, I think there's something wrong. Can't you smell it?"

"Smell what, sir?"

"Something wrong with . . . the feel of things."

"I can't smell anything, sir."

"No, perhaps you can't. Sorry." His eyes were half-closed under wiry eyebrows. "But keep a good look-out, will you?"

Both Ainslee and Mallet-Jones trained their binoculars on the shifting grey line between the sea and the sky and saw nothing that was not always there: the leaping foam-crested waves dancing over the curve of the earth.

Mallet-Jones called, "Bos'n's Mate!"

A fresh-faced sailor with brown hair curling under the edge of his cap stepped forward. "Sir?"

"Pipe hands to dusk action stations in five minutes' time."

"Aye, aye, sir."

Mallet-Jones lifted his binoculars again and shivered, involuntarily, as if something had run up and down his spine.

III

Able Seaman Eric Barraclough had risen as far as he would ever rise in His Majesty's Navy. He was squat, powerful and unalterably opposed to every kind of authority; of the earth, earthy, and generally foul-mouthed.

At action stations in *Conway* it was his task, before each shell was fired, to actuate the mechanism that closed the breech of the second of three ancient six-inch guns situated on the fo'c'sle. As mechanisms went it was not unlike a monumental oven-door and very nearly as clumsy. It was not a task that required any thought or even any particular expertise, but only an unflagging devotion to the principle that the mechanism needed to be actuated at certain recurring points in time, neither sooner nor later, but at a precise split second after each shell and its charge had been rammed home. He performed this task satisfactorily, if to an endless stream of profanity.

When the clangour of the alarm bell had raced through the ship Barraclough had been enjoying a cigarette in the fo'c'sle heads, an eminence he occupied with some frequency, due, as he had contritely explained to the fo'c'sle Petty Officer when last hustled up to the bridge for skulking, to the fact that everything, without exception, gave him the shits.

He had appeared before the officer of the watch, Mallet-Jones, in whose Division he was, and Mallet-Jones, unable any longer to deal with a man who so persistently offended, had referred him to the Commander, who was himself weary of the sight of Able Seaman Barraclough and could think of nothing else to do but refer him to Ainslee, who, at Captain's Requestmen and Defaulters, had said, after the Master at Arms had recited his sorry tale, "This is the third time you have appeared before me in the last three months, Barraclough. Have you anything to say?"

Barraclough had looked at him with his most engagingly innocent expression. "I'm bein' victimised, sir."

Ainslee had stared at him with those screwed-up seaman's eyes of his and snapped, "Three days' cells. We'll see how you like being victimised there."

The Master at Arms had scarcely been able to contain his gratification as his rat-trap mouth intoned, "Three days' cells. On cap! 'Bout turn! Doub-bul march!"

But three days of picking oakum had not significantly modified Barraclough's attitude; he remained bitter, obstinate and, in some intangible way, inconsolable.

Now he hurriedly pulled up his trousers and snatched his tin hat, anti-flash gear and sheepskin coat from the hook of the lavatory door, and moved more swiftly up the ladder than was his custom and ventured on to the exposed fo'c'sle. Curtains of spray sailed over the bow and he waited momentarily in the shelter of the doorway before racing across the intervening space to the rudimentary protection of his gunshield.

He crouched behind it and pulled on his anti-flash gear, and perched his tin hat on top of the white balaclava. Already the rattling spray was running down his neck, inside his coat, wetting his underclothes. He was savage with irritation. "What fer flip's sake's up now?" he demanded.

The gunlayer, sitting on his wet tractor seat, shouted above the wind, "Search me, mate. Maybe the skipper's getting twitch. Enough to give anybody twitch, this lot; and me just gettin' me head down."

Barraclough fastened the remaining buttons of his trousers under his coat and settled down on his haunches under the gun to await nightfall with as much stoicism as he could muster. For a while he appeared, incredibly, to sleep. Then, shifting his position, he said, abruptly, "What d'you make o't' skipper?"

The gunlayer answered, "He's O.K., I reckon."

"I mean, if he was in a scrap of some kind, what d'you reckon he'd do?"

"He'd go slap at 'em, mate, an' give the bastards 'ell."

"Why would 'e do that?" Eric asked.

" 'Cos 'e'd bloody well 'ave to. What else would you expect 'im to do? Blow 'em a kiss? Fart? Crikey, Barraclough, you're always askin' questions. Why can't you wrap up?"

Icy spray spiralled through the gaps in the gunshield and hit the gunlayer in the face. He was a three-badge, leather-skinned Stripey. "Cor, flip this for a lark. I'm soppin' wet through an' all you can do is chunter about the skipper. Look, why don't you go and ask 'im yourself? You've been introduced enough times, 'aven' you?"

Eric lowered his face to his knees and held his legs together with his arms. "D'you think 'e'd bother 'is 'ead about us?"

The gunlayer wiped salt water from the innumerable corrugations of his face and rolled his eyes towards the sky. "What d'you mean?"

"What I flippin'-well say!" Eric was irritated. "Why don't yer listen or 'ave yer got that much cotton-bloody-wool in yer lug-'oles yer can't 'ear any more? Would 'e bother what 'appened to us?" He shouted to make himself heard above the rattle of spray on the gunshields.

"Blimey, Barraclough, you ought to get a job on the wireless. They like blokes like you what can go on yammerin' day an' night. Drip, drip, drip, like a flippin' tap. You could be the forces ruddy sweetheart. 'Ow do I know? 'E's no better nor worse than any other skipper."

"Well, that's just where yer wrong, see? 'E's got a bee in 'is bonnet, 'e 'as. 'E thinks 'e's t'Lord God Ormighty, 'e does. When 'e gets t'bit 'atween 'is teeth 'e'll be off that fast, nowt'll 'old 'im. Should I tell yer fer why?"

"Go on. You tell me, Barraclough. I likes the sound of yer soothin' voice. 'Ere endeth the news read by Able Seaman Alvar Barraclough, the skipper's right 'and man. I asks yer mate, fer the third ruddy time, why don't you wrap up?"

"Medals," Eric said. "Another flippin' medal to nail to t'mast and say it belongs to t'ship. A fat lotta good that'll be when ev'ry sod in 'er's bought it good and proper."

" 'Ey, Barraclough! Ain't you got no machinery in that big 'ead o'yourn? Can't 'e buy it, an' all?"

" 'E doan't look t' kind that snuffs it to me, and anyway, 'e's not worried. 'E's no more worried about 'isen than 'e's worried about you. You'll see. 'E's lookin' fer trouble now, didn't yer know? Searchin' for it, all ovver the 'oggin."

The first green wave poured over the bow and the gunlayer and Barraclough and all the gun's crew were hanging on for life in three feet of raging, baffled water.

Conway ploughed on through the increasing seas, searching with a questing, quenchless intelligence for Ainslee's prey.

Very slowly, the light began to fade.

IV

On what at one time had been termed the Sun Deck—and still bore metal tags to this anachronistic effect—but what was now more accurately designated the Boat Deck, a number of Oerlikon automatic guns had been set up as a defence against enemy aircraft. There were eight of them, four on each side, set in metal pits, and when they were not manned their vicious barrels were locked in a perpendicular position and covered like snakes' heads. At action stations they were each manned by a crew of two and their barrels moved ceaselessly against the colourless sky.

Number One Oerlikon on the starboard side forrard was operated by a forty-year-old Able Seaman who, until war had been declared, had worked as a bank clerk in Leicester where, indeed, he had been born. The beginning of the war had been the signal for his release from a servitude he had long detested and to which he cherished no desire to return. In his own far-from-humble opinion his abilities were formed for greater things than the counting of pound notes; in the opinion of successive managers he was fit for little else. Oliphant found this divergence of opinion inexplicable and disturbing.

But if Oliphant's failures had made of him a man whose nature teetered about in the mental wilderness of the manic-depressive, their affect upon Priscilla, his wife, had been scarcely less severe. She had never learned to live the unassuming life to which her husband's modest income entitled her, and had grown middle-aged before her time hankering after almost everything that remained beyond her reach. Herbert Oliphant had often thought that he hated her, except that the hate was interspersed with such genuine sorrow for her unappeasable condition that it could no longer be termed hate and was perhaps nothing more than an infinite weariness punctuated by an ungovernable irritation.

Yet Oliphant loved, worshipped his gun. When he stood on the firing step of the mounting, strapped to the machine that at the mere compression of a trigger could become a shuddering juggernaut, he was a man transformed: determined, self-confident, furiously happy with the sea-wet wind whipping under his tin hat and the swish and clatter of the waves racing along the sides of the alerted ship in his ears. If he were ever to fire the gun in earnest he would probably fire it in the only ecstasy he had ever known. He leaned back in his leather harness and squinted through the circular sighting rings (see to this lady, Mr. Oliphant, will you?) slowly, lovingly moving the muzzle across the horizon (this is the second time your cash has been short this week, Oliphant) and fingering the cold trigger (Herbert, why can't we go to the Sands Hotel this summer? Do we really have to stay in that dreadful boarding-house?). Atop the plunging vessel, a part of his gun, Oliphant became in a sense more normal, and in another less so. He became a killer charged with the simple task of killing. This, at least, perhaps, he could accomplish well. As long as he was strapped to his gun he knew neither doubt nor fear; separated from it he reverted to his former type.

Oliphant's Number Two on the gun, Reggie Atkinson, came from Carlisle; a bright young boy of eighteen and a half who, by virtue of inordinate sacrifice by his parents, had been a scholarship boy at the Grammar School. His father drove an engine for the London, Midland and Scottish Railway Company and was paid four pounds ten shilling a week for his trouble and skill. He was a CW candidate, a candidate for a commission.

Oliphant hated Atkinson, found him a perpetual, walking affront, and wished him nothing but ill. He could not understand why this boy with the square childish face, this engine-driver's son, should have been singled out for such preferential treatment when he, Oliphant, the bank clerk, whose father had been in insurance, and whose wife had known better days when she was single, had remained so grievously unnoticed—a state of affairs made even more intolerable by a long complaining letter from Priscilla who had read of local boys making good in a similar manner, in the parish magazine.

"Why d'you think we've been called out like this?" Reggie asked.

Oliphant looked down at him from the firing step. He found it difficult to be civil and his sallow stubble-covered face was tense with dislike. "I don't know."

"What's the buzz?"

"The buzz?"

"Yes, the buzz."

Oliphant answered because he was unable to keep silent, because any kind of conversation could lead to a word of revenge. "Oh, I don't know. U-boats maybe. Or aircraft. You never know. Why? Afraid?"

Reggie watched Oliphant and recognised the suspicion of a sneer but did not understand it. "Aren't you?"

Oliphant leaned back in his harness, his hands in the pockets of his sheepskin coat. "I'm asking you."

"I should think most people are a bit scared."

Oliphant's superior attitude was magnificent. "You think so?"

"Yes, I think so. Aren't you?"

"What?"

"Scared."

"No. No, I don't believe I am."

"That's stupid."

"What's stupid about it?"

"Of course it's stupid. If there's a U-boat out there sighting its torpedoes, what are you going to do about it, eh? Tell me that."

"I said nothing about U-boats."

" I didn't say you did," Reggie answered, exasperated. "But suppose there is. Suppose you knew it was there, getting ready to take a pot-shot. You still wouldn't be afraid?"

Oliphant looked down contemptuously. "No."

"Sometimes, Oliphant, I think you must be a bit touched."

The satisfied grin fled from Oliphant's saturnine face. "Watch your tongue, Atkinson. Watch it."

Reggie was overcome with irritation. "You're daft, Oliphant. You're half-way round the bend. You're balmy."

Oliphant's dark face became darker, as if blinds were drawn behind the eyes, shutting out everything but the beseeching consternation. He lifted an arm to hit his tormentor, one short ineffectual arm that was not long enough to reach the angered boy who stood beyond his reach, watching him struggle in the gun harness while the barrel swayed wildly against the sky. Reggie turned his back on him.

"You cheeky jumped-up little bastard," Oliphant squeaked.

Reggie neither turned nor answered but stood watching the mill race of the sea and the advancing phalanx of the convoy astern. He took a tube of wine gums from his pocket and peeled back the silver paper. Later he held out the tube to Oliphant. "Want a sick pill?" Oliphant glowered and looked the other way.

When the glow had gone out of the light and the sky was a uniform matt grey, Reggie said, "Look, Oliphant. I'm sorry. I said I'm sorry, did you hear? Hey, Oliphant!"

But Oliphant was standing erect in his harness, his eyes scouring the sea ahead, chasing the tumbling waves and the spindrift flying ahead of the waves, as if he expected, imminently, to sight the target he had waited all his life to see. He stood with his feet slightly apart, the gun held hard against his body. It grew out of his chest like a monstrous symbol. The beginning of a smile moved on his tense face. He was no longer interested in Reggie or his wine gums or any of his peace offerings; he was interested only in firing his gun.

V

Chief Petty Officer Wilmot, the Chief Bos'n's Mate, in the absence of a single available officer, was in charge of Damage Control Headquarters and acted under the direct orders of the Commander of *Conway*. His station was in what was known as the bridge flat where, in the days of peace, had been situated the Purser's Office.

He was a large imperturbable man with a restful brown face and eyes that shone when he smiled; a generally silent, kindly man who carried out his duties with a despotic benevolence; a stocky upright man who always wore a good-quality, double-breasted, fore-and-aft Chief's Jacket with gold badges; who never deteriorated at sea and had not once in the last fifteen years missed writing his weekly letters to his Mrs. Wilmot in a shipshape little house in Plymouth. He was respected, admired and occasionally feared.

He not only knew *Conway* from stem to stern but also each member of her crew. He knew who were the sheep and who the goats. He knew her weakness and her strength and understood her terrible vulnerability. He felt a personal responsibility to his ship—*his* ship as much as anyone's. He knew her intimately as a man might know a woman and although neither he nor any man can ever wholly know a woman's mind, he was able to sense and even predict her changing moods. As he sat at his desk by the WT board in the old Purser's Office receiving telephoned reports from different parts of the ship, each message reporting Damage Control personnel closed up at action stations, he knew that all was not well with *Conway*.

He did not know why he knew this, unless the intimation came to him from the subtly changing atmosphere generated by the restless Ainslee high up on the bridge. The Captain's behaviour had been noted and watched by a dozen pairs of eyes and the knowledge gleaned from such covert observations disseminated throughout the ship in a thousand speculations. Wilmot did not like the way in which the engines were pounding beneath his feet, driving *Conway* forward through the worsening sea in curtains of spray. And apart from the engines and the creaking girders he did not like the silence.

His men looked at him questioningly. A pen on the desk

36

danced to the fury of the engines and he moved it to a different position and wedged it against the bulkhead. The ship was beginning to rattle and tremble like a demented thing. What in God's name was the skipper up to?

He got up and walked to the scuttle on the port side and peered at the torrential sea. The sky was beginning to darken. When he returned to his station the eyes of his men still followed him, watching him, waiting.

He looked at the youngest, a boy seaman who was being carried as a passenger, who had left his armour-plated cruiser in Norfolk, Virginia, and was being carried back to Chatham in order that he might be trained and later promoted to being a man. He was sixteen, a curly-headed slum child from Newcastle, with a wide mouth and high cheek-bones and small bright eyes set in freckles. The Commander had made him Wilmot's particular responsibility. "What's the matter, boy?"

"Nothin', Chief." And then the youth who was little more than a child asked, "Why are we at action stations, Chief?" He used the word Chief as if it were a synonym for father.

"It's the usual thing, boy. You know that."

He spoke softly and kindly because he liked the cheeky freckle-faced boy, liked him for his cheek and his youth and for his reliance upon him. The boy moved over to Wilmot's bulk and stood by the vibrating deck.

A man said, "She'll go down like a lump of lead if she's 'it with 'owt. There'll be no 'oldin' 'er."

"Stow it," Wilmot growled and looked at the boy's face that was already furrowed with alarm. Wilmot knew that the man was right, that in certain circumstances *Conway* was a floating coffin, a ship with no armour, insufficient water-tight doors and next to no armament. He said, "She has a clean pair of heels, does *Conway*." The men shifted their feet on the deck.

"Just listen to her now," Wilmot said.

Someone answered, "Flip me, Chief! What's eighteen knots?"

Wilmot winced. He did not necessarily object to profanity; through long association he had become impervious to its noise; but not with the boy there—that was not right. He said sharply, "Lead that hose down the starboard passage forrard. Chop-chop!"

The man obeyed and Wilmot looked at the boy again.

"Sailors are all the same, boy. If they've nothing to drip about they're not happy."

The boy grinned wanly at the portly Chief and wished he was the father he had never known.

When it happened the noise of it was like the ending of the world. It was not in the ship but away on the port side, shaking *Conway* as if she were a toy, rattling every bolt and rivet, halting her in her irresistible stride. She gathered herself and flung onward, her engines racing in her bowels towards a new peak of endeavour. The Damage Control Party streamed as one man to the scuttle on the port side—all except Wilmot and the boy, who would never leave Wilmot now.

"Come back, every man jack of you," Wilmot roared. "What d'you think this is? The ruddy boat race?" He glared at them, livid with anger. "Like a lot of bloomin' children at a tea party. Get fell in there and the first man to move before he's told to's in the rattle."

The second explosion was on the starboard side, nearer, erupting like a watery earthquake and flinging *Conway* sideways, appearing to lift her from the water and shift her to a different position in the ocean.

The Damage Control Party was thrown to the deck and the lights went out. Wilmot clung to a stanchion, "Get up," he shouted into the pitch-black uproar. "Get up, you lot of old women!"

The telephone whined. He picked it up and listened briefly and shouted, "Aye, aye, sir."

A voice cried in the scuffling darkness, "What is it, Chief? For Christ's sake, what is it?"

His reply was lost in the thunder of the third explosion which occurred not in the sea, nor in the air outside the ship, but deep in the ship itself. The Damage Control Party ran about like frantic ants in a disintegrating black nest. Wilmot crashed across the office to the emergency lamp and when the boy saw its tiny light he ran to Wilmot's side and hung on to his arm.

Conway opened fire and the light rocked in the racket of the fo'c'sle six-inch. The bridge flat decking jumped beneath their feet.

Wilmot shouted, "They're ours. Do you hear 'em? Listen! On your feet there!"

For a few seconds some order was restored. Wilmot picked up the telephone that connected him to the bridge but it was dead. A man said, "Just listen to them six-inch, all three of 'em soundin' off fit to bust. Jesus!"

Then the third obliterating explosion and the side of the ship opening and the water flooding pell-mell into the bridge flat and Wilmot standing with the boy in his arms, defying it to drown him.

THREE

I

JACOBSON'S disquiet mounted. His ship was too silent (silent, that is, except for the engines and the ceaseless creaking: constant sounds that partook of the quality of silence); even the Radio Office abaft the bridge was like a graveyard. Men talked in hushed voices and shifted their feet gently; they joked less often and with a greater respect for Providence.

He scanned the bridge of the Commodore's ship repeatedly but detected no untoward activity; no signals fluttered in preparation at the foot of her halyards, no man moved with sudden, urgent purpose. Dawson stood like a monolith, his great shoulders hunched within his sheepskin coat, its upturned collar splayed out like a fan, touching the back of his uniform cap. He followed *Conway*'s manoeuvres with undivided attention.

She was some three miles ahead of the convoy now, almost lost in the mists of her own watery slipstream, her stern hard down in the water. She tacked across the advancing front of the convoy, heeling over when she turned, flinging herself recklessly into each new course. Both Jacobson and Dawson were obsessed with *Conway*.

It was not the first time that Jacobson had experienced the apprehension which can overtake a man in the middle of the Atlantic waste, when he becomes more conscious than ever before of the immense distances that separate him from land, his natural environment, however much of a sailor he is; when he becomes terrifyingly aware of the countless fathoms beneath him, penetrable only by dead men, peopled by creatures only dead men have seen. But always before there had been a clearer conception of the immediate danger. . . .

He took a turn across the bridge, erect, pink-faced and alert, and when he had returned to his customary position he rummaged under his coat for his pocket-watch and compared its time with that of the chronometer on the bulkhead behind him. It was almost 16.00; the afternoon watch was nearly over.

Busk stamped on to the bridge to relieve Dawson. He had slept until five minutes earlier and had not yet been drawn into the mood of the watchers on the bridge. He was ebullient and a little too sure of himself, scarcely appearing to listen as Dawson handed over the watch: course, speed, signals, the Commodore's most recent orders and the trend of the barometer. Jacobson felt in his pocket for his pipe and began to fill it with tobacco.

No sooner had Dawson left the bridge than Busk asked, "Permission to smoke, sir?" Jacobson wished his First Officer could contrive to moderate the sarcasm in his voice; but he held up his burning pipe in reply.

"What's *Conway* doing out there?" Busk asked when he had lit his cigarette.

"I do not know. But I think perhaps she expects something."

"Expects something?"

"Yes."

"What can she be expecting?"

"That, Mr. Busk, we should all like to know."

"But, hasn't the Commodore said anything?"

"Nothing."

Busk inhaled from his cigarette and held it cupped inside his hand, seaman fashion. "I see the glass is still falling, sir."

Jacobson nodded, becoming irritated.

"Probably won't go any further. I shouldn't think so."

"No."

Oleron's pitching increased as the growing waves thwacked under her flared bow. The two men stood in silence, Jacobson watching the racing *Conway*, never taking his eyes away from her. Busk's eyes wandered, not yet sensing the magnitude of their danger. "It's beginning to get dark, sir."

Jacobson gripped his pipe with suppressed fury. What kind of donkey did he have on board his ship? Could it not stop its incessant noise? Then, characteristically, he thought: perhaps he is lonely; perhaps he, too, is already afraid and knows that talking lessens the fear; or perhaps it is not Busk but I who have become infected by this . . . tension. He felt a little ashamed and nodded his head in agreement.

"Good Lord, just look at the way she's turning," Busk exclaimed.

Conway was sweeping round to port, almost standing on her heeling stern as her rudder bit savagely into her wake.

"She's hard over," he added, astonished.

Jacobson squared his already square shoulders. "Mr. Busk, please, the engine room; inform the Chief Engineer to stand by for possible increase in speed."

"An increase in speed, sir?"

Jacobson swelled like an enraged turkey. "Yes," he shouted. "An increase in speed!"

Busk looked injured. "Yes, sir."

While Busk spoke to the engine room Jacobson's steward arrived with a cup of tea and placed it on the small table hinged to the after bulkhead.

"Your tea, sir."

Jacobson did not turn but moved a hand in acknowledgement.

Busk replaced the telephone and attempted placatory words. "Why don't you go below, sir? I can manage the First Dog all right."

Jacobson eyed him over his cup of tea, squinting at him through the steam, his brilliant blue eyes almost malevolent, incongruous in so patient a face. "No, not yet. Later, perhaps, when it is dark. We shall be safer when it is dark."

"You think so, sir?"

Jacobson wished that he knew whether Busk was a fool or just one of those lonely ungifted men who, unable to comprehend what they take to be aloofness in others, become themselves unbearable in their struggle to be liked.

"Yes, Mr. Busk, I do."

II

Harris, the one-eyed engineer passenger, stumbled on to the bridge. He wore his uniform cap and a chequered civilian overcoat of gangster cut. Jacobson wondered briefly how he had managed to save his cap when he had last been shipwrecked, how, when he had lost everything, including an eye, he had yet managed, palpably, to save his cap.

"What's all this?" he demanded in his hoarse Midlands voice. Even Busk was astonished.

Jacobson regarded him levelly. "You wish something, Mr. Harris?"

Harris came nearer. "This *Conway*. What's she doing out there? What good can she do all that ruddy way off?"

"Watch your tongue," Busk said.

"You keep out of this," Harris snapped.

Busk would have spoken again but Jacobson intervened, "I do not know what *Conway* is doing. And it would oblige me if you would leave my bridge."

Harris showed no inclination to obey. He just stood there, his hands deep in the pockets of the extravagantly-tailored overcoat they had found for him in Halifax, a half ludicrous, half pathetic mixture of barrow-boy and country bus conductor, his face contorted by what could only be an overwhelming disappointment. He moved even nearer to Jacobson, his voice pleading, "What's she doing there? Tell me that! You're the skipper! Tell me what she's doing!" Before Jacobson could reply or remonstrate he turned to Busk. "No protection! Always the same bloody story. No protection! You can get blown to hell and nobody'll give a damn." He swung and glared at Jacobson. "Why don't you get her back? Why doesn't somebody tell the bastard to come back?" His voice rose still further. "Get her back, damn you! Somebody get her back!"

When it suited his purpose, Jacobson was capable of tremendous self-control. *Oleron*'s bow swung upwards and crashed back into the trough sweeping towards it, knifing the water and the spray into great arcs that fled towards the bridge, the myriad globules hammering like hail against the streaming glass. When the tireless bow rose again Harris and Jacobson were still staring into each other's faces, the one lividly, the other with an obstinate, kindly patience. "Go below, Harris. Go below. There is some tea below."

Harris's remaining eye seemed to soften and its solitary gaze moved away and fastened itself on *Conway*.

"I'm sorry," he said. "I'm sorry. I didn't mean to shout."

He turned and walked slowly away, his slight figure not at all disguised by the shoulders and pinched waist of his overcoat.

III

Schirmer and da Falla were off watch, drinking tea from thick white mugs in the crew's mess. The bulkheads were hung with moving coats and oilskins which, in reality, were the only stationary objects in a world of universal movement.

43

Schirmer said, "Hey, da Falla. Where you come from?"

"Where do I come from?"

"Ya. Where you come from, da Falla?"

Da Falla poured some of his tea into a saucer, blew on it, and looked over the steaming pool at Schirmer's pale, bony face.

"Singapore."

"Singapore? I never been that far East. The skirt, it is good in Singapore?"

Da Falla rubbed the side of his long nose which projected over his mouth like a bird's beak. "Not bad, man. You ought to go. They'd like you there, with that big weapon of yours."

"S'that so?"

"Sure."

"Hey, da Falla. How is Birk?"

"He's all right."

"He does not kick the flippin' bucket?"

"How can Birk kick the bucket?"

"All men the flippin' bucket can kick."

"Birk won't," da Falla said with finality, and sucked at the cooled tea in the saucer balanced on the flat of his hand.

"What is this about Jonah? I do not know her."

"Some guys are so scared they have to think up things like Jonahs. A Jonah? Jesus, I don't know. But when you've got one aboard you've had it. Hopeless, man."

"You think he is not a Jonah?"

"I told you, didn't I?"

"Ya, you told me but all de other guys, they say he is this bloody Jonah."

Da Falla mimicked his accent. "They said so, did they? They told you, did they?" He was suddenly furious. "Get this, Schirmer. Birk's all right. He's our mate. He'll do anything for you, will Birk. If you let him down, Schirmer, by God, I'll fill you in—lah! Got that?"

"Ya, sure, da Falla. O.K. O.K."

"Then don't forget it."

Da Falla drank his tea.

"Hey, da Falla!"

"What is it now, for Chrisake?"

"The skirt. In where was it, Singapore? Ya. Singapore. It is good, eh?"

Da Falla looked at the craggy moon of Schirmer's face and rubbed the side of his nose again with his index finger. "So-so."

"Jesus, da Falla. Think!—Women!—Do I ever tell you about the one in . . ."

"Schirmer, why don't you stop thinking about skirt? Ain't you got nothing else to think about 'cept skirt? I'll tell you what to think about. Think about Birk, 'cos he's goin to need us. Balls, you got to think about Birk."

"O.K. O.K., da Falla. I'll dream about him like he was a fancy piece of skirt."

"You better, man."

Schirmer was suddenly serious. "Do not worry, da Falla. Birk will be O.K. I say so, no?"

"O.K., then."

IV

The Reeds sat in the saloon. Albert reading a paper-backed novel, Alice plucking absently at the loose skin under her chin, waiting for Chan Sam to provide them with strong tea and rock-buns. The prevailing apprehension, like an epidemic, had spread to the passengers; no one, now, was immune. Alice said, not looking at her husband, "D'you reckon everything's all right, Albert?"

He continued to read. "Yes, of course it is."

She sighed, a little helplessly. "Oh, I do hope you're right."

He placed his book face downwards on the tablecloth and smiled at her reassuringly. There was much determination left in both their honest, open faces, but they were getting old and just a little tired. "Everything's all right, mother. You'll see."

Stockmann entered the saloon and seated himself at the vacant table next to the Reeds. He, too, carried a book. His spectacles flashed as he inclined his head. "Good afternoon."

Harris followed him, and when he had divested himself of his extraordinary overcoat, he sat down with Stockmann. "I've just been up on the bridge." He spoke easily, showing no sign of his earlier excitement. He might have been the Captain's confidant, a privileged friend with a standing invitation to the bridge.

"Yes?" Stockmann asked.

"It's a pretty daft way to run a convoy. I can tell you."

"Why so?"

"Bloody escort's miles away."

Stockmann took off his huge spectacles and polished the lenses with the handkerchief he kept specially for the purpose in his breast pocket. His eyes were much smaller without them.

Harris added, "She's so far away you can hardly see her."

Stockmann replaced his spectacles, "That is bad? At least she is now with us."

"It's not only bad, it's madness." Harris was becoming excited again. "You don't want the entire bloody convoy wiped out, do you?"

Stockmann glanced at the Reeds, indicating, it seemed, an irritation with Harris and removed with his little finger a molecule of Harris's spittle from the side of his nose. "Mr. Harris, I am not concerned with your convoy. I am concerned only with this ship and its safe arrival at the other side."

Harris's face fell, like that of a child deprived of a special prize. "What did you say?"

"I am concerned only with *Oleron*."

Harris's voice was incredulous, suddenly outraged, "You're not on our side?"

Wearily: "I am on no one's side, Mr. Harris."

Harris said flatly, "That's your game, is it? Shove off, Jack, I'm inboard."

Stockmann stood up and wiped his lips on his napkin. "If you will excuse me," he said and marched heavily from the saloon.

Harris slumped in his chair and when he glanced tentatively at the Reeds, Alice thought he was going to cry. "You shouldn't speak to him, Mr. Harris," she said in her soothing, sensible voice. "He's not like us, is he, Albert?"

Albert mumbled, "Suppose he's got a right to be neutral, but it don't seem right to me."

Harris did not answer but continued to sit at the table with one fist opening and shutting itself on the white linen.

"Are you all right, Mr. Harris?" Alice asked.

"Yes. Yes, I'm all right. Thank you."

V

Goldstein sat in the tubular-steel chair by Lord Birkenhead's bed. The Negro was covered in blankets and the bandages about his neck shone against the black marble chin. His eyes were open, staring at the white deckhead. Occasionally the thick lips moved in the sculptured face, trying to speak. Sweat glistened on his forehead and when the ship tilted, droplets shifted and gathered momentum and coursed across the skin to the pillow.

"You O.K., Birk?"

The lips moved again and when the voice came it contained none of its former vibrant vitality. "Ah'm O.K., Goldy."

"Wan' anuvver drink?"

"Ah'd sure like another drink. Ah just gotta keep on drinking."

He did not move his head or interrupt his contemplation of the deckhead. Goldstein stood up and took the cup from the ledge on the bunk and put one gentle calloused hand under the invalid's head and slowly lifted it. Then he put the cup against the lips and allowed the liquid to trickle into the red mouth. "Steady does it, Birk. Steady does it." When the lips were surfeited he lowered the head to the pillow. "That better, Birk? That better?"

He sat down and leaned back in the unfamiliar comfort of the armchair, crossed one leg over the other, interlaced his fingers behind his head, and reflected upon his remarkably good fortune. No exposure to wind and weather for Goldstein on this voyage! A wet smile widened over his blubbery mouth. He felt like singing. He hummed to himself,

> It was on the good ship Venus,
> By Gad you should've seen us . . .

Birkenhead shifted in his bunk.

"You all right, Birk?"

"Yeah, Goldie, ah'm all right."

Goldstein relaxed again. The cabin was quiet except for the slow sound of Lord Birkenhead's breathing, creaking decks, and the distant persistent beat of engines. Rivets shifted excruciatingly in their sockets.

"Goldie."

Goldstein, the incomparable nurse, was on his feet at once.

47

"Want sumfink, Birk?"

Birkenhead mouthed the words before the sound came, as if rehearsing them before giving voice. "Svenson. What happened to Svenson?"

"Boy, you really fixed that bastard."

"What happened to him, Goldie?"

"What 'appened to 'im? Crikey, 'e went aht like a light, 'e did. Snuffed it."

Then there was silence again, except that Goldstein could now hear the faraway swish of the swell as it fled past the ship. Birkenhead's eyes were closed, hiding some of the pain. "He's dead?"

"Yeah, 'e's dead all right."

Goldstein patted the sheet near Birkenhead's face and sat down again.

"You can read, Goldie?"

"Sure I can read. I mean, I can read a bit. Why d'you wanna know if I can read, Birk?"

"Can you get a Bible from de Cap'n?"

"A Bible, Birk? You ain't goin' to pass on, so what you wanna Bible for, eh?"

"Go an' get de Bible, Goldie."

"Yer want for me to read the Bible to yer, Birk? You goin' crazy or sumfink?"

"Ah guess you kin read as well as any man here present, Goldie."

Birkenhead smiled, a wondrously wide and charitable smile, and as Goldstein watched him he knew, ridiculously, that if he did not go soon his own eyes would begin to swim with gratitude. He said, quickly, "O.K., Birk. I'll go get a Bible for yer. An' I'll read it to yer, so 'elp me. But I'm warnin' yer, I don't read so good."

He moved towards the door.

"Goldie."

"Yes, Birk?"

"Tell them ah'm sorry about Svenson."

Goldstein grinned in the doorway. "'E 'ad it comin' to 'im, Birk. Git yer flippin' 'ead dahn."

VI

Dawson cautiously opened his cabin door and peered up and down the passage. When he was certain that he was unobserved he stepped out and closed the door gently behind him. He moved aft and when he came to the last door he halted and knocked respectfully on the varnished woodwork.

"Come in."

Gerda Olstein was lying on her back on her bunk, wrapped in a woollen dressing-gown. She had been asleep and he had evidently awakened her. The rich mass of her blonde hair, no longer controlled, lay like bent hay on her pillow. She did not appear surprised that he had come; nor, for that matter, did she appear pleased. But she sat up and swung her legs over the side of the bunk so that she could sit on her hands and look at him. "Yes?"

"I thought maybe you'd like to come and get some tea."

"Tea?"

"Yeah, tea. There's nothing else at this time."

"It is tea time? I have slept."

"Good for you."

He saw the shape of her breasts under the dressing-gown and wondered if she was wearing a brassiere, and when the base of his neck prickled wondered, also, whether his hair actually lifted itself from his skin. He moved nearer, pushing the door closed behind him, and stepped on to the mock Persian carpet. She encountered him with her equivocal stare, expressing neither encouragement nor protest—he saw nothing in her face but a disconcerting absence of animation. She stood up and when she pulled her body erect her breasts were more than ever in evidence, bold, almost intimidating, and when he saw them, or rather the cleft that ran deeply between them, he forgot the vacancy and wanted only to hold her.

She said, "I will have tea with you."

He liked her voice: low, controlled and infinitely precise. "Yeah, sure. I'll wait, huh?"

"If you wish."

She picked up a brush from the chest of drawers and began to run it through her straight hair which fell nearly to her waist. She did not smile, did not betray the slightest measure of gratification or displeasure, did not even appear to notice that Dawson was already sitting on the edge of her bunk, bouncing his fists up and down on his knees, grinning, trying to take a deep breath and receiving only half the air his condition demanded. He watched her coil her hair adroitly on her head.

"The voyage," she said. "It is good?"

"Yeah, it's O.K. I guess. But there's something about."

"About?"

"The enemy. You know, Jerries and things."

"Oh? We are not safe?"

"Search me. Mind if I smoke?"

"No. How long before we reach England?"

"A week, maybe. Maybe a little less."

She was tall, almost as tall as he was, and beautifully proportioned. Everything about her was big; yet she was poised, even graceful. He wanted to hold her and make her sad, beautiful face smile. If only she would demonstrate something other than this irritating docility; it would be better, he thought, if she would hit him.

"That is a long time," she said.

"What is?"

"A week."

"Yeah. Depends how we spend it."

"Who?"

"Us. You and me. Who do you think?"

Her hair in place she turned to face him and untied the girdle of her dressing-gown so that it fell open before him. She wore only her underclothes and no slip. He heard the blood pumping through the bottlenecks in his temples and began to stand up. She said, "Do not move. There is no need to move. It is often that I undress in front of men. You are surprised?"

He laughed, stupidly. "No, I'm not surprised. That is, I don't think I'm surprised. Am I supposed to be?"

Then he was on his feet, grasping her firm arms and pulling her body towards his and pushing his mouth on to hers while his big hands moved over her back searching for the brassiere fastening, and not finding it, and then, defeated, coming between them until they rested, still confounded, on the relentless strength of the protective material. The ship heeled and rolled and when, in consternation, he drew his face away from hers he saw her as he had sensed her, passive, unco-operative, waiting patiently for him to finish, neither resisting nor responding, merely enduring.

"Why, Gerda? For God's sake, why?"

She turned away and pulled on her sweater and climbed into her skirt. While he waited he tugged down his jacket and ran his finger nails through his hair and wiped his mouth on the back of his hand.

"Why?"

"We go and have tea?"

"Sure, sure. Let's go and have tea."

VII

For the hundredth time that afternoon Jacobson swept the horizon with his binoculars and discovered nothing but the intermittent magnification of *Conway*'s churning stern. Now he lowered the glasses so that they hung on the strap against the rounded protuberance of his waist. Once more he delved beneath the stiff skirt of his sheepskin coat and brought out his watch and held it in the palm of his hand while his gaze returned to the horizon and his thumb moved to and fro across the glass face. It was 16.00. He waited, it seemed, at attention, his lips pursed in his pink face, wrinkles of concentration gathering about his eyes.

He was not surprised when he heard Busk's urgent voice singing out in a seamanlike manner, "Signal up on the Commodore, sir!"

As Jacobson raised his glasses, the noise of the wind increased; what had been a variable moan became the precursor of a scream.

Busk's incredulous voice read off the flags, "Emergency turn to port."

"Watch it," Jacobson ordered. His glasses swung back to *Conway*.

"Why an emergency turn?" Busk complained. "We can't have practice turns now. It'll soon be dark."

"Watch it," Jacobson repeated, observing *Conway* execute a maximum turn to starboard.

There was a plaintive quality in Busk's voice. "She's turning again. What's up with her?"

"Watch the signal, Mr. Busk. It is repeated?"

"Yes, sir."

Jacobson kept his glasses trained on *Conway*, concentrating, trying to divine the meaning of the escort's behaviour and already half-perceiving it; trying to anticipate his own reaction and formulate his orders—and already knowing them.

"Messenger. Call the Second Mate."

"Aye, aye, sir."

Conway was standing on her stern, sheering round to starboard, her screws biting deeper into the water, her bow coming up like the snout of an oceanic monster.

"Watch that signal, Mr. Busk."

"Aye, aye, sir."

Busk seemed to encounter difficulty in standing still. He moved continuously, oscillating about a fixed point as if constantly changing his mind, a kind of physical gibbering. But he kept his eyes on the Commodore's signal with commendable zeal.

"What the hell's he waiting for?" he asked savagely. And then, "Signal down, sir."

The hoists on the leading ships fluttered together down wind-taut halyards.

Jacobson waited until the leading ship of his column had turned, and when *Oleron* had taken her place, ordered, "Port twenty."

"Port twenty," Busk repeated.

"Port twenty," the Quartermaster echoed as he swung the wheel. "Twenty of port wheel on, sir."

As the first order was being repeated, Jacobson was already delivering the next, "Two short blasts." He was gratified to see that Busk was ready at the lever; perhaps he was not as excitable as he sounded.

Dawson's great bulk appeared on the bridge as the leading ships' hooters shattered the comparative silence of the wind and sea: hooters fit to sound the final trump, some that whooped with banshee wails, others that simply grunted, like elephants with indigestion—heralds of pandemonium.

Jacobson raised his voice above the uproar. "Mr. Dawson. Man the gun. Prepare the smoke floats."

"Aye, aye, sir."

Busk called, "Another signal up on the Commodore, sir."

Jacobson strode towards him. "Watch it. I take the ship."

Busk hurried out on to the wing of the bridge, breathless now with excitement, apprehension or both. Jacobson watched *Oleron*'s head and the ships on each side jockeying for position. The convoy was rapidly losing shape. He could afford only occasionally to glance at *Conway* sliding down the starboard side.

"Further emergency turn to port, sir. *To port!*" Busk reported.

"Very good. Hold the wheel over, Quartermaster."

"Signal down, sir," Busk called, hurrying back to Jacobson. *Oleron* was rolling like a barrel in the beam swell and Busk's approach assumed a drunken quality.

"What's *Conway* doing?" he shouted at Jacobson as a new crescendo of hooting and grunting exploded in the streaming air. Jacobson feared that Busk was going to take hold of him.

"Take the ship, Mr. Busk."

"What the hell's going on, sir?"

"Take the ship!"

Jacobson brought his binoculars to his eyes and searched the sea beyond *Conway*. She was moving astern now and he was forced to go out on to the starboard wing to see her. He watched her for as long as he dared; then his shoulders hunched, as though he were steeling himself against some physical attack. "There she is. Oh God, there she is!"

He hurried inboard and when he came near to Busk he said, "She is there."

"I can't hear you," Busk shouted. "What did you say?"

The starboard look-out answered him. "Ship abaft the starboard beam, sir."

Dawson was back on the bridge. "Seventy-five manned. Smoke floats ready, sir."

"Very good," Jacobson said, and then to the Quartermaster, "Ease her."

Busk was still shouting. "What kind of a ship? Starboard look-out, what kind of a ship?"

Jacobson growled, "Mr. Busk. Attend to the course."

When the voice of the port look-out reached them, all had already seen what he reported. "Verey lights over the Commodore, sir."

"Christ," Busk shouted, wheeling round. "Scatter! They're scattering the convoy, sir. They're scattering us!" He ran to the starboard wing. Jacobson looked after him as though he would like to kill him. His lips pursed into a perfect circle, the colour in

his cheeks heightened and his blue eyes shone with animosity.
"Mr. Dawson!"

"Sir?"

"Take the ship."

"Aye, aye, sir."

"Emergency full ahead!"

"Emergency full ahead, sir," the Quartermaster answered.

"Midships," Dawson ordered, almost laconically.

Jacobson snatched the telephone from its bracket on the bulk-head and angrily twirled the handle. The telegraph jangled in his ears as he shouted in Swedish to the engine room.

Busk trained his glasses astern. "What is she, look-out?"

The sailor glanced at him contemptuously and shrugged. "What is she, man? I can't see. What is she?" He looked wildly amidships and saw Jacobson and Dawson standing with cool detachment before the wheel, driving the ship through the mêlée of fleeing vessels as if they were merely leaving harbour. He wanted to run back and claw at their faces until they answered him. "What for Christ's sake is she?"

The soundless gun-flashes bloomed like obscene flowers on the horizon. Busk raced inboard. "She's firing! She's firing at us! God Almighty, she's firing!"

Jacobson looked with hard, unforgiving eyes at his First Mate. "And *Conway*, what is she doing?"

"She's ... er ... steaming towards the ... er ... enemy, sir."

"Thank you, Mr. Busk."

FOUR

I

THE blood-red flashes spewing out of the grey shape on the horizon induced in Ainslee a sensation bordering on relief. He had been right! He was about to engage in a murderous battle, a battle which, on the face of it, he could not possibly win, yet he was not concerned with fear or death or even with glory—what was glory?—but only with the precise mechanics of victory. Ainslee's doubts were dissolved by the enemy's fire; those of most of the men who sailed with him were only just beginning.

"Ease to twenty!"

"Ease to twenty, sir."

"Emergency full ahead on both engines."

"Emergency full ahead on both, sir."

He gave the orders before the first salvo of eleven-inch shells from *Leipzig* fell in the water alongside *Conway*.

"Officer of the Watch, make course for the enemy. Pilot, give me the course to intercept."

The Navigating Officer called, "Coming up, sir." Mallet-Jones attempted to tutor his voice to sound as if he were acknowledging an order to darken ship or pipe liberty men to fall in, and smiled, "Aye, aye, sir. Midships."

The engines thundered beneath his feet. Pencils danced on charts, abandoned cups jumped off shelves and water on glass was vibrated into an opaque, excited film; everything rattled and tried to shake itself to pieces in the fearsome delivery of mechanical energy. Never before had *Conway* been lashed into such an inhuman speed, nor, in the opinion of the Chief Engineer, if the present revolutions were maintained for any length of time, would she ever sail at half this speed again—unless, that is, they gave him a new set of engines. The skipper, he said, could have that for a fact. The belching gobs of flame appeared again on the raider's turrets and Ainslee ordered between the flash and the explosion, "Port ten."

The Navigating Officer reported, "Bearing zero-eight-five,

sir. Range, ten miles. Course two-four-zero. Speed five knots. Intercepting course, one-six-zero, sir."

"Very good. Stand by to open fire."

"Aye, aye, sir. Stand by to open fire," the Gunnery Officer answered and added, but only to Mallet-Jones, "All this and heaven too, old boy. Might as well try and pee on it if you ask me."

Ainslee stood forrard by the bridge screens and loosened the huge navy-blue scarf about his neck. The scarf, like the seaboot stockings and the extra-long vest had been knitted for him by his mother. Yet, at that moment in time, it was difficult to accept the fact that Ainslee had ever had a mother or that a mother had ever had him; he was simply a component of his ship like the compass or the mainmast. The others on the bridge had exchanged their caps for steel helmets, but Ainslee seemed unable to find time or thought for such a simple precaution; it was necessary for all but him because all were more vulnerable than he could ever be. He leaned forward a little, balancing on the balls of his feet, flexing his legs as the ship rolled. His eyes never left the sinister presence on the horizon.

Spray displaced by the second salvo rattled about them but his staccato naval bark was clearly audible. "We have to engage her and keep her engaged until the convoy is dispersed and it's dark. What is she, Guns?"

"Looks like the *Leipzig*, sir."

"I thought so."

Leipzig's guns fired again, and until those on the bridge had observed the fall of shot no one spoke, for all except Ainslee were preoccupied with the hiding of their unhideable bodies under the meagre protection of their tin hats.

"Hoist the Battle Ensign."

"Hoist the Battle Ensign, sir."

"Make smoke."

"Make smoke, sir."

"Open fire!"

"Aye, aye, sir. Target still out of range, sir."

Ainslee was furious. "I know, man. Open fire! Give 'em something to think about."

"Fire! Fire! Fire!"

The six-inch guns on the fo'c'sle opened up instantaneously, shaking and jolting the ship as if some maddened imbecile giant were kicking her, trying to prevent her onward flight. Mallet-Jones wondered stupidly whether it would be proper to hold on to his tin hat, like a woman in a gale, and whether, if he didn't, it would jolt right off his head.

The third salvo fell much nearer to *Conway*; the German gunners in their efficient mechanised turrets had already got the measure of their puny David. The limited world of *Conway* was dwarfed by a roaring erupting waterspout. She lurched in her progress and as the water came down so the black smoke billowed upwards through it.

"We're hit, sir," Mallet-Jones shouted, empty and churning inside, wanting to be sick, shaking like the ship in the smoking uproar as water thudded on to the bridge deckhead and the ear-splitting crack of the six-inch pummelled his body.

Ainslee was on the telephone to the engine room. "Speed, Chief! Speed! I don't care what it breaks. Give me more knots!"

It was with something akin to horror that Mallet-Jones discovered that Ainslee was actually enjoying himself. It was preposterous. It was unnatural. But it was true. The blue eyes were narrowed in resolution and about the thin mouth lurked the ghost of a smile. When the raider fired again the eyes did not blink; the German might have done nothing more than make his move in a game of chess. As Mallet-Jones watched Ainslee in the awful period of waiting, he found himself both loving and hating the man and saying silently, "Please God make them miss," and then to the ship, "Get on, you broken-down, tired-out, no-good cow! Get on! Get on! *Get on!*" He gripped the steel rail on the bridge bulkhead, urging the extended *Conway* to greater efforts, to an even greater speed. The thunder of the engines redoubled, the vibrations racing through the bulkheads and along the decks and up through the soles of his boots, tickling his feet in a frenzy of minute movement until he was obliged to stand first on one foot and then on the other, as if, ludicrously, he had pins and needles.

Finally, the approaching whine of the numbered ton-weight shells, and the ship's head already turning in avoiding action, and Mallet-Jones, the prep school teacher not devised by God for this kind of thing or anything remotely like it, standing there erect, still giving orders in a seamanlike manner, no more than a little white-faced, smothering the voice screaming inside him,

"Turn! Turn, you beauty, turn . . . faster . . . faster than this . . . Gwen . . . Where are you, Gwen? It's me, Peter . . . I'm here . . . It's coming . . . Oh God, it's coming. Get down . . . Get down . . . For the love of Christ, *get down*!"

A hurtling locomotive hit him in the small of the back and he was rolling and banging over the jumping deck, entangled with other bodies and with what appeared to be the binnacle and most of the charthouse. What had been the bridge of *Conway* no longer existed.

II

When Mallet-Jones had been a child, his mother had warned him that if he were ever careless enough to fall down the stairs he would probably, as she put it, kill himself. And when, inevitably, he tripped and plunged head first from top to bottom, and arrived yelling in the hall with a bump on the back of his head and the remains of the alarm clock he had been carrying clutched tightly in his hand, the first question he had asked of his mother, when able to draw an agonised breath, had been whether he was now dead or alive.

It was the same in *Conway*, except that on this occasion his mother was not there to reassure him and for some time he was unable to convince himself that he was indeed still alive and not dead. He had lost his tin hat and when he put his hand to his fair hair, in much the same incredulous way in which he had searched for the damage when he had been a child, it came away sticky with blood. His long white face stared at the discoloration with disbelief. Where was he? How had this happened?

Then he was disentangling himself from the smashed wood and the slack scarecrow bodies stretched on top of him, savagely, as if he were drowning in their litter. When he was free of their weight and able to struggle to his feet, he stepped in a creeping lava-stream of blood and slipped and fell against the shattered bulk-head and tore his arm on its jagged edges. Another salvo screamed over the desolation of the bridge and the noise of its passing rivalled the ringing in his head.

The Captain! Where's the Captain? "Where are you, sir? Where are you?" He threw himself into the human rubble as the next salvo passed over the bridge and crumped into the water astern. His hands shook and his teeth would not stop chattering, but with a desperate strength he picked over the bodies like a deranged scavenger, grasping and pulling at blood-wet shoulders and turning the corpses over, lurching as the ship lurched, finally vomiting over the obliterated faces. "The wheel? Where's the wheel? We can't steer without a wheel! We can't do anything without a wheel!" He looked into the wind flooding over the bridge. *Leipzig* was still on the port bow, still moving steadily in a south-westerly direction, going about her business of destruction systematically, closer now, much closer, so close that he could recognise her silhouette perfectly—no longer a spitting grey shape but unmistakably a battleship. He screamed into the wind, "Captain, Sir! Where are you?"

He crouched against the torn edge of the after bulkhead as the ship shied to a new explosion. What in the name of God did one do? His fingers skated over the twisted metal and he put his cheek against its coldness; not a living soul in sight except the automata on the six-inch far below on the fo'c'sle: "All dead, all dead! Why are you dead? God, why are you dead?"

The voice came from the other side of the bridge, weak but still authoritative in the intervals of six-inch fire. Mallet-Jones stayed where he was, crouching against the bent paint-flaking metal, hearing the voice as in a dream.

"Mallet-Jones."

"Hm?"

"Mallet-Jones!"

Then he was stumbling through the wreckage and the slippery mess, slithering to a halt where Ainslee was trying to sit upright.

"Are you all right, sir? Are you all right?"

"My legs, damn it! I'm all right, but my bloody legs . . ."

Mallet-Jones's hands hovered over Ainslee's shins, waiting, afraid of what they might find. But he closed his eyes and grasped the flesh and bones within the torn trousers and sensed the movement of the feet that were attached to the legs like those of a loose-limbed puppet. Ainslee shouted with pain and Mallet-Jones through human contact found himself again.

"They're broken."

"I thought as much. Where's the enemy?"

"On the port bow, sir."

"Still attacking?"

"Still attacking. The bridge is knocked out."

"Anyone still alive?"

"No, sir. I don't believe anyone on the bridge is still alive."

"No stretcher party?"

"I don't think they could have got very far, sir, before being hit."

"I see. Now, listen, Mallet-Jones. We've got to get to the after position. You'll have to carry me, all right?"

"Yes, sir."

Mallet-Jones was not at all certain that he would be able to lift Ainslee, let alone carry him, but he got down on one knee and put one arm under his thighs and tightened the other about his waist and when he stood up he lifted with the strength of ten men. "All right, sir?"

Ainslee was unable to speak and could only mouth the words through the pain, "Hurry! For God's sake, hurry."

Inexplicably, Mallet-Jones found himself moving, sliding down ladders, staggering through littered passageways with Ainslee gasping and groaning into his shoulder; never hesitating however terrible the exploding uproar, but weaving across the boat deck until flung full-length by a shell exploding amidships, and even then, as the mast swayed and sank its trailing bulk into the belching funnel, not stopping but crawling head down in tight circles through the nightmare like a disabled insect, searching and calling for Ainslee who was flat on his agonised face, still moving, dragging himself along with his finger nails deep in the pitch between what remained of the deck-planking. Like an avenging angel, amid the shrieks and groans and dying curses, Mallet-Jones gathered Ainslee into his bent body and reeled aft again as lifeboats were lifted from their davits and flung disintegrating into the sky, aft, always aft, until, after a lifetime, he hurled himself into the after-steering compartment below the wrecked after-platform where the quartermaster lay with his hands on the wheel after a lump of steel the size of a cricket ball had passed right through his head.

"Put me against the bulkhead," Ainslee shouted, his voice timbreless with pain. "Hard astarboard. Hurry, man! Starboard! To starboard! Must get back . . . into . . . the smoke."

Mallet-Jones heaved the quartermaster from the wheel and turned it wildly until it came up hard against the stop. "Wheel hard over, sir."

"Is she coming round?"

Mallet-Jones yelled above the bedlam, "I don't know, sir. The compass is smashed."

"Well, go out on deck and have a look."

"I can't, sir. There's no one to take the wheel. Who's to hold the goddam wheel?"

Ainslee was already shuffling across the deck on his hands and buttocks, his eyes closed as if he were about to faint. He grasped the wheel with one hand and Mallet-Jones fled into the inferno. He was back very quickly. "She's coming round, sir."

"Good. Now try the 'phones and voice-pipes."

He tested each one in succession and obtained a response from none of them; either the wires or tubes were cut, or, as likely, no one lived at the other end to answer them. *Conway* was being systematically reduced to dust and ashes by an incessant rain of high-explosive. "Nothing, sir."

"Right, take over." Ainslee was suddenly irritable, "Christ Almighty, where the hell is everybody?"

Mallet-Jones was irritable in turn. "Almost every man on the upper deck is killed or wounded. You know that, sir."

Ainslee grunted and closed his eyes again, as if the pain were becoming unbearable. "Yes . . . sorry . . ."

"Here's the smoke, sir. We're in the smoke."

The compartment darkened as the swirling oil-smoke excluded what little remained of the daylight.

"Midships."

"Midships, sir."

"Check fire."

Mallet-Jones could scarcely hear Ainslee's voice, partly because of the noise and partly because Ainslee seemed to be weakening. But the order was unnecessary, for Mallet-Jones had no means of speaking to the guns, and their crews ceased fire of their own accord when *Conway* entered the smoke.

"Time?"

"Seventeen hundred, sir."

Another salvo struck the ship right forrard, struck it while it was hidden by the smoke, an unanswerable fluke. *Conway* tried to stop dead in her tracks. Mallet-Jones was flung across the compartment and Ainslee shouted as he rolled over the deck.

"The guns, Mallet-Jones! The guns!"

It was, it seemed, the finishing stroke, and Mallet-Jones was obliged to kneel and put his ear against Ainslee's mouth to hear the anguished voice, "The guns, eh? Have we . . . lost . . . 'em? Did they get . . . the guns?"

"I don't know. But I don't think they can have survived that, sir."

Ainslee rested his head against the bulkhead. "Hard astarboard. Let me know when we sight the enemy."

"But . . ."

Ainslee's head came forward with a jerk and his eyes blazed. "Hard astarboard!"

Mallet-Jones returned to the wheel and put it over. Nothing was important, now. He was unendurably tired. Whether he put the wheel over or not, what did it matter? Whatever they did they were finished. *Conway* was simply pounding to her doom. He looked through the steel walls of his prison towards *Leipzig*: "God damn you, damn you, *damn you!*"

When the smoke cleared he left the compartment and returned with the now matter-of-fact news that *Leipzig* was dead ahead. It seemed as though Ainslee was sleeping but his eyelids moved. "Maintain this course."

Mallet-Jones acknowledged the order and waited in the unnatural silence for the end. There was no sound of gunfire from *Conway*. Mallet-Jones looked down at his hands on the wheel and found great interest there, as if he were aware that he was looking at them for the last time. *Leipzig*'s guns roared at point-blank range and the shells convulsed their target.

"They've had it," Mallet-Jones said quietly as the noise subsided. "The guns—they've had it, sir."

They listened, waiting for a sign and heard nothing but the crackle of flames, nothing but the unappeasable processes of destruction, nothing but this until Ainslee's revitalised voice shouted into the desolation, "No! There! Did you hear? Did you hear it, man? Did you hear?"

It was true! They listened entranced by the sound they heard. Out on the exposed, wrecked fo'c'sle, a solitary six-inch gun fired, and then again, firing very slowly, spasmodically, but nonetheless engaging the enemy.

"We're firing!" Mallet-Jones shouted, uncontrollably overjoyed. "By God, we're still firing. And two Oerlikons!"

Ainslee merely grunted. He had no time for congratulations. "Hard astarboard," he ordered. "Return to the smoke screen."

III

Oliphant and Reggie on Oliphant's gun:

Reggie said, "Oh, my God, just look at her."

Oliphant stared and his only visible reaction was that his hands tightened on the gun.

"Well, look at it! It's a battlewaggon," Reggie went on. "Aren't you afraid now?"

Oliphant turned towards him and smiled thinly and passed the fingers of one hand across the dark stubble of his chin. "No."

After that few words passed between them for little was left for them to share in common. In Reggie's opinion, Oliphant was mad.

When the shells began to arrive, Reggie found that he could no longer stand upright, that he became a hunchback. Even when the shells had fallen and the immediate danger was passed, he could still not pull himself erect, however hard he tried. He wondered whether he would be hunchbacked for the remainder of his life.

He also made a discovery: after the German gunners had bracketed *Conway* and begun to hit their target, the animosity Reggie harboured for Oliphant evaporated and disappeared. He found himself standing nearer to the older man, as if he found protection within his upright, glaring proximity, as if the insane bravery that drove him to stand strapped to his gun not flinching as the ship blew up about him, was no longer a weakness, a form of madness, but a half-wonderful, inexplicable quality that could only be admired and even emulated.

But Reggie could not, dare not, stand upright.

When the salvo burst amidships, felled the mast and split the funnel and wiped out, it seemed, in one terrifying explosion every Oerlikon gun's crew on the boat deck except Oliphant's, and obliterated the dream-like passage of Ainslee and Mallet-Jones across Reggie's astonished gaze, and left only a twisted desert behind it, Reggie began to pluck at Oliphant's clothing and scream that unless he took cover he would be killed. And still Oliphant stood like an immovable colossus, defiant among the destruction, possibly still alive only because he refused even to incline his head to the onslaught.

Then Reggie was coughing in the black smoke lying like treacle on the surface of the water. It swirled about Oliphant's obstinate head like a cloud on a rounded peak as *Conway* sped through its protective opacity. The six-inch ceased fire and the shells from the German no longer rained upon them. Silence; not a particle of sound but the wind in the sea-deadening black treacle moving over the ship and the crackle of flames amidships; a kind of peace. Momentarily they rested, surprised by their sudden security, only half-believing in their reprieve. They even experienced a tiny spurt of hope. Then the freak salvo exploded on the fo'c'sle and Reggie was flung to the deck and the leather thongs of the gun-harness bit deeply into Oliphant's back. The nightmare returned. *Conway* shook herself like a flogged animal and staggered forward, head first into the flames.

"Christ," Reggie moaned.

Oliphant glared with angry eyes, trying to see beyond the smoke, not speaking, just looking as if with equanimity he could kill ten thousand men. The ship heeled and when she righted herself they were out of the smoke, leaving its flattened bulk behind them.

"Where is she?" Oliphant yelled.

Reggie, still bent, pointed forrard. "There! On the port bow."

Oliphant whipped the gun round until the barrel collided with the firing stop. Their Oerlikon was on the starboard side of the ship and a metal frame had been erected about it, within reach of the barrel, to restrict its field of fire—otherwise aerials, masts and even sailors could be shot to pieces by over-zealous and excited operators.

Oliphant's rage was a terrible thing. He crashed the gun on the frame, again and again, and jumped up and down in his harness. "I can't get it round! I can't aim! Shift it! For Christ's sake shift it!"

Reggie, his head tucked in his shoulders, ran towards the muzzle of the gun, grasped the frame and swung on it. It was tough and immovable. He needed an acetylene burner.

"God damn and blast," Oliphant raged. "Look at the bugger! And I can't shoot! Oh God, I can't shoot! Why doesn't somebody turn the ship? Turn it!" He was beside himself with fury. "Turn it! Why can't somebody turn the bastard round?"

Leipzig's guns thundered and after a long time one six-inch on the fo'c'sle answered. And then, by accident and not at all by design, *Conway* did turn through the few degrees necessary to bring *Leipzig* on to her starboard bow.

Oliphant opened fire and kept his hand clamped to the trigger until the magazine was empty. He could see the course of his twenty millimetre shells because every third was a tracer, glowing in the near-darkness. Reggie stumbled about below him as he fired, placing a second magazine ready on the firing step, waiting huddled up until Oliphant finished emptying the first magazine and signalled to him to reload. He could hear nothing but the chattering of the gun, feel nothing but loneliness and an immobilising fear, see nothing but Oliphant's exalted face blurred by the shuddering of the gun.

Leipzig was firing over open sights, the great guns in their turrets depressed below the horizontal, pumping high-explosive into *Conway* in broadside after broadside. *Conway*, a palpitating wreck, staggered towards the shelter of the smoke. Perhaps, Reggie thought wildly, she is indestructible because God is helping her. He became aware that Oliphant was shouting and gesticulating for ammunition. Somehow he propelled his reluctant legs towards the empty magazine and unclipped it.

"Hurry!" Oliphant shouted, possessed by a passion that made waiting impossible, "Hurry, damn you!"

Reggie lurched forward in a mist of fear. He lifted the second magazine to the gun and slid it about on top of the barrel, searching frantically for the elusive clips, afraid that he would never find them before the strength in his arms drained away through the soles of his feet. When, finally, it clicked into place, Oliphant fired immediately, his tin hat dancing off the back of his head as with awesome deliberation he moved the stream of shells in a lazy arc across *Leipzig*'s bridge. He was furious when *Conway* re-entered the smoke.

"Get me out of this harness," he yelled.

Reggie obeyed and unclipped the heavy leather.

"I'll reload this one. Number Two Oerlikon's all right; it's only the crew that's dead. Take that one. Reload before we attack again."

"But . . ." Reggie began.

Oliphant stormed with impatience. "Do as you're bloody well told. God damn it, get on to that gun!"

Oliphant hurled the expended magazine at his feet and struggled up the firing step with a full one and began to clip it into place.

"Did you hear what I said? Get to that gun!"

Reggie stared, still half-paralysed with fear, and then, because someone was telling him what to do, because someone apparently knew what to do (or merely made his voice sound as if he knew), because someone, incredibly, seemed to have maintained his faith and kept his head sufficiently to be able to think and give orders, he began to feel less afraid; and when he saw Oliphant squaring himself at the loaded gun, unaffected by the futility, ready to open fire when his target reappeared, he took courage and raced towards the idle gun on the port side and began to change the magazine. When he was finished and the gun was ready to fire, when the oil-smoke had thinned out and *Conway* stood in for the next bloody round, he looked towards Oliphant and raised his hand in a tentative wave. Oliphant waved back and for the first time in the engagement Reggie was able to take his head out of his shoulders and stand up straight.

Leipzig loomed before them, a great animal waiting for a rabbit to come out of its hole. Reggie heard Oliphant's voice, exultant above the returning uproar, "Fire! *Fire!* FIRE! FIRE!"

The two Oerlikons surged into life together.

IV

Conway emerged from the smoke four times and on each occasion Barraclough, alone on the fo'c'sle, loaded, aimed and fired his six-inch gun single-handedly. It was a stirring, unprecedented performance, accompanied by a torrent of Barraclough's particular variety of unceasing profanity, now directed at the *Leipzig* in particular and at the entire motherless German race in general.

As he raced round the gun, first training and then laying, he was repeatedly immersed in sea-water pouring over the bows. He had lost his tin hat and his sheepskin coat had been nearly ripped from his back by a shell splinter which had left a livid groove across one shoulder as a token of its passing. When he lifted the heavy shells he had great difficulty in keeping his feet on the heaving wet deck; yet, on each occasion, reeling and sometimes falling, he managed to get the shell into the mechanism which lifted it into the maw of the gun before slamming the block home. He worked with an indefatigable strength, derived, not from fear, but from the fury he experienced whenever he saw the dead lying about him. After firing he climbed into the gunlayer's seat to observe the fall of shot and several times registered hits on *Leipzig*. But for most of the time his shots were wide; the interval between sighting and firing was too great, whatever the luck.

Once he was almost washed overboard when a wave and the blast of a shell hit him simultaneously and rolled him over and over the deck until he was hard against the guard-rails with one leg already through them. When he had extricated himself and struggled to his feet he stood for a moment and shook his fist at *Leipzig*, an enraged feeler-flailing insect defying the descending boot. Then he raced back to his gun and put the elevation up a couple of degrees and hoisted another shell into the spout and pressed the firing button and waited for the gun's recoil—which was just about the only way he had of knowing when the gun had fired, because his eardrums were numb with noise.

From time to time he looked up at the bridge for a sign of activity, for some indication of command, but where the proud span of the bridge once had been there was nothing but wreckage. Yet, clearly, some directing intelligence remained, for the engines still raced in a rapidly flooding engine room, and someone must be bringing the ship in and out of the smoke-screen. *Conway*, bless her broken heart, couldn't be doing it by herself. So he carried on, a lonely, frantic figure on the sea-washed fo'c'sle, a Lilliputian holding Gargantua at bay, immune from the German wrath, the sole, comic, inexplicable, unanswerable reason for Ainslee continuing to fight his ship, the moaning, dissatisfied, under-privileged, eternal, unbeatable British bloody matelot doing his duty.

"Cor, flip!"

v

When the water first flooded into the bridge flat, its tidal crest carried Chief Petty Officer Wilmot and the boy down the central staircase to the dining-room flat below and left them helpless at the bottom of a rapidly filling well. Once the breech in *Conway*'s side had been opened, water flooded inboard each time she rolled: untold tons of it tumbling down the turning staircase in foaming, irresistible cascades. The water in the well rose to Wilmot's knees, and then to his thighs, to his waist and then to his chest, and when it reached his chin, when he was having to hold the boy's head above its boiling scummy surface, he had still not reached the staircase, for each time he made progress towards it, some new delivery flung him back like driftwood at the foot of a weir.

When hope was at an end and stark fear approached he caught the bannisters with his fingers, an improbable even if intended encounter. His legs came up and he kicked out strongly, still holding the drowning boy's head above the water. His grip inched up the rail, the rising water itself taking him towards the deckhead, however much new water poured down on top of him until, inch by contested inch, drowning and battered, he came up from below like the Old Man of the Sea himself. When he stood with the boy waist deep in the swirling flood on the deck above, holding on to a stanchion, some forty minutes of the engagement had elapsed. In the interval, his hair had become several shades greyer, almost white.

They ran headlong forrard: the burly Chief Petty Officer and the slight, pale-faced boy; the boy's fingers gripped tightly in the Chief's huge hand, his feet dragging against the impetus of Wilmot's progress through passageways filled with smoking debris and the remains of what had once been able-bodied seamen. They clattered up well-remembered ladders until they emerged on the boat deck, as Wilmot had intended they should, above the level of the hungry water.

Wilmot looked towards the bridge, his ultimate objective. "Christ, it's gone! Back! Back with me, boy!"

They retraced their steps, careering aft in their clinging wet clothing, the Chief's legs short and stocky, the boy's spindly and insecure, stumbling rather than running: this time down ladders and along more sea-swept passageways, through the screams and the explosions and the wreckage and the reverberating racket of a ship breaking up. When they debouched on to the upper deck aft they discovered that the ship was enveloped in smoke. Shortly afterwards the firing ceased.

Wilmot threw himself into the after-steering compartment and only when he was inside its metal protection did he release the boy's hand.

He kneeled at Ainslee's side. "You all right, sir?"

Ainslee slowly turned his face towards him and smiled painfully. "Hello, Chief. Yes, I'm all right except that my bloody legs are broken."

Wilmot looked down at the blood-soaked trousers. "We're in the smoke now, sir."

Ainslee looked pleased. "Where've you been, Chief? It's the third time."

"We were trapped down below. Casualties are very high, sir."

Ainslee did not comment on the casualties. He said, "We've got to get out of the smoke quickly, Chief, before *Leipzig* makes off."

Wilmot ran the tip of his tongue over his lips. "You're not going in again, sir?"

Ainslee did not normally accept gratuitous advice from Chief Petty Officers but Wilmot was an exception. Even Ainslee was ready to ask for his opinion. "We've got to hold her till nightfall, Wilmot. Think we can do it?"

Mallet-Jones shouted, "Out of the smoke, sir."

He ran out of the compartment and when he returned he adjusted the wheel and reported, "Right ahead, sir."

Wilmot said, "As long as we have guns, sir."

They waited.

Ainslee was suddenly furious. "Where's that six-inch? Where the hell is it?"

"Oerlikon fire, sir." Mallet-Jones reported.

Ainslee snorted, beating his fists on the deck. "The six-inch! Why doesn't it fire? Why doesn't it open fire? Chief..."

Barraclough's six-inch cracked in the increasing bedlam.

"Six-inch firing, sir," Mallet-Jones reported.

Ainslee's fists still drummed on the deck, but gently now. His eyes were closed and he leaned his head against the bulkhead. "Thank God," he breathed.

They waited again, listening to the systematic destruction, and when Wilmot could bear it no longer, he said, "We're going to have to abandon ship, sir. You'll have to get those legs into splints first..."

"Back into the smoke, Mallet-Jones."

"Aye, aye, sir."

Wilmot tried again, "You can't go over the side like this or you'll lose them."

"In the smoke, sir."

"Hard astarboard in one minute."

"Aye, aye, sir."

Ainslee was not listening to Wilmot who stood up and ran out on deck. Ainslee wondered vaguely where he had gone but he was too weary of the pain and too preoccupied to think about anything but speed and turning circles. When Wilmot returned he carried pieces of wood and a blanket and lengths of twine—God alone knew where he had found them. He knelt by Ainslee and straightened the legs. He slashed long strips from the blanket with his knife and when he had cut Ainslee's trouser legs and exposed the terrible wounds, he wound the strips round them tightly and secured them with the twine. Then he fixed two splints to each leg and bound them in place while Ainslee shouted with pain.

"You've lost a lot of blood, sir. You'll have to stick with me in the water."

All the disappointment and frustration welled up in Ainslee like a tide. He tried, ridiculously, to get to his feet and succeeded only in lifting his bottom off the deck before falling back, his face contorted.

He addressed himself to Wilmot, "We're not going in the water, Chief. We're not, understand? Bring her round, Mallet-Jones! Bring her up out of the smoke! Bring her up, I say . . ."

They listened to the outburst without comment and Mallet-Jones put over the wheel.

"We'll go in again and again until we're finished. If we're finished, Chief, get outside and let me know when the enemy is in sight."

Wilmot departed. "You wait here, boy."

The boy was crying silently. When he saw Wilmot leaving the compartment he wanted to go with him, even though he was safer where he was. He began to speak, but he was unable to articulate the words through the sobs. "You stay here, boy" the Chief had said. Now he thought he would never see him again.

Mallet-Jones wiped the sweat from his blackened, blood-caked forehead and discovered that his hands were trembling. He wanted something to eat, something to give him strength. His head ached and his fingers were stiff from the pressure they continuously exerted on the wheel.

"Time?" Ainslee asked, his voice quiet again.

"Seventeen forty, sir."

"Ninety minutes."

"What did you say, sir?"

"I said, we've held her for ninety minutes."

"Yes, sir," Mallet-Jones answered. "I suppose we have." Then he said, unable any longer not to say it, "You're going to lose the ship!"

Ainslee did not expostulate. He answered quietly, "Yes, we may lose the ship, Mallet-Jones. But I think we shall not have lost the convoy."

Wilmot returned. "Enemy firing on the starboard bow, sir. It's dark now."

The shells struck *Conway* as Wilmot spoke. The ship heeled and did not this time return. For the first time the engines faltered. Those in the after-steering compartment found themselves standing at an angle of seventy degrees to the deck and were forced to hold on to stanchions and bulkheads to retain their balance. Barraclough's six-inch fired, and then Oliphant's Oerlikons.

"Starboard five," Ainslee ordered.

"Starboard five, sir," Mallet-Jones repeated and put the wheel over. He wished he could do something about the quartermaster's pulverised head. No one had thought to take the body outside. We should have removed it, he thought, with the boy here, poor kid.

Wilmot stood near to the doorway, watching and waiting, close to the boy who was unable to stop his sobbing although he made scarcely any sound. His eyes were wide with terror.

"Hold on, boy," Wilmot said softly.

"That should do it," Ainslee said. "Midships."

"Midships, sir."

Mallet-Jones brought the wheel back to its central position. *Conway*, listing heavily to starboard, her devastated upper deck like the surface of the moon, trundled towards *Leipzig*. Again the broadsides smacked into her, obliterating and then renewing the flames, blow after mortal blow exploding in her guts but still not stopping her. The chaos of noise was punctuated by the firing of Barraclough's gun.

They waited and listened and watched each other. The engines slowed.

The next salvo appeared to detach a part of *Conway*'s stern and in the emergency lighting of the after-steering compartment Mallet-Jones's face tautened as he moved the wheel. He whirled on Ainslee. "The steering! It's gone, sir. Look!"

"Let me see," Ainslee snapped. "It can't be."

Mallet-Jones twirled the slack wheel in exasperation. "Look! See for yourself. It's gone, I tell you."

Ainslee's eyes narrowed and then, abruptly, his chin moved down on to his chest and his eyes closed.

Mallet-Jones saw the blood seeping along the deck from underneath his legs.

"What are we to do, sir?"

Ainslee did not at once answer. Wilmot stared at him and the boy gulped and inhaled through his congested nose.

"Do?" Ainslee asked.

"Yes," Mallet-Jones shouted. "What now? Jesus, what now?"

Ainslee answered after a long time. "There is nothing we can do now, except . . . leave her."

The engines stopped.

Wilmot said to Mallet-Jones, "Look after the boy, sir. I'll take the Captain."

They crawled into the open, Mallet-Jones holding the boy's hand, Wilmot dragging Ainslee along behind him.

"Chief! Chief!" Ainslee was saying, saying over and over until Wilmot heard him above the uproar as *Conway* drifted under *Leipzig*'s guns, "Chief!"

"Sir?"

"Chief, the engine room. You'll have to warn the engine room. There're no telephones. They must be warned."

Wilmot turned very slowly towards him. "The engine room, sir?"

"Yes, yes, the engine room."

Wilmot stood up and looked down at Ainslee and took a deep breath. "Aye, aye, sir."

He doubled away into the flash-ridden darkness and the boy shouted, "Don't go, Chief . . . Chief, come back!"

The three of them sank down behind a cable reel. *Leipzig* was dead ahead, no more than a quarter of a mile away. Every few seconds they saw the wind-driven waves, the ghastly outline of the listing *Conway*, and *Leipzig*'s livid silhouette as her big guns fired. *Leipzig* was discovering that although it is simple enough, given the armament, to disarm a ship, to stop her, as *Conway* had been stopped, even to destroy her, it is infinitely more difficult to sink her. *Conway* writhed as the broadsides tore into her body; but she did not sink.

Tears welled in Ainslee's eyes: *Conway*, his home, his ship, the living extension of his own faith, reduced to a listing shambles. He wanted to cry aloud his love for the dying *Conway*. But if his grief was immeasurable so, too, was his pride in her achievement. He watched her in the darkness and touched her with his fingers. She was not yet dead. She still sliced the seas, her head high even if a little to one side. The battle ensign still flew from the felled mast. She staggered on, and Ainslee could barely speak. "She's finished. God . . . she's . . . finished."

On the boat deck Oliphant clapped his last magazine on to his red-hot gun. He could feel the heat on his blackened face as *Leipzig*, stark in the flame of her own guns, loomed ever larger in his sights. His mood became ecstatic as he reeled at his gun, spraying *Leipzig* from stem to stern, shouting above the din and hearing nothing but the insignificant sound of his own voice grating against the bones in his head. Once, in those last few seconds, he looked towards Reggie, who still stood at his gun, squinting through the circular sights at the towering bridge before him, quietly unleashing murder. There comes a point in every battle where fear is not so much forgotten as transcended. Reggie had become very deliberate in his desire to kill.

Below, Wilmot reached the main door of the engine room and ran out on to the grating and shouted in his stentorian bellow, "Abandon ship! Abandon ship!" In the great cavern of machinery hung with emergency lights he could see the glinting, sloping scum sloshing about below him, creeping up the sides of the engines. "Abandon ship," he cried. "Abandon ship!" He saw the engineers stumbling up the ladder and one of them waved to him and turned round to shout to his companions. "Abandon ship! Abandon ship!" He saw others fighting their way shoulder-deep up the heeling deck towards the ladder, their meagre escape route. He called for the last time, then turned and ran back through the exploding ship in search of the boy he was determined to save.

Leipzig put her stern down in the water and the sea was churned to a boiling vortex under her counter. Less than two hundred yards separated the ships; *Leipzig*'s work was done. She could leave *Conway* now; the sea would soon complete the destruction.

When *Leipzig* was already moving fast, Barraclough the immortal ran out on to the fo'c'sle, a tiny, gesticulating figure hurling imprecations at the towering straight side and black bridge before him, and remained there just long enough to execute one final obscene gesture of contempt before racing back to the shelter of his gun and pressing the firing button for the last time.

Conway turned aimlessly, a drifting, silent hulk. The men left her and she was alone. The sound of the waves and the wind returned, untouched by death, unmoved by sacrifice, a rising, soughing song over an opening grave.

Leipzig made off in the direction of the dispersed convoy. She might find a straggler; with luck two or even three. But she would not find more—the ocean was too big, the night too dark and *Conway*'s triumph too great to be so easily nullified.

FIVE

"MR. BUSK," Jacobson called. "It is necessary to release the smoke-floats over the side. Carry on!"

Busk, not yet recovered from the shock of finding himself face to face with a battleship, was glad of a task, however menial, to divert his mind and moderate his fear. He scooted off the bridge like a scalded cat.

Oleron turned away from *Conway* and her formidable opponent and her passage through the now formless convoy brought forth from Jacobson and Dawson feats of handling and control that in circumstances less urgent would have been deemed homicidal. Jacobson, unable to resist the temptation to leave matters momentarily in Dawson's hands, stumped out on to the wing of his bridge for a final glimpse of the British ship, stern down, steaming towards her adversary. Her insane bravery unnerved him; he was uncomfortable in the presence of such contempt for self-preservation. God knew, he had faced enough danger in his life; but never this cold-blooded deliberate suicide.

He returned to Dawson before the wheel. "What can she do?" he asked. "What can she do against a battleship?"

Dawson shrugged and ordered a slight change of course and only when he had done this did he turn towards Jacobson and answer his question. "Hold her for an hour, maybe more."

Jacobson bit his lower lip and frowned, crinkling the smooth skin of his forehead until it resembled rose-coloured parchment. "But how can she do that, eh? How can she do it? She will be sunk. Of that there can be no doubt. You understand? She will be destroyed!"

On Dawson's face he saw only the sad patronising smile of the believer for the heathen. "Maybe, Captain."

Jacobson turned away, still frowning, tugging at his lower lip with his small, even teeth. He was disturbed by Dawson's apparent callousness. And he was concerned about his own reactions. When *Leipzig* had first been sighted and the convoy had been ordered to scatter, Jacobson had felt nothing but admiration for

Conway; it was only after they had deserted her in her vast arena that he had known this awe that caused his flesh to creep. "What do you mean, maybe? I do not understand. Does it not matter that so many men should be killed?"

Dawson's eyes were fixed on a tanker, too close to the starboard side. He answered, not looking at Jacobson, "There's a war on, Captain. Men are being killed every day and there's nothing either you or I can do about it. Now, let's get the hell outa here, shall we?"

Curiously, Jacobson accepted the implied rebuke. He walked out on to the wing of the bridge again and looked aft, but both *Conway* and *Leipzig* were hidden now by Busk's smoke-screen. At least Busk was managing to accomplish this simple task well—almost too well—for a good deal of the acrid cumulus was billowing back into the ship, enveloping Busk like a stoker in hell. Jacobson smiled wanly at the spectacle.

Then the shells fell into the water a few feet ahead of *Oleron,* drenching her in a moving curtain of spray. Jacobson ran back to Dawson, very erect and stiff-legged and pink in the face. "She's firing at the convoy," he shouted, and having done so could have bitten off his tongue.

Dawson wheeled on him, "Well, what did you expect, Captain? Flowers?"

Jacobson drew himself up to his full five feet, six and a half inches. He could be exceptionally pompous. "You are not to speak to me in such a way."

Dawson smiled apologetically. "Sorry. Guess we're all getting a bit jittery. *Conway* can't hold all her fire power. She'll save some for us."

The ships were spreading out now, fanwise, some to the north of west, some to the south. *Oleron,* under Dawson's expert guidance, moved about a mean course of two-six-five. An explosion occurred over on the port side but they could see nothing for Busk's smoke-screen.

The tanker on their starboard side was the *Southern Star,* very close now, no more than a cable's length away. Jacobson knew her Captain well. He, too, was a Swede who, rather than sail always in Swedish boats, had made a practice (which, to some extent, is the practice of all sea-faring nations with a hard-won expertise to sell) of offering his services to foreign owners. He cared little for flags or companies; his loyalty was to his ship which he strove constantly to improve and fashion into his own unattainable ideal. *Southern Star* was a British ship.

Berenson, her Captain, like Jacobson, had been born in Stockholm. As boys they had attended the same school and had taken the decision to go to sea, together. Yet, although they had remained firm friends they had little else in common apart from their profession. Berenson was a giant, a noisy, sometimes reckless extrovert, who wore his enormous belly above a two-inch-wide leather belt. Jacobson was a shy invariably modest individual who did not take easily to noise of any kind. But for Berenson he held a tremendous admiration, if not always for his jovial nature, then certainly for his daring qualities of seamanship. It was an odd association but, in Jacobson's life, one of peculiar importance.

They encountered each other in the ports of the world but rarely. When they did they would visit and entertain each other with a kind of old-world decorum, sitting together in one or the other's souvenir-cluttered cabin drinking lager beer out of tall frosted glasses and smoking pipe after pipe of expensive duty-free tobacco. They would call each other Captain and Jacobson would enquire about Berenson's present ship, how she handled in a seaway and whether he had a satisfactory crew. Berenson would ask the same questions of Jacobson and then go on to ask about his wife, his home, his garden, his children and inevitably guffaw at the number of the latter. "How many is it now, Captain?"

Jacobson would puff on his pipe and look into his beer and grin a little sheepishly, "Seven now, Captain. There was another one last year."

Berenson would put down his beer and hold his belly with the palms of his hands and roar, "Ho, ho, ho! You'll soon be able to man a ship, my friend!" It was a familiar joke.

Jacobson could see Berenson now, standing on his bridge, an immense figure dwarfing those about him. They had taken a drink together in Halifax and Jacobson, always the more introspective, had wondered whether he would ever see him again. Jacobson had teased him gently about his weight and told him about his eldest son who had now finished school and wanted to enter the Merchant Service—an ambition of which Jacobson could only approve yet felt compelled to hesitate about. There had been long silences in their conversation while they smoked their pipes and pulled at their beer. But this was not unusual.

They had walked to the landing-stage together and before they had gone their separate ways in their separate spick and span boats they had shaken hands.

"Good night, Captain," Jacobson had said. "And a pleasant voyage."

Berenson had answered, before stepping heavily into his boat and reducing the freeboard to negligible proportions, "And good night to you, Captain. We'll meet on the other side."

Southern Star pulled slowly ahead of *Oleron* and Jacobson smiled to himself as he imagined Berenson berating his engine room staff until they piled on enough steam to leave *Oleron* behind. It was a permissible form of swank. They would be able to laugh about it later and remember it in safety. Jacobson raised his hand in salute as *Southern Star* forged ahead and Berenson rolled out on to the wing of his bridge with a loud hailer. Jacobson half expected the tanker to take on a list with so much weight balanced so precariously on her edge. He heard Berenson's voice, carried by the wind but almost drowned by the sound of the sea.

"Good luck, Captain!"

Jacobson shouted back, "And good luck to you, Captain."

Then neither Berenson nor *Southern Star* were there. Their place was taken by an erupting pillar of flame and as Jacobson watched aghast, he seemed still to see Berenson's huge waving figure on the bridge, imprinted in black on the livid flame. He staggered back, his arm across his eyes to shut out the horror, the light and the intense heat. *Oleron* rocked in the blast of tens of thousands of high octane spirit going up in one thunderous explosion which left nothing behind it but a receding, dying inferno, floating in the darkness on the surface of the sea.

When Jacobson took his arm away from his eyes the horror remained in his face. He said, in his clear, precise voice, "The Captain of that ship was my friend. We went to school together. His name . . . was . . . Berenson."

Dawson looked at him, a little embarrassed, not knowing how to answer. "I'm sorry, sir."

"There is no need to be sorry, Dawson." He moved his short fingers over his brow. "I shall be all right . . . I just want to be quiet and . . . think . . . for a little while, that is all."

"Yes, sir. I understand."

Dawson addressed himself to the manoeuvring of the ship, turning *Oleron* about the mean course he had laid off on the chart. He dare not take his eyes away from the sea ahead; there was still a grave danger of collision. But the firing appeared to have stopped. He wished the Captain would pull himself together and accept his part of the responsibility—poor little guy. Meanwhile he glanced at the compass and chided the helmsman. Someone had to take charge of the ship.

Jacobson stood out on the port wing of the bridge gazing at the firelit water. Berenson dead! I should have stopped and gone back for him. But I should not have found anything. It would have endangered the ship. But he may have survived. Berenson could survive anything. But in convoy we are not permitted to stop, not even when we are scattered. Think of the danger of collision. And he could not have survived. But if he jumped overboard, then he might have survived? I should have gone back. But no, it is impossible to go back. Oh God. Berenson dead!

Berenson was a kind man. Only occasionally did he hurt people. I remember once when we were in Rio and he had decided to marry a beautiful singer he had found in a night-club. What was her name now? I forget. He was very taken with her. He had bought himself a new uniform and a stiff wing collar. I remember I tried to dissuade him. But I need not have bothered. On the day of the wedding I found him lashing his crew to a fury of activity to get his ship to sea before the appointed time. He never wore the wing collar. I wonder what he did with it? He was like that, Berenson. Impulsive. Only occasionally did he hurt people. He was a good man. And a great seaman.

Now he has gone.

Oh God, why have they done this?

Why?

Gradually his mood of incomprehension was overtaken by cold rage. The hurt, humble, enquiring expression was replaced by a furious resolution. He straightened his back, pulled his cap firmly down on to his square head, clasped his hands behind him so that his stomach pressed forward through his sheepskin coat and turned towards his Second Mate. "Mr. Dawson?" His voice was assured again, almost brittle.

"Sir?"

"What is the mean course?"

"Two-six-five, sir."

"Cease zigzag."

"Aye, aye, sir."

"Speak to the engine room, please. Tell them there is no longer need for them"—he smiled at his use of one of the few colloquialisms he had learned—"to bust a gut."

Dawson laughed. This was more like it.

"Aye, aye, sir."

PART TWO

PART TWO

THERE were seven survivors, seven, that is, who survived not only the sinking of *Conway* but the subsequent hour alone in the sea, when most of those who had outlived their ship floated on well-inflated and stoppered lifebelts to deaths by cold, water and fuel-oil, deaths deferred and never averted: Ainslee, Mallet-Jones, Wilmot, the boy, Oliphant, Reggie and Barraclough. These seven, since the boats and even, it seemed, the Carley rafts had been destroyed, found no support in the water beyond their own lifebelts, and what appeared to be a door, a flat, dangerously smooth section of planking torn from a deckhouse and deposited whole in the sea with stout brass hinges still screwed to its french-polished frame. They clung to this, not so much to remain afloat as to bind themselves together—a focal point, a refuge about which they gathered in their loneliness and despair, once they had found each other.

That those in the after-steering compartment had encountered the door had been due to Wilmot's sudden, brutal strength in leaving the ship when he did, rejecting the possibility of further delay, carrying the boy and dragging the crippled, protesting Ainslee with him; that those on the boat deck had been able to join them had been due to Oliphant's continuing capacity to think in the presence of disaster; and that Barraclough, still profane, spouting water like an enraged whale, had been able to locate them could be explained only by reference to the inexplicable; it was one of those miracles that occasionally occur at sea.

They came together in the darkness, indescribably thankful that others still lived, loving each other merely for being there.

When *Conway* finally went, stern first, Wilmot said, "She's gone!" as if it were inconceivable that their ship should sink. When the sea closed over her and its surface bore no further indication of the convulsive burial, he said again, "She's gone, sir." But this time there was no incredulity in his voice, only sorrow and an utter finality.

No one else spoke. Ainslee stared into the night like a man witnessing a primitive execution. The others were too concerned with the problem of maintaining their hold on the plunging door, knowing that unless something more substantial than a polished door floated speedily into their tenuous world, none of them had very much time left in it.

The sea poured its ice-cold weight upon them and the spray racing over the sea lashed their faces until they were unable to open their eyes or, for want of air, keep their mouths shut. The door was never still, almost never horizontal, sometimes, as waves swept beneath it, see-sawing from one almost perpendicular position to another, a live thing determined to be rid of them.

Ainslee shouted, "We've got to find something else, Chief!" Wilmot knew this and was already trying to keep his eyes open for long enough to penetrate the spray-filled night, jerking his head round quickly, fearing to look away from the door for when he did the control he held over it jointly with the others tended to disappear. The others stared into the darkness also, humbly pleading with it for salvation, and receiving nothing for their trouble but stinging grey spindrift in their faces.

Ainslee's hands slipped on the door and Wilmot flung an arm about him. "You all right, sir?" Ainslee could not thank him or even acknowledge his help. He could only repeat what was essential before the sea overwhelmed him again, "We've got to find something else."

At the same moment Barraclough shrieked into the wind and flung himself upwards and over and out into the waves, away from the door, swimming strongly into the darkness, carried to the right by the passing crests, sucked back again by the troughs. Wilmot wondered if he had lost his reason. Mallet-Jones shouted, "Come back, Barraclough! Come back, you fool!" It was Wilmot who first saw what Barraclough had already seen: the wallowing shape of a Carley raft.

"A raft!" they shouted together. "God, it's a raft," and at the sight of their insubstantial discovery they wanted to laugh or sing or cry with hysterical relief, as if they were already saved. Yet it represented nothing more than a reprieve, the opportunity to grasp a little more time.

Wilmot was reluctant to leave the door and go to Barraclough's assistance because he feared that either Ainslee or the boy would be carried away if he left them. Those on the other side of the door showed no inclination to leave it. Ainslee shouted furiously,

"Swim, swim and take the door with us!" Although he was unable to move his legs he struck out with his free arm. Wilmot added, like a producer in some blacked-out aquatic extravaganza, "Swim everybody! All together now!"

They all kicked their legs and paddled with their free hands, adding their mite of foam to an ocean of foam, driving their rudimentary paddle-boat crabwise towards Barraclough, whom they could all see quite clearly now, not returning to them but hanging, apparently exhausted, to the rope hand-holds that surrounded the raft. Wilmot kicked his legs like a man possessed. "Faster! Faster! One, two, six, *faster!*"

It was easier for Wilmot than the others because, like the boy, he had come from below decks and neither had been able to collect an overcoat. Ainslee still wore his duffel coat, the others their sheepskin coats, water-logged now, heavy, dragging them down into the sea, but too valuable to be cast off. Slowly, their heads down, the whipped spray rattling against their neck s,they propelled their door towards the Carley raft and the bobbing black shape of Barraclough's head. The raft, with a greater area above the water, tended to move downwind faster than the door. It was also lighter, less encumbered, more easily lifted by the sea, and each time they seemed to be on the point of reaching it some wave bigger than its fellows would pick it up and set it down far away, almost out of sight. When, in this way, the raft was removed from their imminent grasp, they felt cheated and angry and kicked the sea with an uncontainable hatred. They began to chant as they paddled, "Faster, faster, faster!" And Mallet-Jones repeated to himself, in time to the movement of his aching arm, almost weeping with frustration, "Hurry! Hurry! Hurry! Hurry!"

They arrived suddenly, aided by a fortuitous juxtaposition of watery violence. Barraclough glared with red-rimmed eyes at their blurred shapes, as though, now, he hated them, as they, earlier, had hated the sea. His teeth chattered ceaselessly. Ainslee yelled, "Hold it, hold it for God's sake!" Barraclough glared at Ainslee too, and in his own time transferred one hand from the raft to the door so that his body formed the connecting link between them. "Quick," he shouted, "I can't hold them."

Ainslee called to Mallet-Jones, "Get on to the door and hold his arm." He gestured with his head towards Barraclough.

"Quick, for Christ's sake," Barraclough shouted again.

While Mallet-Jones was climbing out of the sea, when the movement of the two rafts was tending to pull Barraclough's arms out of their sockets, Oliphant was pulling himself around Reggie, making his obstinate unheeding way towards the raft without waiting for Reggie to precede him. Reggie was too cold to speak or remonstrate but the expression on his face was compounded partly of terror and partly of rage as Oliphant's heavy body pushed him under the waves. He took a hand from the door and pushed Oliphant with all his strength and would readily have pushed him right away from the door had not Ainslee's voice cut through the noise of the sea. "Stay where you are! You there, get round and help hold the raft."

Reggie stared. He might have been about to say through vibrating teeth, "Who? Me, sir?"

"Yes, you. Jump to it."

Reggie swallowed salt water and began to work his fearful way along the side of the door towards Barraclough. Mallet-Jones was already on top of it, lying full length on his stomach, holding Barraclough's forearm.

Ainslee ordered, "Chief, you go first and take the boy," and added to Barraclough, "Hold on there! What's your name?"

"Barraclough."

"Hold on, Barraclough. Can't afford to . . . be . . . separated."

Barraclough glared in the darkness. Wilmot swam between the rafts, assisting the boy with one arm. At the same time, like a man swaying on a cliff-top, Reggie let go and swam towards the Carley raft. When he was half-way there he appeared to lose his nerve or his hope or his strength and caught hold of Barraclough's shoulders. Barraclough screamed, "Get off, you bloody fool! Get off me! Let go!"

Reggie was petrified, incapable of movement beyond a desperate clinging to Barraclough's stretched shoulders. Wilmot reached the raft and grasped the rope and turned in time to see the door fly upwards and Mallet-Jones slithering head-first down its polished slope and into the water. But he did not let go of Barraclough's arm and when he came to the surface again they were all of them attached, in one way or another, to the raft—all, that is, except Ainslee and Oliphant who remained with the door which was already moving away as the freed Carley raft sped downwind.

Barraclough whirled on Reggie, "Get off, for Christ's sake!"

Reggie spluttered, "I'm sorry . . . I couldn't help it . . ."

"Let go of me . . . or I'll do yer!"

Reggie, thus rebuked, pulled himself towards the raft and held on to the rope. Once there he experienced an overwhelming desire to weep.

Wilmot climbed into the raft. "There're no paddles. God, no paddles!" He threw himself out again and Mallet-Jones yelled, "We'll have to swim with it, Chief."

They set off again, into the wind, following the cries of the men on the door and eventually losing them.

"We've got to find them," Mallet-Jones shouted, "We've got to find them. Where are you? Can you hear me?"

They swam on, furiously, their heavy clothing absorbing much of the power of their limbs, not knowing whether they were moving or not, or, if they were, whether they were moving in the right direction.

Mallet-Jones called again, "Can you hear me? Where are you?"

Wilmot roared behind him, "Captain, sir!"

And still no answer.

"Christ, Christ, Christ!" Mallet-Jones's hand beat impotently against the waves, "We've lost 'em."

Wilmot said, "Let's all call together."

"Right, all together! Where are you? Where are you? *Where are you?*"

Their voices were lost in the desolation of the sea, overpowered by the noise of rushing, toppling water.

"Again," Mallet-Jones said.

"Where are you? Where are you? *Where are you?*"

"Did you hear that, sir?" Wilmot asked.

"No. What?"

"Over there, on the left."

"Is it them?"

"I don't know. We'd better call again."

"Where are you? *Where are you?*"

"You're right! You're right, Chief. Over there, on the left."

They swam with renewed endeavour, dragging their unwieldy

craft round until they were making for the sound beyond the perimeter of their own visibility.

Wilmot counted as they swam, "One, two, three, four, five, six . . ."

Mallet-Jones called, "Can you hear me?"

This time it was unmistakably Ainslee's voice, sounding faintly through the spray, "Over here."

"Keep going," Mallet-Jones shouted to his exhausted crew. "Keep going. We're nearly there."

"Mallet-Jones?" It was Ainslee's voice.

"Coming, sir. Coming!"

Then they could see each other and, after a final terrible effort, the two floating remains of *Conway* touched once more in mid-ocean. This time, it was Mallet-Jones who attempted to hold them together.

Ainslee ordered, "You there! Help him." At that moment Oliphant envied Ainslee his broken legs. They relieved him of so much of the back-breaking, futile labour.

Mallet-Jones began to suffer the agonies that Barraclough had endured. "Help me," he cried. "Somebody do something!" Oliphant splashed away from the door and reached the raft. He grasped one of the rope lanyards and began to swim back to the door, still holding on to the rope. Mallet-Jones saw what was coming and shouted, "Don't touch me! Don't touch me!" Then he felt the strength of Ainslee's fingers on his arm and heard Ainslee's voice, "I'm going to hold on to you. Let go of the door."

Mallet-Jones felt the polished wood sliding from his fingers and the weight of Ainslee pulling himself towards the raft. Then Wilmot was alongside him, helping him to pull Ainslee near enough to the raft to grasp the rope. Oliphant returned to the raft and for a long time they hung there, not speaking, not even trying to clamber inside the raft, just resting and waiting.

They climbed into the raft one at a time. Ainslee saw them all safely inboard before allowing himself to be dragged out of the water. They laid him gently on the bottom boards and waited patiently for him to tell them what to do.

"Barraclough?"

"Sir?"

"Your action station?"

"Six-inch, sir."

"The gun that . . . continued to fire when . . . the . . . others were knocked out?"

"That's right."

"The other guns' crews; were . . . any alive?"

"No, sir."

Ainslee seemed to consider this and closed his eyes and wiped the salt water from his face. "You are the Barraclough who . . . has given us . . . so much trouble? The man I . . . put in cells?"

There was no point in dissembling. "Yes, sir."

Ainslee smiled briefly. "And you? You two?"

Oliphant answered a little before Reggie, but they both said, "Oerlikons, sir."

"That continued to fire?"

Oliphant said, "There were no others."

Reggie said, "Yes, sir," proud now of the accomplishment which in the first place had been Oliphant's.

Ainslee closed his eyes again, "Good! It is good. . . . Good that we are together."

SEVEN

APART from *Southern Star* and two other vessels sunk, the remainder of the convoy escaped unharmed into the darkness, each surviving member losing itself, or hoping to lose itself, in the vastness of the Atlantic. That the convoy had been able to elude *Leipzig*'s enormous fire-power, to avoid what had seemed certain decimation, was due solely to *Conway*'s opposition and the herosim of her crew. But the fact that so many men had died in order that others might live quickly became the cause of much disquiet and self-questioning among the officers and men of the merchant ships; they did not know that *Conway* had been sunk; yet, on the other hand, they could not believe that she had survived. Those who had been on the upper decks of the merchantmen when the action had first begun carried with them an imperishable picture of the stern-down black smoke-belching *Conway* steaming towards her foe, unflinching and undismayed. In the light of such heroism their own flight now disconcerted them. No other course had been possible; yet many wished they could have acted differently. And none was more inclined towards this desire than Jacobson of *Oleron*.

He remained on his bridge throughout the first dog watch when he might more profitably have been engaged in sleeping—except that sleep was impossible as long as *Southern Star* and *Conway* were vivid memories. He tried to fill his mind with routine matters but however much he stumped about his bridge, glancing at the compass, comparing the time of his watch with that of the chronometer on the bulkhead behind him, speaking through the telephone to his Chief Engineer, checking the dead-reckoning track laid out on the chart by Dawson, he returned, inevitably, to the questions that were becoming an obsession: had *Conway* survived; if not, had any members of her crew survived; and, if so, did they still live? He ordered coffee and drank the scalding liquid, hoping, obstinately, that it would alleviate his weariness; he had not slept for thirty-six hours.

When the watches changed Busk arrived on the bridge to relieve Dawson. He appeared unaffected by his curious behaviour during the engagement and to have regained his brash self-confidence. No sooner had Dawson left the bridge than he turned his cadaverous face towards Jacobson and flashed his false teeth in the darkness. "Should I ask for your supper to be sent up to the bridge, sir?"

"What? No. No, thank you. I shall take my supper with the passengers, in the saloon."

"Very well, sir."

Jacobson could see the white gash of teeth in the shadow of Busk's face.

"I see the glass is still falling, sir."

Jacobson turned away and drew on his paper and watched the ghostly spindrift sailing over the water. "I know, Mr. Busk."

"Any news of *Conway*, sir?"

"No."

Busk grinned in the shaded light, as though convinced that Jacobson were enjoying his conversation. If only he weren't so full of himself, Jacobson thought. He's trying to be pleasant, that's the extraordinary thing. It's impossible that he should mean harm. He's simply garrulous to a degree—and a little touched. But if only he would be silent.

"Maybe the swell'll go down later tonight, sir."

"Maybe."

Busk seemed to cast about for some new and engaging topic. "Quite a day we've had, sir. Quite a day."

Jacobson was furious. He wanted to order him to be quiet until given permission to speak, already half guessing at the crassness to come.

"Ah well, sir. All's well that ends well."

Jacobson glared at him, barely believing, fearing to answer, shaking with indignation. "I shall be in my cabin and then in the saloon, Mr. Busk, should I be required. And I wish to inform you that this night is not ended yet." He approached Busk as he left the bridge and actually prodded his chest with the stem of his pipe as he spoke, "I want you to understand that very clearly, Mr. Busk. Very clearly. It is not ended yet."

Busk shrugged when Jacobson was gone and settled down to his watch until Dawson relieved him again.

II

Jacobson went first to his cabin where he removed his outer clothing and washed his hands and face at the small hand-basin that folded into a wooden cabinet. He parted his fair, sparse hair with care and cleaned his nails with a silver contraption he kept on his key ring. Then he sat down in his solitary armchair and filled and lit his pipe and when he was satisfied that it was burning evenly he picked up a book from his bunk and began to read. It was 'Jane Eyre'. He did not have an extensive knowledge of English literature but from time to time he read a book in English and it was always some pinnacle of English letters.

Yet still his mind wandered. His gaze moved round the cabin, idly, almost vacantly. He looked at the photograph of his wife and children, a formal, posed group of which he was very proud. He smiled, briefly, and gestured with his pipe towards his wife because, he believed, when so addressed, she replied and smiled at him from the wooden frame. On the other side of the desk there was a photograph of his mother, an old, benevolent, imperious woman who knew her own mind and never lost her hold upon her son. She, too, sometimes smiled at him from her photograph. He sighed and closed his eyes and leaned his head against the back of his chair. God, he was tired. The pipe grew cold in his hand and for a little while he seemed to sleep, except that the frown of worry never left his pink brow.

Even in semi-sleep he was lonely, separated from his country, his family—no news from them for months on end; even in his own ship divorced by language and nationality from the greater part of his crew and his officers. Even Berenson was gone—and the Lord knew who else. He sighed again and shifted the position of his head and wondered how long he could go on enduring the loneliness. Then he stood up and stretched his short arms and when he yawned he put a pudgy hand before his mouth and patted it.

He consulted his watch and rubbed the glass with his thumb. It was seven o'clock. He replaced the watch in his trousers pocket and looked into the mirror above the wash-basin and set his cap precisely on his middle-aged head. Then he left the cabin. When he reached the saloon Mr. and Mrs. Reed, Harris and Stockmann were already assembled for the evening meal. There was no sign of Dawson or Gerda Olstein. Harris was already drunk.

Jacobson bowed, the bobbed inclination of head and shoulders. "Good evening, ladies and gentlemen." He shook out his napkin as he sat down and prepared himself to receive and parry their questions.

"Oh dear, Captain Jacobson," Alice Reed said, "What are we going to do? I don't know—it was terrible. I saw that tanker go up in flames . . . terrible . . . and all those poor men in the *Conway*. Do you think the *Conway* was sunk?"

Jacobson closed his eyes and ripped his spoon into the soup, distributing the salt through its turbid consistency. "I think it very likely," he said.

Stockmann's small eyes were bright like a bird's behind their pebble lenses. "Where are we making for?"

Jacobson wiped his lips with his napkin and first answered Mrs. Reed. "I think everything is all right now, yes. We are making for Halifax again. We do not take a direct route. We expect to arrive in three days."

Harris put an arm round the back of his chair as the ship rolled and his soup heaped itself on one side of his plate. "You hope."

"Yes, Mr. Harris. We hope. God willing."

"Jerry willing, more like," Harris countered.

The cutlery rattled against the wooden fiddles on the table and in the pantry a plate crashed to the deck.

"What are you thinking, Captain?" Stockmann asked.

Jacobson blinked. "Thinking? Er . . . nothing. Nothing, I assure you."

"Really, Captain?"

"Is there still any danger?" Albert Reed asked, turning his still keen, brisk face towards Jacobson.

"Yes, I fear there is still much danger. There are always U-boats."

"Aye, I suppose so."

Stockmann said, rubbing his hands over the roast pork, "Well, the sooner we get back to Halifax, Captain, the better I shall like it."

"But those poor men from *Conway* in the water . . . if she has sunk . . . there must have been some . . ." Mrs. Reed said.

"What about them?" Harris snapped.

"Yes, what about them?" Stockmann demanded coldly.

Alice wished she had not spoken. She glanced about the table and smiled uncertainly. "I don't know . . . I really don't know . . . but . . ."

Jacobson seemed to urge her to continue. "Yes?"

"Perhaps it's silly," she said. "I know nothing about these things. But . . . I was wondering . . . perhaps we could go back and look for them."

Harris's fist crashed to the table and the plates danced. His face was livid and contorted. He leaned towards her and shouted: "You're daft! You're bloody daft, do you hear?"

"Yes, we hear you," Albert snapped.

Harris turned to him, scornfully. "What do you know about it? Nothing! Those men are dead, do you understand? D-e-a-d! Dead! *You* know that, don't you, Captain?"

Jacobson did not answer.

Stockmann stared at him. "Do you, Captain?"

Jacobson put down his knife and fork. "Mr. Stockmann, I am in command of this ship. I do not yet propose to discuss my actions with you or anyone else. I make myself clear?"

Stockmann breathed, "You do. I believe you would go back. I really believe you would. I fear for your sanity, Captain."

"And so do I," Harris said, and drained his glass.

III

In the crew's quarters those off watch sat over their supper and mugs of sweet tea. Their talk, so far, had been of little but their deliverance from *Leipzig*. They still marvelled that they were yet alive and their ship still afloat. They had gone on to remember similar incidents in which they or men they knew or had known had been involved. They compared these events with that they had just lived through and noted, in passing, that today they had been uncommonly lucky. When their stock of reminiscences was exhausted, when there were no other escapes or battles or sinkings to recall, the conversation flagged and some of the men rose from the tables and climbed into their bunks fully dressed. Others read and two played draughts; one wrote an interminable letter, and the remainder just sat and smoked, or stared, or slowly scratched themselves. Peace came to the mess deck and when it was fully established, when at last there was silence except for the ever-present noise of the ship which no one heard, and the scratching of the pen, the dry, grating voice of the man who had spoken when Svenson had died ended it as a falling stone shatters the mirror-surface of a pond.

"What about Birken'ead?"

Movement ceased abruptly, almost secretly. No one looked at the speaker. Pages were no longer turned, pieces remained un-moved on the draught-board. The scratchy pen stopped in mid-word. Even the men in their bunks ceased to move about in search of more comfortable positions in which to wedge themselves against the movement of the ship.

They waited and the voice repeated itself. "What about Birken'ead?"

Schirmer dared this time to answer. "What about him?"

"Yes, what about him?" da Falla added.

Silence returned, the silence of men looking into tea dregs in mugs or rubbing their noses or watching the patterns their nails made in the white wood of the table, of men doing anything but look at each other.

The speaker's name was Corridon, an orphan of the Liverpool slums, who had grown up and was now growing old in merchant ships. He was undersized, slight, and with a head so narrow that he gave the impression of being viewed through a distorting mirror. His Adam's apple bobbed when he swallowed and his eyes burned as if they were slowly consuming everything in his body. His mouth was a bloodless line, grey like his face. He moved his head slowly, looking at the men about him, fixing them with the lamps of his eyes. None returned his gaze.

"What yer going to do about him?"

"Just now I say what about him?" Schirmer repeated, his voice irritable.

Corridon sucked tea into his mouth and held it for a moment in distended cheeks before swallowing it. He belched and leaned forward, his elbows on the table, his wiry fingers gripping the enamel mug.

"Listen." His voice was low, persuasive and confidential. "We've got to get rid of 'im, that's for certain. Get rid of 'im! I've sailed wi' Jonahs before. I know 'em and when they're black bastards they're worse. They're dynamite. Usually the bugger of it is to find 'em. But this time we know who it is." He smiled and the skin moved over the bones of his face as if it were being pulled upwards from some invisible point on his scalp. "Don't we, mates? We know who it is!"

Schirmer stared at him angrily with his big pudding face and da Falla stood up and moved behind him. Corridon lowered his voice still further, deepening it until it sounded like a gramophone run too slowly. "Listen 'ere. If we don't get shut of that black Jonah, we've 'ad it. I know." He tapped a forefinger against the grey flatness of one temple and his eyes burned in the electric glare. "We'll go to the bottom." His voice rose again. "Jonahs exist. They're real. You've got to get 'em before they get you."

He sat upright and took another swallow of tea and closed his eyes and once the lights in them were hidden his face might have been carved from stone. A cockroach scuttled out from beneath a locker and felt the stale air with its feelers and scuttled back again. The oilskins stood out from the white bulkheads and slowly subsided, and the everlasting globules of sweat jerked down the white paint leaving red-black trails behind them. The engines made the mugs rattle and move on the table. Not a man among them spoke.

Corridon's head came forward again. "Rub 'im out, I say! Rub 'im out if you want to see the beach again."

Schirmer said contemptuously, "Hey, Corridon? What makes you tick? What you got against Birk? How d'ya know? Tell me that. How d'ya know?"

Corridon grinned. The line of his mouth lengthened but remained straight and the thin lips parted a little to show the brown teeth. He snapped like a dog snapping at a fly. "Because this ain't 'is first ship, that's why. Ev'ry ship 'e's been in's bought it. Three times in a year. Di'n't you know that? It ain't natural. An' 'e's a religious. Always readin' 'is Bible an' sayin' 'is prayers, an' that ain't natural either. Thinks 'e's some sort of Jesus Christ or something, always prayin'. An' what d'you think 'e's prayin' about? I'll tell you—that 'e won't go to the bottom when 'is mates do." He smacked the flat of his palm on to the table. "When 'e's good an' ready to send 'em there."

Schirmer said, "Boloney!"

"I'm tellin' you, ain't I? Why don't you listen? Three months ago he was in the *Sea Merchant*, a good ship in the flippin' middle of the centre column of a convoy. Not a ship were lost. Not one. 'Cept *Sea Merchant*. She got a tin fish up 'er backside when she were in a position where it were math'mat'ly impossible to be 'it. She couldn't be 'it because anythin' comin' for 'er would 'ave 'ad to 'it some other ship first—unless the U-boat were right inside the convoy."

The men digested this information and waited for more. They were interested now and no longer quite so ashamed of listening. This Corridon, he had something.

Da Falla said, "Maybe it was."

Corridon turned his burning eyes towards the slight Eurasian as if he not only saw with them but illuminated his field of vision. "An' maybe it wasn't."

There was an almost inaudible grunt of agreement from some of the men.

"An' then again," Corridon went on to the attentive circle of faces, "Before that 'e were in a tanker that sailed smack into a mine in the Irish flippin' Sea. That were the end of 'er. There were on'y one survivor. Guess who? Birken'ead. 'E were picked up in a lifeboat with one other bloke. The other bloke were dead an' as far as anybody could see there weren't no reason why 'e should 'ave been dead unless 'e died of fright."

Da Falla said: "Maybe 'e did."

"Of Birken'ead?"

Schirmer's hands bunched themselves on the table, his pasty face even whiter than usual, a drawn, livid whiteness that Corridon had not seen before, not even when Svenson had taunted Birkenhead. "All this, Corridon. 'Ow you know, huh?"

Corridon grinned again and the skin moved smoothly over the bones. "I make it me business to know. I can smell 'em. I've been at sea too long, matey. I've been checkin' up ever since 'e came aboard. A Jonah! A black bloody Jonah."

The men moved closer to him now, pushing their heads towards the confident mask.

"And before that?" someone asked in the creaking silence. "What about before that?"

Corridon drew a silver coin from his pocket and began to turn it over and over in his fingers. "You ask what 'appened before? I'll tell you. U-boats again. An independently routed ship that they reckoned were too fast for a U-boat to catch. What 'appens? A tin-fish up 'er flue an' again the only bastard to survive is that flippin' black Jonah up topsides. An' all in the space of a year."

"Strewth!"

"Jesus!"

Corridon pulled himself upright on the bench seat, his deadly seed well sown. He spat a shred of tobacco from his teeth on to the table.

"What ya going to do about it?" Schirmer asked.

Corridon's head snapped forward, eyes glittering. "Get 'im. Get the black sod before we're all gonners."

Da Falla moved from behind Schirmer, words tumbling from his lips. "You bastard, Corridon. How many men have been sunk three times in a year? Hundreds! Hundreds, Corridon! You don't think he's a Jonah. Do you, Corridon? You don't even believe in Jonahs. Nobody does. He's the only coloured man in the ship so you want to get him. That's what's eating you, man, eating your flippin' heart out."

Da Falla's brown eyes shone like Corridon's now, alive with passion in the sallow face. Twin spots of high colour developed over his cheek-bones and his brown lips became wet with saliva. He walked towards Corridon, round the men sitting at the table, and as he passed they lifted their blank faces and watched his progress. They had seen fights before and they knew how this would end. Corridon watched him, too, lighting up his approach with his eyes, slowly turning the silver coin over and over on the palm of his hand and grinning.

"You make me sick, Corridon. You ought to be on the other side, you flippin' Nazi bastard. With them it's the Jews and with you it's the blacks. You and Svenson. It were always you and Svenson getting at Birk, who never did any harm. It was his colour you didn't like, not the number of times he'd been sunk. And there are millions like you, Corridon, mean, screwed-up little bastards like you all over the world, getting a kick outa shoving blacks around." He pushed his face into Corridon's. "You think you can swing it this time, don't you, what with this ropey crew an' all . . .?"

"Da Falla," Schirmer called, jumping to his feet while the

others watched with expressionless faces, "da Falla, come away."

But Corridon had already hit da Falla, a vicious upward punch to the stomach, delivered not so much with strength but with an expertise and a sense of timing developed over a lifetime. Da Falla collapsed, wordlessly, his face hideous with pain and lay in a heap at Corridon's feet. Schirmer vaulted on to the table and threw himself on Corridon. He was bigger than his opponent, much bigger and stronger, and would probably have killed him had not half a dozen men risen up from the table and taken his squirming body and punched it and kicked it until it fell to the deck by the side of da Falla.

Corridon stood among them, grinning but not smiling, looking first at his henchmen, and then at those who feared not to agree with him and finally at those who did not know whether to agree or not. There were no others.

"Right," he said. "We get Birken'ead. Anybody got anything to say?"

The oilskins lifted themselves away from the bulkheads and the sweat trickled further down the paintwork. The engines thundered below and a locker door vibrated insanely until a foot kicked it shut. The men waited for Corridon to tell them what they should do.

IV

When the first dog watch ended and he was able to leave the bridge, Dawson lost no time in renewing his acquaintance with Gerda. He tiptoed along the passageway, making quite certain that his journey was undetected, knocked respectfully on her cabin door and waited to be admitted. She was wearing her white roll-necked sweater and rough tweed skirt and since she had worn no other clothes since the voyage began, Dawson wondered briefly if it were possible that she possessed no other outfit; or had she come aboard with nothing beyond the garments she stood up in?

"Oh, it is you." Her voice was flat with disinterest.

Dawson was put out by the sullen emptiness of her face. Sometimes the emptiness disappeared, often when she talked and always when she laughed. But she laughed so seldom. And the emptiness always returned to sit behind her eyes, looking out, brooding and vacant. Her magnificent figure excited him; yet, when she flung out the words "Oh, it is you" he almost shivered, as if being in the presence of so much unhappiness lowered his temperature. Yet he needed to discover the source of her misery, for then he would be nearer to her, capable of loving her. It would be a strange experience; he had never before loved anyone, or even thought that he could. The possibility of loving had never entered his head. Until now. "Everything O.K.?" he asked, grinning.

"Yes. It was very terrible."

"Yeah, not so good. Guess we're getting to hell out of it now, though."

"That is good."

She was standing by the mirror on the far side of the cabin and, quite suddenly, disconcertingly, she smiled at him. He moved towards her, quickly, almost hungrily.

"Gerda, what is it?"

"What is it? I do not understand."

"What is the matter?"

"Matter? Nothing is the matter."

He seized her hands and held them together between his own. "Yes there is. What is it?"

She shook her head and smiled again, but even then a little vacantly, as if she were smiling not at him or at what he had said, but at something of which he could have no knowledge. He pulled her towards him and at first she resisted but when her breasts touched him she seemed to relent.

Almost at once, she was struggling, pushing him away. She was very strong, he found. "Please go . . ."

"But, Gerda . . ."

"Please go. Leave me alone."

His hands hung at his sides and she moved away from him. She picked up a packet of cigarettes from her bunk and offered it to him, absently. He took one and stuck it angrily in the corner of his mouth.

"You kill me," he said.

"Kill you?"

"Forget it."

He struck a match and held it to her cigarette. When she leaned towards the flame he wanted to hold her again but the moment passed and she sat down on the edge of her bunk. He turned away from her, petulantly, feeling like a little boy, and played with her hairbrush on the top of the chest of drawers, listening to the bristles skittering over the polished surface of the wood.

She said, "You like to sit down?"

He ignored the question. "Gerda, you've gotta tell me what all this is about."

"About?"

He gestured, irritably. "That's English. I'll soon not know what goddam language I'm talking. First you let me into your cabin—like a fool I come, but never mind, I come—and you all but undress in front of me. Now you tell me to go. What've I done? You just can't treat a guy this way, Gerda."

He moved towards her and drew her slowly to her feet and as she came up she put her arms about his neck. She said, "Are you a good man?"

He laughed and joined his hands behind her waist.

"No, I don't believe I am, Gerda. But I could be very good for you. The question is, are you a good woman?"

"What does 'good' mean? I do not think so. Not for a long time."

"You're not good?"

She shook her head, her face very near to his.

He said softly, "That makes two of us."

She asked quickly, "Why do we stand up?"

"O.K. Let's sit down."

She sat on the edge of the bunk again, almost demurely, one hand held in the palm of the other on her lap. When he sat by her side he discovered that she was weeping.

"Gerda, what's the matter? I'm sorry . . . did I make you cry? Gee, I'm sorry. Look, why don't you lie down and relax for a while? You're upset."

He laid her carefully on the bunk and gave her his handkerchief. "It's not very clean but it'll have to do. Wipe your eyes and tell me about it."

She said, "Do not leave me. Please do not leave me."

"No, I won't leave you, Gerda. Not just yet, anyway."

"When do you work again?"

"Twenty hundred."

"Do not leave me until then."

She moved her cheek slowly against his as if she were sensing the texture of silk or fur. "I think you are like other men. I am wrong? I think you look too strong and handsome to be kind. You are kind? You will be kind to me?"

"Yes, I'll be kind to you, Gerda."

She tried to stop the tears with the sides of her fingers. "I do not know your name."

"Bill. Bill Dawson."

He watched her, already loving her, loving her if only she would never be cold with him again. He said, "I'm like most men."

"How is that?"

"Unable to do without women."

"How did you say? That makes two of us. In my life there are always men."

"And they've not been good to you, huh?"

"I think I hate all men. But I do not hate now. I can love. One I loved . . ."

"Tell me what happened, Gerda."

"It is a long story. I think you will not like it."

"Don't you understand? You've got to tell me."

"I was a stewardess in a Swedish ship. We sail to South America, to Buenos Aires, and in this ship there is a man. He is a passenger and I love him or I think I love him. He is Argentinian. He is tall and handsome, as you are, and because of his manner I think he must be very rich. He has thick, waving hair that is like wire to touch.

"When we come to Buenos Aires, I leave my ship and go to live with him in his flat. It is small but looks out over the sea and I think I must be happy . . . because I love him. I write to my parents in Sweden. And then, when I am with him and my ship has sailed, when, in a few days I am no more new to him, I discover that all he tells me is untrue."

She propped herself on her elbow so that she could reach over Dawson to the shelf attached to the edge of her bunk and extract a cigarette from the open packet. He struck a match for her and her breasts moved against him. He blew out the match and balanced the ashtray on the flatness of her stomach. "Go on."

"You still wish to hear?"

"Yes, honey. Don't stop."

She tried to smile. "He hit me and made me do terrible things. He kick and punch and scratch—because this is his way of making love and if he cannot kick me and punch me he does not enjoy. There are many such men."

"Yeah."

"Soon he brings home a new girl with a scar on her face and throws me out."

Dawson whispered, "Didn't anybody ever tell you?"

"Tell me?"

"That some men are like that?"

"Then I was young. I do not know."

"When was this?"

"Before the war. Not long before."

"So?"

"I try to find work but I am not lucky. In Buenos Aires there is little work for a woman who can speak only Swedish and very little English. I speak English better now. Yes? I know all the swear-words."

She stopped and stubbed out her half-smoked cigarette and leaned over him again to return the ashtray to the ledge. Suddenly she was angry again: cold, with vacant eyes; pushing him off the bunk with her hands and feet. "You had better go. I do not want to talk. I do not want. Go!"

He sat up and pinioned her arms and leaned the weight of his body upon her and looked into her face. "Go on!"

"No!"

"Gerda, you must go on."

"No! You're hurting. You are like the rest. Hurt, hurt, hurt, always hurting! Can no man do anything but hurt?"

He held her body beneath his own and kissed her, his mouth hard against hers. Slowly her anger subsided and she ceased to struggle. When he moved away from her she was crying again. "I am sorry," she sobbed.

"Go on."

"So, I go to work in a night-club where I learn to smoke and to drink and to go home with men without looking closely at their faces. I learn not to care whether I like them or not. Some of them are kind and cannot help themselves. Some are drunks and cannot sleep until they have a woman to sleep with them.

Some pay me well and some do not pay at all. Some hit me. They like to see the marks where their hands have been."

"Go on, Gerda."

"One night I take a poker to one of the hitters. He is a good customer of the night-club and I have the sack—woosh—next day. I have no money. So I go to a cheaper night-club and then to an even cheaper night-club. In the end there are no night-clubs left where I have not worked. So I go to a bar and then to another bar and then to a cheaper bar until there is not any difference between the last bar and a brothel." She stopped, breathlessly. "You still want me to go on?"

He answered very softly, "Yes."

She smiled to herself, a slow sad diminutive smile on her handsome face. "Sometimes it is nice in a brothel. You have no more to think. There is no worry about food and money. It just comes and there are other girls and they are sometimes kind—when they are not jealous. Sometimes they fight but for most of the time they are friends. They are all in the same kind of trouble. In the brothel I even save some money, enough, in the end, to buy a ticket to Sweden."

"You're going home?"

"To Sweden, yes."

"It's over now, Gerda."

She shook her head and tears ran into her hair at the side of her face. "No, it is not over. I want to be away from men, never to see them again. And yet . . ."

"Yet what?"

"Nothing."

Deliberately: "Yet what?"

"Yet I still want them," she answered in a small voice. "I want you. . . ."

"It's over," he said.

She leaned over him, hammering on his chest with her fists, "No! No! No, it is not over. It can never be over. Help me! Please help me, please . . ."

Dawson fought within himself. That it should come to this! It was silly. He, the hero, or so he thought, of countless beds, that he should come to this! It would be funny if it were less serious. He grinned, "You know what I said?"

She watched his lips, waiting for a sign, or perhaps a miracle.

"What?"

"This makes two of us."

"What do you mean?"

"Never mind. Don't bother yourself with it." He pulled her towards him and wound his arms round her body and kissed her for a long time. She said, "You will not hurt me?" and he breathed back, "No, I won't hurt you, Gerda. God damn it, I won't hurt you. Hell—I love you."

"You had not told me."

"You hadn't asked me."

He kissed her again, aware of his terrible responsibility, as if he were holding priceless china in his hands.

She moved against him and appeared to sleep and he saw that there was something approaching peace in her face. It was sufficient, just to lie by her side. For the first time in his life he knew what he wanted and recognised it when he saw it.

The ship creaked and rolled, plunging westward with a following sea.

v

Goldstein leaned back in his armchair and chewed the end of a matchstalk protruding between his blubbery lips. Lord Birkenhead still lay on his back on the bunk, breathing slowly, his sculptured black face bright with moisture like the surface of a lamp-lit black road in the night, his eyes, white in the blackness, staring at the deckhead. He had not moved for a long time.

"Birk."

The body on the bunk scarcely moved. "Hm?"

"Birk. What's all this crap abaht Jonahs. What's a Jonah?"

"A Jonah?" Birkenhead asked. "You want to know who Jonah was?"

"That's right, Birk. Who was this guy Jonah?"

Birkenhead's voice had grown stronger and was recovering some of its lost timbre. "You still got de Bible, Goldie?"

"Yeah, sure. What you want the Bible for?"

"Open it, Goldie."

Goldstein moved over to the desk and picked up the Bible and sat down again. "I'm 'oldin' the Bible, Birk."

"Start at the beginning, Goldie, and turn over de pages till you come to a list of all de books in de Old Testament."

"I don't know what you want, Birk, but I'm lookin'."

"Found it?"

"I guess so. Reckon this must be it. Crikey! I can't read this lot."

Birkenhead turned his face towards Goldstein. "Near de end of de list, Goldie. Can you see Jonah?"

"Jonah? Blimey, Birk. Is this guy Jonah in the Bible?"

"Yeah, Goldie. He's in de Bible."

"Jesus, Birk, I can't read these names. Ha . . . bak . . . kuk. Ha . . . bak . . . kuk? Who the hell's Ha . . . bak . . . kuk?" He frowned at the small print and pushed his finger slowly up the column. "Yeah, yeah, Birk," he exlaimed, pleased with himself. "I got it. Jonah! Yeah, 'ere 'e is. Jonah."

"What page does it say, Goldie?"

"Page?"

"Yeah, what number comes after de name?"

"Blimey! One thousand and thirty-nine."

"Find de page, Goldie."

Goldstein thumbed through the crinkly India paper for a long time, backwards and then forwards, muttering the numbers to himself as he passed them. Once, he dropped the book and had to go back to the table of contents. It was a long, agonising process. Birkenhead breathed slowly, shifting only when the ship rolled and gently tilted his body, first this way and then that. The lamp fixed to the bulkhead over his head moved, or rather did not move, only appeared to move as the ship moved about it.

"Got it, Birk! Jonah! Got it!"

"Read it, Goldie."

"Read it?"

"Yeah, read it out loud. I wanna hear it all again."

"But I told you, Birk, I can't read."

"Sure you can read, Goldie. You read before. Read and take it real slow, boy."

Goldstein read the small print, slowly and hesitantly: "Now the word of the Lord came unto Jonah . . ." His fingers followed the words of the archaic verses and the rough hesitancy of his voice appeared to add a strange authenticity to the description of that ancient storm. "Wherefore they cried unto the Lord, and said, We beseech thee, O Lord, we beseech thee, let us not perish for this man's life, and lay not upon us innocent blood: for thou, O Lord, hast done as it pleased thee.

"So they took Jonah, and cast him forth into the sea: and the sea ceased her raging."

Goldstein rested the Bible on his thick thighs and stared at the bulkhead. His reading had been a great effort and he felt exhausted. He wished Birkenhead would say something; the silence was beginning to get on his nerves.

"Birk," he said, "what does it mean?"

Birkenhead turned his head and smiled, "It's just a story, Goldie. Just a li'l old story."

"A story? Just a story?"

"Yeah, Goldie, just a story."

Goldstein got up and returned the Bible to the desk.

"Birk, do stories in the Bible ever come true?"

"Sure, Goldie, sure they do."

EIGHT

I

THE temperature in and about the Carley raft was some thirty-eight degrees Fahrenheit—a few degrees above freezing point. The men on the raft could not know this for they had no means of measuring the temperature, but they were inclined to believe that anything colder was a scientific impossibility.

They noted, in their misery, that the wind appeared to be dropping a little and this gave them hope, an iota, a molecule of hope. Yet even now it was blowing, perhaps, at twenty-five knots —force six—and they could scarcely breathe, let alone think, in its bitter pressure. It forced itself against their bodies in an unrelenting stream, piling itself against their saturated clothing and then cutting through it as if it did not exist. None of the men with coats had given them up but, on Ainslee's suggestion, there had been some redistribution of other clothing: Wilmot now wore Ainslee's scarf and Mallet-Jones's sweater, and the boy was given Barraclough's sweater and Reggie's balaclava. But no man would part with his coat, could not be asked to part with it, for upon his coat his life largely depended. Oliphant offered nothing; the others volunteered but Oliphant held his silence—and no one pressed him. A part of the boy's clothing was Wilmot's body which was always between the boy and the wind. The boy never spoke, had become, already, incapable of speech and crouched against Wilmot as if Wilmot were his mother and he an ailing child.

The men huddled about Ainslee, listening to the wind moving over the water, seeking protection, crouching behind the bulbous floats surrounding the rope-slung bottom of the raft. But wherever they moved the wind sought them out and the spray hammered at their bodies like driven hail, immobilising them, stunning them, eventually killing them. They could see no other end.

Both the boy and Oliphant were sick from the violent motion of the raft and their vomit mingled in the wind with the spray, and those on whom it fell were either too cold or too exhausted to wipe it away. They let the sea remove it, carry it into nothingness as wave after wave tipped its foaming crest upon them and swept on into the night. They could no longer control their bladders and had already adopted the physical standards of animals. They did not question their reduction.

They became aware that Wilmot had moved and was cradling Ainslee's shoulders on his knees, and that Ainslee was speaking. It was one of those triumphs of discipline, when a man who has endured it and accepted all its implications, can find the strength, no matter what the effort, when others have passed beyond the power of initiation. Although the men could see Ainslee's shape on the floor of the raft, they could not see his face and could not, therefore, see the pain. But his voice held no hint of the pain: loud and clear in the streaming wind, delivering his appreciation of their situation, and his consequent orders, in a confident naval twang. "Now, listen! Can you hear me? The attack of the *Leipzig* was reported before our aerials were shot away. But there's no shipping we know of within two days' steaming of our position. That means we have to stay alive for two days at least. Even though we might be found by a search aircraft earlier —which is doubtful—we'll still have to wait two days for a ship to pick us up. That's our only hope and it's a slender one. We must keep ourselves alive for two days. In order to do this, while this weather lasts, we must keep moving. We must not sleep. We must not be overtaken by the cold. Any questions?"

Mallet-Jones marvelled at the man's control, astonished that he was able to be so matter of fact lying there as if he were giving his views at a convoy conference. Chief Petty Officer Wilmot was not surprised at all. He expected nothing less. Sometimes in his life he had been disappointed when a superior officer had not measured up to his own exacting requirements. Each successive failure had distressed him—and he had forgotten none of them. But his faith had remained, and this time he had known from the beginning that he was dealing with a man of different calibre.

Oliphant said weakly, "What about the ships of the convoy?"

"They were ordered to scatter. They will not return this way."

"Could one come back?" he persisted.

"Not unless her Captain is mad. No."

They digested this information.

"Right," Ainslee went on, "We'll divide into two parties. Mallet-Jones, you'll take charge of the first, consisting of Barraclough and . . . what's your name?" He put out a hand and touched Reggie's shoulder.

"Atkinson, sir."

"Atkinson. Your party, Chief, will be the boy and . . . your name?"

"Oliphant."

". . . And Oliphant. It will be your duty to keep them active, to keep their circulation going, to make certain they do not sleep. We shall sing. From time to time I shall distribute water. We have enough bully beef and water to last the night if we are careful with it. Right, Chief?"

"Right, sir."

"All right, then. Carry on."

It had been necessary for him to shout above the noise of the wind and the effort had weakened him. Wilmot extricated his legs from under Ainslee's shoulder.

"Pull me back, Chief. I want to sit up."

Wilmot called to Mallet-Jones and together they pulled him backwards so that he could lean against the rounded floats, his broken legs slithering over the bottom of the raft.

"Will you be all right, sir?" Mallet-Jones asked.

"Thank you, Mallet-Jones, yes." He smiled, "I can do my physical jerks better sitting up."

"Yes, sir. Of course, sir."

II

Eight for the April rainers.
Seven for the seven stars in the sky,
And six for the six proud walkers.
Five for the knocking at your door
And four for the gospel makers . . .

Two hours had passed and Mallet-Jones was leading his group in raucous song. Wilmot's party was resting. As they sang they moved their arms as they would in a PT class in barracks except that now their arms moved slowly and drooped as if already they had reached the limit of their endurance. Their heads rolled from side to side and for much of the time their eyes were closed. All of them were sea-sick.

But the wind was still falling and the spray no longer raced quite so violently over the water. They did not feel warmer, but their bodies were less buffeted and for this they were grateful. Ainslee moved his arms in time to the song, trying to keep his trunk still, for each movement of his trunk shifted the position of his legs and then the agony became unendurable. He shouted, "The wind's falling."

The men heard him and a flutter of hope moved in their breasts and for a moment they sang almost lustily.

> Three, three, the rivals.
> Two, two, the lily-white boys,
> Clothed all in green-oh.
> One is one and all alone,
> And ever more shall be so.

Barraclough seemed not yet to be severely affected by the cold. His hands and his face were blue but his teeth did not now chatter uncontrollably as did Reggie's. It was not the first time in his life that Barraclough had been cold, painfully, unbearably cold, hungry and lonely. The sum of these earlier hardships gave him now a greater stamina than Reggie had ever possessed. Reggie had led a more sheltered life and had certainly been better fed and yet, now, the years of care and attention counted for very little; Barraclough was infinitely tougher, had not yet allowed despondency to get the better of him. Reggie wanted only to scream or to be allowed to lie down and sleep and forget. He could see no hope, no possible glimmer of hope of survival. They might as well already be dead. They might as well have died with *Conway*. He was unable to find the strength to defy the inevitable. Yet was it death he wanted or merely sleep? Sleep! The means, the opportunity to become unmindful of the cold and the anguish and the retching in his guts. Sleep! Sleep more than anything. If only he could lie down. Why won't they let me lie down? Why? Why don't they for Christ Almighty's sake shut up and lie down?

Barraclough sang:

> I belong to Glasgie, dear ol' Glasgie toon,
> But there's something the matter wi' Glasgie 'cos it's
>   goin' roon' and roon',
> I'm only a common young workin' lad,
> As anyone 'ere can see,
> But when I get a coupla drinks on a Saturday Glasgie
>   belongs to me.

Reggie watched the moving outline of Barraclough's head and became aware that he hated Barraclough more than any of them. While he might hate Mallet-Jones and Ainslee and even Wilmot for the persistence of their authority, he hated Barraclough for quite different reasons. Barraclough was the low-born tough, a representative of the riff-raff whom Reggie, throughout his life, by constant parental implication, had been taught to despise. But the lowly member of the proletariat was doing better than he, Reggie, would ever do. Reggie knew this with a passionate certainty and the only thing that kept him going was not the hope of ultimate survival, nor Mallet-Jones's constant chivvying, nor Ainslee's invisible drive, but a terrible loathing of Barraclough. It happened quickly and once begun developed furiously.

Barraclough intoned:

> Mr. five by five,
> Five feet tall and five feet wide,
> He don't measure no more
> From head to toe
> Than he does from side to side

In the mists of the sea Reggie began to see not only Barraclough's head but the elementary school he had attended as a child: the bleak stone, the bell high up in a hole in the wall, the asphalt playground. He hated the school, too. When he had been but a child his parents had told him that he would not remain there beyond the age of eleven when, they said, he would win his scholarship and go to the "Grammar". For this reason he had always felt himself to be apart from the other boys in the school; their future, ordained and accepted, was to be less privileged. They sensed his apartness and tended to avoid him.

His way of speaking was different: he swore less easily and was less well-informed on sexual matters. He was unable to stay out in the evening as long as they could, and certainly not after dark, when they would stand in the pools of street-lamps talking endlessly to girls and calling after anyone who invited pity. He had been a lonely child.

Towards the end of his elementary school career, Reggie had made a friend of a pale, sickly youth by the name of Michael Soper. Young Soper had a big head and an incongruously narrow face and ears that stood out like flaps, whose father's mind had been permanently deranged by a lump of rock that had fallen on his head when he had been a miner. The household was kept together by his mother who toiled over washtub and ironing board for fourteen hours each day, who had learnt not to be irritated or even saddened by the sight of her husband sitting endlessly before the fire, smoking his pipe, moving only when it became imperative to empty the accumulated nicotined saliva from the bottom of his mouth into the fireplace where it would sizzle and bubble on the black-leaded bars and throw up little clouds of grey ash.

Yet, for all his poverty, Michael, their son, was possessed of a quiet, gentle manner; like Reggie (or as Reggie liked to think of himself) not of the others. Perhaps this was why Reggie had been drawn to him, partly this and partly Michael's readiness to defer to Reggie's whims.

When the scholarship examination had loomed on the horizon Reggie had seen rather less of Michael—to whom the examination was of little consequence—and had been compelled to stay at home and endure the purgatory of private tuition which his mother and father had scraped and saved to pay for. They would get him through the examination if it was the last thing they ever did.

Reggie took the examination and found it, as he put it, a snip. Then before the term ended, and before the results were announced, he was silly enough or conceited enough to announce that he would not be returning to the school. His companions accepted the news without displeasure, but said that it would be a pity if he were to leave them without their being able to give him something to remember them by.

Reggie could see himself now, propped against the wall in a

corner of the playground, surrounded by a mob of giggling hooligans. He saw his cap being pushed down the drain again, heard the penknife sawing at his tie, felt his flies being ripped open. He heard their voices above the noise of the sea, heard also the voice of Michael Soper who was one of the exultant mob.

"You won't be needin' yer cap yonder!"

"Look, yer flies are open!"

"Yer old man's 'anging out!"

"That's not 'is old man, it's a pimple!"

The hatred clawed about inside his stomach which already ached as if it had been kicked by a mule, a violent hatred, born of self-pity and hopelessness. He was no longer able to control himself. He lunged across the raft and got his frozen hands about Barraclough's shadowy, singing throat which seemed now to be Michael Soper's throat, he above all who had betrayed him.

"Shut up! Shut up! Shut up!" he screamed.

He could think of nothing else to say but this one thing. His hatred had become channelled into one immediate and vital purpose—to stop Soper singing, for if Soper were silent, less alive, less hopeful, the hatred perhaps would be easier to bear. His fingers closed about Barraclough's hard throat, pressing, he thought, like tightening bands of steel, but not pressing hard enough to keep Barraclough down. Reggie felt his body rise up with Barraclough's and in the mist of his hysteria heard Ainslee shouting and felt Mallet-Jones's hands on his, tightening, pulling them away from the muscular neck. Finally, when his hands slipped helplessly away, he heard Barraclough's strident profanity above the noise of the wind: "Jesus wept!"

He sat down and held his head in his hands, his body jerking with sobs. He wanted to be sick again. The singing had stopped and Ainslee said to Wilmot, "See that he's all right, Chief."

Wilmot said, "He'll be all right now, sir."

"Does he have a knife?" Ainslee asked.

"Have you got a knife, Atkinson?" Wilmot asked.

Reggie shook his head.

"I can't hear you," Wilmot said.

"No."

Barraclough shouted, "Flippin' treacherous bastard."

"Pull yourself together, Atkinson. You're not a child," Ainslee said.

"Flip me," Barraclough went on. "'E's not safe. 'E's balmy!"

"Quiet, Barraclough," Ainslee growled.

"Well, 'e is!"

"I said be quiet," Ainslee ordered.

"Flip me!"

Ainslee said, "Mallet-Jones, carry on singing, please."

"Aye, aye, sir."

> Roll me over,
> In the clover,
> Roll me over,
> Lay me down
> And do it again.

"Now then, all together now."

NINE

I

JACOBSON climbed the ladder from the saloon deck at eight bells. He had not enjoyed his supper with the passengers; they had ruined the taste of his food and left him with flatulence. He wished now that he had remained undisturbed on his bridge, except that he would have been obliged, instead, to spend the time with Busk, who, with his bright conversation, grinning dentures and lank curtain of hair falling from under his cap like the sun-shield of a Legionnaire, was in no sense preferable.

He was followed by Dawson, who relieved Busk. Since he had discovered, so to speak, other fish to fry, Dawson had missed his supper altogether. Indeed, he was so taken with the realisation that he was able to love, selflessly, immediately, and without thought of imminent physical reward, that he would willingly have foregone a thousand suppers. That he was able to extend himself beyond the role of the mere philanderer astonished him. His experience had been both novel and chastening and even now, now that he was back on the bridge in charge of the ship, his mind was still half bemused, not with desire or the familiar ribald anticipation, but with an elation that depended for fulfilment upon its being shared with others. He wished he could talk to Jacobson about it.

When his eyes were wholly accustomed to the darkness he could see the white lanes of foam creaming aft on both sides of the fo'c'sle. The wind was falling and the swell, very slightly, was beginning to subside. The waves no longer hammered against *Oleron*'s quarter and with the noise of the wind decreasing he could hear the rush and tumble of the bow waves as they were flung from the cleaving stem, a restful, satisfying sound, denoting progress.

Jacobson stumped into the charthouse and as he examined the chart he mechanically filled and lit his pipe without looking at it, and clipped the patent lid into place. Only the fragrance of Balkan Sobranie would betray the fact that he was smoking in the darkness.

He returned to the bridge and walked out on to the wing and

inspected the sky. No break showed in the cloud blanket; not a star was visible. Dead reckoning could be their only guide. He returned to the shelter of the glass screens and stood with his feet slightly apart, his hands in the wide pockets of his sheepskin coat, his pipe clenched between his teeth, jutting directly forward under his pinched nose.

He had never known such indecision.

Perhaps half an hour went by, neither he nor Dawson speaking to each other. The engines pounded rhythmically below decks. All was well. In three days they would be in Halifax. He ought to sleep. He ought to stop this ceaseless senseless worrying. In the end he would break down and then he would be unable to help anyone. His teeth squeaked on the stem of his pipe as if he sought to bite it off.

"Mr. Dawson."

"Sir?"

"I wonder," he said, in his precise, high-pitched voice, "I wonder if I can ask your opinion on—er—a little matter I have in mind?"

"Sure, Captain," Dawson answered amiably. "Shoot!"

Jacobson winced but did not expostulate. "The *Conway* . . ." he began.

Dawson waited, "Yes, sir?"

Jacobson began again, "Mr. Dawson, what do you think . . . happened to *Conway*?"

"Jeez, Captain. How should I know?"

Jacobson wondered whether he had misjudged his man and a grimace of impatience passed over his benign face. "You must have some opinion, yes?"

"Sure. I guess she bought it. What else could have happened to her?"

"You mean she was sunk?"

"That's what I mean."

Jacobson pursed his lips and looked forward, over the bow. "She could have run away . . . escaped."

"Not likely, sir. Not fast enough. And we'd have seen more of *Leipzig*, if it was *Leipzig*, as they say it was. Anyway, she wouldn't."

"Ha!—She fought?"

"Of course she fought."

"That is what I think, too."

Dawson spoke quietly to the man at the wheel and the course was adjusted.

Jacobson continued, "And you think that if she fought, she was also sunk?"

"Yeah. For sure."

"Now tell me, if she was sunk, you think there are survivors?"

"There'd be some. 'Most always there's some."

"And then?"

"Then what?"

"Well, do you think they still survive?"

"Maybe."

"And what will happen to them tonight, or tomorrow, or the day after that?"

"They'll die."

The promptness of his reply caught Jacobson off balance and for some time he did not speak. He walked towards Dawson and stood before his huge frame in the dim compass-light.

"Quartermaster," he said. "Keep a good look-out. Mr. Dawson, please come with me to the charthouse."

Jacobson marched off into the darkness and pushed his way through the heavy blackout screens at the door of the charthouse. Dawson followed. When they were inside the narrow cabin, which was almost entirely filled by the chart table, Dawson seemed to dwarf the portly Jacobson. He looked down into the worried pink face and wished he could help him. He was a good man, this Captain; if only he would stop worrying about things that did not concern him. And a good Captain, too, for most of the time. Jacobson alternately pursed his lips and stroked them with the tip of his tongue. Now that he was alone with Dawson he did not know how to begin. A pencil rolled over the chart and fell to the deck. A parallel ruler flopped on its rollers, first on to one edge and then on to the other. Dawson lit a cigarette, waiting.

"Mr. Dawson," Jacobson began.

Dawson shifted his huge shoulders and leaned against the chart table. The woodwork groaned. It was becoming a game. "Sir?"

"Suppose those men who . . . er . . . escaped from *Conway* are still alive."

"O.K. Let's suppose that some escaped and that they're still alive."

"Let us say that they are in a boat or on a raft and are able to keep themselves alive during the night."

"Yes."

"Do you believe that we can, in such circumstances, just . . . abandon them?"

Dawson's eyes narrowed and his lips curled over his teeth in an expression of incredulity. "Come again?"

Jacobson blinked. "Sorry, I do not understand."

"What did you say, sir?"

"I said, can we just abandon them, leave them in the sea?"

Dawson began to gnaw at his thumb and Jacobson felt dangerously excited, not understanding why.

"What else can we do?" Dawson asked at length.

Instantly Jacobson was pouring out his plan in a breathless stream, "Look, Dawson. If we do not go back for them, they will die. You say so yourself. I do not think any of the other ships of the convoy will go back for them . . ."

"You're darn right, they won't."

" . . . The only one that might exploded."

"*Southern Star?*"

"Yes, *Southern Star*. We are only three hours' steaming away. We could return and be there by twenty three hundred, certainly before midnight. Then, not every man in *Conway* would be lost. A few would survive, perhaps only one, how do you say?—to tell the tale." Jacobson's voice was eager, intense. "She was a gallant ship. What do you say, Dawson?"

Dawson looked at Jacobson as if he had propounded a scheme so impossible of achievement that only a madman could have devised it. Jacobson saw the hesitation and hurried on, piling his cards on the table. "I have a half-mutinous crew. My First Officer is of no value. I cannot do without you, Dawson. With you, I can go back. Without your help, I cannot."

His eyes glittered in the dim, blue light of the charthouse lamp which made them appear not blue but black, extraordinarily penetrating, avid.

Dawson inhaled deeply and the expelled smoke delineated the beam of the shaded blue light. "You'll never find them."

Again Jacobson was excited. At least he had not yet refused. "We might."

Dawson turned his powerful body away from Jacobson and

moved towards the door. "How long you been at sea, Captain?"

Jacobson said quietly, almost humbly, "More than thirty years."

"And as Master?"

"Nearly twenty years."

Dawson whirled round. "Then you must know that if they exist, these men you want to save, the chances of finding them are nil."

"Nil?"

"Yes, nil! You haven't a chance and you know it."

"That is not correct. We have a little chance."

"And you'd go back, against such odds?"

"Yes!"

"Your crew won't follow you."

"We shall see."

"Your First Officer will let you down."

"We shall manage without him."

"Your passengers will object."

"Perhaps."

"They'll sue you."

"Not if we find them."

"The ocean's lousy with U-boats."

"We have thirteen knots."

"What about *Leipzig*? She's out there, too, or had you forgotten?"

"I doubt if she will find us. She will not expect us there. She will not herself be there now."

Dawson wiped his mouth with the palm of his hand. He looked at Jacobson's mild, determined face and came towards him. Then he banged his fist on to the chart table and shouted, "You can't do it, Captain. The crew! They'll crucify you before they'll go back."

"I shall ask them, of course."

Dawson sneered. He could not help sneering. Jacobson was being preposterous. "Nicely?"

Jacobson answered with dignity. "Yes, I shall ask them nicely."

Dawson laughed. Jacobson held himself very erect. "Why do you laugh?"

Dawson ignored the question. "No."

"But . . ."

"No, I can't help you, Captain."

"But those men."

"To hell with them. There's a war on."

"Is that your final word?"

"It's my final word."

Jacobson grasped Dawson's coat in his fingers and stared into his handsome face. "Is it the woman?"

They stood quite still, close together, the giant looking down into the little man's face. Dawson could feel Jacobson's belly against his. "How did you know?" he breathed.

Jacobson permitted himself a smile.

"A good Captain knows what happens in his ship. If there is no woman, you would go?"

"No, Captain. She has nothing to do with it."

"I ask for the last time. Will you do it?"

Dawson snatched himself away and pounded on the chart table. "No, Captain. I've told you, haven't I? No, no, no! Because it's madness. Don't you understand that? You can't find them! Look at it out there, as black as bloody pitch! And the glass falling. You'll never find them. How many times do I have to tell you?"

"We could save them," Jacobson said sadly.

Dawson moved away from the table and faced Jacobson.

"Look, sir. If there was a chance I'd say yes. If, maybe, there was a one per cent rather than a point one per cent chance, I'd follow you. But there isn't. God, there isn't and you must know it."

Jacobson's body seemed to sink a few inches into the deck and his shoulders sagged. He no longer looked up at Dawson's face. "Thank you, Mr. Dawson. Return to your duties."

II

Alice Reed lay fully dressed on her bunk. Her husband struggled to remove his boots. When his feet were free he sighed and flexed his toes and placed the boots neatly together by the door.

Alice stirred. "I've been asleep, Albert. What's the time?"

Albert crossed to the wash-basin. "A quarter to nine. Aren't you going to get undressed?" He began to remove his teeth.

"Yes, I suppose I'd better."

They heard a discreet tapping on their door.

"Who the Hamlet's that?" Albert asked rhetorically, pushing back his teeth, working them into position with muffled dental clatter.

Alice pushed her legs over the side of the bunk and sat on its edge, smoothing her dress on her thighs with the palms of her hands. "Goodness me."

Albert opened the door a few inches and peered into the obscurity of the passageway. It was Stockmann and Harris. Stockmann was very correct, beaming all over his heavy face. He and Harris appeared to have patched up their disagreement. "Mr. Reed do forgive us for intruding on your privacy at this late hour but Mr. Harris and I would like, if we may, to . . . er . . . talk with you for a moment . . . and . . . er . . . of course, Mrs. Reed."

Albert did not move the door. He just peered at them, the lower half of his face obscured, willing them to go away. Removing his teeth had unsettled him. It was the ultimate act of each day, like the turning of a switch. "It's a bit late, isn't it? We were just going to bed." He swallowed and ran his tongue along the edge of his teeth, pushing the plate further home.

Stockmann smiled. "I can quite understand your reluctance, sir. But we believe the matter to be of . . . er . . . extreme urgency. Don't we, Harris?"

Harris stood half behind Stockmann, looking at the top of Albert's now quizzical head, staring at it angrily (Harris's mutilated face was permanently angry, an interminable Cyclopean anger, inconsolable) and swaying, his shoulder bumping against the passageway bulkhead as the ship moved, and then moodily thrusting himself upright again with the side of his arm. "That's right," he said. "We do."

Albert took his time. To take his time was one of his tricks, like lapsing into the vernacular whenever he was angered. "Well, in that event I suppose you'd better come in."

Stockmann straightened his body within the suave suiting. "I quite understand . . . we shall not keep you a moment . . . good evening, Mrs. Reed."

Albert did not suggest that they should sit down. "Well?" he demanded, his hands in his trouser pockets, his face devoid of all expression, revealing nothing, as if he were facing two men who had come to bargain about the price of cloth or union rates of pay.

Stockmann said, "Mr. Reed, you have doubtless drawn your own conclusions from the conversation at the supper table."

"I don't know that I have."

Stockmann smiled briefly, a nervous, conciliatory gesture. Well, it was the impression of . . . er . . . Mr. Harris, here, and myself that Captain Jacobson was prepared to . . . er . . . entertain, shall we say, the idea of going back to attempt to pick up possible survivors of the *Conway*."

"He's off his rocker," Harris said.

"Was it now?" Albert answered, ignoring Harris.

"Did you not think so, Mrs. Reed?" Stockmann asked.

"I don't know. I didn't think so."

"Well, Mr. Harris and I both had that impression, and we're a little worried over the . . . er . . . possible consequences if Captain Jacobson does so decide."

Albert stood his non-committal ground. "Well?"

Stockmann expostulated mildly, "But, my dear Mr. Reed, consider the danger. And Mr. Harris tells me that there's not a hope . . ."

"Not a hope in hell," pronounced Harris.

" . . . of finding them, assuming, of course, that they are still alive and if, indeed, there were any survivors in the first place—which he doubts."

"He's too drunk to know," Albert said with finality.

Harris's eye burned and he moved towards Albert. There was something pathetic in his angry, puzzled truculence. "What d'you mean?" he demanded.

"What I say," Albert snapped and immediately transferred his attention to Stockmann.

Stockmann said, "My dear Reed, I find it most difficult to agree that the crew and passengers of this ship should be placed in fearful danger simply because the Captain has become . . . er . . . well . . . mentally unbalanced. As Mr. Harris has explained the matter to me, these men—if they exist—may now be anywhere within a radius of ten miles. That means, as I am sure you will realise, anywhere within an area of some three hundred square miles!"

"So?"

"So the idea is preposterous. We can only know our present position—so Harris informs me—from lines drawn on a chart. There is no means of our fixing a more accurate position, either for ourselves now, or *Conway* when she was sunk."

Albert flexed his toes and rose up on them and then let himself down on to his heels. "Tell me, Stockmann, what makes you think that *Conway* was sunk?"

"Of course she was sunk. Harris tells me that she could not possibly have survived."

Albert was suddenly irritated. "Harris, Harris, Harris, all I hear is Harris. Harris is drunk, I tell you. Harris has been drunk for two days. For all I know he's been drunk for months. I'm not interested in what Harris thinks."

Stockmann held out his arm, as if to deter Harris from violence. He shouted, "Why don't you go outside, Reed? Then even you will be able to see how dark it is. Even you will then know how cold it is. We could pass within six feet of men in the water tonight *and not see them*!" He checked himself and smiled again, realising that this was not the way to obtain Albert Reed's agreement to anything. "Forgive me. It is no use our getting excited. Mr. Reed, if Captain Jacobson decides to go back, then, quite frankly, it is our view that he should be restrained."

"How?"

"By we passengers making a joint protest *now*, before it is too late."

Having at last delivered his message, he brought forth a huge white handkerchief from his breast pocket and mopped his moist brow.

Albert said, "What do you think, Alice?"

"I don't know, Albert. I'll leave it to you. But I dare say the Captain knows his job . . ."

"Like hell he does," Harris interrupted.

Albert looked at him sadly, "The best thing you can do, lad, is to go up to your cabin and sleep it off."

Harris glared. Albert turned away from him. Was it right to endanger the ship? No, it was not right. Was it right to leave these men to perish? No, it was not right. Then which, in that event, was the greater wrong? The question was unanswerable. Yet, it was not in the Reeds' nature to weigh the claims of men who *might* die against those of men who would *certainly* die if they were not recovered. He turned towards Stockmann. "I don't agree."

"But surely . . . I have explained the dangers and the problems."

"I said I don't agree."

Stockmann gestured helplessly, alternately smiling and pouting. "Perhaps you still do not properly understand the danger. Your wife, Reed. What does Mrs. Reed think? Surely she should be allowed to express an opinion?"

"Why don't you ask her?"

"Mrs. Reed, what do you think we ought to do?"

Alice looked at Stockmann squarely, almost cannily, as if she were enjoying a joke and yet not yielding to the temptation to smile. "You heard what Mr. Reed said?"

"Of course."

"Then that, Mr. Stockmann, is my answer too. I should have thought you would have known that."

Stockmann had nothing further to say. He seemed to deflate like a balloon.

Harris shouted, "You're all crazy. All of you! This place is lousy with U-boats. Do you know why we haven't been hit yet? Because we're going so bloody fast. We're not in Halifax yet, not by a long way. They can still get us, even at this speed. Easy! Knock off the revolutions and we're a sitting duck."

Albert drew himself up to his full height. The performance, however, lost some of its magisterial effect since he was still without his boots. "Harris, I can excuse you. You've had a rough time. It's a hospital you want and the quicker the better. But you, Stockmann, you make me sick. Good night to you both."

Stockmann passed his tongue over his lips and rolled them together, distributing the moisture evenly over their considerable surface. Then he moved towards the door, shooing Harris before him.

III

In the matter of Theodore Busk the Almighty had blundered. For as long as Busk could remember he had been a lonely, unhappy man. Even as a child he had been deprived of affection.

His father had been a seaman before him, a lost alcoholic soul whose only real solace, apart from drink, was the sea. He was away for years on end. Busk's mother had been a diminutive, amoral shop-assistant with a ludicrously refined accent, a wandering, hapless creature unable to endure the absence of her husband, not because she loved him, nor (after three years of marriage) because she any longer even remembered him, but because the ardency of her own nature led her into a life of more or less continuous concupiscence.

She had therefore forsaken her modest dwelling—it could not be termed a home—and, taking Theodore with her, had camped with a widening variety of men, each a little less fastidious than his predecessor, each a little less inclined to accept the unreasonable burden of little Theodore.

Busk could not recall any part of those early days. Of the years until he was five he remembered only the journey by train through the sunshine of a sparkling May morning. Each insignificant detail of the journey had remained with him, permanently delineated in his mind with incandescent clarity.

He remembered mainly the fear and the loneliness, the realisation that he was being deserted. He remembered the hard hairy material of the carriage seat biting into the backs of his knees; cows grazing somnolently in fields and not looking up as the train thundered by; the sepia photograph of the Giant's Causeway above his mother's head.

He had cried, he remembered, and the taste of the tears that had traversed his youthful cheeks was still a pungent memory. It was his first acquaintance with hate, hatred for his mother and hatred for Aunt Polly to whom he was consigned.

Aunt Polly's dark house swarmed with cats, seven of them, sleek, disdainful monsters padding arrogantly about the house, forever on the move, waiting for the next onset of sexual hysteria when they would curdle the night with their uproar while Aunt Polly lay rigid in her bed, listening, but never interfering. Theodore hated the cats, too.

One day he had killed one of them, the smallest, by strangulation. He had not meant to kill it; he had been lying on his bed when the brute had appeared, tail swaying, staring at him, disputing his occupancy. A sudden fury had compelled him to snatch with tiny hands at the insubstantial neck under the fur and to hold on, whatever the cost. It had taken a long time but in the end he had lain breathless and sobbing with his head in the pillow and the cat dead by his side. He had never forgotten the white foam about its mouth. When he had dared he had touched it, prodded it, pushed it, hating it now, not for living but for having so inconsiderately died.

When his crime was discovered Aunt Polly shut him in his bedroom for the remainder of the day where he cried incessantly into his hot pillow, whispering, saying, calling and finally shouting through the closed door: "I'm glad! I'm glad! I'm glad, Aunt Polly! I'm glad I killed your cat!"

He made few friends as a child. Once he had gone into another child's house on the way home from school. On entering the house his companion had been greeted by his mother with what was perhaps a tactless degree of affection. The frail Theodore had watched with a scowling face until he could bear it no longer. Distracted by grief he had bolted and run all the way home to the spinsterish household of Aunt Polly who had long ago exhausted such maternal devotion as she had ever possessed on her multiplying army of cats. He never spoke to the boy again. He surpassed the comprehension of them all; one so peculiar was never wanted.

Busk was to be accompanied into adult life by a powerful, thwarted gregariousness. He craved, in particular, for the society of women. They were to prove, very nearly, his downfall.

It was to happen many times.

On the first occasion he could see her only indistinctly, sitting beside him below the moving white rods of light in the darkness of the cinema. She was young and he could feel her arm against his on the common arm-rest between their seats. She hunted in her handbag for a cigarette and Busk produced his lighter before she was able to find her matches. She accepted the light he snapped on before her face, without speaking, without even looking at him in the yellow sphere of light that was suddenly extinguished. Then they watched the film, but Busk saw none of it. The tension, the longing with which he was now familiar built up inside him, stifling all processes of reflection, permitting nothing but an ever-increasing magnification of the thing desired. His collar was limp with perspiration. He put out a tentative hand and moved it about before his face, and then abruptly placed it on her knee, his eyes tightly closed, the energy streaming through his fingers like an electric current as soon as contact was made.

And, as if in fact this was the case, having once established contact, he was unable to let go.

By sheer good fortune she did not become hysterical. She grappled furiously with his glued, helpless hand and with a great banging of seats and a hissed imprecation, removed herself from his vicinity. He never knew whether his misdemeanour was reported or not because, in a fever of foreboding, he had slunk out of an alternative exit and disappeared in a taxi.

Later he sailed rather nearer to disaster.

She was a coarse-featured, Glaswegian slum-child who wore her clothes with the tight-fitting grace of a ballerina—which, but for an accident of birth, she might have been. He trailed her through the sodium glare of deserted streets, keeping her in view from one concentration of light to another, a man possessed. He overtook her in the first unlighted street they entered and took up his station by her side. The occasion appeared not unique in her experience, for she paid him little attention. He loped along with his head turned towards her while the click-clack of her heels echoed ever more furiously against the darkened houses. He was incapable of speech until she first said something that required an answer, and when, a street, an alley, an intersection later, she *did* speak, he, in his delirium, mistook the import of the thick Glaswegian words, and seized her arm in his strong fingers. She began to run.

Once in contact with her body, however tenuously, Busk was unable to release her. He was no more able to desist than he had been able not to touch the girl in the cinema or not to kill Aunt Polly's cat.

She stood and fought him, her hard body like a whip in his hands, her mouth hurling obscenities into his sweating face. He did not fight with her but merely held her squirming body against his, not feeling her toes against his shins, not even aware of nails ploughing lividly across his cheek and the blood dripping down on to his shirt, not feeling anything but the pleasure of holding her moving body against every part of him.

"Don't fight me. Please don't fight me. I won't hurt you. Just be still and let me hold you. Let me touch you—I won't hurt you, I promise I won't hurt you—please, please, *please* . . ."

She screamed and when the sound of her scream had ceased to echo among the brick terraces she was gone and he was left standing by her abandoned shoes, deprived of everything but the greater part of her dress still clutched in his trembling fingers. It was almost dawn when he regained his ship. Later, when the sun was up, he was able to read about himself in the newspaper, a brief paragraph in the stop press column. Then his ship sailed and the police doubled their patrols in the area abortively.

Now he stood outside Gerda Olstein's cabin, waiting, waiting and watching, watching for a movement of the light under her door, or the approach of those who would interfere; waiting for the desire boiling up inside him to reach the point where he could hammer down the door and have done with it. The sweat stood out on his pallid skin; he sweated so much on these occasions that he smelled. His hands shook as he took the torn cigarette from his mouth and spat out the shreds of tobacco.

He moved along the passageway, his gaunt body swaying unconsciously to the movement of the ship, and halted by her door and no sooner had he raised his fists than he passed on and stopped at the opposite end of the passageway, still watching and waiting and sweating. The cigarette disintegrated in his fingers and he dropped its sodden mass to the deck and put his foot on it without looking down.

In a moment he thought he might scream. The pressure was building up inside his head as if someone were pumping it full of gas. His mouth was cinder-dry and the sweat rolled off his forehead into his eyes.

He was demented by his love, his God-given, crippling, undeniable desire: "Oh Jesus, Jesus, give me a woman that I might hold her to myself, otherwise, without her, let me die. Let me have her, make her want me."

It was almost time.

He moved towards the door, faster this time, his arms held up before him, and heard, through the thundering in his head the sound of his name. "Mr. Busk! Mr. Busk!"

It was like the scream in the Glasgow slum. He wheeled round with the same expression of astonishment on his ravaged face.

"I should not if I were you, Mr. Busk."

Jacobson stood above him on the ladder. Busk wiped his mouth and then his eyes with the back of his hand and opened his mouth to speak and then closed it again. There was pain in his face, pain and a terrible dumbfounded disappointment.

Jacobson said in a curiously flat voice, "I should like you to turn in, Mr. Busk."

Busk moved towards him and for a moment Jacobson thought his First Officer was going to attack him. Then he stopped and put the palms of his hands against his temples and let the fingers run down the sides of his face. His expression crumpled and he turned and stalked to his cabin, slamming the door behind him. Inside, he removed his jacket and flung himself on his bunk and wept into the Company's bedspread.

Jacobson stood on the ladder, looking after him, wondering what he should do, wondering, too, if *Oleron*'s troubles would ever cease to multiply.

TEN

I

CORRIDON was a rat; a lurking, rodential, two-legged balancing-act; a conscienceless, sea-going hoodlum with a hatchet face and a jaw action that was never still, even in sleep; a maleficent upstart of the streets, untouched by the hand of God or the influence of any ameliorative agency; found, not begotten, fatherless, motherless, kinless, without history, without connection with any living thing; simply *there*—unanswerably, indestructibly *there*: Corridon, the trouble-seeker.

And the men knew it; yet followed him. They followed him, perhaps, in the absence of anyone else able to remove fear from their minds, the fear that Corridon had himself ignited and breathed into flame with his own noxious breath. For the first time in his life he was where he had always wanted to be: in control.

Now he stood by the doorway, his eyes glittering redly, like an animal's eyes in the night. The men stood about him in a ragged circle, some dozen of them, acknowledging their leader, surrendering themselves to the petty Fuehrer who held their strings and pulled them how he willed. Schirmer and da Falla had been dropped in their bunks where they were now asleep if they were not still unconscious.

Corridon's hoarse, urgent voice said, "O.K. We're going to the sick-bay, right? To get Birken'ead. To get 'im, I said, not just scare 'im. We're just going to see 'im, see? To see 'ow 'e's gettin' on. When we're there there'll be an accident, get me? Then we'll be rid of the bastard. Let's go!"

There was something hypnotic in Corridon's commands. There is a quality of leadership even in mobsters, and Corridon was the supreme mobster, incapable of handling more than a dozen men, but master of a smaller number, managing them first by persuasion, then by fear, finally by death—not merely the fear of it—but death itself. Corridon did not flinch from death but only from the possibility of his own. Corridon, as tyrants before him had also discovered, could lead men into courses of action that at any other time, under any other direction, they would vehemently have refused. His voice bored little holes of acquiescence in their bony heads. He owned them, body and soul, possessed them until he failed—when they would fall on him without compunction. It was a dangerous eminence, this tenth-rate pinnacle he occupied with so much aplomb.

He took up his position at the head of his tattered crew and slouched through the doorway and along the passageway that led to the upper deck. The men trooped after him, not yet aware, not yet regretful, not yet sickened—all, that is, except three, who at first straggled, and then glanced at each other in the darkness, seeking encouragement, and finally stopped. A voice said, "I'm flippin' off." They returned to the mess deck and sat down in silence and stared at their hands spread out on the scrubbed white wood of the mess table.

One was a boy of no more than seventeen or eighteen with fair, fine hair and a white face. He appeared underfed but muscles bulged below the rolled sleeves of his jersey. The second was an older man with a black wart the size and texture of a currant on his chin. There were crowsfeet of laughter about his eyes. The third was a wiry little fellow with a face like that of Neanderthal man, known on the mess deck as Chimp.

The white-faced youth was their leader; there was always a leader. He kept lifting his fist from the table and letting it fall with a thump on to the table. He said, "They can't do this."

The others stared with wary eyes at an indeterminate point beyond his face.

"They can't. They can't do it!"

Schirmer stirred, turning in his sleep.

"What's Birkenhead ever done to us?" the youth demanded savagely.

The fist, the knotted white ball of bone and stretched flesh thumped into the table and the mugs danced. "'E's all right, is Birkenhead. 'E's all right, I tell yer. Ain't I right? Jesus, all this crap about Jonahs! Do you believe it?"

The man with the currant-wart shook his head slowly. "No, I don't reckon I do."

"Me neither."

Thump. Chimp began to roll himself a cigarette and when he

licked the gummed edge the saliva spread through the paper, changing it from whiteness to a dull shade of waterlogged grey. He watched the fair-haired youth.

"Listen," the youth said. "We've got to do summut! Do you know that? We've got to do summut! Quick!"

Chimp drew on his cigarette and his cheeks seemed to touch each other internally. The heat of the smoke dried the paper and stained it nicotine-brown. "What?" he asked.

The youth licked his lips and dried them with his fist. "Christ, I don't know. 'Ow should *I* know? What do *you* reckon we should do? Einstein!"

Chimp pulled the sodden stick of tobacco from his mouth and scraped the adhering paper from his lips with yellow teeth. The shreds of paper were drawn into his mouth and reappeared a moment later as a tight little pellet which he spat skilfully at the electric light above his head. The others followed its trajectory. "Nothink," he said. "We just stay 'ere, mate. Keep aht of it. Don't fight 'em. Never fight 'em. If yer can't lick 'em keep aht of it."

The screw thudded heavily as a following sea lifted it out of the water. Chimp replaced the cigarette in his mouth and manoeuvred it from side to side with his tongue. The youth's fist thumped against the table again. "We've got to do summut, I tell you!"

The man with the currant-wart said gently, "There's nothing we can do, son. You must see that. There's nothing we can do."

Schirmer groaned and opened his eyes and immediately closed them again. The youth jumped to his feet and shouted at the other two men. "Come on, 'elp me, for cryin' out loud."

They pulled Schirmer from his bunk and stood in a circle, holding him upright.

"They've gone for Birkenhead," the youth said.

Schirmer looked at him and closed his eyes again and shook his massive head like a swimmer shaking water from his hair. "Let me sit down," he said.

The youth shouted, "They've gone for Birkenhead."

Schirmer grunted and moved towards the mess stool. When he was seated, his head resting on the table in his hands, he said, "Here you! Ya said something. What was it? What ya say?"

"They've gone for Birkenhead. I told you."

Schirmer seemed to consider the statement and replaced his head in his hands. Then he was on his feet unaided, grasping the youth's arms and shaking him. "When? When, for Chrisake? When?"

The youth's head jolted on his shoulders and his words came disjointedly, "A few . . . min . . . utes . . . a . . . go. Just now. Leave off . . . will . . . yer . . . for flip's sake . . . yer 'urtin' . . . sod yer."

When Schirmer saw da Falla his memory connected with the present. He flung himself towards da Falla's recumbent form. "Wake up! Wake up, da Falla! Jesus, da Falla, come to, will ya?"

When da Falla was out of his bunk they gathered round him in a circle. Da Falla pressed his fingers into his eyes and wondered about the roaring in his ears.

"They've gone for Birkenhead," Schirmer said.

"The bastards," da Falla answered weakly, not yet wholly comprehending what Schirmer had said.

"Did you hear, da Falla?" Schirmer shouted. "They've gone for Birkenhead."

Da Falla's eyes swivelled towards Schirmer. "They've gone . . .?"

"Hell, da Falla, why don't ya wake up?"

"Birkenhead, did you say?"

"Ya."

Da Falla was afraid, shifty, like an animal trapped in a situation that offered no means of escape. "We can't fight 'em," he said. "We can't fight 'em, Schirmer. They'd murder us." He looked at the others. "They'd murder us, wouldn't they?"

Chimp licked the disintegrating edges of his cigarette together and the fair-haired youth sucked his knuckles. The man with the currant-wart said, "No, we can't fight them."

Schirmer strode away from them, towards the door, and returned, glaring. He said aggressively, "I'll go to Skipper."

Chimp laughed cynically.

"What can the Skipper do?" da Falla asked.

"I don't know, but I'm going."

"Look," Chimp said. "Don't join 'em an' they can't touch you, right? Go against 'em an' they'll fill you in. Go to the Skipper,

Schirmer, an' you might as well go personally an' kick Corridon in the crutch. He'll kill you."

"Corridon," Schirmer blustered. "What do I care for Corridon. That two-bit Hitler! His neck I will break! Snap!—like that, ha?"

Chimp shouted, "Be reasonable, Schirmer. Corridon's got them men where 'e wants 'em. It makes me sick, but that's where 'e 'as 'em. Like a lot of bloody sheep. Most men I've ever met are like sheep. Corridon snaps 'is fingers an' they get Birkenhead. Next, 'e'll snap 'is fingers an' say, Get Schirmer. An' they'll do it, boy, because 'alf of 'em ain't got the brains of a nit, let alone a flippin' sheep. Jesus, I know 'em. I've known sheep that were flippin' geniuses compared wi' this lot."

He crushed his cigarette into one of the mugs and the man with the currant-wart said into the sudden silence, "He's right, Schirmer."

The youth licked his fist and da Falla stared wildly at Schirmer, knowing what was coming.

Schirmer whirled round and ran towards the door, "I'm going!" he shouted.

They watched him with resigned faces.

Then da Falla was calling to him and running after him. "Wait, Schirmer! Wait, will you? Flip it, Schirmer, I'm coming with you, man."

II

The sick-bay was no larger than a double-berth cabin and was accommodated in a small deckhouse abaft the bridge. When Schirmer and da Falla fled past it some of the men were standing in a furtive group outside the door, each trying to hide himself by standing with his face to the bulkhead, ostrich-like. These were Corridon's sentries, their confidence and efficiency dwindling in proportion to the extent to which their General was out of sight. The ghost-like passage of Schirmer and da Falla went unobserved.

Schirmer led the way up the ladders to the bridge, outdistancing the breathless da Falla; he was neither so young nor so fleet of foot as Schirmer.

When Schirmer rocketed on to the bridge he could see nothing but the pale-blue glow of the compass bowl. He stood for a moment, abruptly undecided, oppressed by the invisible authority that pervaded the place.

Da Falla arrived and slid to a halt behind him, his chest heaving. Schirmer said, "Captain, sir?"

A shadow on the port side of the bridge moved and Jacobson asked, "Yes?" His voice was tired, tetchy.

Schirmer moved towards it, groping in the darkness. "Captain, sir. I have a matter urgent to report. A group of men go to get Birkenhead."

"Birkenhead? The man who is injured? Get him? What do you mean, get him?" The tiredness was gone but the voice was still fretful, as if Jacobson had been detached from more important considerations than the fate of Birkenhead.

Schirmer said simply, "Kill him, sir."

"Yes, kill him," da Falla added, excitably.

Jacobson walked towards Schirmer and when Schirmer could see the pink, astonished face, and the bright lips that regularly pursed and unpursed themselves, Jacobson said, "Kill him? Why should they want to kill him?"

Schirmer stood to attention before Jacobson, his chest pushed out, almost touching Jacobson's coat. "They say he is a Jonah, sir."

Jacobson answered petulantly, "A Jonah? Ridiculous! Mr. Dawson, have you ever met a Jonah?"

"No, sir."

"Nor have I."

Schirmer said doggedly, "But this is true, sir."

"That he is a Jonah?"

"No, sir. That they get him . . . because he is black. That is why; he is different so they think they will get him."

Jacobson turned away and walked back to his habitual position on the port side of the bridge. His voice was weary again. "Mr. Dawson, you must go and investigate."

"Yes, sir."

"Use whatever means that are necessary."

Dawson had sailed with scum before. Jacobson had not. Dawson believed that he knew the crew of *Oleron* better than her Captain knew them. This was a task for a riot squad, not a solitary Second Officer. "But . . ."

Jacobson interrupted, irritably, "Go at once, Dawson. Find out what is happening. We cannot stand here and allow an innocent man to be murdered. I will not have murder in my ship."

"No, sir," Dawson said, thinking of Svenson.

He moved away from the binnacle and approached Schirmer. "Come with me."

Schirmer hesitated. "You want that we come, too, sir?"

Dawson roared, now as irritated as Jacobson, "Come with me if you don't want your precious Birkenhead slung over the side."

"Yes, sir."

Schirmer looked at Dawson's immense bulk in the darkness and decided that he had recruited the only man in the ship capable of standing up to Corridon. Dawson said to da Falla, "Follow me." Da Falla's Adam's apple oscillated and he opened his mouth to speak but by the time any sound came Dawson was half way down the ladder and Schirmer just behind him. He ran after them.

When they reached the upper deck Schirmer said to Dawson, "Do you want to take your coat off, sir?"

"Why should I want to take my coat off—Schirmer, isn't it?"

"Yes, sir. Well, he is an ugly customer, this Corridon."

"We'll see about that, Schirmer."

When they came to the sick-bay the men outside turned slowly towards Dawson, making no effort to move out of his way. They just stood looking up at his height and the immensity of his shoulders, weighing up their chances and deciding that since they were seven to one—Schirmer and da Falla, they thought, would never dare to intervene, even though they had recruited this witless character from the bridge—they had nothing to fear. Dawson was a big man, and powerful, too, but it was their experience that however big and powerful an officer might be, he soon gave up a wholly unequal struggle and walked away, seeing as little as possible; there were none so blind as those who were afraid to see. So they just stood looking at him, not moving.

Schirmer and da Falla executed a circling movement, ready to dance out of the way when real trouble began. They, too, had seen intractable posses of seamen before; they, too, knew what *could* happen. There was no virtue in unnecessary risk.

The men glanced at each other and returned their insolent

gaze to Dawson. Dawson waited. He did not move; none of the performers moved. If the men had been asked why they did not move away or why they were following Corridon instead of Jacobson or why they listened open-mouthed to Corridon's foul talk or what they thought they were going to gain from their mutinous behaviour which in the end could only be futile, they would not have known how to answer. They would have been unable to proffer the slightest reason or excuse for their conduct beyond the fact that they felt like it. They were a rag-bag crew, unknown to their officers, their records mere chronicles of drudgery and punishment for crimes they may or may not have committed which in any event they had been powerless to prevent; unknown faceless creatures, unglorified by war, simply names that signed on not knowing what else to do, not knowing how else to kill the time, whose only comfort was drink and the cash-first-Jack attentions of maritime whores, incapable of sustained thought, vulnerable to the glib claims of mobsters, sea-lawyers and leaders. And all at once they had found themselves a leader—or he had found them—a leader from their midst who, if he gave them nothing else, offered them a fleeting, dubious joy because, for once, they were all together, or nearly so. Their drab spirits were magically uplifted by a novel sense of solidarity. And this was the goodness in them, the generosity and the human need for fellow-feeling that Corridon had extracted, taken, cherished, subverted and made evil. They would kill Birkenhead for love of each other. But they did not know this, nor would they have understood if they had been told. As far as they knew or could ever discern they just bloody well felt like it. And they just bloody well stood where they were, bloody well looking at Dawson.

Dawson began to move. His foot came forward and his weight was transferred to it. Then the other. His great frame moved towards them like a ship, with the same implacable quality of uninterrupted progress about it, and when he was so close to the men that they could hear his breathing, see the details of his wary face, they collapsed and fell back before him and allowed him to pass.

When Dawson entered the sick-bay Schirmer and da Falla went with him, for they felt safer now with Dawson within their sight and calling. They stood together with their backs to the swinging blackout screens and the scene which previously had been all movement was suddenly stilled, frozen. Goldstein was on the deck, pinned on his back by two men who had their knees in his crutch and his neck. Corridon was against the bunk, leaning over Birkenhead's face. Dawson could not see Birkenhead for Corridon's back. Two seamen stood at the far side of the cabin under the scuttle, Corridon's lieutenants.

Dawson said levelly, "Leave him alone, Corridon."

Corridon whirled round and faced him, his hands still clutching the bunk, already poised to leap on Dawson.

Dawson addressed himself to the men holding Goldstein. "Let him get up."

The men glanced at Corridon.

"Let him get up," Dawson shouted.

And when there was no sign from Corridon the men obeyed. The men under the scuttle moved forward.

Goldstein clambered to his feet. "'E's the one, 'e's the bastard who says 'e's goin' to chuck Birk over the side. 'Ow d'yer like that, eh? Chuck 'im over the side!"

"Shut up," Dawson said.

"Jesus!"

"I said shut up."

Dawson's eyes never moved away from Corridon. "That right?" he asked.

Corridon shrugged. The four men moved nearer to Dawson, waiting for Corridon's sign.

"Get away from that bunk," Dawson said.

Corridon did not move but stood holding on to it with his hands behind his back, the heel of one boot against the cupboard below.

He said, changing his approach, "Jeez, me an' the boys was just 'avin' a lark, sir. Nobody ever said nothink about chuckin' anybody over the side. That right, boys? Nar, 'e's got it all wrong. Just a friendly get together. You ask 'em sir."

The men nodded their heads. "Yeah, that's right. We didn't mean no 'arm."

Dawson did not listen. Instead he watched the muscles in Corridon's neck, arms and legs. They stood out like wires under the clothing. "Get away from that bunk."

Corridon smiled insolently, savouring his ridiculous sensation of power. Here he was, with magnificent impunity, defying an officer. Whatever happened now he could not lose. His mind was possessed by an irresistible contempt for all opposition. The bodyguard moved closer. If he played his cards cleverly he would not only be able to force Dawson to leave, but cause him to leave in circumstances that would virtually ensure that he would never breathe a word about his downfall. "An' suppose I don't?"

"I'm coming to get you."

Corridon pushed himself away from the bunk and stood grinning at his huge adversary, brimming over with the self-confidence of the paranoic. Dawson could hear men coming into the sick-bay from outside. Now he was surrounded. A big man in the bodyguard moved closer, shuffling towards him on flexed legs. Dawson watched them, still wondering whether they would attack him. Would Corridon risk violence on him until he, Dawson, had first used violence on them?

"For the last time, Corridon, I'm telling you to come away from that bunk."

The men moved closer and Corridon's yellow-toothed ravenous grin increased.

Schirmer said, "Let's get out of here, sir."

Goldstein was more emphatic: "It ain't no good, they're goin' to do yer good and proper, they are, if you don't take off."

Even Birkenhead, speaking for the first time, added his quota of warning in his deep voice. "Go away, sir. You can't do no good here. You ain't doing nobody any good."

When it happened it happened so swiftly that for a moment no one except Dawson believed it. His left fist came up and round so fast that the men heard it connect before they saw it. It travelled in a wide arc and when it collided with skin and bone it shattered the jaw mechanism of the nearest bodyguard and almost detached his chin from his face. He shot across the tiny room and lay in the corner, holding his chin, screaming. At the same time Dawson had lunged at Corridon and with his other arm sent him spinning away from the bunk. Now he had only Birkenhead behind him. He swung around and waited for them to advance; there were no more advantages to be reaped from surprise.

The fact that one of his men had been brutally injured worried Corridon not at all. He seemed to be enjoying himself more than ever. Now he could deal with Dawson in self-defence. He had witnesses. No one would ever dare to gainsay him. He crouched at the head of his men and the knife appeared in his palm as if by sleight of hand; suddenly, unmistakably there, small and deadly. "O.K., Dawson. If this is the way yer wanta play it, it don't worry me."

He moved towards Dawson still grinning, already anticipating the feel of the knife slipping between the ribs and no one ever knowing that a knife had been used because by the time he was missed Dawson would be at the bottom of the ocean with a steel block about his neck. He came on bent tensed legs, ready to spring. Dawson leaned towards him, arms out, hands open, fingers stretched and splayed. The men did not follow Corridon but stood in a circle, watching, watching as they might have watched a bear-fight, waiting for blood and possible death.

The ship swayed and Birkenhead stirred in his bunk. Schirmer, da Falla and Goldstein had separated themselves from the others and stood on one side. The man with the smashed jaw lay still in the corner, watching over the hand clapped about his chin, whimpering. Corridon's boots creaked as he moved and Dawson could see the globules of sweat on the sallow cheeks which were white below the sallowness, drained of blood. He moved like a duck, his backside moving from side to side as he transferred his weight from one foot to another. Dawson waited for Corridon's unendurable proximity to release the fury within him. Another step and Corridon's grip tightened on the knife, the fingers moving, working themselves into position. Dawson leaned farther forward, his hands closer together and lower now, lower than the knife and Corridon's hands. He waited for the lightning thrust; everything depended on his being able to perceive its beginning, on being able to kill it before it lived. Another duck-like step and Dawson could see the open pores on Corridon's face and the flecks of red in the whites of his eyes, and smell his sweat. The knife steadied, tilted upwards, the blade glinting and sticking out of the knuckle-wrapped hilt like a sting.

Then it moved, this way, that, feinting, deceiving, thrusting, darting, stopping and then gathering itself and streaking invisible through the electric glare towards Dawson, and at the same time Dawson's open hands came up, no less fast, no less invisible, the fingers snaking round the flying wrist and holding on, slowing, stopping the flight and yet still moving upwards until, in a flash of frenzied movement, Corridon's hand was forced high above his head, the knife held loosely in limp fingers. Corridon squirmed and struggled like an insane creature and his men edged forward in consternation but Dawson shouted, "Keep still, Corridon or I'll break your hand off! Keep your men back or I'll kill you."

Corridon's hand went back farther and the knife slipped and fell to the deck. A man lunged forward but Dawson's foot was already upon it. "Get back," he roared, "or I'll kill you too." The man straightened himself and came no further.

Dawson said, "Now get this, Corridon. Get these men of yours outa here. Go on, tell them."

Corridon struggled again and kicked his boots against Dawson's shins but when he felt his fingers moving backwards through their joints he hung acquiescently in Dawson's grip. He clawed with his free hand at Dawson's knuckles but the intensity of the pain dissuaded him from further movement. He needed his knife.

"Go on," Dawson shouted. "Tell them."

Corridon did not speak. Then he screamed with pain. The men heard the snap as the bone of one finger gave way.

"Go on, tell them," Dawson shouted into his ear. "Tell them."

Corridon became maddened by pain and flung himself about like a contortionist in Dawson's immovable grip. He tried to scratch at Dawson's face but the vice about his hand tightened, crushing the fingers against each other until the pain was like liquid fire. He called, incoherently, for support from his henchmen but they had already disowned him. When the second finger snapped consciousness deserted him. Dawson felt him go limp and suddenly heavy and allowed him to drop to the deck. The men watched with astonished eyes and then looked up at Dawson. "Go on," Dawson shouted in disgust. "Take him away. And the guy in the corner. Get them outa here. Go on, jump to it."

The men retrieved their injured leaders and carried them outside. Dawson stood at the door of the sick-bay and watched them move out on to the open deck. A man said, "Drop 'em here, boys. We don't want 'em, do we?"

Some agreed, others demurred. They argued. Finally they picked up their loads again and returned quietly to their quarters. Dawson went back inside the sick-bay and retrieved his cap.

Goldstein gurgled, "Nice work. Luvly bleedin' grub."

"Shut up," Dawson snapped. "And don't let anyone else in here."

Goldstein tried to pull his paunchy body to attention. "Yes, sir. I mean no, sir."

"And you two," Dawson said to Schirmer and da Falla, "get back to your quarters."

Schirmer said, "It is not safe."

"Sure it is. Get going."

Dawson turned to Birkenhead. "How you feeling?"

Birkenhead's ebony face smiled broadly, "Ah'm fine, sir. Ah'm feelin' just fine."

III

When Jacobson had recovered from the shock of Dawson's story—which had offended him exceedingly for he had never before entertained conjecture of the existence of a crew so abominable as that with which he was now burdened—the ultimate crisis occurred.

It was 22.00 and the first watch was half over. The Bos'n had been called and informed of events and had stationed himself outside the crew's quarters with a gun. Jacobson was at his customary position on the bridge and Dawson had walked over to the starboard side and was examining the sea through his binoculars. Dawson could not see Jacobson, nor Jacobson him. They were separated by the entire width of the bridge. The helmsman, in the centre, could just see both their outlines. The ship appeared once more to be at peace. Jacobson watched the bow-wave, beginning to believe that the wind and the sea were getting up again. Dawson watched the magnified white-topped waves, almost lazily. Then he yelled, "Hard astarboard! Torpedoes running."

The helmsman flung over the wheel by reflex action. Jacobson charged on short legs to Dawson's side and clapped his binoculars to his eyes. And there they were, four faint moving white streaks in the sea, approaching from forrard of the beam. *Oleron* began to lurch round. The two men leaned over the wing of the bridge. They had put the wheel hard over in the hope that *Oleron* could pass between the salvo; there was nothing else they could do—except pray.

Dawson shouted into Jacobson's ear. "If they miss it'll be a bloody miracle."

Then they could see them without their binoculars. Dawson hammered with his fist on the rail and Jacobson stood erect and still and the helmsman stood with the weight of his body against the wheel, striving with all the power within him to force it another quarter of an inch.

The torpedoes swept past the turning bow, the others went astern. The men on the bridge waited for the explosion.

When, after a minute, it did not come, they assumed themselves saved. The projectiles could not have missed *Oleron* by very much more than a coat of paint. Dawson wiped his brow and gave orders for the ship to be brought back on to her previous course. For some time, no one spoke. And when, finally, they did speak, they all spoke at once.

Out of the hubbub came Jacobson's piping authoritative voice. "Mr. Dawson, I shall take over the ship. Go below and rouse the passengers and crew off watch. When they are assembled in the saloon, inform me. I wish to speak to them. It is imperative that everyone attend."

"All the passengers and crew, sir? They'll be turned in!"

"No matter, Mr. Dawson."

"As you say, sir."

ELEVEN

He was a bold bad man was our desperado,
From Cripple Creek way down in Colorado,
And he rolled around like a big tornado,
And everywhere he went he gave his war-whoop.

In the raft they were still singing. They had been singing now for three hours, singing and moving their bodies and dying a little with each new song. Their repertoires were not inexhaustible and they were beginning to repeat themselves, unknowingly.

Their weariness was an unrelieved agony, a tentacled deadness spreading through their bodies as if their blood were congealing in their veins. But the singing helped. As a Chinese will drive needles into one part of the body to confuse the pain in another, so the singing tended to lessen their despair—but not very much, enough, only, to decelerate the approach of the end, infinitesimally.

The wind which at first had dropped considerably was violent again, the kind of wind a man can lean against on the deck of a ship and be supported by. It swept in die-straight streams into the valleys of the waves and drove the raft up on to the tumbling crests and toppled it into the belly-emptying voids beyond. It drove onwards in a mist of shattered water, annihilating visibility near the surface of the sea where the men lay huddled and still singing in the noise of its passing. They could not even see the shapes of each other. The temperature had fallen to no more than two or three degrees above freezing point.

There were two leaders on the raft, Ainslee and Wilmot. Ainslee gave the orders and Wilmot ensured that they were executed. Without Ainslee or Wilmot scarcely a man on the raft could have survived thus far; he would have given up long ago—perhaps still alive, but without hope. Ainslee and Wilmot between them kept the hope alive and although the others already half believed that their leaders cherished a raft full of corpses, neither of them would listen. Not a man could dispense with the never-relenting detested pressure of the leaders, lashing him into a perpetual activity. It is possible that Wilmot could have survived without Ainslee; in this respect he was, perhaps, unique. Yet there was still Barraclough; no one yet knew what Barraclough could do.

Half an hour earlier Ainslee had distributed water and a handful of soggy bully beef to each man. Some had wolfed the meat and others had been either too cold or too tired to swallow. They had coaxed the meat down by rubbing their throats. Afterwards they had felt a little stronger, a little renewed, but no less cold.

They had considered the possibility of leaving the raft for the comparative warmth of the sea. There was neither wind nor biting spray in the sea and their bodies would no longer have been such a burden to them. They could have hung on to the lifelines, still safe from sinking, but Ainslee was afraid of numbed hands letting go and no one knowing until it was too late. There could be no question of the occupants of the raft paddling after lost sheep; once a man departed from it he departed also from this life, however much he screamed. They could, too, have secured themselves to the lifelines, but Wilmot was afraid of slack bodies slowly filling up with sea-water and drowning and no one knowing until it was time to climb inboard again. They could even have tied themselves together, and although this, theoretically, could prevent one man from being swept away, it could, on the other hand, lead to their all being swept away simultaneously, murdering each other in the raging sea. It was colder on the raft but safer. On the raft Ainslee could still exercise command. This, he believed, was the most important thing of all.

"Sing!" he shouted. "Sing, damn you!"

> When she's talking, she's talking of no one but you,
> She's so proud, oh so proud of the things you will do,
> Every beat of her heart is somewhere,
> Somewhere in France with you.

"Sing! Sing and keep moving or you'll die!"

They could scarcely hear their faltering voices above the level raging of the wind, nor could they hear Ainslee's fist thumping out the time on the wave-washed wooden bottom of the raft.

"Louder!" Wilmot roared. "I can't hear you. Louder!"

> Onward, Christian soldiers,
> Marching as to war,
> With the Cross of Jesus
> Going on before.
> Christ the Royal Master
> Leads against the foe,
> Forward into battle,
> See, His banner go . . .

Mallet-Jones, if he was not a hindrance, was not a help in their extremity. Although Ainslee had appointed him a leader he had permitted the reins of command to slip wholly into Wilmot's hands. If anything happened to Wilmot or Ainslee he would have to take over again. He doubted whether he could last very long as a leader but he would try. He would have to try. He told himself this in a dull distant way and forced the air from his lungs into his raw throat, singing, singing, singing . . .

> Onward, then, ye people,
> Join the happy throng,
> Blend with ours your voices
> In the triumph song.
> Glory, laud and honour
> Unto Christ the King,
> This through countless ages
> Men and angels sing.
> Onward Christian soldiers,
> Marching as to war,
> With the Cross of Jesus,
> Going on before.

Oliphant was on the other side of the raft from Mallet-Jones. He sat with shoulders bowed against the wind, his saturnine face in his hands, singing into his hands, but no longer moving. In the beginning he had thought of his wife and his home and the bank where he had worked and the paunchy little manager who had been in charge when he had left. It had been warm in the bank. There was a furnace, he remembered, at the back of the building, in the basement. A man named Alf kept the fire stoked and when the water in the radiators was heated in the morning the metal expanded and rang like a cracked bell. He often stood with his hands caressing the fluted top of the radiator when there was a lull in the bank's patronage. It was warm, too, in the train going home in the evening, warm and fuggy and full of still smoke; warm, also, at home where he scooped coal out of the brass scuttle and dropped huge lumps of it on to the fire and watched the sparks fly. Warm. Everything warm. Blood-heat. Priscilla had been warm as he had laid beside her in their double bed with its thick eiderdown. Hot-water bottles. Brandy at Christmas. Toast. Hot butter running down sucked fingers.

Now even these memories passed from his mind. His head became a thundering cavern of resentment; against God, against the sea, against all men, and in particular against Ainslee lying in the bottom of the raft and driving him to ludicrous song. What was the use? Why don't you answer me? Why? The resentment boiled up inside him as, on many occasions in his life, it had boiled up before: wilful, ungovernable.

Ainslee shouted, "Come on, now. Next song. . . . Not to stop . . . not on any account to stop. . . . Sing now . . ."

> Oh you can take a silver dollar and roll it around
> And it'll roll, cos it's round.
> A woman never knows what a good man she's got
> Until she turns him down.
> So listen, ma honey, listen to me,
> I want you to understand
> As a dollar goes from hand to hand,
> So a woman, I said a woman, so a woman
> Goes from man to man.

Oliphant sang the song they had learned at a ship's concert party in Liverpool. He sang it furiously, consumed with a passionate loathing of everything, screaming the words so that he hurt his throat. And then, quite suddenly, with a little spasm of consternation, he became aware that although he was still singing he was making no sound. He was dumb. He shouted to Ainslee, "My voice! My voice, it's gone! I can't speak! Listen, I can't speak!"

His blue-lipped mouth opened and shut in the darkness. "I can't speak! Christ, I can't speak!" His face sagged and his whole body slipped lower into the raft. "Funny! I can't speak at all. My throat . . . Just can't speak . . ."

He did not feel cold, now; just drowsy, floating not on the tempestuous sea but on some soft absorbent cloud. The others drifted away from him. He could hear them singing, but from a great distance, as if they were in some other raft, passing in the night.

He slept.

The boy was already in a bad way. He sat huddled against Wilmot's huge bulk, attempting to sing and move with the others but his voice a mere mouthed whisper and his movements slight. His face was a deep blotched blue, like an enormous bruise, as though it had been trampled on and beaten. Two half-closed eyes peered out through the blueness. Wilmot had opened his own serge jacket and was attempting to hold it across the boy's body but the weight of his arm seemed to be pushing the boy through the bottom of the raft and the coat offered such little protection that it might as well not have been there.

Wilmot leaned over him and put his mouth against the frozen ear. "Try and sing, boy. Come on, try and sing and keep moving."

The boy's eyes flickered towards Wilmot's face in the darkness and his mouth moved as Wilmot sang.

> You are my sunshine, my only sunshine,
> You make me happy, you make me sad,
> Tra-la-la-la-lah, tra-la-la-la-lah,
> Oh please don't take my sunshine away.

The boy was still weeping. He knew he was weeping because the sobs convulsed his body, preventing him from drawing breath, throttling his voice. But there were no tears, neither was there any sound of his weeping. He thought distantly of the pleasures he had missed: a father, a home where he was wanted, girls—even the boy thinking of girls. He had moved only adolescently on the periphery of their society, seeing them, smelling their scent, being intensely aware of their presence, sometimes even touching them; but never knowing them. He had been shy and awkward in their company and although, on occasions, by a glance or a smile or a word, they had lifted him towards an uncontainable ecstasy—unable to think of anything else for days and nights on end—he had not usually dared to speak to them, let alone cultivate their acquaintance.

Once, when he had been on leave, already acting the part of a man, he had lain in a field of fragrant hay with a schoolgirl of his own age. They had talked desultorily of stupid insignificant things and he had not even kissed her but he had put his cheek against hers and the contact had been a kind of magic. When, later, he had lain on his bed in the summer heat of the still day-lit early night, the whole world about him had become a fecund desirable thing, and she its incomparable epitome. For a few days he had loved with a passionate, short-lived intensity. Now, however much he drove his frozen mind, he could no longer recall her name.

But he could see her. He could see her quite clearly in the flying sea-spray mist, unruffled by the wind and the sea, a plain, average girl with a spot on her cheek, a schoolgirl with immature breasts. She smiled at him and came closer, gliding along the wave trough, her lips moving, speaking to him. The smell of hay came to him and he tried to stand up, to call to her, but his legs would not move and he was unable to speak for the sobs in his body. Then, as if lightning had flashed across the sky, he remembered her name: Mary! That was it, Mary! *Mary!* He found his voice and shouted her name, "Mary!"

Ainslee called, "That's right, boy. Try to move. Try to keep moving. That's better. Altogether now."

> Run rabbit, run rabbit, run, run, run,
> Don't give the farmer his fun, fun, fun,
> He'll get by without his rabbit pie,
> Run rabbit, run rabbit, run, run, run.

Barraclough was possessed of infinite qualities of endurance. His curly-haired head stuck up like a rock on a storm-lashed island. He did not even cower before the wind. He sang when he was told to sing, moved when he was told to move, knowing full well that these were the only means of survival, knowing better than anyone that when Ainslee and Wilmot and Mallet-Jones were gone, he would make the others carry on until they dropped. He never for a moment doubted that he could outlast them all.

If he should die, he would die without an overwhelming sense of disappointment. There would be no inordinate fuss. For all his aggressive mien, he was not afraid. He was different from Ainslee and Wilmot in that they had been trained to serve and fight whereas he had been born to it. His strain went back through countless generations of Northern fighting men. They had bred the stamina, the resistance to the cold, the bare-headed effrontery to defy the worst that nature or the enemy or both could devise. They had swept over heather-covered hills to massacre and plunder; they had stormed into peaceful valleys; they had razed castles and fortifications to their foundations and put every man inside them to the sword. And when their turn had come to die they had not themselves shouted for mercy. They had not been appalled by death; death had been their business. And Barra-clough, forged by history, was a weapon of war, their heir, in-destructible. He had something to shout about. He had something to sing about.

"Sing, you bastards! Sing!"

> I've got a loverly bunch of coconuts,
> I've got a loverly bunch of balls,
> Big ones, small ones, balls as big as yer 'ead,
> Give 'em a twist
> Of yer muscular wrist
> And fling 'em right over yer 'ead.

At midnight Ainslee distributed more meat and a further ration of water. They paused in their exertions, lying where they had fallen. Later Wilmot moved, pulling himself upright. He felt at the sleeve of his jacket, running his finger along it and then bending the material between thumb and forefinger. He took his hand away and looked at Ainslee and could see only his legs in the darkness. His fingers crept back to the sleeve and felt the material again, bending it in a different place. His mouth opened and he seemed about to shout. But instead he leaned over so that he could tap Ainslee on the chest. "It's me, sir. Wilmot."

Ainslee turned his pain-glazed eyes towards the shadow above him, "Yes, Chief?"

"It's freezing, sir."

Ainslee's head fell away again, away from Wilmot, so that his mouth was against Oliphant's boots. "Oh God! God, it can't be!" And then, "You're certain, Chief?"

"Certain, sir."

Wilmot waited, never doubting.

Ainslee said briskly, "Start the men singing, will you, Chief?"

"Aye, aye, sir."

Wilmot sat up and shouted in his best parade-ground voice, "All right, now. What about a song? All together now! One, two, three, four."

> Oh Johnny, oh Johnny, how you can love,
> Oh Johnny, oh Johnny, heavens above,
> You make my sad heart jump with joy
> And when I'm with you I can't keep still a minute.
> Oh Johnny, oh Johnny, please tell me, dear,
> What makes me love you so,
> You're not handsome, it's true,
> But when I look at you,
> Oh Johnny, oh Johnny, oh!

TWELVE

DAWSON reported to Jacobson on the bridge, "Passengers and crew off watch assembled in the saloon, sir."

Jacobson nodded gravely. "Very good."

For a little while he watched the ghostly, worsening sea. The high waves were travelling with them, overtaking them, slewing *Oleron's* stern from side to side in their clutching, impatient rush. The wind was mounting steadily, racing over the ship from stern to stem and moaning in the lashed derricks, grasping the wave tops and flinging them onward in an endless grey mist in the darkness. Each moment it became colder. Jacobson pulled his coat collar more tightly about his neck, shuddered, and stumped towards the bridge ladder.

Dawson resumed his station at the binnacle and checked the course.

"And you, Dawson?" Jacobson called, standing at the top of the ladder, "What is your decision?"

Dawson knew why Jacobson had ordered the crew and passengers into the saloon. When the Bos'n had shaken the blaspheming crew and Dawson had knocked respectfully at cabin doors, each awakened sleeper, in his way, had asked why. The Bos'n had answered heartlessly that he would find out soon enough and Dawson had said, "The Captain wishes to speak to you in the saloon but there is nothing to be alarmed about." He had said this, too, to Miss Olstein but only after he had kissed her.

"Well?" Jacobson asked.

Dawson answered quietly, "You're determined about it, aren't you?"

"Yes."

"Then if you're so determined, why do you ask?"

"Because I need your help."

Jacobson moved away from the ladder and approached Dawson. When he was close to him, looking up into his face in the blue light of the binnacle, his eyes below Dawson's chin, he said, "All my life I have been at sea. I have seen much tragedy at sea and always it has—how do you say?—upset me. But never in this way. You know. This evening when we steamed away from *Conway*, when *Southern Star* was sunk, something happened to me. I do not know what it was. But I knew then that I *must* go back. It is as though I have been ordered . . . it is strange . . . very strange . . . but you see, Dawson, I must." He turned away, a tiny corpulent figure beside Dawson, standing very straight and still.

"I see, sir." Dawson did not see at all but it was something to say.

"So," Jacobson said, "I have told you. What do you say?"

Dawson ran his fingers round the glass of the compass. "If you get a majority vote down there, and I don't think you will, I'll support you. If you don't, the matter doesn't rest with me, does it?"

Jacobson smiled and Dawson could see the small, regularly-spaced teeth. "Thank you, Dawson."

Then he was gone, a lonely portly figure, his heels banging first on the bridge decking and then on the steel ladder, growing fainter until they were gone.

The helmsman said, "What's he up to, sir, the old man?"

Dawson answered roughly, "You'll see, soon enough."

II

There was scarcely room to move in the saloon. The crew lounged at the rear in a bizarre miscellany of clothing and the passengers sat in front of them on the dining chairs. Busk stood to one side, on the flank of the passengers, his hair in disorder, his face ravaged and weary.

When Jacobson entered the saloon and stood before them he was removed from the front row by no more than two or three feet. He wished his audience could have been more distant; he had the sensation of standing on top of it. He opened his sheepskin coat, took off his cap, and put his hands in his jacket pockets with his thumbs hooked over their edges. He smiled tentatively, a little bleakly, frowned, and began to speak.

"Ladies and gentlemen, I have asked you to come here at this time of night because I have something very important to say to you. You all know that HMS *Conway* fought the German raider while we and many other ships of the convoy escaped. It is probable that she was sunk, yes? and if she was sunk there may be survivors." He turned towards Gerda Olstein and smiled, swivelling his trunk as if he had a stiff neck. Then, puffing out his chest, he went on pompously, "Well, I, Captain Jacobson, Master of this ship, wish to return and search for them."

A rumble of astonishment, disagreement and some approval swept through the crowded saloon. Each man spoke to his neighbour. Now they knew; there could be no more speculation. Busk's eyes stood out from their sockets, but he spoke to no one. He, too, seemed to be watching Gerda—pale, even in her tawdry dressing-gown inescapably magnificent, sitting silently in the front row, examining the deck about her feet as if she expected to find written there the answer to their joint dilemma. Jacobson wondered briefly if she had understood. His glance shifted to Mrs. Reed who was watching her husband's face. He was abruptly aware that the women on board would be his strongest allies. He wished there could have been more of them.

Harris swayed to his feet and as he spoke his voice rose steadily and a hard pellet of curdled saliva formed on his lower lip and jumped up and down with his words. "Listen to me. If we go back we can't find these men. How can we? They're lost, through, I tell you. Can't anybody understand that? It's bloody nigh freezing up top and if they're not dead now they'll be dead before we get anywhere near them. Dead, I say. What's the use then? What's the use of goin' back for corpses, because that's what they'll be? Jacobson's a fool, I'm tellin' you, a fool who wants to be a murderer . . ."

Strangely, unpredictably, it was Busk who intervened, hurrying on ungainly legs across the saloon to glare angrily into Harris's face. Harris panted and licked the spittle-pellet from his lip, swallowed it and glowered with his solitary eye.

"Shut your mouth," Busk said furiously.

"Shut your own mouth," Harris shouted back.

The two men stood motionless amid the movement of the ship, neither knowing how to continue the interchange. Finally, holding back his anger, Busk said, "Mr. Harris. You're an officer in the Merchant Service. Try and behave like one. Who do you think you're talking to?"

Harris threw back his narrow head and laughed derisively, showing his brown teeth. "Yes, I'm an officer. An' look what I got for it!" He thrust his face and the dead-eye socket towards Busk. "Look! But I know what I'm talking about an' that's more than can be said for that stuffed dummy of a Captain over there . . ."

Busk simply hit him. It was a sorry, ineffectual blow between a punch and a push, but it struck Harris in the mouth and his sharp teeth cut Busk's knuckles. Harris staggered backwards, tripped over Stockmann's feet, lost his balance, and fell drunkenly among the feet of the now-embarrassed crew. Busk watched astonished; it was the first time he had ever hit a man. But then, no one had ever scorned his uniform before—which he took Harris's scorn of Jacobson to be. Busk's uniform was one of his very few real possessions, his badge of membership in a large but exclusive club. It represented his ideal self, his notion of what he would like himself to be, and although he himself might be insulted, even degraded, the uniform—the buttons, the rings, the golden badge—were inviolate, at least from the taunts of others. They were his strength and he was ready to defend them. Therefore he hit Harris and was sorry only that he had been unable to hit him harder.

Jacobson was beside himself. "This will stop at once," he piped, clapping his hands together before the tightness of his jacket. "This is disgraceful."

Harris began to speak as he picked himself up from the deck. No one assisted him, not even Stockmann now.

"Be silent," Jacobson shrilled.

His little meeting was disintegrating in chaos. He was filled with distaste for Harris; in so far as he was capable of hatred, almost hating him. Then he saw the expression on Harris's face changing, slowly at first and then swiftly, no longer angry but subsiding into an uncomprehending misery. He was suddenly humble, a haunted, puzzled little man who had been hurt beyond his capacity to bear it.

Albert Reed got portentously to his feet and looked over his shoulder at his audience. "Captain Jacobson, I don't know much about this sort of thing. Weaving cloth's a bit more in my line, you know. But I agree that looking for these men'll be dangerous. And happen they'll be dead, as Harris says. And happen they won't. We'll have to risk that. Now what I want to know is this: is there a chance of finding them? Because if there is, and I'm not bothered how small the chance is, I'm with you."

Jacobson did not understand everything that Albert said; the clipped syllables were difficult and unfamiliar. But when Albert sat down Jacobson's brow cleared and he nodded his head gravely. "Yes, there is a chance. It is small, but there is a chance."

"That's all I wanted to know. What are we waiting for then?"

Jacobson said courteously, "Thank you, Mr. Reed. I am . . ."

Stockmann interrupted, seeing the decision going the wrong way. "I'll never agree . . ."

"An' I'll second that," a voice from the crew added.

There was a titter of laughter.

"I'll never agree," Stockmann continued, "to support you in putting this ship in such unreasonable danger."

Jacobson sighed and his glance jerked over Gerda Olstein and Mrs. Reed again and then, surprisingly, to Busk. Had he to take a revised view of his First Mate? Busk's face was pallid and drawn. His hair-curtained head rested against the bulkhead.

"Now then, ladies and gentlemen," Jacobson said, "perhaps you have wondered what the name *Oleron* means. Briefly, I now inform you. One of the first—how do you say?—compilations of law about the sea were the 'Judgements of Oleron'. These laws were the decisions of the maritime court of Oleron, an island off the western coast of France. Some say these laws go back to the Vikings. It is very likely. However, that is the meaning of the word *Oleron*.

"One of the laws of the sea, first of the Vikings and later of other men who sailed in ships, was this: imagine, a Viking boat. Its Captain knows that if he takes a certain very dangerous action he may win a great battle or discover a new land, or rescue some comrades lost in the sea. If his decision is very difficult he will call his crew and say to them: 'I think we should do this thing. But we might fail. We might lose our ship—and our lives. It is too great a question for me alone to decide. We shall make this great decision together. What do you think, eh?'" Jacobson's pink face glowed with enthusiasm. "Now, I do the same thing. I ask you to make this great decision with me. If you say No, I shall say, No, it is too dangerous. But if you say Yes, we shall set course for these men without delay."

Stockmann's grating voice shattered the ensuing silence. "But, Captain, we are not Vikings."

Even Jacobson was stung to the acid retort. "That, sir, is very evident."

Again the ripple of laughter.

"Now, ladies and gentlemen, I shall ask for your views . . ."

But Albert Reed rose again and interrupted him, "Just a tick, Captain. There's something I want to know. I take it that if *we* don't go back nobody else will?"

"I do not know. But as long as we do not know, our situation is not altered, yes? I mean, we cannot tell, therefore we must act."

"Yes, I see that right enough. But isn't there any way we can find out? What about the radio? Couldn't we ask on that?"

"Ask who?" Stockmann interjected.

Albert was irritated, "I don't know. How should I know? That's what I'm asking the Captain, isn't it?"

"I fear not," Jacobson explained. "We maintain wireless silence. If we transmit, U-boats can find our position."

"They seem already to have found it," Stockmann said.

Albert turned on him. "Look, Stockmann, would you mind holding your tongue till I've had me say?" He turned back to Jacobson. "I see. Then there's nothing we can do? We can't find out?"

Jacobson shook his head. Albert sat down.

"I must ask now for your views," Jacobson said. "First I shall ask the passengers, one by one. Then the officers. Finally I shall ask the crew for a show of hands. We are ready?"

He looked at them benignly, disguising his fear that their decision might go against him. He had burned his boats now. If they refused to return he had no option but to follow their advice. "Mr. Reed?"

"Aye, I'm with you. And Mrs. Reed. That makes two of us."

"Is that correct, Mrs. Reed?"

Albert was still irritated. "Of course, it is. I said so, didn't I?"

Alice smiled as bravely as her circumstances allowed. "Yes. I'm sure you're right. Yes, of course, I agree."

"Thank you, Mrs. Reed. Miss Olstein?"

Jacobson beamed at her like a father and pink crow's feet gathered at the corners of his intensely blue eyes. He wanted so much to talk to her. She and Harris, he thought, had much in common; they had both been misused, their past hurts over-flowing into the present and the future.

She said gravely, "Mr. Dawson, what does he wish?"

Jacobson swallowed back the womanish 'Ah' that leapt to his lips. "He does not agree or says he does not agree. But that was a little time ago and now he has had time to think. If he were here, I think his answer would not be the same. And in any case he says that he will go with the majority. Does that help you, my dear?"

She smiled. 'My dear.' It was so long since a middle-aged man had so addressed her because, apparently, he liked her, and not merely because he wanted her. She liked Jacobson and wondered at the strange warmth that rose within her. This portly, pink little man was so essentially good, she saw, that she was unable to say anything but, "Yes, I think I agree. I am sure I agree."

"Thank you, Miss Olstein. Now, Mr. Stockmann."

"You know my view perfectly well, Captain. Let us not prolong this farce by asking each other pointless questions."

Jacobson executed a little bow. He could afford it. He already had a majority of the passengers with him.

"Mr. Harris?"

Harris shuffled his feet about on the deck and watched the movement of his pointed shoes. Then he raised his mutilated face towards Jacobson.

"Yes, Mr. Harris?"

Harris just stared, lost in some private speculation, as if he had forgotten what Jacobson's question had been.

"Yes?"

Someone coughed and Busk's head turned slowly against the bulkhead, away from Harris towards Jacobson. A plate vibrated in the pantry. When Harris spoke, he spoke so quietly that they had difficulty in hearing his voice.

"I've done my best to tell you not to do this. There's only one thing to do and that's to get out of here as fast as the engines'll take us. But no, you won't do that, will you? You know better . . ."

Stockmann smirked.

Harris's guilt and misery were uppermost, no longer subdued by drink and Stockmann's baleful influence. He bent his body so that his face was separated from his thighs only by one hand clapped over his mouth and the other over his good eye. He rocked slightly in his chair, forwards and then back again, perhaps to stop himself from shouting.

"Mr. Harris? Are you all right, Mr. Harris?"

His face came up quickly, as quickly as he had hidden it. "Damn you! Damn you, I've got to agree! Those men out there, they're our men. But they're not alive, I tell you! They're dead. Dead!" He began to shout, his nerves shattered by his injury and his month-long drunk. "But I've got to agree. God damn you, Jacobson, I've got to agree! Don't you see that?"

"Harris!" Stockmann said.

Harris turned on him furiously. "Shut up! Shut up! For God's sake, shut up!"

Stockmann shrugged.

Jacobson hurried on. "Mr. Busk?"

"I carry out your orders, sir. Isn't that enough?"

"It is enough. Bos'n?"

"Yes, sir."

Jacobson was elated. He was winning hands down, more than he had ever dared to expect.

"Now, the crew. Those who agree that we should go back will please raise their hands, so."

For a moment there was no movement and Jacobson felt a little stab of fear. One hand jerked upwards, its owner looking round for signs of support. Another was raised and then another. As they appeared, like hesitant flags, Jacobson counted them: "One, two, three, four . . . five . . . six . . . seven. Any more? Eight? Eight. Eight out of how many now? Eight out of eleven."

He pulled his white handkerchief from his breast pocket and wiped his brow and smiled at Gerda Olstein. There was even a round of applause.

"Ladies and gentlemen, our decision is made. You have been very patient. I thank you. Now I must return to the bridge. Excuse me, please."

Stockmann shouted, "What about the crew on duty? They have not been asked."

Jacobson fixed him with a confident, jaunty eye. "Mr. Stockmann, I suggest you go round the ship and ask them for yourself. If my arithmetic is correct, even if they all say that they will not go back—which they will not all say—you will still find yourself without a majority. Does that answer your question? Now, if you will permit me . . ."

He bowed and turned and marched from the room, more erect than ever, pulling his cap on to his head and then buttoning up his coat. He marched along the passageway like a diminutive manifestation of the wrath of God and clattered up the ladder to the darkened bridge. "Mr. Dawson."

"Sir?"

"Steer course zero-eight-five."

"Yes, sir. Zero-eight-five. Hard astarboard."

The helmsman answered. "Hard a starboard, sir." And then, "Wheel hard over, sir."

"Then you won, sir?"

"Yes, Dawson. We won."

Oleron's high stem tilted and swung against the following waves, forcing steep cliffs of steel against the adamant water. The forepeak reared disdainfully, hung for a moment, and then fell back again, crushing the waves beneath it, repulsing them in disarray. The men on the bridge watched the sea swivelling about them, submitting to *Oleron*'s superior power.

"See?" Jacobson cried. "See, Dawson? She *wants* to come round."

Oleron tore into the waves like a ship possessed and as she brought her head up into the wind, so the wind-noise climbed from a moan to a whine to a scream and the broken spray ran in rivers down the bridge screens. The sea about her was white with foam.

"See!" Jacobson shouted again, his voice competing with the sound of the wind and the pounding sea. "See how she comes! Look!"

Dawson shouted, "Midships."

"Midships, sir."

"Steer, zero-eight-five."

"Zero-eight-five, sir."

Jacobson said, "I shall take over. Please work out an accurate course and let me know when we might reach them."

"Yes, sir."

Dawson moved towards the charthouse. Then he stopped and

came towards Jacobson. He said, "I still think you're haywire, Captain. But I wish you the best of luck."

Jacobson did not look round at Dawson, nor take his eyes away from the plunging bow, nor stop stroking the bridge rail. Dawson towered behind him, waiting, and the little man said, "Thank you, Dawson. Thank you. We shall find them. You will see."

"Of course, sir. Sure."

When Dawson was gone and he was alone with the helmsman and the ghostly look-outs, he found himself wishing that *Oleron* could talk; he already believed in a half-sentimental, half-mystical seaman's way that she could think. His fingers moved delicately over the polished wood, consciously touching her, knowing her, believing in her.

He ferreted under his coat for his watch and consulted it in the binnacle light. It was exactly 22.30.

He was marvellously glad and if, at that moment, anyone had spoken to him, he would have been unable to answer, so overwhelming was his gladness.

PART THREE

THIRTEEN

01.00

THE raft was lifted towards the black sky and hurled down into the ravines of the sea. Each minute the violence of its movement increased. Sometimes the singing could not be heard, not even by those who sang, for when a wave flung its leaping crest among the men the noise of the wind and the sea together obliterated all other sound. And when the men opened their mouths to sing the wind snatched the air from their lungs and left them breathless.

> A-tiskit, a-taskit,
> I lost my yellow basket,
> A little girlie picked it up
> And put it in her pocket.

Ainslee still led the musical effort, driving his crew with an unflagging vigour, keeping their numbed, bruised bodies moving until some would have killed him had they been able to find the strength to move through the apparently infinite distance to the source of their torment, and, once there, the power to hold their hands about the offending throat. Yet, at the same time, each man conceded in a corner of his mind that Ainslee was right, and so obeyed him. The men loved Ainslee when they were not hating him.

The boy was the first to die. His weight suddenly increased on the Chief's arm and when Wilmot shifted he toppled sideways like a bird frozen on the branch of a winter tree.

"Boy, what's the matter, boy?"

When there was no answer Wilmot chafed the boy's hands which were rigid and blue and slapped the pinched face which he found in the slopping water. "Wake up, boy! Wake up! Are you all right, boy?" He searched with deadened fingers for the boy's pulse and when he found the veined thinness, when he had held it long enough to become convinced of its lifelessness, he shouted to Ainslee, wonderingly, sadly, "He's dead! The boy's dead, sir."

Barraclough said, "Poor little kid," but he might as well have spoken to himself for no one heard him in the rush of the wind through the spray.

They wondered what they would do with the boy now that he was dead. They searched in their cold brains and found nothing but indifference. After an uncounted measure of time they decided that they should keep him because dead or alive he was doing no one any harm. They did not discuss the matter; the mere presence of each man still living was itself a sufficient influence upon his neighbour. Each man asked himself what the other would do if he himself died, and they decided, thereby, unanimously, silently, to keep him. "Let him alone. He's no bother," they said to themselves, "the poor little frozen bastard," and forgot him except as a corpse. Even Wilmot ceased to remember him as someone who had once lived, and saw only a shifting dead thing they carried with them. The boy fell into the bottom of the raft and when the seas spurted up through the boards the water covered his face and indeed all of his body except one fragile jutting shoulder.

Ainslee roused himself and shouted into the wind, "He was weak. He was only a boy. He died of the cold, do you understand that?" The effort of shouting tired him and some of the men missed the remaining words which fell attenuating from his lips like water from a fountain that is suddenly turned off, "And you'll die of cold too unless you keep moving and singing, do you hear? Do you hear, I said, do you hear? Sing!"

> My eyes are dim, I cannot see
> I have not brought my specs with me,
> I have not brought my specs with me.

Reggie heard. And Reggie answered, answered so loudly that even the men on the other side of the plunging raft could hear him. "Move?" he screamed, "All I hear is move! *You* don't move, lying there with your broken legs. Why don't *you* move! Christ, why aren't my legs broken? I can't move, I tell you. I can't move any more. Or sing. I can't! I can't!"

Ainslee did not interrupt, could not have interrupted even if he had tried. He waited for Reggie to stop. When Reggie's rage subsided he shouted wearily, patiently, "You'll move when I tell you to move, Atkinson," and then, violently, "Do you understand?"

Reggie understood and for the moment was silent.

Eric Barraclough still sang and moved his body.

His behaviour had become a model to the others. In his extremity he had thrown off the burden of his past. He was no longer disgusted by it and began to recall it even with affection.

His father, the drunken loquacious cowman with the perpetual dewdrop on the end of his nose had been called Niffnoff by the villagers. Eric no longer despised him. He found himself remembering the hovel in which they had lived, recalling the smell and the poverty and a particular evening when Niffnoff had returned early from the Barley Mow, not because he was tired of drinking, or full, or had spent all his money, for he had had no money when he had gone there after tea, but because even he, the conditioned scrounger, had become convinced that no one else that night was going to buy him a drink.

Eric was sitting with his elbows on the deep-napped green tablecloth reading the local newspaper in the light of an oil lamp. His sister, then sixteen, sat by the fire mending the only decent dress she had ever possessed, bending over the cheap material and running the tip of her tongue slowly backwards and forwards across her upper lip. When her father returned she lifted up her hard pretty face toward him but did not speak. Neither of them spoke to him now if they could avoid it. Eric watched his sister. He loved her because he thought her to be like his mother before she became witless and took to walking about the village streets in unlaced men's boots and a shapeless trilby hat. He could not remember her otherwise.

"What's for supper?" Niffnoff demanded, picking his way round the table so that he could stand in front of the meagre fire burning in the old-fashioned black-leaded grate between cast-iron ovens.

Edna said, "There's a bit a cheese in't kitchen."

"Then why doan't th' go an' get it, th' cheeky madam?"

"You're drunk," Edna said and went on with her sewing.

Eric added, "And your flies are undone. Did you know that? Can't you even fasten your flies up? 'Appen you can't, at that."

His father pretended not to hear but his hands crept over his trousers, searching for the elusive buttons. "We'er's th' mother?"

When no one answered he yelped, nearly falling backwards into the fire, "We'er's th' bloody mother?"

Edna said, "In bed. We'er' d'yer think she is?"

"'Ere, tha' forward little bitch, who dust th' think tha's talkin' to, eh? Tha's nowt bu' six pennuth a copper."

"Leave 'er be," Eric said.

"What's up wi' thee, lad? I want nonnon th' old buck."

"Leave 'er be," Eric repeated.

Niffnoff turned towards Edna, leaning on his hands planted on the arms of her chair, swaying a little and pushing his drink-worn face into hers. "A'll 'ave to teach thee a sharp lesson, lass. Too much lip, that's t'bloody trouble with 'ee. Yer fast thing. Now go an' get me supper an' look sharp about it afore a lands thee one in th' kisser."

He belched and realised for the first time that he was looking down the front of her dress and that she was no longer a girl but very nearly a woman, and that her breasts, like her face, were cheeky, pert and pretty.

"Leave 'er be," Eric said, his voice rising, his fingers scuttling over the newsprint and clutching it in massive hands. "I'm tellin' yer. Give ovver."

Niffnoff lurched over his daughter, saying like a child discovering a remarkable toy, "A regular little bobby-dazzler, eh?" and snatched with calloused fingers at her dress, tearing it and tugging it from her shoulders and pushing one hand under her arms crossed on her chest. Eric bounded from his chair and threw his father to the floor. Edna sat transfixed. She might, like her mother, have been mad. She held a scrap of material over her breasts which were now too big to be hidden by so small a remnant. Eric breathed, "If you ever touch 'er again I'll kill you. If you ever so much as lays a finger on 'er again, I'll throttle you. An' tha's the truth."

Niffnoff did not answer but lay huddled on the floor, waiting for the walls to stop moving. When they were still he climbed to his feet and left the fetid room, walking painstakingly, almost with dignity, as if nothing had occurred, his misdemeanour already mislaid in the vacuum of his past.

The following week Eric departed from the village to join the Navy, hating everything, mistrusting everyone, holding the whole world responsible for the deficiencies of his father.

Now, miraculously, the loathing was gone and he smiled as he sang in the darkness.

> Let him come, let him tarry, let him sink or let him swim,
> He doesn't care for me and I don't care for him.
> He can go and find another who I hope he will enjoy
> For I'm going to marry a far nicer boy.

They rested and the men in the raft were silent except that Reggie whimpered occasionally. The pain in Ainslee's legs had become a nightmare and for the first time he began to wonder how long *he* could survive. One of his men had died; another, already, appeared to be going off his head. When would his turn come? And what would happen when it did? Would he quietly subside, be alive one moment and dead the next, no one knowing until they asked him a question? Or would he, too, make a scene before finally departing? He thought of Jean, his wife, and saw her as he had left her at the station when he left 'Manningtrees' to return to *Conway*. He saw the gay scarf over the dark hair and her even smile and the light that was always in her eyes. "Jean," he said, as if he were falling asleep. "Jean!" He was abruptly aware that except for his mother Jean was the only person who had ever really liked him. And she had loved him. Others may have admired him but he had always been too certain of himself to be wholly liked—except by Jean and she had loved him. The self-knowledge which he had never before admitted saddened him.

He had showed her his letter of resignation before he had sent it to the Admiralty. When she had seen the unhappiness in his face she had said, "Don't send it, darling. Wait a little. Things won't always be the same." But he had posted it the same day and it had been accepted with alacrity. *He* had never blamed her; but his family had, and he, God forgive him, had permitted her to be exposed to their unreasoning censure.

He remembered them in church when he was married, out in force, the redoubtable Naval Ainslees bedecked in their medals and gold lace, disapproving of his civilian suit and, by implication, of her. He remembered the only time she had cried, when his fool of a brother had said to her, "He would have been Captain now—or, who knows?—of Flag rank." Since the Armada had sailed up the channel the Ainslees had been in love with the Navy; and when he himself had apparently exchanged the object of their service and devotion for Jean, his wife, they would not believe that he could have acted in this way unless he had been subjected to the gravest duress.

"You're wrong!" he shouted. "All of you wrong, wrong, wrong!" Why had he never told them what fools they were. Why before now had he never asked them how they dared to criticise her, to make her unhappy or even merely angry? Who did they think they were, these posturing marionettes, exultant in their fancy dress? God, they were not even able! He did not despise them; but for their attitude to Jean, which previously he had allowed to pass, he could never now forgive them. Something moved against his arm and he shifted his head on the hard raft rim, "Jean, Jean, my darling." Wilmot's voice said, "Are you all right, sir?"

He took Wilmot's arm and held on to it tightly and looked into the shadow of his face. "Chief!" Wilmot felt the hard fingers digging into his muscles. He did not try to take his arm away. "What, for God's sake, Chief . . . are we . . . going to do?"

Wilmot withdrew his arm and Ainslee's hands fell to his side. "Sing, sir. Sing, and keep moving."

"How long can we make them sing?"

Wilmot did not answer directly. He said, "They'll sing, sir. Damn it, they'll sing."

> Oh show me the way to go home
> 'Cos I'm tired and want to go to bed.
> I had a little drink about an hour ago
> And it went right to my head.
> Wherever I may roam,
> On land or sea or foam,
> You'll always hear me singing this song,
> Show me the way to go home.

FOURTEEN

02.00

OLERON had turned at 22.30, six hours after the order to scatter. Between 16.30 and 22.30 she had steamed with the wind and sea, but not all the time at emergency full ahead. Now she was steaming recklessly into the oncoming seas, her engines pounding at the uttermost limit of their capacity and, it was clear to *Oleron's* Chief Engineer, beyond.

Dawson had calculated and laid off the course on the chart with painstaking accuracy. His calculations had shown that if their dead-reckoning position was precisely accurate (which it could never be) they would arrive in the vicinity of the survivors (if any) shortly before 05.00. His calculations allowed for a raft—there could not possibly, he reckoned, be a boat—drifting downwind at a steady two-and-a-half knots. Jacobson had checked the calculations and the allowances made by Dawson for the effect of the wind and the sea on their course and speed through the water. He had worked the problem afresh and found no discrepancy. Their course should indeed be 087 degrees and their ETA 04.47.

Jacobson had clattered out of the charthouse and had stood diminutively by his Second Mate. "087 it is, Mr. Dawson," and Dawson had answered quietly, laconically, "Thank you, sir."

Busk had relieved Dawson at midnight and shadowy figures had flitted across the bridge and tired men had flung themselves into bunks in the warmth below decks. But Jacobson had not moved; through the change of watches and on into the middle watch, and on, it seemed, for ever if necessary, he stood on the port side of the bridge watching *Oleron's* bow plunge through the endless succession of the sea. The ship shook with the turbulence of her engines. The water that came inboard raced in green bores over the fo'c'sle, the breakwaters and the forward well-deck, hurling itself against the foundations of the bridge itself before streaming over the sides in deep waterfalls. The cargo hatches were continuously covered in water and eventually the taut-chained anchor would hammer its way right through the steel sides of the stem. In time, at this speed, into this sea, all manner of damage would accrue. But Jacobson trusted *Oleron* and believed that if she began to break up, the process would not begin until her mission was completed.

Once more the quick ferreting under his coat for his watch, the movement which always suggested a fear that he might at last have lost it, the snapping open of the gold cover and the thumb-rub over the glass: two o'clock. They were more than half-way there. He was excited now, like a child unable to sleep on the eve of a holiday.

His greatest concern was frost. Frost could defeat him more quickly than the wind or the sea or the human enemy. From time to time he called, "Temperature, Mr. Busk?" And Busk would answer, "A degree under," or "Just freezing, sir." The last time he had answered he had said, "Twenty-nine degrees, sir," and Jacobson had frowned and passed his fingers over his brow in a familiar gesture of strain.

Busk said, "I'm sorry about this evening, sir."

"What?"

"This evening . . ."

Jacobson grunted.

"I was a bit . . . overwrought, sir. I'm sorry."

Jacobson grunted again. He had no inclination to discuss Busk's peculiarities at a time like this and even Busk sensed his disinterest. The whole of his attention was devoted to the racing sea. If the wind increased it would whip up the sea even more. To reduce speed would then become imperative. He pondered the question of speed. Less speed meant lost time and the men he sought might die in the interval. He must not reduce speed. But lost speed was better than frost.

He watched the cargo hatch up on the forward well-deck. It was difficult to see anything but the water racing aft, but he thought he saw the ends of flapping canvas. His body tensed, his hands tightened on the bridge rail and he pressed his nose against the water-blurred glass. "Mr. Busk!"

"Sir?"

"Do you see Number One cargo hatch?"

Busk peered obediently through the glass.

"Yes."

"Well, go on man, look at it!"

Busk wiped his hand over the glass to clear it of his own condensed breath. "Jesus," he said, "the tarpaulin's going! It's tearing!"

Jacobson yelped, "Messenger!"

A shadow detached itself from the after bulkhead, and floated through the darkness towards him.

"Shake the Bos'n."

"Aye aye, sir."

"To report to me. Immediately!"

The shadow melted and its feet rattled on the bridge ladder. Jacobson wondered whether he should call Dawson; he would be the right man for work of this kind. But his officers were working watch and watch and it was unreasonable to call them out on their four hours off unless their presence was absolutely necessary. "Anyway, he is likely to be with that woman. I should turn him out . . ." (Gerda, it would be pleasant to be in bed with Gerda, just lying there, touching and occasionally talking.)

He dismissed the outrageous thought and concentrated his attention upon the flapping tarpaulin. It had given way at one corner only but he knew that before long the wind would take charge and rip it to shreds. Then the water, instead of sluicing over the side, would sluice, in part, into the hold.

Busk said, "You'll have to reduce speed, sir."

(Odd, the way he always said, 'Sir'.)

"No."

"Or turn out of the wind."

(No 'Sir'!)

"No."

"But you can't send men down on to the well-deck in this sea."

Jacobson held on to himself. He had been awake for so long now that when crossed he had difficulty in controlling himself. He wanted to scream at Busk. He said, "We shall see." Every word was becoming an effort of control and concentration.

"Sir?"

It was the Bos'n who had approached unheard. Perhaps if he had crossed the bridge on hob-nailed boots and not in rubber plimsoles Jacobson would still not have heard him. Jacobson turned towards the stocky figure and indicated with his finger that he should look downwards through the glass at the disintegrating canvas. "Take four men," he said flatly, "and spread a fresh cover."

The Bos'n looked at the hatch and the water that streamed over it and pushed his cap to the back of his head and ran his fingers through his fine fair hair. "But . . ."

"Yes?"

"You'll have to reduce speed first, sir. Or turn out of the wind."

"Just so," Busk said.

"I cannot do that."

"It is difficult to trust these men," the Bos'n said. "They are a poor lot and can be lost."

"Not if correct lifelines are rigged for them."

"No, sir."

Busk again interrupted. "You can't do that. You'll lose a man and then what'll you do? It's too bloody dangerous down there."

Jacobson stared through the darkness at the Bos'n. "Well, Bos'n?"

The Bos'n was a young man with a career still to make and he had no wish to be found wanting by Jacobson. But still he hesitated. "Do you want me to do it myself, Bos'n?" Jacobson asked. As he spoke he had the feeling that he was becoming impossible. He knew what happened to ships with obsessive Captains on their bridges. But he could not bring himself to reduce speed or turn out of the wind; not yet, oh God, not yet!

The Bos'n sighed. "Aye aye, sir."

He trotted off the bridge and Jacobson returned to his contemplation of the hatch cover.

"Don't you think you'd better have some rest, sir?" Busk asked, apparently accepting the decision now that it was made. Was that it? Was he now too tired to be trusted to make decisions? What was the point of saving a few men from the water if he lost as many in the process? "No, I shall be all right. It is just that we must not lose time."

"Or men," Busk said.

Jacobson answered wearily, "Time, Mr. Busk. I said time. We shall not lose men."

He straightened his shoulders and watched the forward well-deck until he perceived movement other than flapping canvas and swirling water. He was a good man, the Bos'n. One of the best. He reminded Jacobson of himself when young.

He carried two lines, both secured to himself in bowlines about his chest, the first secured at its other end to the super-structure amidships, the other coiled and held ready in one hand. A man held the line attached to the superstructure and paid it out as the Bos'n moved forward, ready to haul in the moment he missed his footing. The Bos'n waited for a favourable juxta-position of waves. Then he ran, knee deep in expended water, and flung himself down on the deck alongside the hatch coaming before the next wave thundered off the fo'c'sle above him. He disappeared under its flood and Jacobson's nose pressed harder against the glass. Then he was moving again, free of the water, at first crawling and then running towards the bulkhead which formed the forrard limit of the well-deck. When the next wave sluiced off the fo'c'sle the Bos'n was below its roaring curtain, furiously bending his freeline to a ring bolt in the deck. He left enough slack to permit movement back to midships superstruc-ture. He could move almost anywhere on the well-deck now without detaching himself from his lines.

The four picked men repeated the process while Jacobson prayed for the tarpaulin to hold together for just a little longer. They were doing nothing that he himself would not have done, would not still do. He considered this. The Bos'n would need help—he had pointed out that his men were a poor lot. Jacobson considered that, too. Suddenly, he called, "Messenger, bring me a line."

Again the shadow rattled down the bridge ladder while Jacobson watched the dark blob of the men crawling over the deck with the folded replacement tarpaulin under their bodies. When, after an eternity, the messenger returned, he said, abruptly, "I am going out on deck, Mr. Busk." Busk stared and swallowed and acknowledged receipt of this intelligence with something between a gasp and a grunt. Jacobson marched off the bridge and made his way down the ladders until he debouched on to the seaswept fury of the well-deck. It was bitingly cold in the wind and the water swirled up to his knees, receded and rose again. The noise was intense. He pulled down his cap until the leather band was like iron about his head and secured his line about his chest, bending the other end to the superstructure.

He stood with his short, sturdy legs wide apart, waiting and watching while his men edged their way along the forrard side of the hatch, flat on their bellies, clinging to the coaming, alternately whipped by the wind and drenched by the sea, still shaking from the cold after the warmth below decks, but not yet numbed by the cold as the men in the raft were numbed. The Bos'n snatched the hammer from his belt and struck at the wedges until the batten holding the forward edge of the tarpaulin was loose enough for it to be ripped away and flung into the sky by the wind but for the men holding it as if they were holding an animal. When the wedges and the batten were sufficiently loose, Jacobson watched the men insert the edge of the new tarpaulin over the old, between the batten and the coaming, watched the Bos'n hammering at the wedges like a half-drowned demon until, it seemed, not all the seas in the world could remove them. Then it happened, just as Jacobson had feared it might.

The tarpaulin secured only at its forward edge, took charge. The wind and the sea rushed into its heavy folds and almost before the men knew that they had lost control, it was taut and flapping in the turmoil of wind and water. Jacobson hurled himself forward and fell upon its harsh strength and cried in a curious high-pitched scream, "Hold it! Hold it!" His heavy body seemed to subdue it for the fraction of time needed for the Bos'n and his four men to regain their balance and join him, their combined bodies pinioning it to the hatch cover. They pressed themselves hard against it, holding on with the insides of their knees and their finger nails, even the cheeks of their faces pressed against its wet sandpaper surface. They grunted and gasped as the water tumbled over them, their minds and their bodies bent supremely to the task of holding on and not letting go, of not being swept away in the continuous flood from *Oleron*'s bow.

When the five men and not the canvas were again in charge the Bos'n moved cautiously towards the after coaming. The others followed, crawling over the hatch while he hammered at the after wedges. They were not surprised to find their Captain lying with them on the open deck soaked and frozen like themselves. They accepted his presence without comment, as men accept almost anything in times of emergency, and were grateful that he was there. When they had first been ordered to the task they had sworn elaborately and called down misfortune on

Jacobson's square head. Their opposition to his authority would doubtless return, but for the duration of their crisis they welcomed him as one of their own.

When the after edge of the tarpaulin was secured and they had begun to wedge the sides, it happened again, once more as Jacobson had seen that it might. One moment the Bos'n was there, his body crouched like those of the others under a mass of surging water; the next moment not there. Before the wave he was with them, after the wave he was gone. The others knew that he had gone when they heard him shout; Jacobson, who was on the well-deck for no other purpose, knew he was going before he made a sound. But he was too late to save him.

The men could not distinguish the words of Jacobson's orders for they consisted of a continuous high-pitched squeaking noise. But his movements made his intentions clear enough. He rose to his feet and ran diagonally towards the port side of the well-deck. The men followed, careering crab-wise through deep water until they came to the guard-rails where the sea was close, heaving towards them as the ship rolled, waiting to take them as it had already taken the Bos'n. Jacobson ran along the guard-rails, still astonishingly stiff and erect, the crown of his wedged cap ballooning like an inflated paper bag on his head, feeling with his feet in the darkness for the Bos'n's lifeline, almost vomiting with the fear of not finding it. Then he had his foot on the taut rope and when he took it in his hands there was a repetition of the squeaking sound and the men gathered round him and grasped the rope and pulled as if their own lives depended upon their efforts. Jacobson shrieked at them, "Heave . . . heave . . . heave . . . heave!" The line jerked in their hands as the racing waves snatched at the Bos'n's inert body. They could not see him but the line was vertical now, reaching down into the darkness of the sea, not running aft as when they had found it. "Heave, damn you! Heave!" Slowly the swinging, turning body left the sea and was pulled up to the guard-rails where five men who could scarcely keep their feet in the bucking and rolling of the ship bent down and grasped his arms and head and shoulders and pulled him through the rails until he lay like a seal on the sloping deck.

"Get back to the hatch," Jacobson shouted. "I shall look after him."

The men stood in the howling wind, bereft now of the Bos'n's business-like lead. "Go!" Jacobson squeaked. They turned and raced back to the hatch, glad, perhaps, to be away from a man who might be dead.

Jacobson crouched by a guard-rail stanchion, his arm crooked about it, his back to the wind and sea, and looked into the Bos'n's Swedish face and knew a rare relief. He had not been lost over the side as a result of his, Jacobson's, unreasonable orders; he, Jacobson, had retrieved him and all that remained for him to do was to bring him back to life. In his gratitude he wanted to stroke the man's fair face. "Thank God," he whispered. "Thank God, we found you." He grasped him by the shoulders and pulled him round and began to drag him towards the port shelter-deck. The water cascading off the fo'c'sle swirled and roared about him. Once he slipped and fell but did not feel the ventilator striking him viciously in the small of his back; the pain would come later. He rolled over like a beetle in a flooding drain but never released his hold on the Bos'n whose body hard against the ventilator saved them both from being swept overboard. He scrambled to his feet when the worst of the wave had passed and travelled backwards over the endless expanse of the well-deck, step by uncertain step in a black world of violence, his mild face held down, contorted with effort; he did not even feel cold any more.

When he came to the shelter-deck he reached the limit of the Bos'n's lifeline and untied it. Then he pressed on to the athwart-ship-passage entrance and after a titanic struggle with the heavy metal door succeeded in pulling the Bos'n over the coaming. He untied his own lifelines. Once inside the warmth and comparative peace of the ship he threw off his coat and began artificial respiration. Thirty minutes later, when the men came in from the well-deck, he was still performing the persistent, patient movements on the inert body spread-eagled on the puddled deck. A man offered to take over but Jacobson worked on, afraid of the interval that would occur, afraid, too, to take a chance on a man's as yet unmeasured skill. Later, when the Bos'n's eyelids rolled upwards in life, the men picked him up and carried him to Jacobson's cabin where they gave him an enormous tot of brandy and wrapped him in blankets after they had removed his wet clothes, and left him to sleep in Jacobson's bunk, a little drunk now as well as more than a little drowned.

When the men had gone awkwardly from his cabin Jacobson slowly stripped off his wet clothing. His weariness was becoming an agony. He moved slowly about his cabin, his pink belly glistening in the light of the reading lamp, shaking a little as he crossed the carpeted deck. He poured water into the basin and washed his hands and bathed his smarting cheeks.

He dressed slowly, almost painfully. When he was ready he examined himself in the mirror, pulled down his reefer jacket and straightened his tie; it was typical that even now he should wear a tie, that cufflinks should gleam in his white shirt, that his shoes should be so highly polished that the whole of the cabin was reflected in them. He pulled on his cap and made quite certain that the Company badge was in the precise centre of his forehead. Before he left the cabin he looked back at the sleeping Bos'n and the suspicion of a smile moved over his cherubic features.

He climbed the ladder like an old man. But when he arrived on the bridge his shoulders went back and his whole body gained an inch in height. It always did, whatever the weariness. If anything he was even more determined now, beyond all contrary persuasion.

He did what he did because he saw it to be right. And no one could gainsay him.

FIFTEEN

03.00

THE wind streaming across the flat sea-world became a gale, destroying the flatness and pushing the malleable water into moving ranges of wild and corrugated mountains.

The men in the raft had forgotten the boy. His body moved as the raft moved and sometimes it rolled on to their feet, but they did not know what it was that pressed against them until they tried to move their legs. Then they cursed and heaved him away. He was naked now; little by little, as they had overcome their scruples, they had undressed him and shared out his clothing and wrapped it about their exposed bodies. They would have taken any part of his body, too, if they had believed that it could make them warmer. Wilmot, who had no coat, took most of the clothing and tried to still the thought in his head that it was a pity that a man with a coat had not died instead of the boy.

Wilmot was the leader now; pain and bleeding had wrought their effect upon Ainslee who lived now only because he clung fanatically to what little life remained; but he still sang—or at least his mouth opened as though he were singing—and he still moved his arms, but he issued no orders now, too ill, too weary to speak, let alone command.

Wilmot's voice was not what it had been. Before it had been young, younger than his body, and powerful; now it was hoarse, almost plaintive. He, too, was coming to the end of his tether. The cold was a dull pain in his body, a pain no longer identifiable as mere cold, but a body-possessing anguish that never ended, not restricted to a limb or a joint or to any part of the body, but a part of his being. It was killing them all no less surely than a fire kills a man who is roasted over its flames, and just as painfully. The temperature had fallen to twenty-five degrees Fahrenheit; there were now seven degrees of frost.

They rested. The rests were tending to become longer and more frequent, and now it was always Wilmot who lashed them back into activity like a sadistic galley-master. "Right, now! Sing! Don't loll about like a lot of old women."

Roll out the barrel, we'll have a barrel of fun,
Roll out the barrel, we've got the blues on the run.

"MOVE, I say, MOVE!"

Sing, boom, ta-ra-ll, pour out a glass of good cheer,
Now we're going to roll the barrel, 'cos the gang's all here.

"The gang's all flippin' 'ere all right," Barraclough said when the verse ended. The wind snatched at his voice but Wilmot heard and said, "What's the matter, Barraclough?"
"Let's 'ave a decent song, Chief, for cryin' out loud."
"What d'you mean, a decent song?"
Their voices were weak and they could only just hear each other above the wind. Ainslee stirred, listening.

We'eer 'ast'a bin sin' I saw thee?
On Ilkley Moor baht'at.
We'eer 'ast'a bin sin' I saw thee?
We'eer 'ast'a bin sin' I saw thee?
On Ilkley Moor baht'at!
On Ilkley Moor baht'at!
On Ilkley Moor baht'at!

They all sang and when they had worked their way through the interminable verses they rested again. Barraclough still retained the most energy, the greatest apparent reserve of strength, but even he was silenced by the effort of recounting the morbid cycle of Ilkley Moor.

Of the seven men in the raft no close friend or relation was aware of their predicament but Third Officer Gwendoline Baker who worked in the Plot in Liverpool. She might not have known that Mallet-Jones still survived, freezing to death in a Carley raft, but she would have known that *Conway* had been sunk; of this Mallet-Jones was quite certain. And knowing this would also have understood that the possibility of his being still alive was remote.

The ghastly signals, duplicated in blurring purple print, would themselves have fluttered on to her desk—first, the sighting report, and then, almost immediately afterwards, Ainslee's laconic communication, "Am engaging the enemy." Mallet-Jones wondered what those in the Operations Room had said when they had received this second signal: "What with?" as likely as not.

His speculation on Gwen's knowledge began to occupy the whole of his attention. She would have waited after the arrival of the two signals, waited for some other message that neither she nor anyone else could ever have believed possible. But she would have waited, nonetheless. Finally, despondent (he felt no conceit in seeing her despondent), immune to the mumbled words of encouragement or even, by now, commiseration, she would have walked back to the wrennery.

When she reached her room he saw her more clearly than ever before, shining in his darkness. Two tears gathered in the corners of his eyes to be swept away repeatedly by the sea. His lips moved, "Oh God! Oh God, Gwen, come to me!"

She began to undress in the cold room. "Why haven't I cried? Aren't I supposed to cry?" She removed what was left of her make-up at the mirror above the wash-basin and tried, deliberately, to cry and found herself tearless, like a stone. "Why now? Why me? We were going to be married; God, we were already married. Why do I have to know and no one else?"

"Gwen, Gwen, my darling, come to me."

She hated those who were yet spared the pain of knowing. She moved quickly towards the bed and it suddenly seemed thoughtless, unmindful of the dead, to get within its warmth and comfort. "I loved him and he loved me and now he is dead." Her whole body shuddered and she wanted to stand all night in the concrete chill.

"Come to me, Gwen: please come to me!"

She kneeled by the side of the bed. "We were going to be married and my name was to be Mrs. Peter Mallet-Jones and one day when the war was over we were going to have a house and children and we'd even thought of their names." She caught sight of her uniform lying on the chair where she had dropped it and hated it with a peculiar intensity. "Dear God, will it always be like this?"

"Gwen, Gwen, come to me, Gwen. I love you. Please come to me."

She sat on the edge of the bed and pulled the taut sheets and blankets away from the pillow and pushed her feet under them until the whole of her body was in the bed and her face and fair flowing hair on the pillow. She lay still and rigid and then, slowly at first, the tears came, creeping in a glistening sheet over her white face. "Darling. Where are you, my darling? I love you. I love you. I love you."

In the screaming darkness Mallet-Jones held her in his arms and kissed her and protected her with his body from the wind and the sea.

"Sing," Wilmot shouted, "Sing, damn you!"

> You take the high road and I'll take the low road,
> And I'll be in Scotland before you,
> Where me and my true love for ever want to be,
> On the bonnie, bonnie banks of Loch Lomond.

Reggie now sat in a foetal attitude with a suspicion of a grin on his face. He saw, constantly now, not his mother (as his mother would profoundly have hoped) or his father or his aunts or any of the people he had known as a child or a youth, however good or kind or loving or forbearing they had been, but a little bit of a girl he had met in a dance hall in Liverpool, a slight, pretty child with a thick Lancashire accent and a mass of red hair and adolescent breasts that had pushed disturbingly against his jumper. After the dance, before she had disappeared into the mêlée of the Ladies' Cloakroom, he had asked with trepidation in his heart, "Can I see you home?" and she had answered, "If you like. O.K."

He had held her hand as they had walked along the drab, wet streets until they had come to the terrace dwelling that was her parents' home, and hers, too, until she was able to leave it with someone like Reggie. They had stopped in a nearby shop doorway (or rather Reggie had stopped and she had not appeared reluctant to stay with him) and he had leaned against the door with his cap flat aback and held her and kissed her hungrily. The recollection of the taste of her lipstick-perfumed mouth made him grin now like a frozen Cheshire cat, as if he were going mad with the memory of it. "You're a one, that you are," she had said, and the sentiment had pleased him.

When his hand had wandered down her frock and on to her thighs he had dreaded the anticipated refusal, but when his fingers had encountered the elastic barrier she had only pressed herself more closely against him. There had been some delay while he had fought wildly with the abominably unfamiliar female clothing but somehow he had inserted his hand inside it and she had moaned, "There, darling, there!" and Reggie had known a kind of ecstatic lust which he would never forget. "There, darling, there!" had been the measure of his triumph.

Later, she had said, "I shall 'ave to go in now or me Dad'll be after me."

Conway sailed the following day.

Now he sat in the raft with the stupid grin on his frozen face, seeing and feeling the only girl he had ever known, a little slip of a thing with red hair, small breasts, a Lancashire accent and not much sense. She was the token by which he would remember the world. He knew an immeasurable sadness. The pictures and sensations ceased and he pitched forward on to Ainslee's legs.

"Chief," Ainslee shouted in agony, "Get him off my legs, for the love of God get him off!"

Wilmot struggled with Reggie's body in the moving raft and let it fall at Ainslee's side. He stooped and put his fingers on Reggie's wrist and said, not wonderingly this time, nor even sadly, but with a fierce finality, "He's dead, sir . . . Like the boy, he's dead!"

They did not hesitate to take Reggie's clothes; they were bigger and offered more protection than those of the boy. Like body-snatchers, they were becoming accustomed to their trade. And at last Wilmot had a coat.

Barraclough sang plaintively:

> Mother, may I go out dancing,
> Yes, my darling daughter.
> Mother, may I go romancing,
> Yes, my darling daughter . . .

SIXTEEN

04.00

JACOBSON stood on the port hand of his bridge, deep in thought.
It was near to the time now; soon he would need to begin his
search. His resolve had not weakened during the night, nor,
indeed, had his confidence. But he found himself becoming
increasingly obsessed with the possibility, the fear of failure. The
necessity of finding the men had assumed a position of such overwhelming importance in his mind that the mere thought of
failure was intolerable. Yet the thought was there all the time,
never going away, exhausting him more than all the days and
nights of standing on his bridge.

He sighed in the darkness, reluctant to look even at the dim
binnacle light for fear of losing a little of his ability to see in the
dark. It was almost four o'clock. At four o'clock the watches
would change and all now awake would then sleep; all, that is,
except Jacobson and his insoluble problem. He sighed again,
a short, explosive exhalation of breath in the racket of the night.
Another hour, two or three, perhaps, and it would be over. But
what would he do if, in that time, he failed to find his men? Or
if he found them dead of the sea and the unbearable cold?

He did not know and the realisation that he did not know
terrified him.

Busk glanced at his still form, a bulbous, distant shadow, and
considered speaking to him. But the little man was unbearable,
snapping and complaining when he was not wrapped in his
unapproachable silence. *Oleron* and her strange Captain were
beginning to get on Busk's nerves. Here they were, up to their
necks in the most perilous exercise imaginable, an exercise which
they had all—or nearly all—supported once Jacobson had
explained himself and his plan, and all he, Jacobson, could do
was to stand like a corpulent statue on the far side of the bridge.

"What's the matter with him? What's he got to be so silent
about?"

Busk braced himself as the ship tried to stand on her nose and then lifted herself slowly under a nearly intolerable weight of water.

"Why doesn't he talk? Just say something? Does he think he doesn't need us? I don't think we're going to find these men. Harris was right; he must be touched. I'm not going to put up with this for much longer. Somebody will have to stop him. Suppose we come across a U-boat, what then? Christ, what are we going to do?"

Busk's scalp began to crawl and the sudden coldness in the small of his back caused his whole body to twitch.

II

Dawson's wrist-watch alarm buzzed as the bridge messenger knocked on his cabin door, opened it, entered, and found only an empty uncrumpled bunk and no Second Mate. He retreated, nonplussed. Dawson slid off Gerda's bunk and stilled the alarm all in the same movement and sat for a moment with his head in his hands. Then he dressed rapidly.

Gerda looked up at him and smiled sleepily, her body moving slowly as the ship tilted rhythmically. He said to her, "Gerda, I want you to get up and dress and put on your life-jacket. You're not to take it off until I tell you to. If anything happens come to the bridge. O.K.?"

She smiled and stretched her long body under the sheet. "Yes, I understand."

When he was dressed he leaned over her and put his arms about her shoulders and pulled her towards him. "I don't want to lose you," he said. "I've only just found you and I don't want to lose you."

He felt the desire rising inside him and knew he should go now if the going were to be easily accomplished. He put his lips against her ear, "Remember what I've told you, Gerda. If anything happens, come for me before you do anything else."

She moved her lips against his stubbled cheek. "I shall come for you, my darling."

He put on his coat and gloves and when he was ready to leave he said, "This Captain, he's a funny little guy. There's no knowing what he'll do next. You see, he wants to find these men. Somehow, he's *got* to find them. Something's eating him, making him go back even though he knows—he must know, damn it—that he'll never find 'em. Don't ask me why he should do this. He ain't even officially in the war. Maybe he's just a bit crazy. Maybe we're all a bit crazy. Then, perhaps he *will* find 'em. His kind of dumbness—which isn't so dumb—sometimes pays off."

Gerda watched with wide eyes, understanding only a little of what he was saying half to himself, "I shall come for you," she said.

III

Albert Reed listened to the engines thudding in his pillow, then opened his eyes and looked at his watch. He could hear Alice in the bunk below him, the cycle of her breathing a shorter, sharper sequence than the creaking of *Oleron*'s bones. The waves thumping against the bow made the ship sound like a hollow shell, as if someone were beating an immense empty tank with a sledge-hammer.

He wondered whether to get up or not. It had been his intention to leave his bunk once the ship reached the search area, but he was warm and comfortable and the thought of going out into the night was not a welcome prospect. For some time he watched his coat alternatively hanging perpendicular and then rigidly lifting itself away from the door, like an endlessly repeated trick of levitation. He made up his mind suddenly, swung his legs over the edge of the bunk and dropped awkwardly to the deck.

He began to dress and, although he made no noise, Alice opened her eyes. "Are you off, Albert?" she asked.

Albert nodded as he pulled on his trousers, hopping about like a drunken stork in the centre of the cabin. "Aye, might as well see what I can do."

"Be careful, lad, won't you? There's no need to take risks."

"Now, you go to sleep, Alice. There's no occasion for you to get up for hours yet, and you know you can't see in the dark."

"No. I can't see in the dark at all. Albert, I do hope the Captain finds those men."

"He'll find them. Whatever else they say about him he's a sticker." He tied his boot laces and stood up. "Well, I'm ready. You go to sleep now."

Alice closed her eyes. "Take care, won't you? Keep yourself well wrapped up. It's bitter outside."

"Aye, I'll keep myself wrapped up. Go to sleep now."

On his way to the bridge he passed the cabins of Harris and Stockmann. He did not think to wake them. But even if he had he would probably have said that at a time like this sleeping dogs were best left undisturbed.

IV

Goldstein twitched in the sick-bay chair, his fat thighs quivering convulsively as if he were in the middle of an erotic nightmare. Once a beatific smile passed over his slack features. His head was thrown back and his mouth open. Once every five minutes his mouth closed and he swallowed wetly and the sound was like the sound in miniature of the sea sucking against *Oleron*'s sides.

Lord Birkenhead lay on his back with his eyes open, the deck-head light casting pools of brilliance on his skin. His head might have been cast in black metal. The bandages about his neck shone against the blackness, focusing attention on the weakness in the indestructible strength.

"Goldie."

Goldstein snorted and shifted the position of his body.

"Goldie!" Birkenhead's voice was stronger now, less laboured, and some of its magnificent resonance was returning.

Again Goldstein stirred but did not wake.

"Goldie!"

Goldstein might have been stroked with an electrically charged wire. His arms and legs were pushed in front of his body and for a moment he balanced precariously on the fulcrum of his bottom. "Birk? Did you call, Birk? What is it?"

Birkenhead spoke gently, as he would speak to a child. "Nothing, Goldie. Nothing. Ah just wanted a drink. Can you get me a drink of water, Goldie?"

Goldstein was on his feet immediately, splashing water into the tumbler and crossing to the bunk. "Sure, Birk. Sure. Here y'are, Birk. Got it? Jesus, you gave me a fright."

Birkenhead drank the water slowly and returned the empty tumbler to Goldstein's hovering hand. "We must be nearly there now."

"There? Where?"

"Where dese guys are in de water."

188

"Oh, yeah. Yeah, I guess we're nearly there, now, Birk."

"What time is it?"

"Soon be five o'clock."

"Ah don't know how de Skipper thinks he can find anyone on a night like dis. Can't you hear dem waves, man?"

"Yeah, I can 'ear 'em."

"You know sumpin', Goldie? I guess de Skipper's hoping for a miracle."

"D'you reckon it's dangerous?"

Birkenhead slowly nodded his massive head against the pillow. "It's dangerous, boy."

"What we doin' 'ere, then?"

"Looking for dese men."

"Yeah, I forgot. We're lookin' for these poor bastards in the drink. Like the Skipper said."

"That's right."

Goldstein sat in his chair again and when Birkenhead closed his eyes the words dropped like stones into pools of silence: "Birk! All this stuff about miracles. It's all crap, ain't it?"

"What do you think?"

"I'm askin' you."

"Ah reckon miracles can happen, Goldie. Like ah told you."

"Yeah?"

"Do you?"

"Me? That kid's stuff. Not me."

Birkenhead smiled and closed his eyes again and before many more waves had thrown themselves in tumult against *Oleron*'s bow, Goldstein was asleep.

v

Corridon's eyes burned redly in the darkness above his bunk. His hand was too painful for him to be able to sleep and his mind was a turmoil of hate. He was filled with a pitiless ire and his childlike need for violence was a need for fulfilment. He lay like a wounded animal intent on the elimination of his enemies, Birkenhead and Dawson. Now he was biding his time. Soon, when he was rested, when the hatred within him had risen to unbearable heights, he would leave his lair and stalk them and pounce on them and eventually kill them.

A tear rolled down his thin fox face and he wiped it away with the tip of the index finger of his good hand.

VI

"Mr. Dawson?"

"Sir?"

"Reduce speed to eight knots."

"Reduce speed to eight knots, sir."

Jacobson held himself erect. "We shall commence our search."

"Aye, aye, sir."

The telegraphs jangled in the depths of the ship and the bow sank a little lower in the water and the distant thunder of the engines became instead a rhythmic thumping.

Jacobson gripped the bridge rail and stared into the night and said silently to himself, "Oh God, let me not fail these men. If You are merciful, let me not fail them."

PART FOUR

PART FOUR

SEVENTEEN

05.00

IN the raft the singing had stopped. The men huddled about Ainslee, their bodies pressed heavily against the shifting wet heaps of dead flesh and bones that had been the boy and Reggie. They heard Ainslee's voice from far away, a hoarse monotonous whisper in the wind. "We've got to sing. Sing! We've got to keep singing. Do you hear that? And we've got to move. We've . . . got . . . to . . . keep . . . moving. We're freezing! Freezing to death! Sing . . . and . . . move . . . and sing . . ." The men paid no need. They were no more able to sing than Ainslee, for all his strength. Not even Wilmot could sing now.

The raft plunged and gyrated, shipped and unshipped water, rode the wave crests like an obese surfboard, wallowed in the troughs like a dead duck in a millrace, yet still remained afloat, a ghostly vessel unbowed by the tumult. And the men sailed with it, inseparable, even in death.

Distantly, bubbling in the cold spray's hiss and the universal roar of water, Oliphant heard the sound of his own voice. "I can hear you," it said quietly, almost reasonably, but the sound of it rising, "I can hear you going on and on about singing and moving but I've finished singing and moving. I'm never going to sing again whatever anybody says. How do you like that, eh?"

No one heard him for nothing occurred beyond a rasping passage of air through paralysed membrane. "How do you like that, Ainslee? You make me think of all the managers I've ever had. Oliphant . . . er . . . yes . . . Oliphant . . . sorry to say this . . . your work . . . not up to standard, is it? . . . don't get on with your colleagues, do you? . . . Are you happy at home? . . . No problems? Ha! That's . . . what they asked . . . patronising. . . . Scream inside my head until I thought my head . . . burst. . . . Want to hit him . . . but said, always said, 'Yes, sir . . . sorry, sir.'

"But not any more. Christ, not any more. Not even for you, Ainslee. I'm too tired and I'm too cold."

By a superhuman effort of will he rose up in the raft and leaned over Ainslee and screamed. He screamed as he had always wanted to scream: abandoned, bereft now of even that modicum of control that had always saved him before. But he uttered no sound. Wilmot looked up slowly and saw the dim shape jerking over Ainslee and then falling upon him, the two bodies indistinguishable in the darkness and the hammering spray. He heard Ainslee grunting and shouting and finally screaming as Oliphant's weight set his broken shin-bones grinding. Wilmot heaved himself to his feet so that he could half stand, half lean over Oliphant and pull at his shoulders. "Oliphant! What're you doing, Oliphant? You're killing him! Get off!"

He leaned all his weight against him but it was insufficient to move Oliphant's flexed body. He was too weak and too cold. He began to beat Oliphant's head with one fist, holding on to his shoulder with the other hand to retain his balance. Oliphant did not even feel the ineffectual blows. Both Mallet-Jones and Barraclough seemed to be asleep, or, if not asleep, then incapable of reaction.

"I'm going to kill you, Ainslee . . ."

Wilmot pounded obdurately at Oliphant's bony head like a blacksmith at an anvil, punctuating the inaudible words.

"Yes, sir. . . . No, sir. . . . Three bags bloody full to overflowing. . . . Kill you, Ainslee."

Wilmot shouted into Oliphant's ear, "You're mad, Oliphant! Insane! Don't you know that? You're *insane*!"

The words, if not the physical violence, penetrated Oliphant's derangement and his hurt face came up into Wilmot's, so close that Wilmot thought he could smell the madness as well as feel it. He stopped hitting him and peered into the unreasoning eyes. Oliphant's lips moved. "You, too? You, too, you bastard?"

Wilmot said, not understanding that Oliphant was attempting to speak, "Steady, man. Try to get a hold of yourself."

Oliphant actually laughed, a choking, indeterminate sound between a sneer and a sob, and swayed to his feet. Wilmot watched him but before he was aware that Oliphant had even moved he felt the hard fingers fastening themselves about his throat; they were surprisingly strong for one who had spent all his life counting money in a bank.

Wilmot threw his superior weight against him, snatching and

jerking at the immovable fingers. Oliphant's strength was the unmanageable strength of madness. The raft swayed as the big waves swept beneath it and the weight within it shifted. Wilmot began to punch Oliphant's stomach. But it was the violence of the raft's movement that granted him a reprieve; perhaps afraid of losing his balance, Oliphant's hands flew from Wilmot's throat and clutched at his clothing. Wilmot sucked air into his body. "Sit down, Oliphant . . . an order! Don't you hear me? . . . Sit down, I said!"

Wilmot was vaguely aware of his feet kicking against dead bodies, of his heels sinking into slack faces, of skin splitting over compressed flesh, vaguely aware, too, that this did not disturb him. His mind was numb as well as his body, and nothing mattered beyond being warm again and controlling Oliphant and not dying.

"You're going to kill us, Oliphant . . . overturn the raft . . . fool. Pushing me overboard. Stop it . . . Christ, Oliphant, sit down!"

He felt Oliphant's breath against his cheek and his sluggish brain registered the fact that it was no warmer than the wind, like air out of a refrigerator.

"Going overboard, Oliphant. . . . Can't hold you. . . . Can't. . . . God . . . can't hold you. . . . Help me! . . . *Look out . . . fool . . . fool . . . fool!*"

Wilmot sank to his knees and at the same time felt his back arching over the bloated hard edge of the raft. Oliphant seized his advantage and flung his wiry weight on top of him.

"Please . . . Oliphant . . . Please . . . Can't hold you."

Wilmot knew he was going to die, and for the most ridiculous of all reasons. The knowledge made him unhappy, no more; it was not insupportable. It was not unnatural that he should die, even stupidly; he simply wished, a little wistfully, never fiercely, that he could have seen Judy again before he died, or his wife who knew nothing of Judy, or even his house by the sea. "Please . . . Please . . . Oliphant."

His body snapped and he felt himself falling as if from a great height, falling for such a length of time that he was able to wonder why the water did not at once engulf him. When he reached it he found it strangely comfortable, like a warm bed. It streamed into his mouth and nose and killed his shouting dead.

He struggled in the water and in due time his life-jacket lifted his head above the waves and he was able to breathe again. Then a wave swept over him and more water ran into his lungs and when he came up again consciousness was almost gone. It was so warm in the water that he closed his eyes to sleep but no sooner did he sleep than another avalanche of water awakened him. "Judy! I'm sorry, Judy. It was wrong. . . . I suppose it was wrong. But it was good while it lasted. Wasn't it? Wasn't it, Judy? I loved you, Judy. Where should we go tonight, this last night? . . . I shall never see you again, Judy . . . Judy . . . Judy. . . ." His head projected momentarily above the water and the wind lashed his face like a many-thonged whip.

He became aware that something was attached to his legs, something that pulled and tugged maddeningly at his ankles. He wished that it would stop, that he could be left alone to sleep and smile to himself in the water and think of Judy in her uniform and Brighton and the promenade on a summer's day, the sound of children and seagulls and the warm touch of sand, the sight of old men selling newspapers and ice-cream and tickets for deck-chairs in the sun, the black pier against the incomparable blue smoothness of the sea and the first time, nervously, half-paternally, he had kissed her. . . . "Judy!"

His face scratched against the harsh side of the raft. This surprised him for by now he should have been a long way from the raft, lost in the night and the mountainous water. His hands sought for the lifelines and found them and when his fingers were fastened about them the tugging weight on his feet was removed and he sank into an upright position alongside the raft.

Hands searched for his and pulled. It took a long time because he was too weak to climb into the raft unaided and the man above not strong enough to pull him in. But together they managed it. He rolled over the raft's edge and lay with the bodies of the boy and Reggie, groaning and retching. When he had finished vomiting water he climbed painfully to his knees and found the face of the man who had saved him and ran his fingers over its shape in the darkness and recognised it. "Where's Oliphant, Barraclough?"

"Christ, Chief . . . you O.K.?"

"Where's Oliphant?"

Barraclough did not answer.

"Where is he?"

"I 'it 'im."

" . . . hit him?"

"I 'ad to, Chief. I 'ad to 'it 'im . . . what else could I do?"

"Where is he, Barraclough?"

" . . . there was nothin' for 'im . . . to 'old on to . . ."

"What . . . happened?"

"'E's gone, Chief . . . gone . . . over the side . . ."

Wilmot panted and his head fell on to his chest. He wondered whether he, like Oliphant, was already mad with the cold. He heard Barraclough's voice breathing into his ear. "Listen, Chief . . . Christ . . . oh, Christ . . . listen!"

Far out among the waves Oliphant had found his voice. "Help! . . . Help me! . . . Don't . . . leave me. God, God, God . . . don't leave me! . . . Don't . . . Jesus, gentle Jesus . . . don't . . ."

The words stopped abruptly and Wilmot looked at Barraclough's invisible face. Barraclough said, "'e took 'is coat with 'im." Wilmot hated Oliphant briefly for his selfishness. Then he lay down with his face against Ainslee's head, his lips touching a cold ear. "You all right, sir? Answer me!"

There was no sound from Ainslee, nor any movement. Wilmot grasped the wet clothing and shook the body inside it. "Answer me, damn you!"

The head turned slowly and the mouth moved and Wilmot put his ear against the whispering lips. "It's . . . no . . . use . . . Chief. God . . . it's . . . no . . . use."

Wilmot was too tired, too numb to answer. His body relaxed and rolled over the boy and before it was still he was asleep.

EIGHTEEN

06.00

THE men of *Oleron* had been searching for an hour and a quarter and they had seen nothing in the night but the white-flecked grey sea. *Oleron* trundled through the water at a reduced speed, breasting the great seas when they were ahead, rolling to them violently when they were abeam, slewing and yawing against them when they were astern. From whatever direction they came they were a mounting source of danger for there was a limit to the pounding *Oleron* could take before her plates buckled before the onslaught and opened themselves yearningly to the sea.

Jacobson had abandoned his customary position and stood now before the compass, his trunk motionless, only his head moving slowly from side to side as if driven by a clockwork motor. His eyes never left the sea except to glance occasionally at the well-deck hatch when the seas were ahead. A look-out had been posted on each wing of the bridge and another at the mast-head. They were changed every fifteen minutes. Dawson stood on the port side of the bridge and Busk on the starboard, both equipped with binoculars which almost never left their eyes. Albert Reed stood to one side of Jacobson and a little behind him, intent, like the others, on the racing sea. The engines were a mere repetitive thump against the soles of aching feet.

Oleron, conned by Jacobson, steamed in expanding squares, doggedly moving round the perimeter of an ever-widening box. The system worked only as long as *Oleron* was not deflected from her rigid course. But since she was undoubtedly deflected, large areas of sea inevitably remained unscrutinised. But it was the best that *Oleron* or her Captain or her Second Mate or any of the men on her bridge could do. There was no other way.

During the middle watch Jacobson had decided upon the courses to be steered when the search area was reached and had calculated the times when each alteration of course would be made. The courses were 040 degrees, 130 degrees, 220 degrees and 310 degrees, a right angle between each, together a box.

Jacobson had jotted down on a piece of paper the precise sequence of times and this, at progressively greater intervals, he consulted in the binnacle-light. His high-pitched voice ordering each change of course and the quartermaster's hoarse reply were the only words spoken; Jacobson's quick inclination over the compass and the quartermaster's rapid turning of the wheel, the only movement. *Oleron*'s bow would begin to turn into or away from the seas and the new course would be announced. Then, once more, the silence amid the uproar, the stillness amid the violence.

The quartermaster was relieved each half-hour and during his trick dared not remove his attention from the compass; each time the wind or the sea hurled *Oleron* off course he unconsciously braced himself to receive the brunt of Jacobson's wrath. But it never came; Jacobson understood the futility of commenting upon the inevitable. He would only complain when the quartermaster did less well than he himself could do.

"Steer 040."

"040, sir."

Oleron turned and the seas thundered against the starboard bow. She rolled, as Dawson put it, like a whore in bed. The seconds passed and then the minutes and then the quarter-hours. The look-outs and the quartermasters relieved each other, and then again. Soon they had been trundling round their box for two hours, and the tension had become an electric, tangible thing, born of a search in which none but one man now believed, and he fanatically, irrationally.

Albert Reed began to think that Jacobson was growing smaller. The erect stance was still there, the head held just as stubbornly, but the little man was shrinking within his heavy clothing. He seemed to order the next change of course in a smaller, less vital voice. When the alteration had been made and the quarter-master had reported *Oleron* on her new course, Jacobson passed his finger tips over his forehead, a gesture he had not used since the search began. Albert wondered if it indicated the point where Jacobson's determination began to ebb, as, in the end, it must. He said, "Don't worry, lad." The words were out of his mouth before he could stop them, but Jacobson looked round and Albert assumed that he smiled in the darkness for he did not snap as earlier he would have snapped but answered gravely, gratefully, "Thank you."

Jacobson was finding it difficult to think. He saw his ship and he saw the seas pounding themselves against her sides and he saw the shapes of the men about him, and realised with a spurt of terror that there were moments when he actually forgot what they were all trying to do. He shook his head but it only increased the pain above his eyes. He mumbled, "If only I were not so tired. I should have slept earlier. I had time to sleep then. I should have slept for an hour."

A familiar voice sliced through his meandering mind. "Sir."

Jacobson tried to focus his attention upon the detested sound. "Hm?"

"Sir."

"Yes, Mr. Busk?"

"There's no sign of them."

"No, not yet."

"May I have permission to go below, sir?"

"No, Mr. Busk, you may not."

Busk walked towards Jacobson, speaking with a mock reasonableness. "But this is silly, sir. We'll never find anybody. The weather's getting worse. Just look at it! We'll steam in circles for ever. Don't you think you ought to give up, sir?"

Jacobson was alive to his danger and answered without hesitation, "Return to your position, Mr. Busk."

"But . . ."

"You hear my order, Mr. Busk?"

"Yes, I hear you. But I still say it's bloody silly. We've done our best. Why can't we pack it in now?"

Jacobson was almost speechless. He moved towards Busk's dark shape and looked into the narrow, denture-slit face. "Be silent," he squeaked. "Obey my orders and be silent."

Busk said deliberately, "Don't you know what danger we're in? Damn it, don't you know? Haven't you ever heard of U-boats?"

Dawson called quietly, "Drop it, Busk."

Busk flared back, "You keep out of this. Who do you . . ."

"I said be silent," Jacobson squeaked again.

Busk muttered, "What're you trying to prove, Captain. That men don't die when they're frozen to death?"

Jacobson trembled with consternation. He lifted one short arm, for the first time in his life aching to knock a set of false teeth down a man's throat.

Dawson called, "Take my place, Reed." Albert hurried to Dawson's position and Dawson ran across the bridge to Jacobson and Busk.

"Listen, Busk. You may be the First Mate but you obey the Captain. I'm telling you because I intend to see that you do."

As he spoke he saw the lurking, curiously beseeching fear in Busk's face, the fear that could so easily become contagious and uncontrollable.

Busk breathed, "Get stuffed!"

Dawson thrust his head down towards Busk. "Say that again! Go on, just say it again! Because if you do I'll break you in two."

Busk held his ground. For a moment it seemed that he would, indeed, say it again. Instead, he said quietly, "All right, Dawson. And you too, sir. If we ever get out of this mess, which I doubt, I'll see to it that you never go to sea again. Just remember what I've said, that's all."

Dawson did not move his head away from Busk's face. "Get going, Buster."

Busk stared into the big face, then turned rapidly and walked back to his station. Dawson returned to the port side of the bridge. Jacobson plodded towards the binnacle, an old man now, weak with worry, weariness and disappointment. He fumbled for his piece of paper in his pocket, consulted it, and ordered a further change of course.

Jacobson said to himself, "As long as I have Dawson I shall be all right. But if I should lose him . . .?"

His speculation was interrupted by the urgent voice of the starboard look-out. "Something on the starboard side, sir! Something moving!"

NINETEEN

07.00

IT was Barraclough who discovered that Mallet-Jones was dead.

"Mallet-Jones," he had called, "Mallet-Jones! What's up, Mallet-Jones?"

When Wilmot had collapsed beside Ainslee, Barraclough was the only man still conscious, the only man in the raft not dead or nearly dead. He discovered quite suddenly that no one remained to whom he could speak and that the only apparently living things were the wind and the sea and these avid for his destruction. He scrambled over the accumulated bodies in the bottom of the raft towards Mallet-Jones, took his icy face in his hands and tried to see its dead-whiteness in the night, and when he could see only a shadow between his unfeeling palms, he shook it violently. There was no response and when Barraclough released the face, the head fell forward and the weight of it overturned the body so that all of Mallet-Jones tumbled stiffly on to the floorboards and caused the raft to sway as it passed through a wave-trough. Barraclough bent over him, aghast, afraid now, feeling for the half-submerged face in the sucking, regurgitating water and shouting, "Mallet-Jones, for flip's sake, wake up! Jones, I'm talkin' to you!"

His hands ran over Mallet-Jones's body, trying to identify the frozen components. He whimpered as he searched. "Mallet-Jones, wake up! Wake up, Mallet-Jones! And then, suddenly, viciously, "You're dead! You're dead like all the rest! You're dead, Mallet-Jones!" Finally, the return of grief and unutterable disappointment. "Why are you dead, Mallet-Jones?"

He knelt by the dead body and flung his arms about his own frozen trunk and worked them backwards and forwards until he thought he might faint with the effort. "I'm cold. I'm so cold, it's killin' me, too. It's freezin' me blood. Christ, I'm cold!" He began to remove Mallet-Jones's coat and as his frost-bitten fingers worked at the buttons he saw for the thousandth time the procession of pictures that had passed through his mind all night: his sister, the children he had known at school who were all men and women now, the shop where he had bought sweets on rare occasions, which was also the living-room of an almost uncountable family and where the sweets were kept in bottles on the sideboard with a coloured picture of the Crucifixion and an advertisement for cigarettes, his father and his father's bucolic employer who drank too much and paid too little but who was a gentleman for all that—or so they said, those who were able to recognise a gentleman when they saw one—and his mother's face whenever he had come home on leave, full of love and a hopeless, crumbling emptiness, knowing him and yet not knowing him. "Oh, Mammy, Mammy, Mammy! They're all dead! I'm 'ere all alone. I want you, Mammy! Save me, Mammy!"

He remembered the village in the sun in the summer-time and the conical sludge-grey slag-heaps in the winter, and men with smiles on red-lipped black faces cycling home from the pits. He remembered the school and the church he had never attended and the way other people dressed themselves up on Sundays. And more than anything he remembered the girl in the village to whom he had written, awkwardly, arduously, ever since he had left home; a well-built, rosy-cheeked daughter of a farm labourer. They had never found a great deal to say to each other but he had always felt strangely at peace in her company; he had lain for hours in fields with her, not speaking to her, not even looking at her, but gently touching her until he wanted to go on touching her for the rest of his life. Only once had things gone further than this and he had immediately regretted it. But she had submitted readily enough, as if she, too, had been anxious for the experience and could think of no sensible reason to refuse. "Madge! I'll never see you again, Madge! Where are you, Madge? Let me touch you, Madge; just once. You're beautiful, Madge . . . beautiful . . ."

He was angry again, still kneeling in the raft and shouting into the wind, "Christ, why didn't anybody come back for us? Why didn't any bastard look? You, you in your warm ships, leaving us when you could've come back! Bastards! Didn't you think? Didn't you think of anybody but the'selves? Christ, didn't you think we might be 'ere? Didn't you? We'd 'ave come for thee. The Skipper'd've come for thee. 'E wouldn't 'ave left you like this!"

He seemed to become aware that he was shouting and stopped abruptly and began to whimper again, a sound scarcely audible above the wind. "I'm not going to die! D'you 'ear? I'm stronger than they are, a lot stronger an' I'm not going to kick the bucket, I'm not, I tell thee . . ." He struggled into Mallet-Jones's jacket. "Look, I'm a bleedin' officer now!"

He dragged himself over the bodies again, still whimpering, pulling on two coats over Mallet-Jones's jacket. Once he lost his balance and rolled among the bodies and lay in the rising, falling water long enough to want to close his eyes and never open them again. But he roused himself and moved towards Wilmot's bulk. He leaned over the slack face and slapped it repeatedly. "Chief! Wake up, Chief! Not you, too? Wilmot! Don't die! Don't leave me! The skipper said you'll die if you sleep an' 'e's right. Wake up, Chief! Don't leave me!"

He began to pant. He hit Wilmot's unflinching face again and again and when he still did not move or speak or show any sign of life he took his shoulders and shook the corpulent middle-aged body until the head bumped against the boards of the raft. *"Chief! For the love of Christ, wake up!"*

Wilmot stirred. "What's . . . matter? I was . . . sleeping."

Barraclough was beside himself. "We're dying, Chief. Sit up! You'll die if you lie there." He grasped the front of Wilmot's jacket and shouted into his face, "Get up, Chief. *Get up, get up, get up!*"

Wilmot struggled and Barraclough helped him. They slipped and fell over the bodies and lost their balance in the heeling raft but eventually Wilmot rose to a kneeling position and waited for Barraclough, the new leader, to tell him what to do.

"Wake the Skipper," Barraclough shouted. "We've got . . . wake him."

Without waiting for Wilmot, Barraclough threw himself over Ainslee in a paroxysm of anxiety. "Captain! Captain! You've got to wake up! Understand? Wake up, I . . . say! Wake . . . up . . ."

Wilmot tried to move his arms, returning slowly from his dream world of warmth. "What's . . . the . . . matter with him?"

Barraclough stopped shouting and his head turned towards Wilmot, "He's dead, Chief. T'Skipper's dead. That's what's the flippin' matter. He's dead!"

Wilmot wanted to cry. All Ainslee's efforts had been to no

avail. In Ainslee Wilmot saw not only the man but the Service of which he was a part; Ainslee's death was partly his own. He said, as if it were an epitaph, "He was a good Captain." And Barraclough answered, as if it were a response, "Sometimes I 'ated 'is guts, but 'e were a good Skipper."

They waited on their knees and the frost ate further into their bones. Later, Barraclough said, "Got to sing, Chief . . . got . . . sing!"

They sank down among the corpses and Barraclough began this song, perhaps because his mother had crooned it to him as a child, before she became feeble-minded.

> Old soldiers never die, never die, never die,
> Old soldiers never die, they simply fade away.

They shouted aloud their quenchless hope of living and the sound of their voices was snatched by the wind and broadcast over the desolation of the sea.

> Old soldiers never die, never die, never die.
> Old soldiers never die, they simply fade away.

Barraclough yelled to Wilmot in an ecstasy of survival, "*And again, Chief. And again, by Christ, again!*"

> Old soldiers never die, never die, never die,
> Old soldiers never die, they simply fade away.

TWENTY

THE men on *Oleron*'s bridge turned as one man towards the look-out's distant cry. Jacobson ran on short legs down the tilting deck to the starboard wing and forced his way into the howling sea-wet wind. He leaned over the look-out's shoulder. "Where? What is it? Where?"

The look-out pointed a gloved hand a few degrees abaft the beam. Jacobson jerked his glasses to his eyes again and fiercely examined the sea. "Where? Where man? I see nothing."

The look-out peered hopefully through his glasses in the same direction, hiding his puzzled but still righteous expression behind his thick gloves. Whatever he had seen was no longer in view. Jacobson shouted, "Spare look-out?"

No one answered.

Jacobson shouted again, imperiously, his voice rising, "Spare look-out?"

A man came running. "Sir?"

"Take over." Jacobson tapped the shoulder of the existing look-out. "You, you come with me."

"Yes, sir."

Jacobson marched inboard, followed by the shambling look-out whose body was grotesquely bulbous in its protective clothing. Jacobson resumed his position before the wheel and waited for the man to attempt a position of attention.

"Well," he snapped, "What did you see?"

Busk edged towards them, the teeth in his half-open mouth glinting in the darkness.

The man was Swedish and replied in his own tongue.

"What does he say?" Busk demanded.

Jacobson ignored Busk and asked a further question. The answer came with a disturbing certainty; the man was very sure of himself.

"What does he say, sir?" Busk demanded again. There was the slightest edge of hysteria in his voice.

Jacobson's voice piped, "Emergency full ahead."

"Emergency full ahead, sir."

The telegraph sounded. Jacobson said to the look-out, "Return to your duties. Perhaps you have done well." The man hurried away, thankful to be no longer the focus of so much attention. Jacobson pushed Busk from his path and snatched the engine-room telephone from the bulkhead.

"You'll smash up the ship," Busk complained. "What are you trying to do?" But Jacobson was shouting into the receiver and all that Busk heard above the sound of his own voice was the repeated, insistent word, "Speed . . . speed . . . Chief . . . speed!"

Jacobson banged down the receiver and glared at Busk with blood-shot eyes. "Yes?"

"What did the look-out say, sir? Surely, as the First Officer of this ship I have a right to know."

Jacobson turned half-away from him, resuming his station before the wheel. "He thinks, Mr. Busk, he saw the conning-tower of a U-boat."

"But aren't you going to alter course?"

Jacobson squared his plump shoulders and momentarily closed his eyes. "No."

"But the U-boat?"

Wearily: "We shall see about the U-boat—later."

Busk exploded, "But don't you understand the thing's hostile? It's out to get us! My God, where've you bin all this war? Don't you know there's a war on?"

Jacobson answered with deceptive patience, "At the moment, Mr. Busk, we steam away from the U-boat. At full speed. It does not matter in which direction we steam, we steam away from it. In a little while we shall turn but still we shall be steaming away from it. And I am aware there is a war on."

"But then," Busk persisted, "when you alter course again, and again? Then we shall be steaming towards it!"

"Let us wait and see, should we?"—and then, quietly furious, "*Let us wait and see.*"

Dawson had not entered into the altercation with Busk; Jacobson would have liked to have known what Dawson thought of the matter but shrank from questioning him.

"Mr. Dawson?"

"Sir?"

"Can a U-boat overtake us under water?"

"Not at this speed, sir."

"At what speed can a U-boat move under the water?"

"Maybe seven knots, not much more."

"It follows, then, that if it pursues us, it must pursue on the surface?"

"Right first time, Captain."

"I thought U-boats submerged in this kind of weather."

"They do, usually."

"Could it be, then, that this one is already damaged, unable to submerge?"

"Could be, Captain. Could be."

"But we cannot be certain?"

"No."

"Mr. Busk?"

"Sir?"—a very surly 'sir'.

"Warn the look-outs to keep a close watch astern."

"Sir."

"And, Mr. Busk?"

"Yes?"

"Report to me afterwards."

Almost inaudibly, "Yes, sir."

It was the episode of the torpedoes all over again: indisputable evidence of danger only spurred him on, galvanised him into greater irrationality. Or was it simply that he would not submit to the sea or anything that went upon it or even under it? It was possible to adumbrate a dozen theories—and Albert Reed did— but not even Jacobson could have said which one held the greater truth.

II

In the raft Wilmot was sustained by Barraclough. He sat with his head held against his bent knees, taking the force of the wind and the water on his back where, he believed, there was a hole like a wind-dug crater. The wind was funnelled into the crater, freezing his lungs and his stomach until there was nothing in his consciousness but the pain of being cold irradiating from the crater in his back. His body was older than Barraclough's, already partly worn. Now, its power to survive was spent; not even the desire to be warm again remained. He could not live without Barraclough and Barraclough could not live for long: ten minutes, perhaps; fifteen; half an hour; not more.

Wilmot wore Ainslee's jacket now: a Captain RN and a Lieutenant RNVR adrift with four nude bodies. Barraclough held Ainslee's duffel coat about their shoulders so that it added some protection to their backs. Wilmot could not feel it.

Barraclough shouted, was certain that he shouted, but only whispered, infinitely slowly, "Come on, Chief. Got to sing." Wilmot's greying head moved feebly. The raft swept up to the peak of a flying wave and swooped down its other side, drowning them in frozen spray.

Barraclough sang, followed by Wilmot: two cracked, feeble voices, dirge-like, dwindling,

> All people that on earth do dwell,
> Sing to the Lord with cheerful voice,
> Him serve with fear, His praise forth tell,
> Come ye before Him and rejoice.

III

Harris and Stockmann appeared on the bridge simultaneously and Stockmann announced their presence by querulously demanding, "Well, what is happening?"

When no one answered, Stockmann repeated his question. Jacobson turned and glowered at him. Curiously, it was Albert Reed who dealt with him, a tough, uncompromising Albert who might have been dealing with two of his mill-hands. "If you chaps want to help, you'd best get one each side of the bridge and act as look-outs unless the Captain has other plans for you. If you don't want to do that, then get out't'road." Albert's colloquialism was growing dangerously; its appearance was like the hoisting of a flag, denoting determination, a total absence of inclination to suffer opposition.

"Did you hear that?" Stockmann asked Jacobson.

"Yes, I heard," Jacobson said.

"I'm glad you heard," Stockmann retorted. "It all adds to the evidence against you, Captain."

Dawson crossed the bridge and stood furiously before Stockmann. "Did you get what Reed said? Did it penetrate that thick skull of yours?"

"How dare you speak to me like this?"

"Did you hear, I said?"

"Yes, of course I heard. I'm not deaf."

Dawson roared into his face, "Then do it! On the double. Either do it, or beat it!"

The unexpected ferocity of Dawson's attack left Stockmann momentarily speechless, an unusual condition. Harris said plaintively, "Come on, Stockmann. We'd better try and help."

"I shall report you too, Dawson," Stockmann spluttered.

"Do that," Dawson answered.

"Come on," Harris urged.

Stockmann allowed Harris to lead him to the starboard wing of the bridge and when Harris turned to leave, Stockmann said urgently, "No, stay here, Harris. Do not leave me alone. You will be of no use over there, not with one eye. It is safer if we stay here together. I am not always like this; it's just . . . the . . . fear . . ."

Harris shrugged and stayed with him.

Every male passenger and deck officer was now on the bridge. Eight-and-a-half pairs of eyes gazed searchingly into the spray as *Oleron* plodded doggedly about her growing box. And no one saw anything but an infinity of water, a grey, foam-slicked moving wilderness.

IV

In the raft Wilmot was sustained in Barraclough's arms. He saw in the dimness of his mind his first meeting with Judy on Brighton pier and heard the cry of the child who had rolled its ball under their seat and brought about the conversation that had trapped them in a futureless love, he, a middle-aged Chief Petty Officer with a wife and no children, she a desirable thirty, her husband dead at Dunkirk.

Afterwards they had gone to a crowded café on the promenade and later walked along the edge of the cliffs where the wind had blown her fair hair into disarray. Wilmot had wanted to touch her, to hold her hand in his, but he had not dared, not even yet believed that she would ever permit it. He had found her incomparably beautiful in her A.T.S. uniform.

When they were back in the town he said, "What time do you have to be in?"

"Not until midnight."

His heart lurched. "I should like to see you again, Judy. Could we . . . I mean . . . perhaps we could meet later and have some food? I'm sorry—I shouldn't ask you."

"But I should love to."

He experienced an overpowering urge to kiss her. "Let's meet in the Ship, then. What time do you think? Half-past seven?"

Then he rolled away on his short seaman's legs and she stood for a moment, watching him, her head a little on one side, as if she were saying, "He's nice. He's very nice." She was as eager as he was to meet again.

Wilmot was waiting in the bar of the Ship by a quarter-past-seven, resplendent in his number one suit and gold lapel badges. He drank a beer as he waited, unable to understand this astonishing thing that had happened to him.

"Hello, Chief." She was always to call him Chief. "I'm not late, am I?"

He looked, already lovingly, at her freckled face, "No, you're not late, Judy. I was early."

"Good."

"What will you have?"

"Chief, I'm feeling reckless. A Bloody Mary."

"A Bloody what?"

"Vodka and tomato juice."

"Great Scott!"

They were to meet many times again before they departed on their different ways from Brighton, and she was to love her chunky fatherly Wilmot as he from the beginning had loved her. It was a strange, moving affair that no man believed in until he saw them together, and then even the most ribald members of the Chief Petty Officers' mess could only stand before them with wonder.

When he was drafted to *Conway* she had taken a week-end leave and gone up to Liverpool. It was the last time they had seen each other. They talked very little; it is difficult to talk when there is no future. He went with her to the station on the Sunday evening and waited with her on the platform. They stood very close together in the railway gloom, she in her greatcoat, he in his blue waterproof. When the train approached in a welter of noise and steam he kissed her. He could still feel her lips on his. "Take care, Judy darling."

The tears moved slowly over her cheeks, "I said I wouldn't cry, Chief. I'm sorry."

He held her tightly and said, almost humbly—he had always been a little humble in her presence—"I can never thank you, Judy," and then, as if he felt that this would not do at all, added, "I'll write until we're gone." She nodded and swallowed and allowed him to lead her towards the train and help her into the carriage. He stood on the platform while she leaned out of the window and dried her eyes and tried to smile.

As the train pulled out of the station she called, "Goodbye, Chief," and he saluted and answered, "Goodbye, Judy. For God's sake look after yourself."

She was unable to speak and watched him grow smaller on the platform by the swaying train. He took off his cap and waved it until he could see her no longer.

He slipped deeper into the raft against Barraclough's legs.

"Judy . . . Judy . . . Judy."

His head fell forward against the bloated gunwale and the sweeping water left his hair plastered in thick lines over his brow.

"Judy . . . my Judy . . ."

The duffel coat fell away from them but neither had the strength to replace it. Neither of them felt cold any more.

"Judy . . . my darling . . . I'm sorry . . ."

Wilmot drifted into oblivion and Barraclough swayed about on its verge and was not tempted to come away, for across the verge there was a prospect of unimaginable comfort. But he still sang. No one could have heard the song but himself. But it sounded in his head and his lips still moved.

> Side, side, *Conway*'s ship's side
> Jimmy looks on it with pride
> He'd have a blue fit
> If he saw all the shit
> On the side of the *Conway*'s ship's side.

This is my story, this is my song,
We've been in commission too ruddy long
Roll on the *Nelson*, *Rodney*, *Renown*,
This one-funnelled bastard is getting me down.

V

Jacobson said to Dawson, "You have thought about the gun?"

"Yeah, I've thought about it."

"You know what we have to do?"

"You tell me, Captain."

"We have to man the gun."

Dawson's answer was immediate and emphatic. "You can't, sir. You just can't."

Jacobson's reply was equally simple and direct. "We must." He had finally become godlike in his demands.

"Who'll you get to do it? Who'll even attempt it?"

"That, at this moment, I do not know."

Dawson was unable to resist the muttered sarcasm. "That's something, at any rate."

The gun, the solitary, precious gun, at that moment, was under five feet of rushing water. It was an ancient French 75mm. relic of the 1914-18 war, set high up in the bow among the anchor cables on the steel-decked fo'c'sle like a harpoon gun in a whaler, firing, when suitably coaxed, a six-pound shell. It had been given to *Oleron* as a last-minute gesture by the Naval authorities in Liverpool and urgently affixed to her cluttered deck. Jacobson had been promised more guns when he returned; meanwhile he was to be patient, to try to make do with what God offered.

In one sense the fo'c'sle was as good a place as any in which to site *Oleron*'s at once main and sole armament; it commanded a maximum field of fire and was at the business end of the ship. Those on the bridge could see it, and therefore, in some measure, control it. Yet, in foul weather, its position became untenable; the wind could blow hard or the gun could be fired; the two phenomena could not occur simultaneously.

Jacobson had caused two selected men to be trained as the gun's crew during the first Atlantic crossing. To some extent it had been a case of the blind leading the blind, for no one on board knew how to manipulate this strange contraption, but by the time *Oleron* sighted the North American continent, the gun's crew were fairly confident that they knew how to open the breach, load the gun and aim it. What happened when they pulled the firing lever was still a matter for speculation since they had had no shells to spare for practice shoots; but they assumed that the missile would be ejected from the muzzle at a considerable velocity and in roughly the desired direction.

Understanding the perils of the fo'c'sle in bad weather, Jacobson had wisely selected for his gun's crew the two biggest and strongest men in the ship. It was unfortunate, and not in any way foreseeable, that neither of these men should now be available— the first, Svenson, now deceased; the second, Birkenhead, now incapable of leaving the sick-bay.

"What are we going to do?" Jacobson asked Dawson, already knowing what he would do, already knowing what Dawson would answer, but nonetheless asking the question because some arrangement had to be made and he wanted Dawson to agree with what he had already decided.

"Don't ask me, Captain."

"If we encounter a U-boat the gun will have to be manned."

"Yes, sir. But who will man it?"

"There is only one answer."

Dawson was all attention, "Yes? Who?"

"Yourself. No one else is strong enough."

"Now, just wait a minute, Captain. You just can't send anybody down there, neither me nor anybody else. We wouldn't last thirty seconds; we wouldn't even get there! Christ Almighty, you saw what happened to the Bos'n? You nearly lost *him*! And he was only on the well-deck. Captain, when does it get to your saying, I'm through?"

Jacobson's mild face watched the towering silhouette against the flying grey sea. He sought in his mind for the right English words. "You refuse? Is that what I understand? You refuse?"

Dawson thought quickly. "It all depends where the ship's head is."

Jacobson again warmed towards his Second Mate and moved nearer to him, his voice which a little before had been all weariness now speaking quickly and confidently. "Of course it does! When we find the survivors we run for Halifax. The sea will be astern. You see what I mean? The gun we cannot man now, but we can man it when the sea is astern. *We have to find the survivors before the U-boat finds us.*"

Dawson was angry. "And how, for crying out loud, do we do that?"

"I cannot answer you . . ." Jacobson said mildly. "But . . . what do you say?"

"You've asked me that before."

"I know. But what do you say?"

"I'll think about it. I want that good report. I'll let you know nearer the time; it'll depend on the weather."

Jacobson put a tentative hand on Dawson's arm. "Thank you, Dawson. Thank you."

Then the cry, stopping hearts and stilling breath, "Object on the starboard side, sir."

VI

Corridon waited in the lee of the sick-bay, consumed by a passionate longing for violence and revenge. He smouldered with an uncontainable anger, his desire like the slow heat of a wet haystack. Yet he was content to wait for his opportunity, to wait all night if necessary. All he wanted was Goldstein to leave the sick-bay, just for a moment, for just long enough for him to be able to dart inside and get his hands about Birkenhead's throat. It would not take long; with luck, no one would ever knew who had done it—if, indeed, it was not simply assumed that Birkenhead had died of his previous injury.

He moved nearer to the door and when he had his hands on the cold clamps the desire to see the great Birkenhead lying on his bunk as if he were a slab in a morgue became irresistible. He turned the retaining clamps slowly, and felt the silent squeak of metal against metal in his palm. He just wanted to see, to gloat. The clamp clicked and the door swung free. He pushed it open. Soon he was able to insinuate his spare body between the door and the blackout curtain and when he had both legs over the coaming, he began to pull the stiff material imperceptibly to one side.

Goldstein still slept in the chair, his mouth open, saliva dribbling down his fallen chin. Birkenhead's great muscles stood out under the sheets and blankets, his chest moving rhythmically as he breathed. Corridon's eyes burned and blood pumped in his temples. His anticipatory pleasure was almost unendurable. But he waited. And as he waited the human form under the sheets began to rise in the bunk, slowly, deliberately, like the body of a man still sleeping, first the sculptured-bone head, then the bandaged column of the neck, then the mighty shoulders and the black body. Corridon watched astonished, a little afraid now. Then the legs moved out from under the bedclothes and Birkenhead was sitting on the edge of the bunk. He slid carefully to the deck. Corridon pulled back his head and squeezed through the door and retreated into the darkness abaft the sick-bay.

Then the engines stopped and the seas swept over the silent *Oleron* from stem to stern.

VII

Alice Reed fell asleep again when Albert left their cabin but she did not sleep for long. When she awoke she found the cabin eerie and oppressive. She listened to the throb of the engines; then she got up and dressed. She was a gregarious creature, not accustomed to being alone, and when she was ready she made her way to Gerda Olstein's cabin and tapped gently on the door.

"Come in."

Alice entered. "Can I come in?" Gerda was up, wearing the same skirt and sweater. She also wore her life-jacket.

Alice said, "I'm sorry to disturb you, love, but do you mind if I come and sit with you? Albert's up on the bridge. I don't know what the Hamlet he's doing up there—getting in the way, I shouldn't wonder—but he *would* go."

Gerda frowned at the strange diction. "I'm sorry?"

Alice saw her difficulty and laughed. "I'm that Yorkshire, I don't suppose you can understand a word I'm saying. Can . . . I . . . come . . . and . . . sit . . . with you?"

She indicated the chair and Gerda smiled. "Of course. I am very happy that you come."

She offered Alice a cigarette.

"No thanks. I don't smoke. Do you think I should be wearing my life-jacket?"

"I think so. Mr. Dawson tell me to wear it."

"I'll go and get it in a jiffy."

Gerda was glad that Alice had come.

Alice said kindly, "Are you going home, Gerda? I can call you Gerda, can't I?"

"Yes, I'm going home."

"That's nice. You'll be happy going home. We're both going home, Albert and me."

"You have been for a long time away?"

"No, not all that long. But long enough. I shall be glad to be back."

Gerda said impulsively, like a child making a new friend. "I have been happy on this ship. Every person is very kind to me."

"Well, why ever shouldn't they be?"

Gerda shrugged her shoulders.

Alice said slyly, "I've seen that young officer. We're not blind, even if we are getting on." She laughed and Gerda responded as Alice had hoped she would. Alice was an extraordinarily wise woman, even if a little garrulous.

"Mr. Dawson? You know him?"

"Well, of course, I've never spoken to him. I'm too old for *that* sort of thing."

Gerda said gravely, "He is a very good man. But I think he has had a difficult life."

"I'm sure he's a good man, Gerda."

"Thank you."

Alice said, "You're such a beautiful girl, Gerda. You have such a lovely face when you smile. Did you know that? You looked so sad when you came on board. I felt right sorry for you. But I can see I needn't have bothered, need I?"

Gerda answered with the same impulsiveness, "I was a stewardess in a Swedish ship. I left the ship in South America. I was to marry."

"I'm ever so sorry. But you'll find that everything's for the best in the long run. You'll see."

"Is it?"

"Yes."

They listened to the engines and Gerda said, "I hope everything is all right. Please . . . nothing will happen, will it? You see, we are going to marry, Mr. Dawson and I . . ."

Alice laughed, "Nothing'll happen to us, lass. You forget that Admiral Reed's on the bridge. Oh, Gerda, I'm so happy for you. You must both come and see us in Yorkshire. We've got plenty of room and we'd be that glad to have you. Will you do that?"

They both knew a great happiness, a happiness induced almost wholly by danger. Danger formed odd alliances, rendered human relationships strangely free of human failure. Without danger, Alice and Gerda almost certainly would never have spoken to each other; now they came as near to loving each other as two normal women could ever come.

The engines stopped without warning. When they were silent, Alice's voice sounded louder than it had ever sounded before, strident in an empty cavern. They clung to each other in the tiny cabin as *Oleron* swooped and lunged in the maddened sea. "Happen it's the raft," she whispered. "Happen they've found them."

She tried to stand up but Gerda would not let her go and they sat in the silence of the ship, waiting for a sound of life.

VIII

Oleron's engines started again almost immediately, but this time astern, shaking the ship in a frenzy of vibration. Jacobson ran once again to the starboard wing and clamped his binoculars to his eyes and trained them in the direction indicated by the look-out.

Dawson remained amidships and put the ship hard over, willing her to come round before whatever the look-out had seen disappeared into the night. The vibrations of the ship tickled his feet and caused his teeth to chatter.

"Jesus, Captain," he shouted, "what is it?"

Half a dozen voices answered, "It's a raft. My God, it's a raft. It's there! There!"

Jacobson's voice piped above the hubbub as he came towards the wheel. "Mr. Busk! You know what to do. The scrambling net is ready?"

"Yes, sir."

"Lose no time. Go!"

Busk hurried away and Jacobson said to Dawson, quietly now, "It is a raft, Mr. Dawson. Thank God, it is a raft. I saw it. I saw it with my own eyes."

"Good for you, sir. What now?"

"It is out of sight, of course. But we cannot bring her round faster."

"No, sir."

Oleron rolled as if determined to turn turtle. The men on the bridge could no longer stand unless they held on to rails and stanchions and the waves seemed to rush unimpaired over her superstructure, drowning her in water and spray. When nearly all the way was off her the seas moved astern and Jacobson ordered, "Slow ahead."

Again the tension and the absence of human voices, the striving to see the unseeable, the hopeless attempt to see through the murk that covered the sea like an endless blanket.

Jacobson muttered, "Where? Where for God's sake is it?"

"Hold on, sir," Dawson said, sensing the hidden fury in Jacobson's voice.

The look-out's voice reached them from the wing, barely audible.

"What does he say?" Jacobson snapped.

"Raft on the port bow, sir."

"Full astern!"

The telegraphs sounded.

"Full astern, sir."

"Hard astarboard!"

"Wheel hard astarboard, sir."

Oleron began to turn, bringing the seas on to her quarter, striving to turn in time to bring the raft up on her starboard lee. Jacobson fled towards the starboard wing and when he was out in the wind that seemed to tear through and not round his body, he looked down and saw the raft first in a trough and then coming up towards him as a crest swept below it. He waited with one hand held above his head. When it flashed downwards he piped, almost screamed, "Stop engines!"

The ship was silent and the men on the bridge, with the exception of Dawson and the helmsman, gathered behind Jacobson.

"Where?"

"I can't see anything."

"Yes, there it is!"

"There!"

They held on to each other, falling from one bulkhead to

another, a compact swaying mass behind Jacobson who was leaning outboard, striving to see the operation below him. He shouted, "Hurry, Busk. Hurry!" and at the same time heard Dawson's bellow, "For the love of God hurry, sir, or she'll turn right over. She can't roll like this for ever. Hurry!"

Jacobson became aware of shouting on the well-deck below. "What is it?" he called.

A reply came at once but he was unable to distinguish the words. He heard only an excited shouting, not only from Busk, but from all the men on the well-deck. Then it stopped. He pushed his way through the men behind him and reeled inboard again. "Mr. Dawson, something is wrong. Go below and report to me. I shall take over."

Dawson answered, "Sir. But please, *please* get her off this beam sea. She won't take it. She won't take it, I'm telling you."

Jacobson lifted his head, pomposity incarnate, "I am in command, Mr. Dawson. Please do as I say."

Dawson persisted, "You've got to get her off . . ."

Jacobson screamed at him, "Go! It is an order!"

But Dawson, it appeared, had had enough. He did not go. He stood against the binnacle, watching Jacobson. "Helmsman," he ordered, "Slow ahead, hard astarboard."

"No!" Jacobson shouted. "I gave no such order."

Jacobson's rage was beyond control. He rushed at Dawson, "That is not my order." The helmsman's voice intoned the repetition, "Hard astarboard, sir. Slow ahead." The telegraphs jangled on Jacobson's exhausted nerves and his body collided with Dawson and the binnacle. Dawson put down one hand and held him off as if he were deterring a child. He said, "It's no use, sir. You can't keep her beam to the sea." He spoke gently, as if he were genuinely sorry that he was unable to comply with Jacobson's demands. Jacobson shouted, "I know my ship. I know *Oleron*. I know what she can do." But Dawson still held him.

As *Oleron* turned her tired head away from the sea Busk arrived on the bridge, shouting as he came. Jacobson turned expectantly towards him. "What is it, Mr. Busk?"

"That raft's empty! There's no bastard in it! Jesus, there's nobody in it, do you hear?"

IX

Birkenhead tested his legs in the sick-bay and found that they did not collapse beneath him. He held his neck quite still. He searched for his clothes and found them rolled in a pathetic bundle by the side of the desk. He stooped and felt blindly for it with his hands, not bending his neck, and when he touched it he picked it up and carried it back to his bunk. He dressed slowly and silently. Goldstein slept and dribbled in the chair.

When the engines were put astern it seemed inevitable that Goldstein should wake, but he slept through the uproar and when the engines were put ahead Birkenhead was ready to leave. He was sadly ill-equipped for the weather on deck; he wore only a pair of old shoes without laces, a faded boiler suit and a grey roll-neck sweater beneath it. The prospect of the intense cold did not appear to deter him.

Before he moved towards the door he stood for a moment looking down at his nurse's unlovely face. He put out a hand and placed it gently on Goldstein's shoulder and the trace of a smile passed over his huge face. Then he went to the door and let himself out into the night.

The wind whipped under the flimsy boiler suit but Birkenhead did not flinch. He turned forrard, walking carefully, sedately, as if he carried an invisible load on his crown. When he emerged on the forrard side of the superstructure the sea was astern and he found it easier to keep his balance. He rested for a moment, leaning his body against the wet bulkhead, his head thrown back against the metal, exposing the white bandages at his neck. He could see the waves racing past on each side of the well-deck, travelling from stern to stem as if *Oleron* were belting full speed astern and not slow ahead. The cold wind seemed to give him strength and his only discomfort was the dull throbbing in his neck.

Corridon emerged from the passageway on to the well-deck, just as Birkenhead had expected he would. He saw the red eyes in the darkness and sensed the knife in Corridon's crippled hand travelling upwards towards the bandages at his neck. Birkenhead scarcely moved his body but one bunched black fist flashed upwards and hit the underpart of Corridon's arm so that the knife still gripped in the crushed fingers flew upwards and Corridon found his face and his body exposed to Birkenhead's fury.

But nothing happened. Birkenhead said softly, resonantly, "Drop it, Corridon. You're comin' wid me."

Corridon danced backwards and crouched with the knife. "You black bastard. You 'eard what the men said? They said you was a Jonah. I don't give a flip whether you're a Jonah or Jesus Christ. I just 'ate your guts."

"You're wastin' time, Corridon. Ah said, you're comin' wid me."

"Over the flippin' side, you mean? Don't make me laugh."

Corridon moved forward again, the knife still held awkwardly in damaged fingers, and lunged. Birkenhead reacted in the same strangely lackadaisical way, leaning motionless against the bulkhead while his hand came up like the paw of a tiger. Corridon yelped with agony and fell back again.

"Jesus, you black swine!"

Oleron began to turn again, bringing her port side up against the sea. The water raced and tumbled over the fo'c'sle and on to the well-deck. Corridon attacked for the third time. The knife was very near to Birkenhead's throat when the fist tore into Corridon's muscles, paralysing his arm so that the knife flew upwards unattended by the fingers. Corridon squealed with pain and knifeless fear, discovering at the same time that Birkenhead's fingers had closed about his upper arm and were forcing it inexorably upwards and backwards, tearing the muscles, smashing the bones—nearly; desisting only when the arm would move no further in the socket. Birkenhead let him go and struck the thin fox face with the flat of his hand. Corridon sprawled across the iced deck.

When he picked himself up he found Birkenhead standing over him, swaying as the deck heaved.

"Get up!" Birkenhead said. "Get up and come wid me."

"Up yours, you bastard!"

Birkenhead hit him on the back of his head, harder this time. The blow hurt Corridon's eyeballs and he wondered mistily if they had shot right out of his head.

"Get up!" Birkenhead said.

Corridon did not answer but just lay prone on the deck.

Birkenhead stooped and picked him up by the scruff of the neck and held his face against his own. "You comin' wid me, Corridon? Or do ah have to kill you?"

Corridon was incapable of speech. Birkenhead ran over the well-deck dragging Corridon behind him through the avalanche of water that now came over the side. They reached the bulkhead below the fo'c'sle but the seas drove them back to the guard-rails. Corridon found his voice and screamed, "Get back, you fool, get back! We'll be over the side. You're crazy! Get back!"

Birkenhead screwed the clothing tighter about Corridon's neck and braced his great body against the guard-rails. When the brunt was past he strode like Goliath towards the ladder that led up on to the fo'c'sle and reached it simultaneously with the next deluge. They disappeared beneath the water but before it was past Birkenhead was climbing the ladder, holding Corridon with one hand in the receptacle of his clothing.

The wind screamed over the fo'c'sle but when the sea was abeam the high sides offered a greater protection from the waves than the shallow well-deck. Birkenhead ran again, right up into the bow, hauling Corridon with him, and when he reached the gun he threw himself down in its lee and grasped the canvas cover.

His neck throbbed violently and he put a hand to the bandages and felt the wetness; then he put a finger in his mouth and tasted not salt but blood.

He yelled to Corridon as a mountain of water descended from the sea above them. "Hold on yourself, Corridon. Ah can't hold you all de time."

Corridon whimpered and clung to the harsh gun-cover while Birkenhead patiently unlashed it. When, eventually, in the unceasing turmoil of wind and water, it was freed, the wind took it and flung it into the night. Birkenhead lay flat against the deck on his stomach in the lee of the gun and shouted into Corridon's ear. "The shell locker's behind you. All you gotta do is hand me dem shells when ah says ah want 'em. O.K.?"

"Flippin' black lunatic," Corridon shouted back.

He felt Birkenhead's fingers tightening at his throat, felt the pain at the back of his eyes again. "Are you goin' do as ah say, Corridon? You can't get off dis deck on your own, boy. You just ain't strong enough. Are you goin' to stay here and hand me dem shells? Or do ah just have to let you go wid dese here waves?''

"O.K., Birkenhead. But I'm tellin' you, I'll get you for this. Jesus, I'll get you for this."

Birkenhead took his fingers away from Corridon's throat. He said, "You ain't gotta stay here for long, boy. Just a little while an' then it'll all be over."

Corridon thought that Birkenhead smiled in the violence of the sea. He began to shake with fear and his damaged fingers dug into Birkenhead's muscles for protection.

x

Barraclough was singing his final song.

He saw in the darkness of his mind a picture, a picture that faded and then glowed, that faded a little more each time the light flickered in his mind, a picture of those he had known, a part of the procession he had witnessed all night: Niffnoff, his father, his torn waistcoat open but the scarf he wore at his neck tied neatly over his shirt, and on his face a concerned, contrite expression that said, 'I'm not wholly bad, just weak, and I am sorry for what I have done'—and his son saw his face and forgave him; and his mother, like her son with curling hair and eyes that still looked kindly at her husband, the man she had loved or thought she had loved before she had lost her mind, wearing a black satin dress she had bought at a Mothers' Union rummage sale which neither suited her nor fitted her, but was better than anything she could ever otherwise have afforded, loving it and stroking its shiny smoothness, pleased that she was dressed up— and her son was grateful to her for being dressed up, for that was how he chose to remember her; and his sister, she of the develop- ing breasts and the too-thin, stick-straight legs in a flared skirt, she with the insolence of her brother but none of his gentleness, some of his bravado but none of his strength, the same peasant capacity to endure but none of his charity, she with the hard, half-adult, pretty face, which, for all its hardness, smiled—and her brother acknowledged her smile and was thankful; and yet a fourth person, the girl Barraclough had known in the village, with whom he had walked and lain in warm fields of hay and long grass, whose body he had known and wanted and almost loved, a buxom, country-bred girl with a coarse voice and a merry laugh, she, too, was there—and Eric was glad she had come. They sat in a circle before the fire in the living-room that smelled of life and warmth and human dirt. The fire burned brightly and all felt its heat in their faces. They were happy in each other's company.

Barraclough's lips moved and he sang with his mother and father, his sister and his girl, as once he had sung at Christmas time.

> O come, all ye faithful
> Joyful and triumphant.

His lips moved slowly and one hand crept on to Wilmot's and fastened itself about the stiff fingers.

> O come ye, O come ye to Bethlehem.

His eyes were closed and he sang even more slowly, his lips barely moving and no sound coming in the rushing wind . . .

> Come and behold Him
> Born, the King of Angels.

A wave with white fingers climbed above him and then leaped downwards and tore through his hair and ran like daggers inside his clothing and moved his body with their weight; but his hand did not let go of Wilmot's hand.

> O come, let us adore Him,

and louder!

> O come, let us adore Him,

and louder!

> O come, let us . . .

His lips were still and he sang no more.

XI

Pandemonium ensued on *Oleron*'s bridge when Busk delivered himself of his ominous pronouncement. The men who had formed his party on the scrambling net had followed him when he had bolted for the bridge, for they, too, were of a not dissimilar inclination. They stood behind him now in a close-packed mob on the bridge access ladder, swaying heavily in the darkness as *Oleron* rolled to the seas. They were in no mood for explanations or persuasion. They wanted only action and an end to Swedish lunacy.

"It's empty!" Busk yelled. "Empty, God damn it! There weren't any survivors. There wasn't a bloody thing in that raft but sea-water. We might have known."

He was furious, nearly out of control with anxiety and frustration, and the mood of the men behind him incited him, pushed him further into his monstrous indiscipline. At any other time, on any other occasion, he would have reviled such behaviour, castigated those guilty of it, deemed himself incapable of anything remotely resembling it; the honour of the Service, his precious uniform, the tradition—all would have been in danger and he would have defended them. But now, in the last resort, afraid and mob-infected, trapped in the blind alley of his own incorrigible self-deception, none of his high principles held a particle of water. He was beyond the comforting influence of his day-dreams. And, ironically, for the first time in his life, he was leading a body of men through sheer power of leadership.

"That raft," he shouted, "might have been floating around in the ocean for weeks. The Atlantic's full of them, and boats, too, and bits of ships. But there're never any men. Never!"

Jacobson shrank within his sheepskin coat and Dawson released his arm. He was a very small man now, a small man in a huge coat, bewildered and hurt. "No one? No one, did you say? You looked, and there was no one?"

"No one," Busk said vehemently. "I've told you."

Albert Reed said, "No one? You're sure of that?"

"How many times do I have to tell you? Of course I'm bloody well sure. Ask these men."

The men behind him chorused a gruff assent and pressed forward behind Busk, forcing him further on to the bridge.

Jacobson half turned towards Dawson. "I cannot believe it. There is some mistake, perhaps? There must be another raft. This is . . . just the . . . wrong one . . . that is all. There must be another."

"We can't hear you," one of the men said.

Dawson roared, "Pipe down!"

A voice answered, "Aw, nuts!"

Dawson strode towards Busk and the men behind him, but found Jacobson's arm stretched before him, imploring him to wait.

"There must be another raft. Nearby, you understand? It must be near to us, near to this raft. We cannot give up when we are so close to it."

Busk approached and stood closer to Jacobson than he had ever dared to stand before. "Are you suggesting, *sir*"—his old trick— "that we stop and look for it? Because if you are, I'm telling you that the crew won't stand for it. They've had enough. And so have I."

Jacobson regarded him with troubled eyes, still preserving an outward composure, only his tongue darting over his thin lips betraying his anger.

"That right?" Busk called over his shoulder to the men.

"That's right," they answered. "We won't do it."

Jacobson became the pompous captain. "They will not, as you say, stand for it? Is that what you say? But it is not up to them, or you, to stand or not to stand for anything in this ship. I am still master of *Oleron*, Mr. Busk."

Busk leaned even nearer to Jacobson, enjoying his new-found power, not yet in a condition to be cognisant of his irretrievable error, "Listen! Let's get out of here! Do you think these men don't know about the U-boat? Do you? They know all about it. There's a man here who saw it. They know the danger we're in, and they know it isn't justified. It's my duty to tell you that they won't obey your orders, not any more, not one of them. I'm just warning you, sir."

Jacobson knew that unless Busk and his rabble ceased to offer their provocation his fury would seethe uncontrollably to the surface. He wanted to sweep his arm about his body and mow them down, to a man. He was not concerned with whether any of his crew or his passengers were right or wrong. This thing was inside him, this unanswerable will to find the men of *Conway*. He might not be able to sink U-boats. But he could find these men. He *would* find them. He would go to the ends of the earth to find them. "Have you forgotten *Conway*, Busk? Have *you*, you men there? You forget how she fought, how she went on to the end so that you could escape? Did you see her fight?" He grasped Busk's coat with his pink fists. "Did you, Mr. Busk?"—unconsciously falling into Busk's trick of accenting the 'Mr.'— "Did you see what happened to *Southern Star*? Disappearing in flames? *Southern Star* was commanded by my friend, Captain

Berenson. Only because of *Conway*, and the men in her, did that not happen to you!" He began to shake Busk's body backwards and forwards, his voice hoarse with fury. "If only because of *Southern Star*, I am going to find these men! I will not give up. Do you understand? I will not give up. I will find them, *dead or alive*!"

Before Busk could speak he was interrupted by the cries of men at the foot of the ladder and then by the hullabaloo of their ascent. Schirmer passed through the knot of men like a rocket, closely followed by da Falla and a breathless Goldstein travelling less boisterously in the vacuum of his wake. "Birkenhead," Schirmer shouted into the darkness of the bridge. "He has gone: he is no more in the sick-bay!"

Goldstein's hoarse voice added, "They got 'im, got 'im while I were sleepin'."

Jacobson shouted above the confusion to the helmsman, "Hard astarboard. We shall continue the search. You men there! To your stations! Mr. Busk, we resume our quest." He was like a school teacher vainly attempting to induce order into a mob of children on an outing.

Busk yelled, committing himself totally now, "No! No! We refuse!"

Jacobson's voice piped in anger. "I ordered hard astarboard, helmsman. Hard astarboard, I said."

Schirmer's voice shouted in the background, "Captain! Sir! They have got Birkenhead. What are we going to do?"

The helmsman hesitated long enough for Jacobson to become aware that the notion of refusal was in his head, but when Jacobson flung his bulbous weight at him he gave way without resistance for even though, with the support of an officer, he was prepared to defy the Captain, he was not, when it came to the point, prepared to fight with him. Jacobson took the wheel and swung it violently in a clockwise direction and held on to it, hard against the stop. *Oleron* heeled over until half her upper deck was awash.

He did not need human allies, not when he had *Oleron*, strong and resilient beneath his feet. He had fought with the sea all his life and if this should be his final battle, well, he would go as the men of *Conway* had gone. But he would not go; he would defeat the wild ocean, as he and his ship had defeated it before.

He shouted above the chaos of voices. "The search will go on!"

He heard Busk lunging towards him, smelt his breath on his face, felt the words piercing his eardrums, "Stop him! Stop him! He's mad. Get him away from the wheel!"

The men at the head of the ladder did not rally to Busk's aid. They stood sheepishly in the darkness, afraid, like the helmsman, to lay hands on their Captain. Only Stockmann came to Busk's assistance. His soft hands and arms grasped Jacobson about his middle and failed to meet about the squat rotundity. "Help me!" Busk yelled, aware that the men had already betrayed him. "Help me hold him! He's mad! Don't you understand that he's mad? Christ, doesn't anybody understand?"

The biggest wave in the Atlantic on that memorable night then swept beneath *Oleron*, a monster, a towering avalanche of water holding *Oleron* like a toy ship on its flying peak. And when the greater part of *Oleron*'s hull was exposed to the wind, her solitary screw threshing and shaking itself to pieces in the back-breaking void, she began to fall sideways, the momentum of her fall increasing as she slid down the wave's endless slope. When she arrived in the trough, she was on her beam ends. All that moved in *Oleron* slid in maniac confusion to the starboard side: men, their possessions and the tools of their trade; Jacobson felt his hands snatched from the wheel and knew himself to be sliding towards the starboard wing, his body still intertwined with those of Busk and Stockmann. When he thudded against the bulkhead, every particle of breath knocked out of his tired body, he heard Busk's hysterical voice, "He's done it! I told you, he's done it! She'll never come back now. Jesus, she'll never come back. She'll stay like . . ."

The noise stopped abruptly and Jacobson heard Dawson's voice. "Shut up. Another word and I'll break your goddam neck."

"The wheel," Jacobson gasped. "There's no one on the wheel."

But his voice was so weak and the noise of the wind and the sea on the exposed wing so great that Dawson could not hear him and continued to bend his efforts towards dragging Jacobson up the fearful slope towards the shelter of the bridge.

Meanwhile, close to the binnacle, a strange alliance had formed. It came about without fuss, without preliminaries of any kind, as if no other relationship had ever existed between the two men. Harris shouted, "There's nobody on the wheel. It's unattended!" And Albert Reed, hanging on to the binnacle, the intensity of his accent doubled by the nature of his predicament, answered, "Dust tha' know what to do wi' it, lad? For if tha' does, for God's sake, get 'oald't'bloody thing." Harris scrambled and slithered towards the wheel, and he and Albert together clung to its spokes and forced the rudder amidships and beyond until *Oleron*'s indomitable old bow began to push its way up into the seas again, and slowly—terrifyingly slowly—the ship began to right herself.

A voice shouted in the darkness, "It's that bastard, Birkenhead. The flippin' Jonah. If somebody filled 'im in, they didn't do it soon enough."

Then da Falla's shrill voice, "Balls, don't be crazy, man. What's Birkenhead to do with this?"

Once the ship was on a moderately even keel, Jacobson and Dawson ran towards the wheel and when they reached it they found Harris and Reed behind it, unruffled and composed: they might have been there all the time. They held *Oleron*'s head dead into wind. Harris shouted, "I'll keep the wheel, sir. Mr. Reed, look out for that bloody raft or whatever it is and don't come back till you've found it."

Albert hurried towards the bridge screens and put his binoculars to his eyes. "By golly-'eck! It were worth it just to have that bugger Harris come to his senses. He'll be as right as rain now."

Jacobson said to Dawson, "Get these men off the bridge."

Dawson roared, "Get below, all of you." He ran from one end of the bridge to the other. "Get below. Get off the bridge."

In ones and twos, slowly, sheepishly, they went, leaving behind them a crumpled black heap in one corner of the bridge which was Busk, their leader, the failure, still unconscious from the blow he had received from Dawson. Jacobson had won, or at least he had beaten the men; he had not yet beaten the sea.

He was beyond tiredness now, functioning like an automaton, his reflexes and reactions slow, his brain sluggish, but his will unimpaired. He turned to Harris. "How long was the wheel unattended, Mr. Harris?"

"A couple of minutes, maybe more."

Jacobson smiled in the darkness. He said, "You know what this means? If we find the men now, it will not be we who have found them, but *Oleron*. For two minutes, perhaps more, she pursued her own course, and perhaps for this very reason, we shall find . . ."

Albert Reed's voice ended Jacobson's prayer like an axe severing a hawser. "I can see summut! It's ovver there, on't right. D'you see it? It's a raft! Yes, it's a raft! Can you hear me? It's another raft! Quick, stop t'ship . . ."

"Hard astarboard. Full astern."

Harris answered Jacobson's order and the telegraph rang.

"Take the scrambling net, Mr. Dawson. I shall try to bring the raft up on the starboard side. Mr. Reed, keep watch! Keep me informed of the raft's position."

Dawson clattered off the bridge.

Oleron's engines thundered astern and as the seas came on to the beam the ship heeled over against their continuous impact.

"We're too far away," Albert cried. "I can't see it any more."

Jacobson answered calmly, "In a moment, Mr. Reed. I shall make another approach. Keep a good look-out."

He put the engines ahead again and held the wheel over to starboard and when, as he would have put it, *Oleron* told him that she was ready, when he judged, as all natural seamen are able to judge, whatever the magnitude of the violence by which they are surrounded, that the precise split second had arrived, he reversed the rudder and put the ship astern. "Can you see them"— already 'them'—"Mr. Reed?"

"No, I can't."

"They should be on the starboard side now."

"I can't see a bloody thing."

"Look, Mr. Reed. Look!"

"Yes," Albert cried. "Yes, there it is. Down there. Very close. You'll have to go backwards a bit or you'll over-shoot."

Jacobson held the engines astern. Albert ran out on to the wing and peered down and saw the raft alongside the well-deck and raced inboard again. "Stop! Stop t'ship! It's just down there."

Jacobson stopped the engines and Albert ran out on to the wing again almost weeping with relief. Dawson's stentorian voice came up to him through the wind and when Albert had received the message, he waved a hand in the darkness. He sensed Jacobson behind him. "It's them," he shouted into the wind. "It's them! It's full of bodies! Full, Dawson says!"

Jacobson did not speak, could not speak, could only feel an inexpressible thankfulness and lean avidly over the bridge rail and try to see what was happening on the forrard well-deck through tears that filled his eyes. *Oleron* lunged from sea to sea and Dawson himself was lowered on a line to the raft so that he with his immense strength could secure it to *Oleron* before being hoisted inboard again.

They heard his bellow above the noise of the sea when he regained the deck and Jacobson stumbled inboard to the telegraphs and put *Oleron* dead slow ahead, sufficient to maintain steerage way, with the seas on her port bow.

He rang the telegraph himself because he dared not trust himself to speak, but when he altered course he was obliged to speak and Harris could not believe that the choked small voice came from Jacobson at all.

They sailed in this way for more than twenty minutes. A man was lowered into the raft and, safely secured to a line, bent an additional line to each man he found and saw him hoisted inboard. Jacobson stood out on the wing in the piercing wind as the operation proceeded, watching the black shadows below him. When, after a long time, he did not speak, Albert said to the lonely bundled-up figure, "It'll be all right. I'm sure they'll be all right. You shouldn't worry." He put out a hand and touched the bent shoulder. Jacobson turned towards him. "We found them, Mr. Reed. Whatever was said, we found them. And now . . . now that we have found them . . . they must be alive. We have not failed. . . . *But if all are dead?*"

Albert mumbled, "They won't be dead."

"Some will be dead, Mr. Reed. There are always some who die quickly. But there may be others . . ."

"Would you like me to go downstairs and see?"

"No. No, Mr. Reed, thank you. Dawson will tell me . . . soon enough."

When the last man was safely inboard and they heard Dawson's powerful voice again, the raft was cast adrift in its rightful element. Jacobson put the engines to half ahead. "Starboard twenty, Mr. Harris. You see . . . we can go home now." His voice was strangely dispirited, his words disjointed, as if, at last, utter weariness had won its battle of attrition. Harris confirmed the order in his best seamanlike manner and when the wheel was over and *Oleron*'s head beginning to turn out of the seas, he said what Albert had said before him, said because there was nothing else to say, and even this ludicrously inadequate, "I hope they're all right, sir."

As he spoke the sea and the sky and *Oleron* were lit by an exploding blood-red light that came from the starboard hand. It illuminated Albert Reed out on the starboard wing, Harris erect at the wheel, and Jacobson's haggard face. It vanished as quickly as it had come. Then it reappeared, vividly, murderously.

Harris yelled, "Christ, it's the U-boat! Firing at us!"

XII

The men on the fo'c'sle lay in the lee of the gun and clung with deadened fingers to the inadequate platform and pressed their faces against the ice on the deck. Birkenhead shifted his great head so that his lips touched Corridon's ear.

"De ship's stopped, Corridon. I guess they've found de men they were lookin' for. That's fine. Don't you think that's fine, Corridon? We have to watch out now, not let 'em jump us. You know about de U-boat, don't you Corridon? I guess you do 'cos every son-of-a-bitch on board knows about de U-boat. Some of de guys even seen it. Maybe it's comin' to get us, Corridon. If it does *Oleron*'s goin' to depend an awful lot on you, boy."

Birkenhead did not have to shout. He spoke easily in his rever-berating voice, his protruding lips so close to Corridon's ear that Corridon thought he was going mad with the noise and his own ceaseless shivering. The water snatched at his injured fingers and tried to pull his arms out of their sockets. It was water that pre-vented him from answering Birkenhead because Birkenhead's voice only stopped when the water thundered on top of them. When the waters sluiced away, it started again, taking up where it had left off.

"You're no good, Corridon. You ain't no good to man nor beast. Except tonight, eh? Tonight you're goin' to do something you ain't never done before. For one thing, you're goin' to do as you're told, boy. And for another, maybe you're goin' to die. Hey, Corridon, can you hear me talkin' to you? Ah said, maybe you're goin' to die. An' ah'm here, case you're wonderin', to see dat if you does die, you meets your Maker in a decent manner."

Corridon wanted to jump up and scream and flee from the black giant at his side, but all he could do was twist his body against the metal and squirm away from Birkenhead. When his body moved round the gun he exposed it to the murderous seas, and Birkenhead always followed him.

"I guess, Corridon, you wishes you had your knife now. But if dat U-boat comes a knife ain't goin' be much use to you. Only dis here gun can help you now; if you passes me dem shells when ah says ah wants 'em. Listen, Corridon! De ship's goin' faster now. I guess dey got all dem men inboard. Listen to dem engines turnin' over faster an' faster. Ma neck's bleedin', Corridon. It's been bleedin' all de time ah've bin up here. If dat U-boat don't come soon ah guess ah'll bleed all away. What'll you do if ah dies first, Corridon?"

Corridon lifted up his rat-like head and screamed into Birkenhead's face, "Yer savage black bastard! You can't 'old me 'ere. Yer can't do nothin' to stop me goin',—you with yer neck bleedin' like a stuck pig. I'm flippin' off . . ."

The sea flung down on them again and held Corridon's thin body against the deck and when the water was gone he could not find the courage to move. He heard Birkenhead laughing at him.

"Hey, Corridon. You still reckon ah'm a Jonah? I guess you soon goin' see if ah'm a Jonah or not. You still believe in Jonahs, Corridon? Ah don't care if you still believe or if you don't still believe. Not now. It don't matter any more. But Corridon, you just remember dis: you'll be better off dead! You ought to thank me, Corridon."

The flash erupted into the night and Birkenhead's great hand closed about the scruff of Corridon's neck and his bull voice roared, *"On your feet, boy, and pass me dem shells!"*

XIII

Alice Reed and Gerda Olstein clung to each other in Gerda's cabin.

"Bill says if anything happen we go to the bridge."

"Well, love, nothing's happened yet, except that the engines have stopped. I think we'd better wait a bit, don't you?"

"I think so. I wonder how long they stop? It is dangerous when the engines stop."

"Hark, they've started again."

"I am in a ship once that is broken down for two days because the engines they do not go."

"I'll bet you were sick of the sea before they got them going again, weren't you? I should've been."

"Yes."

"What are they playing at? Stopping and starting the engines, as if we were a 'bus. First we go this way and then we go that, what's the matter with them? You don't think Bert's getting in the way, do you? He will, you know, if he's given a chance. I've never known a man like him."

"What do we do?"

"Do? We stay here. They don't want us women up on the bridge seeing what a mess they're making of it all. They'll be swearing that hard it wouldn't be fit for us. We'd best stay where we are."

The sound of men's voices raised in anger came to them from the deck above; then there was comparative silence while Jacobson pleaded with his crew. Finally *Oleron* rolled and the roll seemed never to end. Alice fell backwards and struck her head against the bulkhead and when she regained a modicum of equilibrium she found herself lying more on the bulkhead than on the bunk which stood almost vertical at her side. Gerda was holding Alice's head in her hands. "Are you hurt, Mrs. Reed? Are you hurt?"

Alice leaned against the cold metal. "No, I'm not hurt. I just bumped me head a bit, that's all."

"Do you think we must go?"

"I don't know, lass. I don't know what's happening. The ship's not turning over, is it? *Gracious, it's not turning over?*"

"I think we must go. Come. Come with me."

Gerda pulled her from the bunk and when they were on the tilting deck they began to crawl towards the door. Gerda went first, more certain of herself than Alice, knowing more about ships and their unpredictable behaviour. The opening of the door was on the downard side and it was necessary for Gerda to struggle with it before she was able to get her shoulder beneath its weight. She called to Alice to crawl through into the passage.

Alice said, "It's coming all right again. The floor'll soon be level. Happen we'd better stay where we are after all." Soon the door swung freely on its hinges. Gerda laughed self-consciously. "Yes, perhaps we must stay. It was just a big roll." They sat down on the bunk again and held on to each other in the rolling that followed.

Alice talked for they both felt more at ease when one of them was talking: " . . . he was such a handsome man was Bert when he was young. I don't always call him Bert; just sometimes. You wouldn't think it, would you, but I started off in one of his mills. I was a mill-hand. Just fancy that! You know, Gerda, I used to see him striding through the mill, very purposeful, his eyes glinting, not missing anything—and some of those girls were born idle— and do you know, I used to say to myself, one day I'll marry that man. Of course, I could never have spoken to him; I was too shy. I didn't know how, not in those days. But one day he came up to me and said, 'I've had me eye on you, lass.' And I said—I remember my very words—'Oh, and what've *I* done?' And he said, 'Nothing. There's no occasion to be afraid. What about coming out with me tonight?' I thought I was going to cry. But somehow I managed to say, Yes. And that was that. My mother ironed my dress and I washed my hair and I always reckoned that when I met him that night he didn't recognise me at first. I was that changed. And everything's worked out just lovely. I wouldn't ever've changed me life, not for anything. He's a good man, is Bert, and he's been a good husband, except when he's busy interfering. Like now. It'll be the same for you, Gerda, you'll see . . ."

The sky was lit with the bursting blood-red light but the women did not see it; and then, reaching *Oleron* faintly through the bluster of the storm, the sound of the gun arrived, but the women did not hear it; and many more flashes and reports followed as Alice chattered on and Gerda listened to the soothing words, but the women did not see or hear or even dream of any of them; until one shell, one evil, bullet-shaped, barrel-hot projectile sped from the U-boat's sea-washed deck and traversed the distance between the U-boat and *Oleron* in less time than it took for its flash to come and go, and entered *Oleron*'s exposed side below the bridge and, because the vicious nose was diamond-hard and armour-piercing—not that there was any armour to pierce—it passed right through the hull intact and through a steel bulkhead and on through the steel bulkheads of Gerda's cabin into the cabin next door and there exploded. For one infinitesimal particle of time the women stared with incredulous faces at the point where the hole appeared. Then they fell to the floor like puppets deprived of their strings and lay still among the wreckage that rained about them.

XIV

When the enemy opened fire Jacobson had already returned to his favourite position on the port side of the bridge. He had been standing there, his small beak-like nose almost touching the glass, his hands gripping the bridge rail so hard that his knuckles stood out in white relief in the pudginess, watching *Oleron*'s head come round to the homeward course. He had still appeared small, smaller than when the voyage begun, his back less straight, his bearing less martial, but on his face there had been a secret smile, part triumph, part relief. He knew a marvellous sense of oneness with his ship. He was *Oleron* and *Oleron* was Jacobson. He even knew a little peace.

And now this! Oh God, no! The gun! How was he to man the gun? How was he to solve the problem that had exercised his exhausted mind for days, the problem that was essentially insoluble?

"Full ahead, sir." Harris's voice was still firm and alert but had risen half an octave.

The U-boat fired again and for a fraction of a second they waited but the shell went wide or overshot; at such range it was inconceivable that any shell could fall short.

The hair stood up on the back of Jacobson's neck and he shouted in Swedish into the engine room telephone and even as he spoke the thunder below decks increased in violence and *Oleron* began to tremble with the strength that was in her.

"Hard astarboard!"

"Hard astarboard, sir."

Albert Reed, on the starboard side of the bridge, was beginning to understand the language. "But it's on the starboard side!"

Jacobson snapped, "I know. That is why we turn to starboard."

The sea was on the port beam and *Oleron* lunged forward in a series of desperate rolls. The U-boat was on the starboard beam

237

and when the gun fired again they saw the low shape of the conning tower and the seas breaking over her casing.

Dawson charged on to the bridge, followed by the man who had been the helmsman. "The gun! The gun, sir!"

Jacobson screamed at him, "Man it!"

"But your course!"

"I said, man it."

Dawson held his ground, "If you turn into the sea it can't be manned. I've told you that! How do I know you'll stay out of the sea?"

Jacobson was beside himself, "I shall look after that. *Man the gun, Mr. Dawson.* Get to it or we shall be too late."

"It's already too late."

The wind moved astern. Jacobson came near to Dawson, raging, "Look! The wind is astern. The sea is astern. The gun can be manned."

Dawson came to meet him. "But you can't keep it astern. The sub'll just trail you. You can't stay out of the wind. And any man on that fo'c'sle when you're into the wind can't last ten seconds."

Jacobson's face was livid, his nose extraordinarily pinched. He grasped Dawson's coat. "You refuse?"

"You've asked me that before, Captain. . . . Yes, so help me, I refuse."

Jacobson's body subsided and his arms fell to his sides. He walked slowly back to the bridge screens.

Dawson came after him, "I'll go on one condition, Captain."

"Yes?"

"That you come with me."

"You do not trust me?"

"With you up here and me down there, no."

The two men stared at each other, each striving to see into the mind of the other—Jacobson, distraught, pompous, concerned for his dignity; Dawson, insolent, concerned for his life.

Birkenhead's gun fired as the German shell smashed its way through Gerda Olstein's cabin and exploded.

Jacobson shouted in amazement, "The gun! . . . Who? . . . Who?"

"That shell," Dawson shouted, holding on to the binnacle as *Oleron*'s stern was lifted high out of the water, "It was just below, in the cabins."

Jacobson called, "Mr. Reed, please go below and see that the women are safe. Mr. Dawson, who is manning the gun?"

The U-boat fired again and the shell struck *Oleron* amidships. Each shell bursting in her side hurt Jacobson as if he himself were wounded. The enemy's fire was erratic, as was to be expected from a vessel subjected to such violent movement from the sea, but *Oleron*'s entire starboard flank was exposed to the U-boat's bow. *Oleron* was being flung about by the sea, too, and for this reason Birkenhead's aim could be no more accurate than that of his adversary; and his target, in comparison, was pathetically small. His gun cracked again and again, but since he could not see his target, except when it fired, he did not know whether his aim was good or bad or indifferent. But he worked away over open sights, assisted by Corridon, for even Corridon was afraid to leave the gun now.

Jacobson snapped, "Midships."

Harris answered, one furious eye glittering in the binnacle's light, "Midships, sir."

"Has Reed returned?" Jacobson asked.

"No," Dawson answered and added, eagerly, "Should I go and see what's happened?"

"No. Not yet."

The U-boat fired from astern and the shell found its mark aft. *Oleron* shook herself and fled onwards.

"Now what're you going to do, Captain? There she'll bloody well stay and we can't answer back."

"We shall see. Ring the engine room. Demand more speed!"

Oleron charged north of west, flung through the water by her racing engines, carried by the sea from wave-top to wave-top. Yet, no matter to what unreasonable pinnacle of revolutions the Chief Engineer drove his faithful machinery, no matter how helpful, now, the following sea, the rating who sat glued to the U-boat's hydrophonic apparatus never once lost contact with *Oleron*, never once allowed the roar of the sea to confuse his judgement. The men of the U-boat had been a long time finding *Oleron* again; they had no intention of losing her through incompetence.

The gun fired regularly and two more shells struck *Oleron*'s stern.

Dawson shouted, "We'll be on fire if this goes on. What's keeping Reed? Harris, what's the answer?"

"There isn't any answer. You either clear off like we're doing and hope the bastard loses you or you go round in circles with him in the middle. Then at least you're firing at him—but we're such a big target he can't miss. Christ, don't ask me. What *can* we do but make off and frig about a bit from side to side."

Dawson shouted, "Where's Reed? Where, for God's sake is he?"

"There's something the matter with them women," Harris muttered, "or he'd be back by now."

Dawson strode towards Jacobson who was immersed in his own thoughts by the bridge screens, immersed in them even when under fire from the enemy. "I've got to go below and see what's happened to the women. Do you understand what I'm saying, Captain? I've got to go below."

Jacobson said, "We've got to turn into wind."

Dawson answered furiously, "I wasn't asking that! I was telling you that somebody must go and see to the women. The women, remember? Reed isn't back."

"Yes," Jacobson agreed sadly, "you must do that."

Only then did Dawson comprehend what Jacobson had said. "You can't. I've told you, you can't. I've even told you why you can't. Whoever's on that gun'll be lost if you do. It'd be me if I were there, wouldn't it?"

Jacobson asked, "Do you know who's on the gun?"

"No."

"Perhaps you should find out."

Dawson planted his feet wide apart against *Oleron*'s pitching. "Look, Captain. To begin with, I was all for you. But there're limits. I've taken just about as much as I can stand on this ship. I'm going to see to the women. And if you turn this ship into the wind while I'm gone, I'll see that you turn it out again. I mean what I say, Captain. I'm not fooling. This way, we've a chance. The other way that sub'll pound us to bits and you'll lose the men on the gun. I'm warning you, so don't try anything."

He strode from the bridge, not waiting for Jacobson's reply.

Stockmann, whom no one had noticed for a long time, said, "Are you going to turn, Captain?"

Jacobson did not bother to look at him. But he said, "What is it to you?"

"Nothing. But one by one the men are turning against you.

You cannot go on like this for ever. We are already in terrible trouble. You cannot make it worse."

"I do not require your advice."

"Captain, why have you not asked how many of the men we picked up were alive? Because you are afraid to ask? Because you are afraid they are all dead?"

Jacobson stared out over *Oleron*'s side. The fat fingers moved shyly to his brow and wiped away the moisture they found there and transferred it to his pocket. Oh God, how many? How many? How many are dead? It is true! I am afraid to ask, afraid to know. Stockmann could barely hear his voice. "How many?"

"There were six men in the raft. Four were dead. Those who were dead wore no clothes. Of the two who were alive it is unlikely that the elder will live. It looks as though you have saved only one man, Captain."

Jacobson's small eyes closed and his fingers forced themselves into tight fists. It was difficult to speak; there was so little air about him. He loathed Stockmann's suave voice, but once it was begun, he was driven to continue the conversation. "One? Only one, did you say?"

"Only one, Captain. Do you now consider that it has been worth it?"

"Worth it? Did you say, worth it? It is not a question of worth. It is a question of what is right."

Stockmann grunted in the darkness. "And if you lose your ship, your men, your passengers, even the man you have saved, will it still have been right?"

Jacobson's fist pounded on the bridge rail; he was like a man in a dock seeing his case go the wrong way. "Yes," he said quietly, "I do." Then, curiously, he smiled. "Yes, oh God, I do!"

Stockmann said, turning away, "You astound me, Captain."

Jacobson watched his shadow retreat. "Mr. Stockmann! Dawson has arranged for them to be well cared for?"

"As far as I know, yes."

"Dawson. It is always Dawson. I could not go on without Dawson."

"But he is against you now."

"Dawson?"

"Yes."

"No, he is not against me. In spite of what you have seen and heard, he is not against me. Nor is my ship. *Oleron* and Dawson, that is all I need. And Mr. Harris. Mr. Harris!"

"Sir?"

"Zigzag twenty degrees on each side of the course."

"Aye aye, sir."

Oleron's head swung away to starboard and then, as if she had swung deliberately into the gates of hell, the bridge exploded about Jacobson's head.

XV

Albert Reed crawled through the shattered cabin door and among the wreckage lying deep on the deck he found first his wife, and then, when he was quite certain that Alice was still alive, Gerda Olstein. He lifted Alice's shoulders and held her head in his hands, and ran his fingers over her body, at the same time, characteristically, pulling her dress over her knees. As he held her he whispered to himself like a child in the dark, "Ee, Alice, lass, what 'as tha' done, what 'as tha' done, what 'as tha' done to tha' self?"—a strange monotonous song, an incantation, endlessly repeated.

Later, when he lifted Gerda's shoulders as he had lifted Alice's the incantation became an unbroken sob. His stomach reeled and he released what remained of her head. It cracked sickeningly against the deck. For a moment he watched it moving as the ship moved, and wiped the blood from his hands on to his trousers.

He returned to Alice and sank down beside her. As far as he could see her only injury was a long gash on her temple. The blood had run from the wound and flowed down her cheek and was already coagulating on her chin. He smiled, infinitely briefly. "We'll have to get you out of here, lass. You can't stay here, can you? You can't stay here at all."

Later, when he had pulled her body through the broken door and lain her in the passage, he heard Dawson clattering down the ladders from the bridge. He stood up, waiting for him, his back to the door. He said, "Mustn't go in there."

"Why? Why not? Your wife! Is she all right? Is Gerda all right?"

"Yes, Alice'll be all right. But you mustn't go in there."

"What's the matter, for God's sake? It's Gerda! Tell me! I'm going in."

"I said 'No', lad."

"Get out of my way."

Dawson put out an arm and pushed against Albert's shoulder and Albert felt a kind of panic rising up inside himself. "I said 'It's better not to go in'!"

Dawson swept Albert away from the door and shook it violently and when it did not open bent down and began to crawl through the hole from which Albert and his wife had just emerged. Albert grasped the great shoulders with strong hands, shouting, "No! No! No!"

"Let go, Reed. I've got to see her."

Albert threw himself on top of Dawson, shouting hysterically, as if this were a culmination of all that had gone before. "Don't go in, Dawson! For the love of God, don't go in! You can't see her!" And when Dawson's body continued to move he added, beyond control, "*You can't see her! She hasn't got a face, Dawson! She's dead!*"

For some time Dawson neither moved nor spoke. Albert wiped his mouth and climbed to his feet, waiting for Dawson to come away from the door.

When they stood before each other in the passageway Dawson's unbelieving eyes moved aimlessly over Albert's face. "Dead? No, not dead! Please God, not dead."

"She's dead."

"Did you know . . . we were going to be married?"

Albert looked down at Alice. "I know, lad."

Dawson shouted, his voice a compound of grief and rage, "It's Jacobson! That self-willed bastard, Jacobson. Jesus, we needn't be here! It need never have happened!"

"No, not Jacobson, son. It's not Jacobson. He didn't do it. You know that."

Then the shell struck the bridge and most of what had been up above seemed to fall down the bridge ladder. Albert ducked and attempted to cover Alice's body. Dawson walked deliberately into it and stormed up to the bridge.

XVI

Jacobson felt the blood running over his hand before the pain in his arm. He was unable to remember what had happened and was surprised to find that he was lying in the bridge scupper. He could hear the wind tearing through the broken glass of the bridge screens above his head; but he did not know that they were broken, nor could he think why the wind, suddenly, should be making so much more noise. He could hear excited voices; but he could neither recognise them nor understand what they were saying. He tried to call to them but his mouth would not move. And although he experienced the will to stand up he was unable to transmit the messages of his mind to his muscles. So he remained there, wedged in the channel that ran along the forrard edge of the bridge, on his back, helpless, like a beetle.

The voices about him increased in intensity and twice the ship jumped and shuddered as if she had been hit. Heavy feet ran past his head, irregularly, as if what they carried was in a perpetual state of imbalance.

Then the pain began, pain so great that he was able to move his other hand and put it on the mess under his torn sleeve.

Finally, reality returned. It was odd that it should return in the shape of Busk.

"Sir! What's the matter? You've been hit. Can you get up? You must try and get up; we're being pounded to bits. We can't stand this for long. Get up, sir!"

Jacobson's mouth moved. "Busk? Mr. Busk?"

"Yes?"

"Is it you, Mr. Busk?"

"Yes, it's me. You're the only one who can get us out of this mess. You got us into it; you've got to get us out. Can you get up?"

"Help me, Mr. Busk."

Busk rolled Jacobson out of the scupper and got his arms under his shoulders and hoisted him to his feet. Jacobson did not faint, nor did he actually scream with the pain, but he thought that if the pain went on he would become insane. Biting a jagged hole in his lower lip was a relief.

"This way! I'll hold you. Hold on to me, sir."

Busk led Jacobson towards the wheel and turned him round

so that he faced the bow. The gun on the fo'c'sle fired again, almost into their faces.

Harris, still on the wheel, yelled, "I've turned beam to sea, sir. It's no bloody good running away. He just gets under our tail. We've got to keep turning. We'll have to turn again in a minute. Christ, if there weren't something wrong with that sub it'd dive."

"Are you all right, Mr. Harris?"

"Yes, I'm all right. Are you?"

The pain in Jacobson's arm was less now that he was upright, now that his arm was no longer being pulled or rolled on. But it was still worse than any pain he had ever thought possible.

Harris yelled, "Take these. You'll feel better with a shot."

Jacobson took the pills in a mist of pain.

"Go on. Eat them. They'll take some of the pain away. I've carried them ever since my last do."

Jacobson put the tablets in his mouth and gulped them down. He had difficulty in focusing his mind; he had, for example, forgotten about Dawson.

"Where's Dawson?"

Harris said, "He came to fill you in."

"Fill me in?"

"Yes, clobber you."

"I do not understand. Where is he?"

Harris added, "He's on the gun if you ask me. He was so mad, the gun's about the only thing he could do."

The next shell came from right astern and fell in the water alongside the bridge and exploded deep down. A tower of water shot upwards and fell back on *Oleron* and the men on her bridge.

"We've got to turn," Harris shouted. "We've got to turn so that we can fire back. Which way, sir? Which way are we going to turn?"

Then the whole problem returned to Jacobson: how to fight the U-boat? To flee or steam in circles? To run away or stand and fight it? That was it! This was what he had been trying to solve when he had been hit. He had got to the point of deciding that there was not more than half an hour's darkness left. Soon it would be day. Then *Oleron*'s chances would be negligible.

He fought back the waves of pain and nausea. "Mr. Busk, you will have to do something with my arm."

Busk had apparently already thought of attending to the matter for he had produced a length of twine and proceeded to bind it tightly about the terrible wound in Jacobson's forearm, forcing the tattered clothing and his own scarf against the torn flesh and bone to staunch the bleeding. Then he pushed the dangling wrist and hand between the buttons of Jacobson's coat so that Jacobson in outline, became truly Napoleonic. Busk's hands trembled uncontrollably.

"The shell, what damage did it do?"

"You, mainly," Harris answered. "Broke all the glass and took the deckhead off. But apart from that, not much. But, which way are you going to turn?"

Jacobson tried to see the gun in the darkness. He must answer; turn to starboard, out of the sea? Or turn to port, into it? It was better to make a wrong decision than not to make a decision at all. But then, had he not ordered a zigzag, the bridge might never have been hit; he might not have had his arm half ripped off. The saying was not always true. Do *something* was not always good advice.

He said, "Hard astarboard."

Oleron's head responded at once and the violent rolling began to be replaced by an equally violent pitching.

Jacobson moved nearer to the unglassed frames of the screens and as *Oleron* came out of the wind he felt the diminution of the wind-speed on his face. He put his feet apart and held on to the bridge rail with his good hand. Busk watched him intently and so did Harris, and Stockmann, who was still a little shell-shocked. What was he going to do? Now that *Oleron* was faced with imminent destruction, Jacobson was beginning to assume the nature of a saviour.

"Tell me when to straighten out," Harris yelled.

"Keep the wheel hard over, Mr. Harris."

The U-boat fired from the starboard quarter. Birkenhead's gun replied instantly. The U-boat fired again and once more Birkenhead's answer was instantaneous.

The sea came from right astern and Harris called, "Straighten out, sir?"

Jacobson replied quietly, but loud enough for his voice to be heard above the storm with which they travelled, "No, Mr. Harris. Hold the wheel over."

The flashes of the U-boat's gun came from nearer the beam now and the sea crept round to the starboard quarter.

Busk said, "What are you doing?"

For a moment Jacobson did not answer, as if he were preoccupied with some mental problem, but when he spoke his voice had taken on a new quality of assurance and command, "Speak to the engine room, Mr. Busk. Order them stand by for emergency alterations of speed. Ask them for the greatest speed of which we are capable. We must have it now. Then stand by the telegraph."

Busk was so taken aback by the whiplash voice that he forgot to accent the 'sir'. "Aye aye, sir."

Oleron was beam to sea now. Gusts of wind whistled round the corner of the starboard wing of the bridge and Busk began to miss the scarf he had wound round Jacobson's arm. Jacobson peered into the night, watching the sea, trying to see the men on the fo'c'sle. When the U-boat fired again it was almost on the starboard beam, doubtless steaming towards them, keeping inside *Oleron*'s turning circle. Birkenhead's gun answered—he never knew where the U-boat was until it fired—and this time he seemed to score a hit, for there was an explosion on the submarine which was clearly not another shell being fired.

"He hit it," Harris shouted.

"Christ, did you see that?" Busk added.

Jacobson said nothing; the hit, if it were a hit, had not disabled the U-boat, for in a moment it fired again. But the Captain of *Oleron* seemed to grow a little larger, a little higher and more alert, tending now, in spite of his injuries, to stand on the balls of his feet with his heels off the ground, willing *Oleron* to an even greater speed, an even tighter turning circle.

"Speed," he muttered, "Speed! Speed! Speed!"

"Wind's abeam, sir," Harris reported.

"Straighten out, sir?" Busk added, the faithful echo.

"Wait," Jacobson said.

The wind careered from one side of the bridge to the other like water through a high-pressure hose. The men braced themselves against it and rubbed the salt water from their eyes.

"She's coming up into the wind now, sir. They'll go overboard if you don't turn back."

247

Jacobson ignored Busk but shouted to Harris, "Hold the wheel where it is."

The U-boat was now on the starboard quarter; in spite of their constant turning they were not getting any nearer to it. Another shell left the U-boat's gun and almost simultaneously erupted on *Oleron*'s fo'c'sle. It could have missed the bridge only by a hair's breadth.

Jacobson stared helplessly into the night, waiting for *Oleron*'s gun to answer, and when, finally, it did, his fingers moved slowly to his brow and found ice-cold sweat there.

He looked down, trying to estimate the damage, trying to see into the gaping crater into which untold tons of sea-water would shortly empty themselves. The waves were already crashing over the fo'c'sle and rushing in torrents on to the well-deck. In less than an hour enough water could run through the shell-hole to make *Oleron* nose-heavy and unmanoeuvrable; and there was nothing this time Jacobson could do about it, except pray—and hope that the forrard bulkheads would hold up against the increasing pressure of berserk water—and stand on the balls of his feet.

And then, in the midst of the sea and the arrant wind and the insane rolling, the miracle occurred. Jacobson heard a voice, a loud, thunderously resonant voice down on the well-deck, and when he looked with expectant eyes towards the voice he saw at first only a white, strangely luminous patch moving in the darkness, but when he leaned out through the broken frame of the screens he saw also the dim form of a giant of a man with white bandages about his neck.

"It's Birkenhead," Jacobson shouted, holding up his arms for silence, as if the gesture could silence the wind or the sea.

Busk ran up to Jacobson and leaned his body over the smashed woodwork. Jacobson's voice yelped in anger, "Get back to the telegraph."

"What is it?" Jacobson called to the voice below, his voice lost and helpless in the wind.

The voice answered, booming up to the men on the bridge so that even Harris and Busk could hear it, "Don't be afraid, Cap'n. Turn her into de wind now."

Jacobson waved. It was his only method of communication. His voice was useless in the increasing uproar.

The voice came again, "Turn her quick, Cap'n! Turn her . . . turn her . . . turn her . . . NOW!"

Then the voice and the shape of the man and the moving white column of bandages in the darkness were gone and Jacobson turned on Harris and Busk like a diminutive General at the head of a poised army, "Emergency full astern."

Busk began, "Captain . . ."

Jacobson shrieked at him, "*Emergency full astern, God damn you!*"

The telegraph rang and the engines were silent and *Oleron* made way through the water at an angle of forty-five degrees to the sea under her own engineless momentum, but still turning to starboard, inch by tortured inch. The ship was deathly quiet without the comfort of her engines and the noise of the wind seemed to increase a hundredfold.

Jacobson chanted to himself, "Hurry, hurry, hurry!"

Albert Reed stumbled on to the bridge and came near to Harris and grasped his arm for support, "My wife's injured. The girl's dead. I've got to look after the wife. Tell the Captain will you? I've got to go."

Before Harris could answer he was gone, plunging headlong down the bridge ladder which was still strewn with wreckage. "What's he say?" Busk called and Harris answered, his hands like claws on the wheel, "Never mind."

Jacobson's fist opened and closed on the bridge rail, "Hurry, for God's sake, hurry!"

They waited for the men in the engine room wrestling with great clutches, grease-wet wheels and ponderous controls, and even though they knew that the engineers were reversing *Oleron*'s engines in less time than ever before, knew in their bones that this was so, they could not help but curse their slowness. *Oleron*'s head wallowed in the seas, ceased to move to starboard, became stationary, and began to fall off to port, away from the wind and the clamouring sea.

Jacobson shouted to himself, "What in the name of heaven is keeping them?"

They felt the movement of the engines in the soles of their feet first, a slow, hesitant shaking that developed quickly to a thundering climax as the reversed screw hit into the water piling against it. "Hard aport," Jacobson yelled.

Harris swung the wheel like a one-eyed fiend and when it banged against the stop reported, "Wheel hard aport, sir."

When the engines were astern it did not make a great deal of difference where the rudder was, but *Oleron* tended to follow her rudder astern and reversing it clipped a few seconds off the time taken to turn *Oleron* about and was therefore justified.

Jacobson was still impatient. "Come up, damn you! Come up!"

But *Oleron* knew what to do—or to Jacobson she seemed to know what to do. She forced her head into the seas, and when the U-boat fired again it was much closer and forrard of the starboard beam.

Harris shouted, excited and jubilant, "He doesn't know we've turned!"

"Stand by," Jacobson answered.

The wind screamed into the open bridge and fled out of each wing. When Jacobson had been wounded he had lost his cap and his thin hair stood upright on his scalp. *Oleron* shuddered as the seas hammered at her bow and the noise of water sluicing off the fo'c'sle became a roaring nightmare.

He yelled into the wind again, holding up his good arm which the others could not see. "Stand by!" They heard the tail end of his voice and understood before the wind took it and flung it into the sea. *Oleron*'s head came round still farther and when the U-boat fired again the shot went wide.

"Look," Harris yelled, but audible only to Busk, "he's on the starboard bow."

Birkenhead's gun fired in reply and the U-boat commander was left to speculate on whether *Oleron* had, in fact, turned, or whether a gun mounted on her fo'c'sle had become endowed with magic properties and was able, also, to fire from her stern.

Jacobson hurtled across the heeling deck towards Busk and Harris, his arm outstretched, his feet wide apart. "Emergency full ahead!" He skidded to a halt before the wheel. "Hard astarboard!" He did not hear their answers but he heard the metallic clangour of the telegraph and was satisfied that his orders had been obeyed and ran back to his forrard position. The engines stopped and again *Oleron* was overtaken by her own terrible silence. The U-boat fired as the men on the bridge waited, and then again, and the movement of the flashes was clear and unmistakable: he had realised his error and was turning to port.

Again the interminable waiting, the impatience; the slowing, the stopping and finally the falling off of *Oleron*'s bow. Somehow the men contained themselves and even Stockmann was moved to take a closer interest in the proceedings and to enquire of Harris whether *Oleron* could, in his opinion, survive the U-boat's assault. Harris advised him to ask Jacobson but Stockmann appeared not to accept the advice, which was perhaps as well.

And then, as if there can never be a miracle unless it is redressed by a compensating calamity, a lucky shot went straight through the well-deck hatch and set the cargo of foodstuffs alight. Jacobson staggered backwards, his free hand clapped to his forehead where a piece of shrapnel had gouged the flesh to the bone. Busk caught him, more by accident than intent, and helped him stay upright. When Jacobson discovered that he was still alive, that this injury, although bloody, was not serious he ran back to the screens and looked down into the smouldering ruins and shouted for his engines. As he watched the dull red glow it developed into palpable flames, growing and burgeoning and licking upwards through the wrecked cover towards the bridge so that Jacobson could feel the heat of them in his face.

"The engines," he screamed. "Where are the engines?"

The U-boat was presented with a perfectly illuminated target, a target so big that its gunners, exposed and sea-swept as they were, could scarcely miss it. This was Jacobson's doom. This was his nemesis. He had run his wild course of wilfulness. Now he would pay for his foolhardy behaviour, his disregard of the most elementary laws of probability, his unconcern for his officers, his crew or his passengers, his persistent flying in the face of danger. The trouble was, he would not pay alone; the ship and everyone in it, the innocent, the guilty and the merely hapless would all pay with him. And no one now could prevent it. This Jacobson had asked for; and this Jacobson was going to get, whether he liked it or not.

Or so Busk thought, a Busk roused to a crescendo of fear by the sight of flames jumping above his head. But he did not think; what he took to be thought was a mere torrent of emotion rushing about in his head. It incited him until he wanted to scream, to rush at Jacobson and fling him overboard; yet he never would, for even as his screams ricocheted about the tunnels of his mind, he knew that Jacobson was the only man with the power to keep his head until the end. Even Busk, in his extremity, clung to Jacobson, for Jacobson was his only hope.

The U-boat fired furiously and another shell tore into the superstructure below the bridge. The ship danced in the detonation. At the same time the engines began to turn again and their distant thunder increased rapidly in volume. *Oleron* began to move through the water in the light of her own flames. The U-boat turned towards her, anticipating the kill, closing in on the cornered prey until she was so close that not even a storm-tossed torpedo could miss.

Oleron gathered way and charged into the great seas, elbowing, shouldering them aside, tossing them over her head. The water rushed over the fo'c'sle and on to the well-deck and down into the hold, but there was either not enough of it or too much fire, for the flames remained before Jacobson's eyes in spite of the water.

In the light of the flames Jacobson could see the three men on the fo'c'sle: Birkenhead, another giant he took to be Dawson, and Corridon. He did not recognise Corridon. They worked feverishly, loading and laying and training and firing and unloading and watching, and then doing it all over again. *Oleron* was steaming directly into the wind now and the seas approached like moving mountains, no longer parting when they met *Oleron*'s bow but inundating all before them. Each time the waters passed Jacobson watched for the movement of the men and thanked God each time he found them there, flattened against the deck, their lives hanging on the gun like distended laundry on a line, half-drowned, half-dead, but still there, still indubitably, gloriously there; even Corridon glorious now.

Oleron passed the eye of the wind and she began to turn faster and at the same time the Commander of the U-boat perceived the nature of his previous mistake and saw that *Oleron*, his nameless adversary, was still very much alive and kicking, even though burning. But his steps to rectify it were still unhurried; doubtless conjecturing that *Oleron*'s persistent little gun could do less harm to his craft if he remained to the windward of it, he began to turn to starboard, sheering off instead of coming closer. But this, again, was a mistake. When his previous decision had been taken *Oleron* had been apparently stationary—and no one who was not a lunatic or simply disabled would stop in a sea like this; now, without warning, she was proceeding towards him at an unbelievable rate of knots. Like Jacobson, he called for more speed, but not quite so urgently, not quite urgently enough.

Jacobson could not hear his own voice above the frantic noise about him. *Oleron* began to shake like a ship about to disintegrate. The vibrations entered the bodies of the men on board until their teeth became rough with infinitesimal oscillations. The engine room staff opened their throttles until the quivering machinery threatened to jump out of its bed. The screw thundered in the sea and when it came out of the water the whole of *Oleron* hammered like a road-drill. The speed was insane. It could not last. In a very short space of time *Oleron* would be reduced to a broken wreck, without the aid of the U-boat's gun. But Jacobson did not spare her; it was her hour of trial as well as his.

He ran back to the wheel. "Midships! Can you see her? Aim for her, Harris! Aim for her!" He ran forrard again and looked into the hold. The flames were dying, doused by immense quantities of sea-water. But in their light he could still see the men on the gun. The gun fired. And then two men were running aft between the seas, a big man and a small one, but he was unable to recognise them.

The U-boat, now no more than three hundred yards away, fired as she turned further into the wind. Jacobson crouched over the bridge rail, the flames lighting his face like that of a fat-faced devil sitting over the stoke-holes of hell.

"Faster!" he yelled.

"We're gaining!" Harris shouted.

Now that things looked brighter even Busk was persuaded to comment, "Yes, we're gaining!"

Two hundred yards.

"We're breaking the ship up!" Harris shouted. "She'll never last at this rate."

Jacobson ignored him, almost climbing over the bridge rail in his terrible excitement. This was *Oleron*'s doing; and he, Jacobson, was her exultant instrument.

One hundred and fifty yards.

Progress was slower now because the U-boat was gaining speed, approaching *Oleron*'s never-before-achieved fourteen knots. Jacobson's hair stood up on his head. His shoulders were square, his back rigid and straight, held not by strength or even will but by a consuming fever. When this was over, however it ended, he would probably collapse. "*Oleron! My Oleron!*"

One hundred yards.

The U-boat, apprehensive, manned her after gun and fired at point blank range into *Oleron*'s bow. The shell struck the stem above the water line and the noise the men on the bridge distinctly heard was the sound of the anchor carrying away. The gun fired in reply. Jacobson ignored the consequences; nothing now could still *Oleron*'s gun.

He shouted to the ship, the men, the night, the storm, "He is still there! We are still firing! Did you hear them? We still fire!"

Oleron fired again and the range came down to fifty yards.

Dawson, saturated, raced on to the bridge.

"It's Birkenhead down there! He's bleeding! You're killing him, Jacobson! He won't come away. Christ, he can't last and he won't come away."

Jacobson yelled back, "I am not killing him. He is of the ship! He will never come away!"

Dawson stormed off the bridge. "I'm going to get him!"

Another shell found its target and exploded in a lifeboat on the starboard side. Jacobson shouted above the rattle of debris, "A little to port, Harris! Just a touch to port."

Twenty-five yards.

"She knows! Oh God, she knows!"

The fire flared up again and Jacobson could see Birkenhead again, a towering black figure by the gun. At the same time Dawson appeared on the well-deck. Birkenhead fired the gun and this time he achieved a direct hit on the conning tower. The submarine lurched but did not at first appear to slacken speed. Instead, it mounted what was probably the biggest wave in the world that night, and when it had passed over the crest the entire blundering weight of the wave fell upon Birkenhead. He disappeared beneath it and Dawson scurried back to the shelter of the superstructure. Jacobson bit his hand in agony as he watched, imagining the great sinews straining and tearing against the invincible water, even those magnificent muscles not strong enough, not hard enough to hold on, but slipping, slackening, sliding, parting like taut lines, and finally releasing the gun, paralysed by the magnitude of their effort, and being carried away inside the tumultuous wave, over *Oleron*'s fo'c'sle, over the well-deck, and over the side into the deep voracious ocean.

Birkenhead was gone, a Jonah returned to the sea, and once he was gone the world of *Oleron* was a different world, and while men watched aghast where Birkenhead had been, saw the water draining in torrents from the fo'c'sle and the well-deck, saw the gun stark and unattended, *Oleron* seemed to lift her head higher than ever before and with one mighty plunging effort flung herself over the wave crest into the unknown.

The U-boat, broached to by that monumental sea lay athwart her course and as *Oleron*'s stem passed through its helpless carcass there was about the final cataclysmic meeting a sense of terrible inevitability. *Oleron* destroyed the U-boat before Jacobson and the men on her bridge knew she was there.

U 39 sank in two halves, one each side of *Oleron*'s crippled quiescent bow. And when it was done Jacobson cried aloud with grief and stumbled wordless to his cabin in a stupor of weariness, sorrow and pain. The men on the bridge watched him go and none of them dared speak to him.

Dawson took four survivors from the water and, in the light of dawn, turned *Oleron* towards Halifax.

may break the tumultuous wave, over Oliver's face, over the well-deck, and over the side into the deep torrents ocean.

Blanchard was gone, a Jonah returned to the sea, and once in that great black world of ocean waste without world, and while motion watched upheld alone like a ghost and here, saw the sluggish in currents from the to-side and the well-deck, saw the movement unattended, Oliver strained to lift in it and it, but then once before wild, with one sudden upturning, there sling herself over the wave crest into the unknown.

The Cudworth, too, proached to be, that unattended sea at sea all went her course vast as Oliver's seen passed through to Halifax's canvas limp was about the final catastrophe meaning it some cheap like inevitable, Byron destroyed the U-boat below. Jackson and the men on her bridge knew she was there.

Olivia sank in two halves, one each side of Oliver's crumpled quickened bow. And when it was done, Jackson had cried aloud to her grief and stumbled wordless to his cabin in a stupor of weariness, sorrow and pain. The men on the bridge watched him go and none of them dared speak to him.

Dawson took four survivors from the water, and in the light of dawn gained Oliver toward Halifax.